HEAL You

MELISSA TEREZE

First Edition June 2025
Published by GPC Publishing

ISBN: 978-1-915242-49-5

Cover Design: Melissa Tereze
Editor: Charlie Knight

Find out more at: www.melissaterezeauthor.com
Follow me on Twitter: @MelissaTereze
Follow me on Instagram: @melissatereze_author

"Love comes to those who still hope after disappointment, who still believe after betrayal, and who still love after they've been hurt."

— Anon

Also by Melissa Tereze

Another Love Series

The Arrangement (Book One)

The Call (Book Two)

Before You Go (Book Three)

Mrs Middleton Novels

Mrs Middleton

Teach Me (Co-write with Jourdyn Kelly)

Vanessa

The Ashforth Series

Playing For Her Heart (Book One)

Holding Her Heart (Book Two)

The Stepmother Series

The Stepmother (Book One)

The Show Must Go On (Book Two)

The Hush Liverpool Series

Discovery (Book One)

The Hideout (Book Two)

A Little Light (Book Three)

Any Kind of Life (Book Four)

The Study You Series

Study You

Choose You

Other Novels

Life After

It's Always Been You

It's All About Bex

Privately Investigated

Behind Her Eyes

At First Glance

Always Allie

Breaking Routine

In Her Arms

Forever Yours

The Heat of Summer

Forget Me Not

More Than A Feeling

Where We Belong: Love Returns

Naked

Titles under L.M Croft (Erotica)

Pieces of Me

CHAPTER 1

Humming lightly as she tilted her face towards the sun, Jan rested against the bonnet of her car and smiled. God, she loved pleasant weather. More than anything, she loved pleasant weather *and* good people. Friends, family, even her employees most of the time.

Today was the beginning of a new week, and Jan had everything to look forward to. She had a husband who had dedicated every second of his time to her over the weekend, and she planned to see Gillian and Finn in a couple of days. What more could she need right now?

Oh, you have it all.

Jan pushed off her car and took the steps up to the office. Gillian, her best friend, often told her she was out of her mind to be stepping over gravel in her expensive heels, but this was all second nature to Jan Bartlett. All she had known for over twenty years was this. The business. The daily commute down the motorway to deal with plant hire and housing developments.

"Love?" Phil opened the door to his office—an outside portacabin —that he was currently residing in while his usual one was being refurbished. He swapped and changed depending on his mood, but he would know about it the moment the summer arrived. He would be cooking in that tin can. "Can you bring me the files on The Mews development when you have a minute? I forgot to pick them up when I got here earlier."

"Of course. Give me ten to get my things sorted, and I'll be over."

"Thanks." Phil regarded Jan with a loving smile, his gaze lingering. "You look gorgeous today, by the way."

Jan smiled to herself as she allowed the compliment to sink in. "Thank you. I'd say the same back at you, but you've always been a handsome bastard, and that'll never change."

Phil winked and turned back inside the cabin. He had been extra attentive this weekend, surprising Jan at the last minute with a spa weekend on the outskirts of the city. It had been just what they'd needed, given how busy they'd been recently. Jan didn't require much in the way of relaxation, but she *did* need a day or two to recharge on occasion.

She quickly rushed inside her own office and took her phone from her handbag the moment she was sitting behind her desk. Gillian had wanted an update on the hotel they'd just been to, and if Jan didn't take care of that right now, Gillian would be calling her for most of the day.

Hotel was amazing! The treatments were exceptional. Throw the hint to Finn and I'll expect a call from her for hotel details soon. Love ya! x

Jan locked her phone and looked up at the door when someone knocked. She caught sight of Gareth through the small window and waved him inside. Gareth was one of the business' couriers who handled the delivery of office supplies. He was here at least twice a week, usually delivering reams and reams of paper or ink cartridges.

"Hi, Gareth." Jan sat back in her seat and clasped her hands on her knee as she crossed her legs. "Nice weekend?"

"He...hasn't told you."

Jan frowned. "I'm sorry? Who hasn't told me what?"

Gareth's face had suddenly turned very pale. Jan's concern was instant, so she shot from her seat and helped Gareth into the one on the opposite side of her desk.

"I'm sorry, Jan. I really didn't want to be the one to do this." He scrubbed a hand down his face as his voice broke. "Fucking coward!"

"Okay, take a breath, and tell me what's going on." Jan returned to her seat and perched her elbows on her desk. She had no idea what Gareth was talking about, but he seemed almost... haunted by whatever this was. "Has something happened? Are your family okay?"

"Y-yeah. Mum is doing really well, and Dad has been a diamond looking after her."

Jan smiled. Gareth's mum had recently undergone treatment for cancer. Jan and Phil had given him any time he needed off so Gareth could be there for appointments, so to hear that things were going well was always a plus. "That's great news. Please send them our love, won't you?"

Gareth stared at Jan. That look on his face hadn't changed. It was only growing worse. "I, uh... I caught them, Jan. In bed together."

Jan smiled. "Caught who?"

"Anais and Phil."

Jan sat forward a little. She thought for a second that Gareth had said her husband's name. No, he couldn't have done. "Anais and who?"

"Phil. Your Phil."

Jan laughed, mostly with nerves...but also because that just couldn't be true. "My Phil? No, you have it wrong. We've just been away for the weekend to a spa hotel. It wasn't him."

"It...was last weekend." Gareth swallowed as his eyes filled with tears. "She told me she was away with friends for the weekend, so I decided to stay with Mum and Dad. Give Dad a break, you know?" He shook his head. "I called home on the Saturday morning because I'd forgotten my razor and wash bag. They were there, in bed together."

Jan's heart sank. Phil had also been away from home last weekend. Only for Jan, that was nothing out of the ordinary. Phil often travelled for work, usually to finalise contracts or to source land for new developments. Still... "No, you have it wrong. Phil would never cheat on me. We're celebrating our twenty-fifth wedding anniversary in a few months. W-we're taking our friends away on a cruise."

Only you haven't booked that cruise yet.

Not because they hadn't decided on where to go but because Phil kept putting it off. Was that because he was planning to leave Jan for Anais? No. This just wasn't something she could comprehend.

"I'm sorry, Jan. I told them they had the week to tell you, or I'd come to you myself. I thought he may have done the decent thing and come clean, but it seems not."

Jan didn't show it, but inside, she was slowly dying. Phil, her husband, had been having an affair with their employee? For what reason? Just...why? *This has to be a mistake.* "Can you give me a few minutes please?"

Gareth rose to his feet. "Of course. I'm sorry. This is a lot for you."

"No, no. Take a seat, and I'll be right back." Jan composed herself and left her office. It would take her all of ten seconds to knock on Phil's door, but she found herself taking her time. Was she worried that this was true? No, not at all. But she was trying to figure out how to run this by her husband without accusing him. Only, as she reached his door, she wasn't sure it was possible to say this in any other way.

She poked her head around the door. "Do you have a minute?"

"For you? Always." Phil smiled where he stood behind his desk, his hands braced against it as he studied floor plans for their most recent development. As Jan stepped inside the office and closed the door behind her, he said, "Did you bring the files for The Mews?"

"No, um...could you come to my office for a few minutes so we can clear something up?" Jan threw a thumb over her shoulder. "Gareth is in there, and I think he's a little bit confused."

As Jan watched her husband, the way he shifted uncomfortably and wrung his hands, her heart sunk further. "Jan, I—"

"It's true, isn't it?" Jan's voice boomed in her ears, her pulse hammering throughout her entire body. Shock was the first thing she felt, sheer humiliation the second. "Answer me!"

Phil visibly swallowed as he slowly lowered himself into his seat. "I wanted to tell you. I just didn't know how."

Jan took a step back and walked directly into the door. Her back connected with it, but it barely registered in her mind. "You've been sleeping with another woman..."

"I'm sorry. It was a mistake."

Jan laughed weakly, staring back at a man she had spent so many years with...but now felt as though she didn't know at all. "Was it a one-off? Were you drunk?"

Phil lowered his gaze to the desk strewn with their business plans. Their hard work and dedication.

"How long, Phil?" Jan dug her nails into the door, sure she would break them any second now. "How fucking long?!"

"A year, I don't know. Maybe a little less."

Jan pushed off the door, crossed the room, and braced her hands against Phil's desk. "I want a divorce."

"Wait, love. We can work this out. Nothing is lost. We just... have to work this out between us. I can't lose you."

"You've already lost me, Phil. The moment you even looked at that fucking woman out there was the moment you lost me.

You're now just realising it—that's all." Jan turned and walked away, glancing back over her shoulder. "Twenty-seven years together, and you ruin it all by dropping your fucking pants for your receptionist."

"Jan!"

"Don't. I'm not interested in anything you have to say." Jan left the office and looked to her left. Anais sat at her desk, chancing a look over the top of her computer screen. "No need to hide. I know the truth. I hope you'll be *very* happy together."

She strode out of Phil's office, determined not to break down until she was alone. Right now, she had Anais' distraught husband sitting in her own office, and she would have to deal with it whether she wanted to or not. As she stopped outside her door, gathering herself *and* her thoughts, Jan's throat grew thick with emotion. What the hell was she supposed to say to Gareth? What the hell was she supposed to say to herself about all of this? God, she couldn't begin to imagine the state she would be in later today.

With her shoulders pulled back and a quick check of her makeup in the barely visible reflection in the door, she walked back into her office and pressed her back to the door once it was closed. "I'm sorry, Gareth. I don't know what to say to you."

"Don't apologise. This isn't your fault."

Wasn't it? It was hard to believe anything else when her husband had found what he needed in another woman. Shouldn't she have seen it coming? After all, they'd been going through marriage counselling recently. Perhaps Jan had pushed Phil into Anais' arms simply because she had wanted counselling. "I...need to get my things together so I can leave."

"Leave?"

"Mm." Jan smiled as she rushed around her office and gathered what was visible to her. "I need to go home and pack some of my belongings."

"You're leaving him?"

Jan spun around and frowned. "You're *not* leaving her?"

Gareth drew in a deep breath and shrugged. "To be honest, I hadn't thought that far ahead. I don't know what to do for the best."

"That's understandable. But for me, there is no coming back from this. I don't even intend to try to fix my marriage with him." Jan took a calming breath, hoping her heart rate would begin to settle. She needed Gareth to leave so she could figure out the next step, but he didn't look to be in a good way at all. "Maybe you should take the rest of the day off. Give yourself some time to come to terms with this. It's out there now, so you can begin to decide what's best for you."

"Will you be okay?" Gareth asked as he got to his feet and shoved his hands in the pockets of his cargo pants. "I can stay, or we could get a coffee somewhere and talk about this..."

"I appreciate that, but I also hope you can understand that I need to be alone for a little while. I didn't come to work this morning expecting to find out my husband has been having an affair."

Gareth pulled one hand from his pocket and held it up. "Of course. Of course."

"Whatever you decide to do, you'll take care of yourself, yes?"

Gareth sighed and backed up towards the door. "I will. You will, too?"

Oh, Jan was sure as hell going to look after herself. If *anyone* thought she would fall apart because of a man, they had another thing coming. "Of course."

Gareth nodded and left Jan's office, the silence in the room now deafening. Jan expected Phil to come bursting through the door at some point, but she wouldn't be around long enough for that to happen. The only thing she knew for sure right now was that she had to leave. The office and the house. If Phil had been fucking Anais in Anais' bed, then there was no telling what had happened in their own home when Jan wasn't around.

She gathered some bits and pieces from her desk drawers and

shoved them into her handbag. Choosing not to take any work with her—she had no idea if she'd ever return here—Jan turned out the lights and stepped out into the open office she managed. It was quiet, people were getting on with their jobs, but Jan couldn't look any of them in the eye. The moment she did, she would break down.

CHAPTER 2

Gulping down an entire pint of water, Morgan looked out at the rooftops from her kitchen window and sighed. Her shift in the bar downstairs really needed to go smoothly tonight or she was going to lose her head. Nine times out of ten, The Corner Bar was the only thing that kept her sane—it was her pride and joy after all—but lately, it was just bad memories. Memories of Amanda and the day they'd met downstairs. Memories of inviting her up here, knowing what would come of it. She hadn't been interested the day her customer walked into the bar, but after a few drinks together and many laughs, Morgan found herself a little more interested. She found herself hanging on every word that fell from Amanda's mouth.

She'd been significantly older than Morgan, but that wasn't an issue. It never would be. Morgan preferred to connect with women like Amanda. Women who knew who they were and what they wanted. So, when Amanda had hinted at a little fun with Morgan, Morgan found herself unable to turn down the request. As she turned and scanned her open plan living room and kitchen, dread sunk into the pit of her stomach.

Never again. No way.

She shook her head and moved towards the door. Morgan had a shift to start and Tyler, her bartender, had to leave on time for his late-afternoon college course. She appreciated that he'd even been available to come in at short notice today. It wasn't often she got lucky like that.

Morgan took the stairs that led to the bar and opened the door. It was always nice to see a friendly face sitting waiting for her, and today, that face belonged to Finn Ashton. They'd known one another for a few years now, and what Morgan liked about Finn was that she often told it as it was. Still, she wasn't ready to discuss Amanda with anyone yet. God, Finn had only just found out Morgan was fooling around with her. She wanted to pretend a little longer.

"Hey!" Finn grinned. "You really look like you want to be here this afternoon."

Finn had that right. Morgan would rather be *anywhere* else. "Long night. Didn't get much sleep."

"Oh. Amanda, huh?" Finn wiggled her eyebrows and sipped her beer. "Things going well between you two then?"

"I didn't see Amanda last night." Morgan stepped behind the bar and wiped down the area. Tyler was pulling a pint for another customer, so she would leave him be for a moment. "And like I said, it's nothing serious. It'll never be anything serious."

"Fuck them and then drop them. The story of Morgan Tate's life." Finn lifted her pint and held it up in mid-air. "Cheers to you, the commitment-phobe."

Morgan leaned over the bar and said, "Just because you're tied down now, don't take it out on me."

"Pfft. I'd rather be tied down with Gillian. Trust me. She's great when it comes to knots." Finn winked and then laughed. "But in all seriousness, you should see where it goes with Amanda. I didn't think I'd be in a relationship with Gillian, let alone call her my wife one day."

"You and I are different people, Finn." That was a lie, Morgan would love nothing more than to find someone she really connected with, and ultimately settle down, but that was hard to do when she worked this bar almost every day. "You're happy. I'm happy. Let's leave it at that, yeah?"

Finn shrugged. "Mkay."

"How *is* the wife? My number one fan."

Finn rolled her eyes as she finished the beer in her glass. "I don't know how many times I have to tell you that Gillian *doesn't* dislike you."

"She needs to tell that to her face then whenever you and I are talking." Morgan gave Finn a knowing look. It was no secret that Gillian wasn't fond of Morgan. Morgan had a feeling Gillian believed her and Finn had slept together at some point in the past, but Finn really wasn't Morgan's type. They were friends and that's all they'd ever been to date. "I'm serious. If looks could kill, I'd be six feet under by now."

"You can ask her yourself when she gets here." Finn checked her watch and smiled. "She left campus twenty minutes ago so she should be arriving any moment now."

Morgan's heart rate spiked ever so slightly. Whenever Gillian came here lately, she usually had her best friend, Jan, in tow. Morgan could happily stand around all day admiring Jan, but she knew it was a lost cause. After the first few occasions—once Jan had found herself comfortable here—it had been a struggle for Morgan to concentrate on anything else. They'd chatted, they'd laughed, and Morgan had realised that she was enamoured by Jan.

Yeah, until she turned up here with her fucking husband.

Morgan sighed inwardly. She was forever finding the wrong women attractive.

"You okay?" Finn clicked her fingers in front of Morgan's face, her brows drawn. "Lost you for a sec then."

"I'm fine. Just trying to figure out how long I have left on my shift." Morgan lied. "Too long, is the answer."

"What time are you here till?"

"Until close, unfortunately." Morgan briefly turned and pressed the espresso button on the coffee machine behind the bar. She sat a cup under it while the beans were grinding, and then she turned back to Finn. "What do you guys have planned for the rest of the afternoon?"

"Gillian is coming here for a glass of wine, and then I'm taking her out to dinner. She had a busy weekend working from home, so we didn't get much of a chance to wind down. This week looks less busy for her, so I'm stealing her away from her office for the rest of the night."

"That sounds nice." Morgan rested her forearms on a beer pump and sat her chin on them. "Jan coming over with Gillian?"

"No. Jan doesn't do day drinking. She'll be at the office still. She's just been away for the weekend with Phil. I've asked Gillian to find out what the hotel was like so we could potentially book it. Jan is really into her spa treatments so if the place is good, she'll tell us."

Of course Jan was into her spa treatments. That woman had looked like an angel the last time she strode through Morgan's bar door. That had been the night when Morgan accidentally let a wine glass slip from her hand, and it was the crash of the glass that had brought her back down to reality. Jan was striking. Her long blonde hair was natural, and those blue eyes were like nothing Morgan had ever come across before. And she'd come across many people in her time behind the bar alone. But it was the dress Jan wore that had caused the wine glass incident. Morgan hadn't been able to focus her eyes anywhere else for the entire night. At one point, she'd considered closing up early just so she didn't have to ogle any longer. A little black dress and heels would always have Morgan salivating. Put those items on *Jan* and Morgan was having palpitations.

Finn clicked her fingers again. "What the hell is going on with you? I lost you *again*."

Fuck. Morgan had to stop doing that. "Like I said, I didn't sleep much last night."

"Sure. You keep telling yourself that. But I know you well enough now to know that *something* is going on inside that mind of yours."

Morgan exhaled a breath and left Finn sitting at the bar. If they kept talking, Morgan was going to blurt out the latest with Amanda, and she honestly wasn't ready to have that conversation. She approached Tyler and laid a hand on his shoulder. "I'm here now so you can get going for your course."

"Thanks, Morgan. I appreciate it."

"I appreciate you coming in at short notice for me today. I owe you one."

With the greatest sense of loss settled deep in her chest, Jan knocked back the dreg of wine in the bottom of her glass and lifted a hand to catch Morgan's attention. She had spent the last two hours sitting in this very spot, watching people come and go, unable to fathom the idea of going home tonight.

What home? You don't have a fucking home anymore!

Jan swallowed down the emotion in her throat and closed her eyes. This day had been the furthest thing from her mind from the moment she'd met Phil. In all honesty, Jan had to wonder whether she was dreaming. But then the realisation sunk in all over again, and now Jan sat here on a Monday night...*actually* alone for the first in twenty-seven years.

Morgan approached from the other end of the bar and rested her arm on a beer pump. "You've been here a while now and you're *still* sitting on your own. You want me to call Finn and find out what the hold-up is? They were both in earlier, but I thought Finn was taking Gillian out for dinner. She didn't say they were coming back here."

Jan smiled as she looked up at Morgan. She had spent many nights here with Gillian and Finn now. It was their 'local' even though it was nowhere near their homes. Morgan was great, she'd hosted some amazing nights here since Jan started to frequent the place, so she'd found herself walking towards the bar a couple of hours ago. "I'm not meeting them tonight."

"No? Waiting for the husband? Phil...was it?"

Jan tensed at the mention of her husband's name. He had also frequented The Corner on several occasions with Jan, Gillian, and Finn. "No. Phil won't be joining me either."

Morgan frowned. "Then why are you sitting here drinking my bar dry?"

"Do you ask everyone that?" Jan eyed Morgan as she held up her empty wine glass. "I can go elsewhere if I'm putting a downer on the atmosphere in here."

"That's not what I was implying," Morgan said as she took Jan's empty glass and refilled a fresh one with wine. "You know you're *always* welcome here, Jan. I'm just not used to seeing you on your own or looking so sad. Did you need to talk to someone?"

What was the point? Jan didn't even know if she could speak the words. She was yet to inform Gillian of her day so far. "N-no. But thank you. I appreciate your concern."

"Well, I just need to change a beer barrel and then I'll be right back." Morgan regarded Jan with a gentle smile, her deep brown eyes soft and caring as they always were. Jan understood, though. Morgan was probably used to playing therapist for the lonely souls who ended up sitting here night after night.

Jan couldn't believe she had just become a part of that particular group, but here she was, unable to comprehend what her future looked like. She'd had it all planned out. She'd never imagined anything different. But here she sat, with the knowledge that her husband had been having an affair with a woman sixteen years younger than him.

She turned her phone over and looked at the screen. He'd texted her again.

Jan, please come home, love. I want to work this out with you. I made a terrible mistake.

Jan scoffed. Phil hadn't made a terrible mistake and they both knew it.

She swallowed as she exited her message thread and instead brought up Gillian's number. Her best friend would know what to do, and if she didn't, they always had the option of Finn kicking Phil in the bollocks to fall back on. Jan would pay good money to see that happen.

The call connected just before it went to voicemail. "H-hello?"

That wasn't Gillian's voice. It was Finn's, and she was *very* out of breath.

"Hi, Finn. Is Gill around at all?"

Finn cleared her throat. "She, um...she's a bit busy at the minute, Jan. Can I ask her to call you back in a little while?"

Jan heard Gillian moaning in the background, then Finn giggling. She couldn't deal with this tonight. She loved Gillian and Finn more than anything in this world, but Jan wasn't in the right headspace to make some kind of dirty comment. She just wanted to talk this through with the very woman who had stood by her side for so long. "I...it's okay. I'll call her in a few days."

"Sure?" Finn asked.

"Yes, I'm sure. H-have a lovely night, both of you." Jan hung up before she heard something else she didn't need to hear.

As she looked down at her screen, she saw a notification for a memory on one of her social media apps. She opened the app and read the notification, tears sitting in her eyes as she stared down at the picture. The very woman her husband had been having an affair with was pictured with Jan during a teambuilding day last year. They'd all gone out for lunch and drinks, and Anais had spent most of the afternoon sitting with Jan. To know that Phil had been sleeping with this woman, it sent a shiver up Jan's spine.

She shook her head and locked her phone, looking up from it to find Morgan watching her from the other end of the bar. Jan smiled, then lowered her gaze to her fresh glass of wine. Maybe she should just buy a bottle and get a hotel room for the night. She sure as hell wouldn't be going back to her marital home. Not in a rush, anyway. The thought of seeing Phil's face right now had anger flaring in the pit of Jan's stomach. Going home was *not* a good idea.

"Hey, Morgan?" Jan called her over, quickly brushing a tear away that had escaped down her cheek. When Morgan stopped in front of Jan, she sniffled. "Can you recommend a good hotel nearby?"

Morgan ran a hand through her light brown hair, her tongue poking out and playing with her lip ring. "The guesthouse two blocks down is decent. It's not five-star, but it's clean and safe. I believe they do a very good breakfast, too."

A very good breakfast, Jan thought. She wasn't sure she would be able to stomach a coffee in the morning, let alone a breakfast. "Do you know the name of it so I can call and see if they have a room available?"

"Tell me to mind my own business, but you don't even have any belongings with you. Is...everything okay, Jan?"

"Define okay..."

Morgan cocked her head and stared back at Jan with those pretty eyes. "I'm locking up in thirty. Hang back and we'll have a chat, okay?"

It meant a lot that Morgan was willing to do that for her. They knew one another, Jan had spent enough time in here now to say that, but she still hadn't expected the offer. "You don't have to do that, but thank you."

"Trust me, I could do with a chat, too. I find it hard to wind down as soon as I lock up, so I'd appreciate the company."

"Okay. That would be nice." Jan ran a fingertip up the stem of her wine glass, unable to gaze into Morgan's eyes any longer. She hadn't noticed it before today, but they were strikingly beautiful. Almost mesmerising. "Could I buy a bottle of wine to take to wherever I'm going before you cash up for the night?"

"Any drinks once I lock up will be on the house. If you still want that bottle once we've had a chat, then it's on me." Morgan winked and walked away, clearing up behind the bar while people finished their drinks.

Jan relaxed into her seat, ignoring her phone as another message from Phil flashed on the screen. She turned it over again, screen faced down, and sighed. If she could just get through the next twenty-four hours, she would kick herself up the arse and prepare for a life she had never imagined. A life...without Phil Bartlett.

CHAPTER 3

Morgan turned away from the entrance to the bar once she'd double-checked each lock was secure. Jan still sat on a stool, her shoulders hunched and looking like a lost soul, but Morgan was determined to get to the bottom of whatever was going on. She may not know Jan as well as she wished she could, but Morgan was happy to listen and help. She would just have to push the whole husband thing to the back of her mind. She knew it couldn't be anything Phil had done; he'd always appeared attentive in Jan's company. Then there was the fact that Gillian and Finn were good friends with him, too. Finn wasn't the kind of person to accommodate someone she didn't like, so, no, there was no way Jan was having husband trouble.

As she took a moment to watch Jan, or the back of her at least, Morgan couldn't recall her ever being in here on her own. She had been surprised by just how quiet Jan had been since she'd arrived, too. Jan was usually the life of this place whenever they all came in for a drink. Jesus, she'd even been the one to get everyone up dancing just a few weeks ago in here. Morgan's bar wasn't always a dancing type of venue, but she would admit that the atmosphere that night had been electric. Mostly because of Jan's gorgeous smile, but Morgan would never divulge that. Jan was a married woman, and Morgan didn't pine after married women. Not knowingly, anyway.

As she turned down the lights—her license only allowed the bar to be open until Midnight—she cleared her throat and approached Jan. They had all spent so much time in there that Jan's perfume had become familiar to Morgan. Subtle but very pleasing, just like the woman wearing it. "You wanna come up with me?"

"Up...where?" Jan looked back at Morgan, utterly confused.

"To my place. Above the bar. I...live here, too."

Jan took her clutch bag from the bar and slid her phone into it. "O-oh. Right. I didn't realise."

As she lowered herself from her stool, Morgan quickly wrapped an arm around her waist when she stumbled. Jan rarely appeared drunk, usually only having a few glasses of red wine before she switched to water, but Morgan guessed tonight wasn't one of Jan's usual nights. Not judging by the dullness of her usually gorgeous blue eyes. "Whoa. You good?"

Jan placed a hand on Morgan's chest, her cheeks red as she nodded. "Yes. Sorry about that. My legs didn't want to work then."

"I mean, you have sat there for the last few hours, unmoved. I'm not surprised they're not working." Morgan grinned back at Jan, her gaze lingering longer than it should. "Think you can make it upstairs without me carrying you?"

Jan blushed further. "I'm sure I can manage just fine."

"Come on then." Morgan turned the lights off above the bar and opened a door to the side of the counter. Once they'd safely made it upstairs, Morgan turned back to Jan. "Another glass of wine?"

"Do you have anything stronger?"

Morgan gave Jan a knowing look. "I own a bar. I have whatever strength you need tonight."

"Maybe a whiskey? No ice if it's scotch. Just a drop of water." Jan suddenly frowned and shook her head. "I'm sorry. You own a bar. You know how to make a drink."

"People like what they like. That's not for me to decide. So, whiskey with a drop of water is coming right up." Morgan moved towards her kitchen and took a bottle of scotch from the counter in the corner. She poured herself a glass too, then returned to Jan. "Have a seat. Make yourself comfortable."

Jan lowered her bag to the side of the coffee table and took her glass from Morgan. Once she was sitting down, her eyes tired and half-lidded, Morgan took a seat beside her.

"Come on. What's going on with you tonight?" Morgan turned side-on and propped her head in her hand against the back of the couch. "You're usually the one cheering me up when I've had a rough day. This isn't the Jan I'm used to."

Jan scoffed. "No, I know. It's not the Jan I'm used to either."

Morgan remained silent, aware that Jan was going over things in her head, but she did place a supportive hand over Jan's where it rested on Jan's knee.

"I found out this afternoon that my husband has been having an affair."

"Shit. I'm sorry." Morgan would usually have some smart-arse response about men, but she'd also found out something very similar yesterday...only it was a woman. It seemed that gender was irrelevant to this conversation. *Anyone* could be a scumbag. Still, this wasn't about Morgan. Jan needed an ear, and Morgan was happy to offer both of hers. "Does Gillian know?"

"Not yet. I don't really know how to tell her. I was there for her through her divorce, but I *cannot* imagine going through this myself." Jan shook her head and sighed. "You never think it'll be you, do you?"

Morgan puffed out her cheeks, reminding herself of how she felt yesterday. Only her situation was entirely different from Jan's. To a point, anyway. Morgan certainly hadn't been married to the woman who had hurt her. Or overly attached. This was a whole different ball game. "No, you don't."

"And the worst of it is that he's been having an affair with a woman I work with. She...works at our company." Jan frowned. "H-his company. I guess it's nothing to do with me anymore."

Morgan could understand that Jan had probably had several knee-jerk reactions to everything since she found out, but was Jan really considering ending it all? On the very day she had found out. "You're not going to work it out with him?"

"I can abide many things, but a cheater is not one of them."

"No, I get that. It just seems a shame to throw it all away so quickly, you know?" Morgan was partly speaking from her own experience. While she knew she wouldn't be intimate with Amanda ever again, it didn't mean she wouldn't remind herself of everything they'd shared the next time they came face to face. It may have been nothing more than fucking between them, but Morgan *did* have a heart. She *did* care about Amanda. "Maybe sitting down and talking to him is a good first step."

Jan shook her head. "I can't even stomach the thought of being in the same room as him."

"How long have you been together?"

"Together twenty-seven years and married for twenty-five." Jan's voice broke as she said that. Morgan immediately plucked a tissue from the box on the coffee table and handed it over. "Thank you."

"Could it have been a one-off? You know, a drunken mistake or something like that?" Morgan didn't know why she was trying to back Jan's husband up. She guessed it was the 'bartender solving a crisis' in her. Quite frankly, she couldn't give a shit about Jan's husband. If he could do what he'd done to his wife, then he didn't deserve respect from anyone.

"I thought so. Hoped so. But he admitted to me that it's been going on for almost a year." Jan dabbed at her eyes. "Gareth came to see me today. Her husband. He works for a courier firm that brings a lot of goods into the office. Anais works in the plant hire department within Phil's company. When he pulled me to one side this morning, I didn't know what to do or say. I actually laughed at him at one point, and then I realised he was distraught, and I had a feeling it was true." Jan puffed out her cheeks and slumped a little more. "I asked Phil outright, but he didn't even deny it. He just kept apologising."

Fuck. That had to hurt. Morgan wasn't quite sure how to respond.

"Have you ever been cheated on?" Jan looked up at Morgan, the sadness in her eyes almost taking Morgan's breath away. It took a lot of strength for women to be vulnerable in front of other people, but Morgan was used to this. She had sat and listened to many of her customers over the last few years.

Only Jan didn't feel like a customer. She almost felt like a friend. Someone Morgan wanted to know. Someone she wanted to help through this. Of course Jan had Gillian and Finn, but maybe this was the perfect opportunity for Jan to process it *without* friends who knew her husband. Morgan was neutral in all of this, really.

"I...don't know," Morgan said, frowning as she stared into her glass of scotch. "I guess my latest situation could mean that. Yes."

"Your latest situation?"

Morgan wasn't sure it was the right time to discuss this with Jan, it could go one of two ways, but she wanted Jan to know that she kind of understood how she was feeling. In a fucked up way, at least. "I was seeing a woman. Well, seeing her is a bit of a stretch. We've been sleeping with one another on and off for about six months now. I found out yesterday that she actually has a husband, and I never knew anything about it."

"I'm sorry." Jan turned her hand over and entwined her fingers with Morgan's. "Feels terrible being the other woman, doesn't it? Even though he was *my* husband for twenty-odd years, *I* feel like the other woman."

"Right now, I just feel sad about it all. I'd never knowingly get involved with a married woman. *Ever.* I mean, it's always nice to admire women...I've admired you on way more than one occasion, but I'm not the kind of person who would cheat. I feel...dirty, you know?"

Jan searched Morgan's face, a slight crease between her brows. "You've admired *me*?"

"Yep." Morgan lifted a shoulder. She just hoped Jan didn't think she had other reasons for inviting her up to the flat. Yes, Morgan found it hard to look anywhere else the moment Jan was in her bar, but that wasn't what this was. She *did* want to be a friend in this moment. "You're gorgeous."

Jan snorted. "Tell that to my husband."

"If he's been seeing someone else, then he's a fool. A complete fucking idiot."

"I should have known something was going on," Jan said before sipping her whiskey. "Gillian and Finn don't know, but Phil and I have been seeing a marriage counsellor for almost seven months. I just...felt as though I was losing him, and I couldn't put my finger on why."

"Oh." Morgan's brows shot up. So, Jan had been suspicious of something. She just didn't know what. "A marriage counsellor."

"I know. It's ridiculous, the money we wasted on it. But it was the only thing I could think of in that moment. That moment when I knew everything had become routine and a little bit lifeless. Then I saw how happy Gillian was with Finn, and I wanted my own marriage to be like that."

Morgan completely understood. Gillian and Finn were so in love that Morgan rolled her eyes most of the time. But really, she was just jealous she didn't have a relationship like that. She'd love to be in that position, of course she would, but there never seemed to be enough hours in the day *or* the right woman walking through the door. Amanda had been the perfect remedy, really. "I'm sorry you've been going through this alone."

Jan smiled as she mindlessly and most likely subconsciously stroked her thumb across Morgan's knuckles. "I've always been the problem solver. I've always been the one people come to when they need advice. Now that I'm in this position, I don't quite know what to do with myself."

"That's understandable. When I found out about Amanda yesterday, I hid away for a few hours. Even though it wasn't anything serious between us, I was still hurt by it. And like you, I didn't know who to turn to."

"Then I'm sorry you've also been dealing with things alone."

Morgan smiled and squeezed Jan's hand. "Look, I've always been a loner. I'm used to it. But when it comes to you...I *am* here if you need to vent."

"That's very sweet of you, Morgan. Thank you."

"Top up?" Morgan eyed Jan's glass, instantly switching into bar owner mode. She didn't like to see people with empty glasses.

"Why not. I have no home to go back to." Jan handed her glass over, choosing not to down what remained in it.

Morgan busied herself in the kitchen, her hand tingling where Jan had been holding onto it so tightly. She didn't think Jan was aware of what she was doing, but Morgan wouldn't complain. That soft skin pressing against her own...God, Morgan *itched* just to have a conversation with this woman most of the time.

As she turned back to the couch, Jan was looking down at her phone. "He's fucking unbelievable."

"Your husband?" Morgan asked, placing both glasses down. "Has he contacted you?"

"Yes." Jan handed her phone over to Morgan. There was a message waiting on the screen.

Look, Jan. You may not want to see me or speak to me, but you cannot possibly blame me for all of this. We were stale, love. We had no fun in our lives. I thought that by giving in to the attention from Anais it would spice things

up for us. I did it for us. Please come home so I can make it up to you. I still love you.

Wow. What a piece of shit. Right now, Morgan hoped that Jan wouldn't fall for her husband's bullshit. How could he possibly shift the blame onto her? He'd been the one who couldn't keep his dick in his pants. "That's...yeah, I don't really know what to say to that."

"Maybe *I* should find someone to fuck tonight and throw it right back at him. See how he likes it!"

While Morgan would happily insist Jan assume the position, spread out naked on her bed, now wasn't ideal. She lay a hand on Jan's knee this time, hoping she felt the support in her touch. "Hey, don't even rise to him. It's probably what he wants, so he can use it against you."

"How can he say that to me? And if that's what he *truly* believes, then it clearly didn't work out for him." Jan scoffed. "He did it to spice things up? I'm not sure he knows the meaning of the word!"

"Why don't you stay here tonight? It's one less thing for you to worry about, and I don't really like the idea of you leaving this bar on your own and not knowing what the plan or next step is."

"No, I couldn't ever ask that of you."

"I offered. I'd sleep much better tonight knowing that you're safe in my bed."

Jan's cheeks reddened as she dipped her head and looked down at her hands in her lap. Then her gaze shifted to Morgan's hand on her knee. "Is that why you invited me up here?"

"Oh, fuck. No. I swear it wasn't." Morgan swiftly pulled her hand away and inched back on the couch a little. She may be into Jan, but she absolutely hadn't invited her up here with any intentions of sleeping with her. She hadn't even known that Jan was technically available until *after* they'd reached her flat. "I meant that you could take my bed, and I'd sleep here. On the couch."

"I'll take the couch. If you're sure you don't mind."

Morgan wanted to argue that Jan should sleep in her bed and not on the couch, but she didn't want to scare Jan off. So long as she was warm and safe tonight, Morgan didn't care what happened next. The likelihood was that Jan would wake up in the morning and see things differently, and Morgan would never be alone with her like this again.

Don't let this become another Amanda situation all over again.

"If you want the couch, the couch it is."

CHAPTER 4

Stretching her back, Morgan groaned and rolled over, almost falling off the couch. She'd woken up as the sun streamed through the windows about an hour ago, wondering what the hell was going on, and then she remembered that Jan was here...and had ultimately agreed to the bed last night rather than the couch.

As she sat up on her elbows, her neck stiff, the bathroom door opened, and Jan strolled out in one of Morgan's fluffy but *very* short towels. Jan froze, gripping the towel against her. "O-oh. I took a shower. I hope you don't mind." She dipped her head. "I'm sorry. I didn't mean to wake you."

Fuck. Jan could wake Morgan up looking like that on *any* morning she wished to. It would be an honour to have this woman walking around her flat naked. It truly would.

"And thank you again for last night."

A lazy smile spread on Morgan's lips as she said, "Any time."

With red cheeks, Jan stared back at Morgan. "I'll just get dressed and head off. I need to go to the house and get some belongings, then find a place to stay. I didn't have the energy yesterday once I got there. I just sat on the edge of the bed for hours, wondering what was going on."

"You're welcome to stay here, you know. I work most evenings, so you'll have some space and that." Morgan didn't often share her space with anyone else, but she couldn't get that look of heartbreak in Jan's eyes out of her mind. If offering her a place to stay could ease the load for Jan, then Morgan would do that for her. "It's really no problem. I can be invisible."

"That's a very kind offer, but I shouldn't. I'll need to find a place eventually, so I should start that process now. Though, I think it'll just be a hotel for the time being."

Morgan sat up and ran a hand through her messy hair. She toyed with her lip ring, wanting to stand up and move closer to Jan. Could she do that? Probably, but Jan would likely run a mile given what she'd said last night when Morgan offered her bed to her. Maybe she should just stay sitting on the couch, and hopefully, Jan would join her for some breakfast. She would need the fuel for the day ahead anyway. They both would. "Okay."

"And if you should happen to see Gillian and Finn in the coming days, could you keep this to yourself please?"

"Of course. It's not my business. I just wanted to offer a shoulder last night and be there for you. I'm sure you'll tell them when you're ready to." Morgan wanted Jan to know that this could be a safe space when she needed it. There was no ulterior motive here, even if Morgan *did* want to show Jan a thing or two that her husband likely couldn't. "Take your time. No rush to get out of here, okay?"

Jan rested against the doorframe of Morgan's bedroom. "I can't believe I'm about to go home in the clothes I was wearing last night. I'm forty-eight, for the love of God."

Morgan lifted a shoulder. "I wouldn't worry. You looked *gorgeous* in that dress last night."

As she watched Morgan from across the room, still holding her towel in place, Jan narrowed her eyes. "I have a feeling you're quite the womaniser, Morgan."

"Me? Nah. Used to be back in my early twenties, but I can't be arsed with it anymore. It gets too messy. I think the whole Amanda situation has just reminded me that I'm better off single. That fucking around isn't for me anymore."

"You won't be going back for another helping if she shows up here?" Jan quirked a brow.

Fuck, that was sexy.

Morgan shook her head. "Absolutely not. I'm not getting tangled up in her marriage. No way. If I'd known in the beginning, I never would have slept with her." She did rise to her feet this time, opting for the coffee machine while Jan was getting dressed. Once she'd powered it on, she turned back to Jan. "I'm going to write my number down for you, okay? If you need anything at all, just send me a text, and I'll help in any way I can."

"Thank you, but I don't plan to be reliant on anyone if I can help it. People have their own lives to deal with. God knows Gillian and Finn have had enough going on to last them a lifetime. I'm not sure I even want to tell them."

Morgan understood that Jan probably felt embarrassed by all of this, but she had no reason to be. Her husband was the one in the wrong, and if Morgan knew Finn and Gillian the way she thought she did, they'd be upset knowing Jan was dealing with this alone. "You'll have to tell them at some point. Gillian is your best friend, and if Finn finds out I knew about it down the line, she'll kill me."

"And when that day comes, I'll take the blame. Since I'm taking the blame for everything else right now, what difference will it make?" Jan's shoulders slumped as she said that, the defeated look in her eyes painful to witness.

Morgan crossed the room and stopped in front of Jan. She smelled of white tea and mint, Morgan's favourite shower gel. "Hey," Morgan said as she lifted a hand to Jan's cheek. "You don't take shit from him, okay? Whatever bullshit he feeds you, you walk away with your head held high. He's the one who fucked up, not you."

Jan subconsciously leaned into Morgan's touch as her eyes closed. "I feel worthless."

Morgan stroked her fingers along Jan's jawline and brought them to her chin. "Look at me."

When Jan's eyes opened, the blueness of them had Morgan's heart pounding. "Don't *ever* feel worthless. You've done nothing wrong, and if he can't see what he had and is now losing, then I feel sorry for him. *He* should feel worthless. *He* should feel ashamed. Not you."

"I spent so long reminding Gillian of the things you've just said, but deep down, I know he needs more. He must do." Jan sniffled. "Twenty-seven years together, and he's getting his kicks elsewhere. I was so in love with him that I chose to look past his faults, *our* faults within the marriage, and now look at me."

"He has a mouth, Jan. If he chooses not to use it to communicate, then that's not on you. You did the decent thing and went to marriage counselling." God, Morgan hated seeing Jan like this. Her prick of a husband didn't deserve her at all.

"I...have nothing left." Jan whimpered as she lowered her eyes. "I even work with him. How am I supposed to keep doing that, knowing he's around and Anais is probably around, too. He's not going to fire her. *That's* a lawsuit waiting to happen."

"The important thing right now is that you concentrate on yourself. Look after *you*, not him or anyone else. You *have* to allow yourself the time to process this."

"I don't know how I would have got through last night without you." Jan took the hand resting under her chin and pressed her lips to Morgan's knuckles. The sensation it caused had Morgan's stomach somersaulting, but she couldn't focus on that. Whatever she *felt* was happening here...wasn't. "Thank you, Morgan."

God, even the way Jan spoke her name had the hairs on the back of Morgan's neck standing to attention. But Morgan knew Jan wasn't interested in her. She was straight—Morgan was certain of it. "You're welcome." And now she had to create some distance between them. "I'll put some breakfast on for us while you're getting dressed."

Jan turned for the bedroom and closed the door behind her. Morgan remained in her place, pressing a palm to the wood separating them, and sighed. Right now, Jan's well-being was the priority. Once she had left, Morgan could give herself a moment to process her own feelings. Until then, she would treat her guest the same way she would treat anyone else. With respect and a line between them.

With a shaking hand, Jan slid her key into the lock and opened the front door. Everything remained as it had always been, not an item out of place, but her heart was aching in her chest. She'd always wondered what a broken heart felt like, and as she stood in her bright, vanilla-scented hallway, she now knew. It wasn't something she would wish on anyone. *Just get some things together and leave.*

What a dreadful feeling to have. The house she had poured so much love into with Phil felt alien to her. She didn't feel as though she belonged in it anymore. Would Anais move in with Phil? Would he break things off with her? Jan didn't know any answers right now other than the fact that she needed to leave as soon as possible.

As she placed one foot on the stairs, the back living room door opened suddenly. "Thank God you're home." Phil sighed with relief, then frowned. "Where the hell have you been dressed like that?"

Jan looked back at Phil with utter disgust. "Why do you care where I've been?"

"Of course I care. You're my wife, and you didn't come home last night."

"Oh! *Now* I'm your wife? When it fucking suits you!" Jan

didn't want to get angry, she didn't have the energy for it, but how dare Phil say something like that to her? "And since you care so much, I stayed with a friend."

"Gill? She knows? Great!"

Jan almost laughed at that. If this hadn't been such a serious situation, she *would* have laughed. But this was a mess, and she had no idea where she would go from here. Nothing about this was remotely funny. "Gill doesn't know anything. I feel too fucking embarrassed to tell her. So, thank you for that. I have nobody to fall back on because *you've* made me feel so fucking humiliated that I don't want to face my closest friend."

"This has nothing to do with anybody else. It's between you and me."

Jan narrowed her eyes. "And Gareth and Anais."

"Love." Phil reached out a hand, but Jan shifted away.

"Don't dare touch me. You've been fucking another woman for a year, so don't you *dare* lay a hand on me, Phil."

He held up his hands and took a step back. The light caught his wedding ring, but it only made Jan sick to the stomach all over again. She lowered her clutch bag to the stairs, then removed her custom-made wedding and engagement rings. She dropped them into his palm, then looked back up to meet his gaze.

"W-what are you doing?" Phil stared down at the platinum in his hand as his bottom lip trembled.

"Thank you for ruining the twenty-seven years we spent together. Do whatever you like with those. I have no use for them anymore." Without another word, Jan took the stairs slowly, the weight of what was happening crushing her shoulders. She felt tired and drained. She felt...hopeless.

"Jan! We need to talk about this! You can't just walk out on me."

Jan turned around when she reached the top of the stairs and glared at Phil. "We have nothing to talk about, and I *can* just walk out on you." She scoffed and shook her head. "And take this as my notice. I resign. Don't expect me to work the four weeks required either."

"Jan, love. Please."

Jan walked away and directly into the bedroom. She eyed the bed, consumed by so many questions. Had Phil ever brought Anais over here? Had that woman been in her bed? She balked at the thought, rushing into the ensuite and emptying the contents of her stomach into the toilet. As Jan lowered herself to the floor and pressed her back against the bath, tears slowly worked their way down her face.

What the hell am I supposed to do now?

She stared at her knees as she brought them to her chest, her eyes burning when fresh tears appeared. How long would crying last? Would she ever stop, or would the pain of her marriage ending consume her forever? Gillian had pulled through, but then again, Gillian had found someone ten times the person Dave ever could have been. Jan didn't feel as though she was in a similar position. Gillian hadn't been happy with Dave, but Jan? She'd worshipped the ground Phil walked on...even when she felt something was off within their marriage. Perhaps that had been where she'd gone wrong. Unconditionally adoring someone could only ever bring disappointment. At the end of the day, *nobody* was perfect. On reflection, Phil certainly hadn't been.

The only thing she knew with certainty right now was that there was no coming back for them. Other people may be willing to give that second chance, but Jan couldn't. She would forever wonder what Phil was doing and who he was with. That trust had been obliterated, and there was no going back.

She exhaled a shaky breath and wiped the tears from her face. "Time to...start over."

CHAPTER 5

Morgan held her phone in her hand, staring down at the screen. Amanda was calling her, but she was praying it would ring off before she found the courage to answer it. She didn't want to deal with her own life. She'd spent enough time helping Jan out with hers. Yes, she was avoiding the situation, and no, she didn't care. Amanda was just...too much for her today. She would have an answer for everything Morgan threw at her, and right now, Morgan didn't have the attention span for that kind of conversation. All she wanted when the time came to confront Amanda was the truth. Plain and simple.

She's going to bullshit her way out of this. I know it.

Morgan lowered her phone to the shelf beneath the bar and got back to work. In the grand scheme of things, her situation with Amanda wasn't that important. Morgan had specifically avoided any sort of attachment with her because she didn't want to be tied down. With the right person, she would love nothing more than that, but there had always been something about Amanda that just about kept Morgan at arm's length. Today, she was grateful for that.

She groaned when her phone pinged. If Amanda didn't stop

the constant calls and messages, Morgan was going to block her. That wasn't really what she wanted to do, she would prefer to move on with her life without adding to her never-ending block list, but it was something she was considering.

Only as she lifted her phone again, it wasn't Amanda. It was Jan.

Hi, Morgan. Thank you for everything you did for me the other night and the following morning. I don't know what I would have done without you. I owe you dinner when you're available. Jan x

Morgan tried to suppress a smile but failed. Jan wanted to take her for dinner to say thank you? Well, Morgan couldn't turn that down even if she knew she should. Jan's situation was going to be complicated, Morgan wasn't stupid, but that wasn't her main concern. No, her biggest issue was the idea of being alone with Jan again. That woman knew how to dress, she knew how to present herself, and fucking hell...she was hot. Four days on from Jan showing up here, and Morgan had her firmly on her mind.

Morgan had always thought Amanda was hot, and yeah, she was. But Jan? Oh, Jan was on another level entirely. Before last night, Jan's confidence whenever she walked through the door to Morgan's bar was like nothing she'd ever come across before. But it wasn't a confidence that intimidated you or made you question the kind of person Jan was. It was just a sexy 'I'm an older woman, and I know my worth' kind of confidence. Amanda, on the other hand, knew she was attractive, and she didn't care who she looked down her nose at.

She tapped her foot against the floor, trying to find the right words to respond to Jan. Morgan had almost put herself in it the other day when Jan had gone up to the flat with her, and she really didn't want Jan to think that she was doing this for her *because* Morgan was a lesbian. Yes, she'd been accused of *that* before today. Morgan appreciated women—how could she not?—but she would never try it on with someone going through so much.

Throw in the fact that Jan was straight, and Morgan knew it was a recipe for disaster. That had been the very reason she'd put anything she felt for Jan to the back of her mind the *second* she knew she was a married woman.

Hey! Great to hear from you. I couldn't let you leave last night. You weren't in the right frame of mind to wander the streets. You know I'm around if you need anything.

Morgan chose not to add a kiss to the end of her message, even though Jan had put one at the end of hers. She would simply play it cool and leave it at that.

Her phone buzzed in her hand.

He was home when I got here. I thought he would be at work x

Morgan winced as she read that message. With the mood Jan had been in that morning, she didn't imagine seeing her husband was really what she wanted. The pain in her eyes, the shake of her hands, it just...felt devastating. This didn't even involve Morgan, but her heart *did* break for Jan.

She responded immediately.

Are you okay?

As she waited for a reply, the bar door opened, and Amanda walked through it. Morgan clenched her jaw. She didn't want to do this now. Not while she was working and certainly not in front of the few daytime paying customers she had dotted around the place.

"Why aren't you answering my calls?" Amanda lowered her handbag to the bar with a thud. "I told you the other week that I'd be here for a couple of days with you. You didn't let me know what you wanted for dinner, so here I am, empty-handed."

Morgan's brows rose. Even though Amanda had no idea Morgan knew the truth, she was still surprised Amanda had walked through the door. "Could I have a word with you out the back?"

Amanda smirked. "Sure. *A word.*"

"No, I'm serious. I *do* want a word with you, so whatever ideas you have in your head about what's going to happen out there, you can get rid of them right now." Morgan recognised the look in Amanda's eyes as she rounded the bar counter and stepped through the door Morgan held open for her. It led to the cellar; it was cold and damp, but this wouldn't take Morgan long at all. She would be back in the warmth of the bar in mere moments.

"What's going on?" Amanda folded her arms across her chest and leant against the wall.

"Okay, so...let me explain this to you." Morgan carded a hand through her hair and cleared her throat. "You're going to go back out into the bar, get your bag, and leave."

Amanda scoffed. "Excuse me?"

"You're married, Amanda. You have a fucking husband. Did you not think that was something I should know? Did you not think it was important for me to have this information so I could decide if I wanted to do this with you?"

"H-how do you know about my husband?"

Morgan couldn't believe this woman. Did it really matter how she knew? "I found out last weekend. One of my regulars saw you leaving the flat, and they know you. They also know that you've been married for *thirty* years."

"That's nobody else's business!"

Morgan nodded slowly. "It's *my* business, Amanda. I can't do this with you if you're married. I know we've had *a lot* of fun, but it stops now. Right now. Please, don't come here again."

Amanda snorted and pushed off the wall. "You've no idea what you're walking away from. You'll be sorry."

"Sorry to walk away from a cheat? Nah, I don't think I'll regret this decision at all." Morgan opened the door again and ushered Amanda back out into the bar. "Take care of yourself. I have a job to do."

Amanda stood on the other side of the bar, dumbfounded by Morgan's reaction. She blinked repeatedly, but Morgan wasn't discussing this any further. Amanda was married, and that was that. It didn't *need* any further discussion.

"Morgan, can we work this out?"

"Nope. We can't." Morgan lifted her phone from the shelf and found two messages waiting for her.

Am I okay? That's quite the question to ask. The honest answer is no. I'm not. Still, I have no choice but to pick myself up and move on with my life. I don't know what that looks like yet, but at least I'm not staying with a man who sleeps with other women. That's something, I guess x

Then came the other message, timestamped almost ten minutes later.

I'm sorry. That was too much. You don't need this. Thank you again x

Shit. Jan must have thought that Morgan's lack of response meant she didn't care or that this was all too much. Only she did care, and she would care a whole lot more the moment Amanda left her bar. She quickly started writing out a reply.

Would you like to come over tonight?

Jan likely wouldn't take her up on that offer, but Morgan secretly *and* stupidly hoped she would. She could be an adult and offer *another* shoulder to Jan, right?

Morgan looked up. Amanda was watching her intently. "Are you going to leave?"

"No, I'm not. I'm not leaving until we've talked about this." Amanda moved closer and lowered her voice. "You have no right to judge me when you take a woman up to your flat who has only come into your bar for a drink! Because that's what happened, Morgan. *You* encouraged me up those stairs."

"Mm. I did. And *you* had no issues using your legs and taking yourself up them, did you?" Morgan sighed. She couldn't be bothered with drama. "I really need to get on and serve my customers."

Morgan's heart jumped when Jan responded.

I think you gave me enough of your time on Monday night.

Chewing her lip, Morgan thought about how best to approach this. She wanted to spend time with Jan again to find out what the next step for her was, but she didn't want to sound desperate.

Look, I'll be here all evening. If you find yourself at a loose end and want to talk, you know where I am.

Satisfied that her response was good enough, she locked her phone and shoved it into her back pocket. "Right, I'm off to do some work. Please leave, Amanda."

Amanda took her bag from the bar this time. "I'm not done with this. I *will* be back."

Oh, I'm sure you will, Morgan thought. "And when you do, I'll tell you the very same thing again. Whatever the fuck we were doing...*has* ended."

Armed with a huge arrangement of flowers, Jan stepped inside The Corner bar and looked around. Damn it. It seemed Morgan wasn't working tonight. Jan didn't really know why she was here; she wasn't sure it was the wisest idea in the world, given the fact Morgan had revealed a few things to her earlier in the week, but Morgan seemed to care. She seemed to want to be there for Jan. At the moment, it felt as though Morgan was all she had when it came to someone she could talk to.

She still found herself unable to reach out to Gillian and Finn again, so here she was...hoping for the support Morgan had so selflessly offered on Monday. Right now, Jan only hoped she didn't find herself an emotional wreck in Morgan's flat, as she had on the previous occasion. Even though she rarely showed her emotions, she felt safe doing so with Morgan. Jan couldn't put her finger on *why* she'd felt drawn to come here this evening, but she was just going to go with it. It was just a drink, and Morgan had already invited Jan over. Maybe she would even gain a friend out of this.

Your real friends are going to hit the roof when they find out about this.

Jan had her reasons for keeping her separation from Gillian. Finn, too. They'd had a rough time of it over the last several months, and she simply didn't have the heart to put this on them. They were just getting back into life with one another. Jan's issues could wait. She could deal with it all herself.

She cleared her throat and stepped towards the bar. A guy she'd seen working here before smiled back at her, and then he approached. "Hi. What can I get you?"

"Oh, I'm looking for Morgan. Is she out tonight?" Jan frowned, both disappointed *and* relieved. Morgan wasn't expecting her, Jan hadn't even bothered to send a message before she'd left the house, but Morgan *had* said she could show up.

"R-right. I see." He grinned and took his phone from his back pocket. "I'll just let her know you're here." He eyed Jan as he tapped the screen, that smile not fading. And then Jan realised that Morgan *was* here, and she was about to come face to face with her, flower arrangement and all. "You seem much nicer than the other one. For a start, you've brought her flowers. Nice touch."

Jan looked down at the flowers and then back up at the bartender. "I'm sorry?"

"You're her date, no?" He frowned. "I mean, nobody else brings her flowers."

"I, uh...I'm just a friend of Morgan's." Jesus. Did Morgan put herself about, or was this guy just not selling her very well? "If she's busy, though..."

"She's not. She's upstairs, on her own, in that bloody flat. She rarely leaves this building unless she has to get supplies in." His phone pinged. "She'll be down now."

Jan hesitated between the bar and the exit. Was she making a mistake coming here? Had Morgan really wanted to invite her over, or was she just being polite? Either way, Jan appreciated it. Then there were the very brief thoughts she'd had since Morgan had told Jan she'd been attracted to her. Of course Jan had noticed Morgan the first time she walked through the door and on several occasions since, but Jan hadn't been with a woman in what...thirty years? A very brief fling during her university years with a woman called Antonia had been probably the greatest sex of her life, but that had been a long time ago. She'd lived an entirely different existence since then. Jan couldn't even say she was bisexual. There had been precisely *one* woman in her forty-eight years on this earth, and as she stood here, she wasn't sure she could even remember what to do when it came to sex with another woman.

Oh, I bet you Morgan could show you a thing or two...

Whoa. Where the hell had that thought come from? Jan swallowed as she looked at the bartender, wondering if she'd said something out loud that should have remained firmly in her mind.

"She shouldn't be long." He smiled. "Have a seat, and I'll get you a drink?"

The door to Morgan's flat suddenly opened. She looked up at her, flashing a full smile when Morgan rested against the doorframe and stared back at Jan. "H-hi. I'm sorry for just showing up."

Morgan poked out her tongue and ran it over the ring in her bottom lip as she lifted a brow. "Nice flowers. They're not from the husband, are they?"

Jan snorted. "God, no. Even when we were together, he rarely brought me flowers." Jan started towards Morgan, suddenly feeling a little hot and bothered. Morgan wore nothing but a tank top and a pair of short gym shorts. "They're for you. From me."

"Oh, Jan." Morgan tutted as she stepped closer and took the flowers from Jan. "You do realise that when you bring a lesbian flowers, it means we'll be living together within the next two weeks, right?"

That was precisely what Jan needed tonight. Humour. Actually, she suspected that humour would be her go-to for the foreseeable future. "Oh, two weeks?" She sighed. "I have my luggage in the car. I was hoping that *you*, the strong lesbian, could take it up the stairs for me. I wouldn't want to break a nail."

Morgan barked a laugh and stepped aside. "It's good to see you again."

"I came over because I thought you were working. Sorry to interrupt your night off." Jan felt stupid for not texting Morgan first. If she'd known she had the night off, she would have left her in peace. "Anyway, I just wanted to bring the flowers over and say thank you again for Monday night. It meant a lot."

"The flowers are gorgeous, but you didn't have to do this. I invited you up on Monday because you needed someone to talk to. And I'd do it again." Morgan reached out and squeezed the hand at Jan's side. "You're not alone, okay?"

Jan chewed her lip as she looked back at Morgan. "I'm sure you don't want to, but would you like to go for a walk or something?"

Morgan wore a huge smile. "You know what, I would. I'd like that."

"Okay, well, I'll wait here until you're ready." Jan hopped up onto a stool and placed her bag on the counter. "Don't rush or anything. I don't exactly have anywhere to be."

"You can come up if you like?" Morgan threw a thumb over her shoulder as she half-turned. "I just need to throw some pants on and grab a jacket."

Jan decided to decline. Morgan wore the bare minimum, and Jan found herself looking in places she shouldn't. It wasn't anything to worry about; Morgan was an attractive woman, but Jan still knew it would be for the best if she waited down here. With the headspace she was in, she had no idea what she could be capable of. "Really, I'm okay here."

CHAPTER 6

Quietly strolling around the streets of the town, Jan looked up at the clear night sky, appreciative that Morgan had joined her for a walk. When she had texted her earlier, Jan wasn't sure if Morgan had really wanted to respond. They'd been chatting...until they weren't. "Thank you for joining me tonight."

"I enjoy spending time with you. You're good company."

"Oh." Jan was surprised by that. "I wasn't sure if my texts were too much earlier."

"No. Not at all." Morgan smiled as they crossed the street. "While I was texting you, Amanda turned up."

"Amanda is the woman you were seeing but not seeing, yes?" Jan didn't like the idea of Morgan being involved with a married woman, but she did believe her when Morgan said she was completely unaware of the fact. They didn't know one another. She had no reason to lie to Jan.

"Yep. That's the one. I didn't think she was going to leave, to be honest." They stopped outside a bar, and Morgan cocked her head towards it. "Fancy a quick drink?"

"Yes, okay." They made their way inside, and Jan found a table for them. When Morgan returned and Jan had a glass of Merlot in her hand, she relaxed into the environment. "Do you see any kind of reconciliation with Amanda?"

"No. It was nothing serious anyway. There was always something about Amanda that I couldn't quite put my finger on, so I was never all in. Neither was she. It was just...fooling around, if you will."

"Genuine question," Jan said as she shifted in her seat a little. "Is that something you enjoy? No strings...casual?"

Morgan sipped her beer and lifted a shoulder. "Sometimes it's all I can have. The bar is my life, and even though I love being there and meeting all kinds of new people, it does affect my love life."

Jan stared down at the rich red liquid in her glass. "I don't even know what dating looks like these days. It's not something I've had to worry about for a long time."

"You'll be okay. It's not as scary as you probably think it is."

"Oh, I don't know. Gillian and Finn certainly didn't have an easy time." Jan couldn't bear the thought of taking an interest in someone that society saw as risky.

"Well, unless you're a lecturer and planning to sleep with your student, I wouldn't worry about it being anything remotely similar."

"No, you're right." Jan smiled.

"What is it that you do? If you don't mind me asking..."

Jan lowered her wine glass to the table. "I worked with Phil. He has a housing development business and a separate security business. I took care of all things office-related on the housing development side of things."

"You're really not going back to work with him?"

"It's not something I can even begin to imagine." The day Jan walked back into the office, she knew she would fall apart. Everyone would know about the affair—news always travelled fast in those settings—and she didn't want everyone whispering about it behind her back. "But I don't know what the plan is right now. I'm taking it one *hour* at a time."

"You *will* be okay, you know, Jan. It'll take some time to find your feet and find a new normal, but in the end, you'll thrive. I'm sure of it."

"How can you possibly say that? You know practically nothing about me."

Morgan angled her head. "Well, I know that you light up my bar every time you step foot inside it. I know that you're great fun to be around. I know you're very close to your friends and you'd probably do anything for them. I could go on, but I won't."

Oh, Jan wished Morgan would continue. For the last few days, Jan had felt unsure of herself. If Morgan believed in her, then she would take it. She dipped her head and smiled. "Thank you."

"Your husband may have royally fucked up, but don't let it defeat you. You have so much to look forward to. You just have to be patient."

Jan knew she would find herself again. She just didn't know how that would happen. "You know what, can we just forget about my failed marriage tonight?"

"That sounds like a good idea to me." Morgan inched her glass towards Jan's as Jan picked hers back up and clinked them together. "Cheers to being amazing women who don't take shit from anyone."

Jan could only allow the warmth she felt inside as Morgan gazed back at her. "Mm. Cheers to that."

Morgan shoved her hands in the pockets of her jeans as they left the bar, aware of how she'd felt as she sat across a table from Jan. If she didn't do something with her hands, she was worried she would reach out and take one of Jan's. Spending the evening away from the bar had been good for Morgan, but it only left her wanting to do it more often. She couldn't recall the last time she had taken her jacket from the hook behind her door and strolled around the local area. The fresh air was a nice change from the smell of alcohol.

They crossed a side street and passed by the closed shops. Morgan didn't want to head back just yet, but Jan looked tired. She hadn't seemed that way when they'd been talking, but Morgan understood that Jan's days were likely a lot to deal with lately. If this was the end of the night for them, then so be it.

"Thanks for inviting me out. It's been lovely."

"I know you said the bar is your life, but does that also mean you work a lot, too?"

Morgan held up a hand. "Guilty."

"Then we should do this again when you're available. It gets me out of that stuffy hotel room and you away from the place you spend most of your time."

Morgan smiled as she side-eyed Jan. "I'd like that."

"Please tell me to piss off if you don't fancy it, though."

It would take a lot for Morgan to turn down an evening like this with Jan. Unless she was severely sick in bed, she was going to make herself available for this woman whenever she could. "I'll always fancy it."

"I will tell Gillian and Finn soon. I'm just trying to sort things out in my own head before I have to have that conversation. Gillian is going to be just as shocked as I was when I found out." Jan suddenly linked an arm through Morgan's. "Once they know, you won't have to feel obligated to do any of this with me."

Morgan tightened her arm and effectively drew Jan closer to the side of her. "Do I look like this is any trouble for me?"

"Well, no." Jan smiled, and if Morgan's eyes weren't deceiving her, she would say she was blushing a little, too.

"Then I don't know why you would think I feel obligated to do this with you."

Jan sighed. "I guess I'm just surprised by how accommodating you've been. How much you've helped me through recent days."

"It's just who I am. Always there to help everyone other than myself." It was true. She was forever doing something for someone or making sure everyone else was okay, but when it came to herself...Morgan generally pushed what she wanted to the back of her mind.

"Why is that?"

"Because I know how things usually go for me." Morgan lifted a shoulder as they turned a corner and landed in front of the local park. She expected Jan would want to separate here since her hotel was nearby, but Jan just continued walking. Morgan wouldn't stop her. It meant they got more time alone with one another. "Even the smallest part of me is jealous that you'll have the chance to date soon."

"Correct me if I'm wrong, but you must have so many women on offer. You own a bar, for the love of God."

"Mm. All straight, it seems. Or...straight again once they've taken what they want from me." Morgan glanced in Jan's direction, admiring her profile against the streetlights. "I've lost count of the number of times I've found myself attracted to a straight woman." Morgan locked eyes with Jan as Jan turned her face to her. "Case in point."

"I still don't know why you've *ever* found me remotely attractive." Jan laughed as she said that, almost as though it was self-deprecating. "But I am sorry you've had those experiences with women."

Morgan could reel off all the reasons she'd found Jan attractive, but what was the point? She would rather befriend Jan than make it awkward between them. Because inevitably, it *always* ended that way. Morgan didn't want to risk that here. Jan was great company, regardless of the fact that Morgan was into her. "I'm sure I'll live."

"And love, at some point." Jan winked as they took the gravelled path around the park. It was a mild night, only requiring something light in terms of layers, but Morgan would have been warm anyway. Jan was one of those women who was unassuming to some people but drop-dead gorgeous to most others. Morgan fell into the latter. Her temperature had risen the moment she'd laid eyes on Jan standing in the middle of the bar, holding the most gorgeous flowers. "Did you feel anything for Amanda at all?"

"Oh, yeah. I cared about her. Of course I did." God, Morgan didn't want Jan to think she just fucked her way around the city. It really wasn't like that. "We both knew what it was. We agreed. I just wish she'd been forthcoming with me about her marriage."

"I think that if it worked for you at the time, then you shouldn't let it get to you. Like Phil, she's the one in the wrong. Neither you nor I should feel guilty about anything."

Morgan appreciated that. "You're right. It's easy to blame yourself, though. I'm sure you'll agree."

"I've been the master of blaming myself recently. But then I sat there in the hotel room, wondering why I should lay the blame on myself. I didn't drop my pants for anyone other than my husband."

Oh, I wish you'd drop your pants for me. Morgan batted that away and shook her head. "You did nothing wrong."

"And neither did you." Jan gave Morgan a knowing look. "If I find out that you've taken any blame whatsoever, you and I will fall out."

"Nah. This one is *all* on Amanda. I know that."

"So, what does the rest of the night have in store for you?" Jan was still linking Morgan's arm with her own. Did she even realise she was doing it? Morgan wasn't about to alert her to the fact.

"Not much. Home, maybe some TV, then bed. Same old, really."

"I'd invite you over to my place, but I don't have one of those at the moment." Jan laughed. Morgan was glad she could find some humour in this situation. Then again, she guessed Jan would cry if she wasn't laughing about it. "Maybe one day soon I'll be able to return the favour."

"And when that day comes, I'll be the first on the doorstep with the best bottle of red I can find."

Jan smiled. "It's a date!"

CHAPTER 7

Jan arched her back, moaning into the silence of the room as she came down from an intense orgasm. For the first time since she'd left Phil, Jan had found herself overcome with arousal. Unable to concentrate, she had taken to her bed some two hours ago, only now releasing the pent-up tension her body had been holding onto.

She pressed a hand to her forehead and panted. She hadn't expected to come so hard, but it was what she was focused on that had her worried and confused. As she'd slipped her fingers inside herself, Morgan had been solely on her mind. As she'd forced her heels into the mattress and sunk deeper, she had imagined Morgan's fingers inside her. Bringing her to the edge as she whispered filth in her ear.

Jan shuddered and relaxed into the bed. Did she need to process whatever this was she was feeling? Most probably. Only she didn't want to. It had been a *joy* to have Morgan on her mind in that moment. Jan just prayed she would be able to look Morgan in the eye the next time they saw one another.

"Oh, this is a mess."

In her head, perhaps, but when Jan was with Morgan, she

found herself unable to focus on anything other than the woman in question. Morgan made her feel as though everything wasn't so terrible right now. She made her want to pick up her life and move it onto a path far more exciting than what she'd subjected herself to over the last few years. Jan wasn't ready to admit her marriage had been falling miserably, but it was true. For the most part, it seemed Jan had been holding onto the beautiful weekend she'd recently spent with her husband. But if she pushed those very few days to the back of her mind, the affair was beginning to make sense. It didn't absolve Phil of anything, but it did make sense to Jan. Perhaps 'sense' was the wrong word for her realisation, but Jan *was* beginning to understand that the life she'd portrayed hadn't quite been so truthful.

She turned on her side and spied her phone on the bedside table. She hadn't seen Morgan for a couple of days now, but that wasn't anything unusual. Until last week, they hadn't really had much of a conversation with one another. Jan had briefly found herself looking in Morgan's direction, but no sooner had she done so...she had stopped. She hadn't allowed her mind to wander when it came to women in *many* years, but around Morgan, she found it too easy. She found it normal and natural. Morgan, the beautiful bartender, certainly made Jan feel some kind of way.

A way she wanted to explore.

But a way she knew would cause a lot of confusion.

She reached for her phone and chewed her lip. Could she drop Morgan a message to say hi? Could she ask if she would be free in the coming days? Morgan had given Jan her number, and they'd already exchanged a few messages, but Jan wasn't sure sending a message out of the blue would be wise. She never wanted Morgan to think she had to respond.

She told you she enjoys being with you.

Jan smiled as she held her phone to her chest and rolled onto her back. She *had* noticed the way Morgan looked at her. She also had the reminder of what Morgan had said at the back of her mind. Morgan...found Jan attractive. *God, you're out of your mind if you think anything could happen between you*. Jan sighed, aware that she wasn't in the right frame of mind for anything meaningful at the moment. She could just about manage to find the strength to leave her hotel room since she'd left Morgan outside the hotel the other night. But—and she had to wonder if this was true—she believed she was dragging her feet this weekend *because* she had no concrete plans to see Morgan.

Fuck it. Text her.

Jan brought their very short message thread up on the screen and scrolled through the conversation they'd had since Morgan had so kindly handed her number over to Jan. She smiled as she read the messages, reminded of just how supportive Morgan had been so far. Yes, it had only been a week—*almost*—since Jan had left her marriage, but she had been there for Jan, regardless of the length of time.

Hi.

Jan tutted and deleted the single word she had written. What did she even say to Morgan? She couldn't exactly start with, 'Hi, I've just fucked myself while I was thinking about you'. Maybe if they knew one another better and something had happened between them, then that would be the perfect conversation starter, but *nothing* had happened, and nothing would.

Jan sat up against the headboard and closed her eyes. This wasn't healthy, and it wasn't sensible. But she'd spent a significant number of years being the sensible one. So what if she wanted to let go and enjoy life for the brief moment it was possible.

Hi. I don't know if you have plans, but I wondered if you'd like to see one another at some point this week? As you are aware, I have very little to do with my time, and we seem to enjoy the spontaneity.

Okay, that wasn't too much, right? Jan quickly hit send before she could delete the message again. She didn't expect Morgan to reply any time soon—she was likely preparing the bar for opening

—but she would look forward to a response at some point later this evening.

As Jan locked her phone and lowered it to the bed, it pinged. Her heart shot up into her throat, but most of all, she was wet all over again at the mere thought of Morgan.

Hey! I was just thinking about you. I'm working tonight, but you're welcome to come over here and grace my bar with your beautiful presence.

Morgan had been thinking about her? *Oh my.* Jan felt her cheeks beginning to heat. She didn't know why Morgan made her feel that way, but she was a very attractive woman. Perhaps she was just choosing to focus on that fact without realising it.

You wouldn't mind? I don't want your customers to talk...

Morgan started to reply immediately.

Talk about what? Whether I'd ever be lucky enough to call you mine, or whether you're considering an AA meeting?

Jan squeezed her thighs together.

Why would Morgan hint at something like a relationship if she wasn't thinking it?

The latter. I could be accused of sleeping with worse people.

Jan considered whether that was too forward, but if she was learning anything about Morgan, it was that she found the humour in most situations.

Now, now, Jan. Don't hint at a good time!

Jan laughed out loud at that. Morgan had responded exactly the way Jan hoped she would.

Then, another message came through.

Seriously, you should come to the bar this evening. You help my shift to go much quicker when you're here.

God, Morgan was going to make it painfully difficult to be around her. Jan felt it as she stared down at the screen.

Maybe I'll surprise you. Who knows?

She locked her phone and threw it to the end of the bed. If she couldn't reach it, she wouldn't continue texting Morgan. The longer she did, the more she knew she would end up flirting with her.

Jan shifted back down the bed and smiled. Whatever she was feeling, she was running with it. It sure as hell beat sitting here thinking about the worst she was dealing with. She slowly lowered her hand down her stomach and moaned when her fingertips reached her clit again. Fuck, she was sensitive. Her body was craving something far more than this. But for now, she would enjoy being in the most beautiful place in her head. A place where Phil and her failed marriage didn't exist, but Morgan did.

Rushed off her feet, Morgan served customer after customer, dying to reach out and grab the coffee she'd made herself well over thirty minutes ago. Tyler was taking care of one end of the bar while Morgan focused on the other. She'd always known showing football matches would bring in more people, but she hadn't expected the bar to be *this* packed tonight. It was only a league game for a championship team.

She handed change to one customer and moved along to the next. Ben had been pulling pints of their bestselling beer, ready to hand out as soon as one was ordered, and he was now on his fifth lot of pulling. *At least*. Morgan eyed him as she took one of the few left beneath the bar. "Thanks, Ben. This was a great idea."

"Most people want beer. It just made sense to have some ready to go."

Morgan didn't know what she would do without her bar staff most of the time. She would also admit to not pre-empting the sheer volume of people. Still, they had a good system going now, and the match would be over soon. Once the TV was turned off,

Morgan would have a minute to gather herself and get back to work. She likely wouldn't have the chance to grab something to eat until she finished in a few hours. Thank God she wasn't working until close.

As Morgan set two beers down on the counter, she took a ten-pound note from her customer and rang it up. It was becoming a mindless task now. And then she caught that familiar scent. Jan's perfume. Morgan turned her head to the right, beaming a smile when Jan stood waiting patiently. "Hey!"

"Busy tonight." Jan leaned over the bar a little, her blue eyes captivating against her dark eye makeup. "Makes sense, though. This *is* the best bar in town, after all."

"Yeah. It'll quieten down soon. It's because of the footy," Morgan said, thrilled that Jan had decided to turn up. She also appreciated the compliment about the bar. "Do you have a seat?"

"You must be joking. I just about made it through the door."

Morgan eyed the guy who had been sitting on the high table in the corner for the last couple of hours. He had a spare stool, even if several people had already asked if it was in use. Morgan knew it wasn't. He often came in here, and he was always alone. She approached him and smiled. "It's okay if I take this?" She nodded towards the stool as she lifted it. "It's been free since you walked in here now."

He shrugged and murmured something, but Morgan didn't have time to ask him to repeat what he'd said. She took the stool and positioned it right next to the small walkway entrance behind the bar. She held out a hand and helped Jan up onto it.

"There you go. Now, you have no reason at all to leave." Morgan winked as she turned away from Jan, poured a glass of red, and then set it down in front of her.

"Thank you." Jan smiled. "For the drink *and* the seat."

"I look after my customers. Especially the pretty ones." Morgan knew she was flirting, but she didn't care. After spending several moments with Jan over the last week, it had only heightened everything she'd been pushing down. "How are you?"

"Good. I've had a relaxing day."

Morgan groaned inwardly. She would give anything for a relaxing day at the minute. There always seemed to be one thing or another that she needed to tackle. "Maybe I'll have one of those in the near future."

"No days off on the horizon?" Jan wrinkled her nose as she brought her glass of wine closer. "Don't forget that *you* are the owner, Morgan."

"I have tomorrow off. I just know I'll end up taking care of something that crops up. I usually do." Morgan was aware that she needed to make time for herself. But once she ended up down here, it seemed easier to help out if she had no plans.

"Well, you'll have to make yourself available tomorrow evening. No ifs, no buts."

Morgan eyed the date on her watch and frowned. She didn't have anything planned, and if she did, she was certain she hadn't mentioned it to Jan. "Do I? Why?"

"Because I'm coming over." Jan shrugged and scanned the bar. "If it'll keep you out of here for the night, I can suffer through it."

Morgan smirked as she approached Jan. She turned her face away from the customers and dipped her head towards Jan's ear. "If you keep showing up here, I'm going to find it very hard to bury the attraction I've always had towards you. I hope you realise that."

Jan turned her own head until their cheeks were pressed together and said, "You'll just have to learn to keep your hands to yourself."

Morgan took her bottom lip between her teeth while Jan couldn't see her doing so, hoping to God the arousal wouldn't be evident on her face when their eyes met again. She gathered her thoughts and took a step back. "So long as I don't wake up again to find you half-naked in my living room, I think we'll do just fine."

"That wasn't intentional."

Morgan cocked her head. "Well, that's a shame. That was the best morning I've had in a long time." Morgan looked at Jan's lips, then back up at her eyes. "I was waiting for you to drop the towel."

A redness spread on Jan's cheeks, but it didn't seem as though she had any intention of admonishing Morgan. She just smirked and dipped her eyes. "Should I repeat what I said to you that morning?"

Morgan couldn't recall what that was, so she simply shrugged.

"I called you a womaniser." Jan narrowed her eyes slightly. "But now that I know you a little better, I was wrong."

"Oh?" Morgan quirked a brow, aware that customers were waiting to be served. "What makes you think that you're wrong?"

"I've been in here now when many women are around, and you haven't once done anything to give me that impression of you."

Huh. Good observation. "No, I reserve the womanising for certain women in particular."

Jan pursed her lips and looked away, but Morgan could see the slight smile she wore. God, she loved that smile. "Interesting."

"It...could be." Morgan winked and turned to one of her customers. "What can I get you?" She chanced a look in Jan's direction as he reeled off his order, surprised that Jan was staring back at Morgan with an unusual look in her eyes. Was that... arousal? Surely not. She snapped out of her thoughts and smiled at her customer. "Coming right up."

CHAPTER 8

The laughter that rang out throughout Morgan's flat was something that rarely happened. She spent so much time here alone, in the silence, that she was sure her bartender was going to complain about the noise at some point. Jan had texted her this morning, reminding Morgan that they had plans together tonight, and now here they were, spending another evening together up in Morgan's flat. Today marked one week since Jan had found out about her husband's affair, and she seemed less harrowed by everything.

One thing Morgan had noticed was how much she'd loosened up since she took a seat on the couch some two hours ago. Really, this night couldn't be going any better. Jan was great fun; she had the most intoxicating laugh, and Morgan had almost spewed her drink down herself on several occasions tonight just because of Jan's humour. The most important thing was that Jan was comfortable here.

"You know the other day when I texted you before I brought you flowers?" Jan's face turned serious all of a sudden. Morgan had no idea what she was about to say.

"Yeah."

"I did mean it when I said I owed you dinner."

Morgan smiled. "I'd love to go for dinner with you."

"Perfect. Just let me know when is best for you. I'm flexible at the moment."

Morgan would be sure to let Jan know her availability. She had thought about Jan's offer a few times since she'd received it on Friday, but she wasn't sure if it was the right idea to bring it up. Jan had already thanked her with the most beautiful arrangement of flowers. Dinner no longer seemed necessary. "I will. For sure."

"You don't leave your flat much, do you?" Jan asked as she sipped her wine. "I say that because your bartender implied it when I turned up last week."

"I don't. When I'm not working, I'm too tired to bother going out anywhere. Around here, it's mostly other bars. Spending my life working behind one means I'm sick of the sight of them when I finish work or have a day off."

"I can understand that."

"But I have friends who come here to hang out. Finn, for example."

Jan narrowed her eyes at Morgan. "Did you and Finn ever… you know?"

Morgan choked on the sip of wine she'd just taken. "Fuck each other?"

"Mmhmm."

"No. Finn has always been complicated and kinda standoffish. We used to flirt, but I don't think anything would have ever come of it. We're not each other's type. She's heavily into femme women, and well, so am I." Morgan would consider herself a tomboy rather than anything else. It would take a lot for her to dress up, but she wasn't completely opposed to the idea. "Put a woman in sexy heels and a dress, and I'm all hers. Finn is the same. Hence her attraction towards Gillian."

Jan sighed and ran her fingertip around the rim of her wine

glass. "Must be nice having someone like Finn who would do anything for the woman she loves."

"Finn and I are very similar in personality. I think it's why we get along so well. We don't go out of our way to hurt people, and any woman we're in love with becomes the centre of our universe."

"So, you *don't* only do no-strings?" Jan asked as she searched Morgan's eyes. "You *do* have a heart for someone out there?"

"Of course I do." Morgan wished someone would come along and steal her heart. She wished someone would want to be the centre of her universe. Seeing Finn with Gillian just reminded her of everything she craved. "I may appear to be a bit of a flirt, but that's just the bartender in me. I'm not like that if I'm involved. I'd *never* flirt with anyone or make my girlfriend feel uncomfortable. It's not my style."

"Women just have more respect, don't they?"

Morgan wanted to agree with Jan, but based on recent experience with Amanda, she couldn't. "I'd like to say so, but... Amanda."

"Is she not maybe an exception?" Jan wrinkled her nose, and Morgan had to wonder why Jan was asking these questions. She almost seemed hopeful that Amanda was the exception.

"Most of us are genuine. Most of us don't fuck around behind someone's back. I certainly don't, and I know Finn never would either."

"Tell me about Amanda. Something must have drawn you to her."

Morgan puffed out her cheeks, then emptied the last of her wine down her throat. "You want me to be completely honest?" Jan nodded. "I'm attracted to older women, and that's precisely what she was. I just find it hard to connect with people my own age. They all have a wandering eye. Amanda wanted to fuck, and she wanted to have fun. It worked perfectly for me at the time because I wasn't looking for anything serious." Morgan hoped that didn't make her sound like a player. "Like I said, I struggle to find the time for a relationship. If I'm in, I'm *all* in. I can't give someone my all when I work as much as I do."

Jan gazed back at Morgan with the most beautiful smile spread on her lips. "How old was she?"

"Fifty-two." Morgan wasn't the kind of person to give a fuck about someone's age...provided they weren't younger than her. "Look, women are exceptional. I adore every last thing about them. Throw in a good fifteen years or more experience than what I have, and I'm putty in their hands."

"And now I understand why Finn was so insistent with Gillian." Jan laughed, but then her smile faded again. "Does it make me a terrible person to feel jealous about them?"

"What exactly are you jealous of?"

"That my best friend has a woman in her life who loves her more than anything in this world. That they have that love a lot of people can only dream of...me included."

"You didn't have that love with your husband?"

Jan shook her head lightly. "No. Phil was a wonderful husband, he really was, but when it came to romance and that kind of thing, he just didn't bother. Sadly, I'm only just realising all his faults and failures as a husband. I chose to look past it all, and now I find myself in this position."

"I'm sorry." Morgan lay a hand on Jan's knee and regarded her with the slightest of smiles. "I guess we all want something to last, and when it doesn't, you look back on things differently."

"Hindsight and all that."

"I guess so, yeah." Morgan hoped Jan wouldn't regret her marriage. For the most part, it must have been enough for her. She would have left before now if that hadn't been the case.

As Jan placed her hand over Morgan's, her eyes suddenly lit up when the track on Morgan's sound system changed. Morgan didn't recognise it, but Jan did, and she was tugging on Morgan's hand as she got to her feet. "Dance with me. I love this song."

Morgan wanted nothing more than to dance with Jan, but this

song—God, this slow, *aching* song—wasn't making it easy. Her hands twitched at her sides, struggling to know what to do. She would never overstep, *never* push, but every encounter with Jan lately seemed to leave Morgan feeling conflicted. Was there something there? A hint of something unspoken? The questions Jan had been asking tonight had her head spinning, yet here she was, following her into the middle of her living room.

Jan's arm slid around Morgan's waist, her fingers clutching possessively at her side. She took Morgan's hand, said nothing, and hummed along to the track as she rested her head against Morgan's shoulder. The warmth of her cheek seeped through the fabric of Morgan's shirt, and all Morgan could do was surrender to the moment. Forget what she, herself, wanted. Jan *needed* this comfort. That was enough.

But then Jan lifted her head. Her blue eyes locked onto Morgan's with a sadness so raw that it ached deep in Morgan's chest. That smile, soft but worn, *almost* undone her. This woman...she didn't deserve any of this pain. Her husband's affair had shattered her, and Morgan hated him for it.

Lifting her hand, Morgan brushed her knuckles gently across Jan's cheek. God, she was beautiful tonight. *She's beautiful every night.* The way Jan's arm lingered around her waist, her fingertips grazing lazily across the small of her back—it was driving Morgan insane. She swallowed hard, her voice barely above a whisper. "Don't ever think less of yourself because of him, okay?"

Jan's lip quivered, and then her eyes closed as though she was warring with herself. "Morgan..."

"Talk to me," Morgan urged. "What's going through your head?"

Jan's long lashes fluttered as she opened her eyes, her gaze flickering to Morgan's lips before she took her own between her teeth for a very brief moment. Fuck, that was sexy. "I shouldn't say."

Morgan tilted her head, cupping Jan's chin with a cautious touch. If she was reading this situation wrong, she had to know she could lie her way out of it. "You can tell me anything. No judgment. *Ever.*"

Jan closed the sliver of space between them, pressing herself against Morgan. Her stare became intense, as though she'd finally decided *something*. "That night...when I came up here with you. You said you'd admired me."

"Yeah. I did say that."

"Did you mean it?" Jan's voice was small but steady.

"Every word."

Jan's brow furrowed. "Why? What could you possibly see in me?"

"Why *wouldn't* I? You're gorgeous." Morgan regarded Jan with a soft smile. "And your laugh? It's one of those laughs that gets inside you and makes everything feel...lighter." She paused, careful of her words. "It's *always* a pleasure when you're in my bar."

"You've never said anything..."

"I knew you were married." Morgan shrugged. "Flirting would have been disrespectful."

Jan's hand rested on Morgan's chest, her palm warm. "It's been so long since anyone flirted with me. I probably wouldn't have noticed."

"Oh, you'd have noticed." Morgan's smile turned into a smirk, her lips dangerously close to Jan's. "Trust me. I'd have made sure."

Jan's breath hitched, her gaze flickering downwards to Morgan's lips once again.

"Hey," Morgan whispered as she leaned towards Jan's ear. "If you'd walked into my bar single and even *hinted* at being interested in women, we wouldn't be standing here like this."

Jan's brow rose. "No?"

"No." Morgan tipped her head toward her bedroom door. "We'd be in there." She let those words hang between them, the air thick with the possibility that something may just happen here. "But more than anything, I need you to know that no matter what, you're so fucking beautiful, Jan. Don't let him take that from you. If he can do what he did, you deserve better."

Jan's arm tightened around Morgan's waist, her fingers digging in as though she feared Morgan might slip away. Her breath was hot and ragged against Morgan's neck, each exhale sending a shiver down her spine.

"Oh, God," Jan whispered, her voice rough with need.

Morgan barely had time to answer before Jan's lips found hers —soft at first, almost like a question. But then Jan pressed harder, her mouth far more urgent and demanding. The tension between them snapped like a rope that had been pulled too tight. Jan's tongue swept inside Morgan's mouth, warm and slick, and Morgan's resolve crumbled.

Morgan threaded her fingers through Jan's hair, tugged her closer, and dragged her nails along the delicate, smooth skin at the nape of her neck. Jan let out a low, breathy moan that vibrated against Morgan's lips. God, that sound absolutely ruined her.

Morgan felt Jan's body moulding to hers, those soft curves pressed against her, a thigh slipping between her legs just enough to make her head spin. Jan's fingers snaked beneath Morgan's shirt, tracing a path of what could only be described as fire up her back, and it left her skin tingling.

"F-fuck, you're driving me crazy," Morgan murmured against Jan's lips, her voice hoarse with desire.

"Good," Jan moaned, her teeth grazing Morgan's bottom lip before she kissed her again. Only this time, it was deeper. *Hungrier*. Each press of their bodies felt like a spark igniting something dangerous, something wild that neither of them wanted to extinguish. It didn't matter how much Morgan wanted to have these moments with Jan over and over again; she knew it couldn't be. Jan was dealing with too much, *and* she was straight.

Morgan broke away just enough to catch her breath. "Are you drunk?"

"N-no," Jan stammered. "Just a glass and a half of wine."

"You sure? It's just... I'm trying to figure out how the fuck that happened."

"I'm sure." Jan's smile spread wider. "I kissed you because I wanted to. Because I was tired of feeling miserable."

Morgan narrowed her eyes, searching her face for doubt, but she found nothing of the kind. "Jan, you...you're straight."

"I *have* been with a woman before," Jan admitted, her eyes painfully dark. "A long time ago, but I never forgot how it felt."

As Jan allowed that admission to sink in, she found herself staring back at Morgan. A slight space had been created between them, but Jan didn't feel terrible. She didn't hold any regret. No, she felt as though a spark had just ignited. One that had her palms clammy and her entire body aching with anticipation. She didn't quite know what had possessed her to kiss Morgan in that moment, but she had wanted it to happen.

If she'd realised anything since last week, it was that Morgan paid more attention to her and was far more honest with her than Phil had probably ever been. That was sad on reflection, but Jan couldn't change Phil or his personality. And for the most part, she hadn't wanted to. She had met and fallen in love with Phil, knowing and understanding who he was. She had spent twenty-seven years with him *still* aware of who he was, but maybe this was her perfect opportunity for change.

Is now really the right time for change?

Jan had always been of the opinion that there was no time like the present, but she'd had a huge shock just a week ago today. She knew her marriage wasn't something she could simply move on from. As she stood there, the taste of Morgan still on her lips, she hoped Morgan didn't think she was nothing more than a rebound. Jan was nearing fifty. She didn't do rebounds. Morgan made her feel good about herself, and she couldn't change that.

"I...can't believe you've just kissed me." Morgan tugged her bottom lip between her teeth. "Or did I kiss you? I-I don't know."

Jan grinned. "I kissed you. Don't worry."

"And, um..." Morgan puffed out her cheeks as she frowned and looked down at her bare feet. "You wanted to do that, right?"

"Do I look like I didn't want to do it?" Aware that Morgan was potentially about to panic, Jan took her hand and guided Morgan towards the door. "How about we rustle up a few shots downstairs? To calm your nerves if nothing else."

Morgan nodded. "Y-yeah. Shots. That's a good idea."

Jan wasn't convinced it was a good idea; she couldn't be sure that another kiss *wouldn't* happen again...or more, depending on how much they drank, but she was one hundred percent sure that this feeling she had was a good feeling. Morgan made her feel wanted. She made her feel less alone and less humiliated. "Come on. Relax."

Thankful that Morgan was following her out of the door, Jan decided it would be best if she put one foot in front of the other and focused on making it down the stairs. Her legs were like jelly, her mind was whirring, and her blood...well, it was pumping hard in many places right now. God, Jan couldn't recall the last time she'd felt so aroused.

But she wouldn't tell Morgan that. Not just yet. She had a feeling Morgan needed a moment to gather her thoughts. What may have been shocking to her just moments ago wasn't quite so shocking to Jan. Perhaps she just didn't care anymore. Perhaps Phil had done the best thing for them without either of them realising it.

"Hey, um...we're okay, right?" Morgan took Jan by the hand as they landed inside the dark, closed bar. She visibly swallowed, slight frown lines present. "Like, you're not going to freak out and run out on me, are you?"

Instead of reassuring Morgan with words, Jan tugged her closer and drew her into another kiss. Morgan trembled against her, but that was a mistake. Because now, Jan wanted to continue kissing her whilst preparing herself for so much more. If she could find a woman who trembled from a simple kiss, then Jan would be out of her mind to not enjoy it. She pulled back and ran her tongue along her bottom lip. "I'm not going to freak out, and I'm certainly not about to run away, either."

"Okay. Good." Morgan wrapped an arm around Jan's waist and smiled. "I don't know what the fuck is happening here, but it's all on your terms, okay?"

"Our terms," Jan said as she turned out of Morgan's arm and stepped behind the bar. "So, what do I need for these shots?"

Morgan remained in her spot, blinking repeatedly. "Um."

"Earth to Morgan." Jan waved a hand in front of Morgan's face, choosing to ignore the wetness between her own thighs.

"I'm sorry, but you can't kiss me like that and then expect me to function like a normal human being after it." Morgan shook her head as she closed her eyes. "I need *at least* a minute."

"Okay, well, you take that minute, and I'll see if I know how to pull a pint."

Morgan suddenly stepped up behind Jan as she lifted a pint glass from the shelf behind her. "No, no. I'll show you." Morgan's arms came around Jan's body as she carefully took the glass from her, her breath washing over Jan's ear. "You can't just pull a pint. You have to know what you're doing."

"Mm. You know what you're doing." Jan turned her face to Morgan, their lips barely an inch apart. "I have a feeling you *really* know what you're doing."

Flustered, Morgan eyed Jan and cleared her throat. "And *you* have to concentrate."

"Oh, I am." Jan stood mesmerised by Morgan's soft brown eyes. She'd found herself gazing into them often now, but in this moment, it was far more intense. If Jan could read people the way she believed she could, then she knew Morgan was feeling the very same effects that Jan was. "I'm definitely concentrating."

"O-on the beer. You should be watching the beer. Me... pouring the beer." Morgan groaned. "Fuck, now *I* can't concentrate."

Jan turned her face away and watched Morgan's shaking hand hold the glass. She pulled the arm on the pump, and Jan watched the amber liquid cascade from the spout. When Morgan was finished, she set it down on the clean drip tray beneath and settled her arms around Jan's waist.

"I know that kiss was unexpected, and I know you're going through a lot, but just so you know...I didn't want it to end." Morgan stroked her thumb against Jan's skin where her blouse had ridden up slightly. "I'm also finding it very hard to keep my hands to myself, so can we make those shots before I lose my mind?"

Jan brought one of Morgan's arms from around her waist and guided her hand lower. It rested on the waistband of her jeans, the tremble barely present now. "Just so *you* know, I'm more than happy for those hands you can't keep to yourself to explore wherever they need to explore." Jan heard Morgan swallow again, and then Morgan slowly dipped her hand and cupped Jan through her jeans. "O-oh." Jan tried to arch her back, but Morgan held her flush against her. "M-Morgan."

Morgan turned her face towards Jan's ear and whispered, "I'd really love to touch you."

Jan could only nod, her lips parting as her head rested back on Morgan's shoulder.

"*Can* I touch you?"

"Y-yes." Jan's heart rate spiked when Morgan popped the button on her jeans and slid her fingers past the waistband, directly inside her underwear. She stroked Jan's wet lips, moaning her approval as she kissed Jan's neck. "Oh, God."

Jan hadn't known what to expect, but she was finding it difficult to take a normal breath every time Morgan moved an inch. "You're soaking. Just how I like women to be." Jan felt Morgan smirk against her neck. "Tell me what you need..."

Oh, fuck. Jan couldn't begin to explain what she needed. The more Morgan teased her fingers up and down her lips, the wetter Jan became. "More. I need more."

Morgan obliged, pressing two fingers against Jan's clit. The moan that left Jan's mouth was far more than surprising to her. She didn't think she was capable of being so vocal, but here she was, whimpering as Morgan rolled her fingers a little harder over her clit. "I think you need a lot more attention than you've been getting." Morgan inched lower and eased a finger inside Jan. She tightened, her world spinning as her entire body came alive. *Truly* alive. "And if nobody has ever told you before, you feel so fucking good that I'm trying to hold back." Morgan nipped at Jan's earlobe, forcing her closer to the edge. "May I fuck you, Jan?"

Oh, my. Was this really what Jan had been missing all these years? A woman who knew exactly what she was doing. A moment with someone that could redefine who Jan was? Jan gripped Morgan's wrist and urged her deeper inside as she sunk down. "P-please."

"You have to say it..." Morgan teased

"Please, Morgan." Jan's entire world tilted on its axis as she closed her eyes and enjoyed the feel of Morgan inside her. "I need you to fuck me."

With her free hand, Morgan grabbed a handful of Jan's breast and eased another finger inside. Jan forced her jeans and underwear over the curve of her arse, granting Morgan all the access she desired. She wasn't shy when it came to sex, but behind a bar was a very new experience.

Morgan widened her stance ever so slightly, her sole focus on Jan's pleasure. This was all she'd wanted over the last few years. Someone who wanted to see Jan in this light. Someone who wanted to watch her come undone in a split second. Phil had been a wonderful lover, but Jan had a feeling Morgan was about to show her a world she wasn't familiar with. Jan...would never be the same after this night.

Forcing Jan's blouse open, Morgan tugged on Jan's lace bra and exposed her nipple. She pinched and teased, breathing heavily in her ear, aware that Jan was being driven closer and closer to the edge. She felt her walls squeezing Morgan's fingers, but she didn't want this moment to end. She wanted to feel Morgan inside her for as long as it was humanly possible. "R-right there. Fuck! Oh, Morgan." Jan's knees started to shake, the intensity of her orgasm building in the pit of her stomach. "Shit, I'm close." Jan lowered her hand and lashed her fingers against her clit. "Y-yes, I'm coming."

"Mm. Fuck, you are." Morgan forced herself deeper and quickly wrapped her arm around Jan's waist to hold her up. "That's it. Give it to me."

Jan's knees gave out on her, but it wasn't enough. She didn't need the shots, she didn't need to try her hand at pulling a pint, but she *did* need to be naked with this woman in the next few minutes. "Fuck, I can't." Jan gripped Morgan's wrist and tried to hold her in place, overly stimulated as Morgan withdrew her fingers and rolled them over her clit. "P-please, I need a minute."

Morgan lifted her hand and spread the wetness coating her fingers across Jan's lips. "Tell me how you taste."

Jan's entire world exploded. Morgan...was a revelation. "Morgan, I—" She poked out her tongue and cleaned herself from her lips as she panted, "I...you...we need to go upstairs right now."

Morgan turned Jan around, pressed her back to the bar, and dropped to her knees. She took a slow, teasing lick up the length of Jan's pussy, then sat back on her knees and nodded. "Fucking delicious."

CHAPTER 9

Placing her palm to her forehead, Morgan stared up at the ceiling, too terrified to move. She knew what was going to happen this morning. Jan would wake up, realise where she was, and run for the hills. It was inevitable, but Morgan had allowed herself to get caught up in the moment last night, and she wouldn't change any of it.

She hadn't known what to expect when it came to intimacy with Jan, but fuck, that woman could go all night long. And she had. Now, as Morgan lay here, she had to wonder exactly what Jan's reaction would be. She desperately hoped it wouldn't be anything too heartbreaking. Morgan wasn't sure she could handle being kicked to the curb right now. Still, she had to prepare herself for the potential. Jan's head was up her arse, and that was a guarantee.

As she slowly and *carefully* sat up on her elbows, she spied the coffee machine through the open bedroom door. She was going to need caffeine soon and, ideally, some breakfast. *At least lie to me and have breakfast with me*, Morgan thought as she slid out from the cover and pulled a hoodie on. She quickly stepped into a pair of shorts and tiptoed across the room. Once she was safely outside, her heart pounding, she closed the bedroom door over and moved further into her living room. Jan's blouse and jeans were situated on opposite sides of the open plan space, her underwear hanging from the coffee table.

It had been a long time since Morgan had enjoyed a night like last night. Or rather, it had been a long time since she'd spent the night with someone she *genuinely* cared about. Someone she felt she knew well enough to allow herself to care. Someone...Morgan would really love to see again. But then she swallowed and braced her hands against the kitchen worktop. Finn was probably going to smack her when she found out about this. Morgan would like to think nobody would know about it, not unless Jan wanted them to, but was life really that simple? Around here...absolutely not.

Knowing Morgan's luck, Finn or Gillian themselves had probably caught Jan and Morgan fucking in the bar last night. It didn't matter if the shutters were down, and it didn't matter that the place was locked up. Morgan was known to be *that* unfortunate.

She exhaled a deep breath and pushed off the counter. She really needed that coffee she'd been thinking about. As she powered the machine on and waited patiently for the light to stop flashing, she felt a presence in the room. Jan, without a doubt, was watching her.

She turned and revealed her best fake smile. If Jan was getting ready to leave, Morgan refused to show her disappointment. They hadn't even had the chance to talk about whatever the hell they were doing with one another, and that was *before* Morgan had let go and found herself deep inside Jan. "Hi."

Jan leaned against the bedroom doorframe, her blonde hair tousled. "Good morning."

"Can I get you some coffee?" Morgan tried to inconspicuously shake her hands at her sides, hopefully forcing away her nerves at the same time, but Jan's stare pinned her in place. "Or something to eat?"

"Do you have somewhere you need to be?"

Morgan frowned. "No, why?"

"Then I'll just take coffee for now. Maybe we can make breakfast once you've got some colour back in your face." Jan pushed off the doorframe and crossed the room. "Would you like me to take care of the drinks?"

"N-no. It's all good. I've got it." Morgan cleared her throat and nodded slowly. "Before I get on with this, I...wanted to ask if you're okay."

"Should I not be?" Jan lifted a brow when she stopped beside Morgan and mirrored her position as she rested back against the counter. She wore one of Morgan's T-shirts and a pair of boxer shorts she must have taken from the chest of drawers.

"I hope you are, but last night was..." Morgan sighed. "Last night happened, Jan. While I wouldn't change any of it, it happened, and I *need* to know you're okay."

Jan turned and cupped Morgan's cheek. "I'm okay. I'm great, actually. A little sore in places, but very okay."

Morgan relaxed instantly. She knew Jan would be open and honest with her, but that worry had still been at the back of her mind. It was hard not to hold space for it when Jan—a *technically* married woman—had woken up naked in her bed. The fact Morgan had thought Jan was straight was the furthest thing from her mind today. Jan was *not* straight.

"Hey," Jan said as she pressed herself to Morgan. "Are *you* okay?"

"Yeah. Just worried that you're going to realise you've made a huge mistake." Morgan smiled weakly, but Jan took her hands and brought them up between them. "But if you're sure everything is okay—"

"I'm sure that everything is okay. That everything is going to *be* okay. I don't regret last night if that's what you're wondering."

"I hoped you didn't, but I had to expect the possibility, you know?" Morgan cast her gaze on their hands. "I had the most amazing night with you."

"Likewise."

"And I don't know. I...kinda wanna see you again whenever I can." Morgan didn't know why or when she had become so needy for this woman, but it was true. Jan was all she thought about lately. "If you'd like that."

"I would like that."

"Yeah?" Morgan's world lit up in a multitude of colours. Jan, Gillian's best friend, wanted to see her again? *Fuck!* "You...want to see me again?"

"Mmhmm." Jan blushed as she shook her head and smiled. "I can't believe *you* want to see *me* again."

"You've got to be joking. You have met you, right?"

Jan reached around Morgan and sat a cup under the spout of the coffee machine. She pressed the button, and the beans started to grind. "I have met me. Right now, this me is a little bruised but not broken. If you can give me whatever time I need to figure everything out, then I'll be in a much better headspace to figure *this* out with you. Because I don't know about you, but it all means something to me."

"It means something to me, too."

Jan took the cup and handed it to Morgan, then made her own coffee. "You felt the connection, too, right?"

Morgan lifted herself up onto the counter and gazed down at Jan. "For me, the connection is strong." While Morgan enjoyed being with women, it wasn't often she slept with them so quickly. Not anymore. Even Amanda hadn't brought out the desire Morgan had last night. "If at any point it's too much for you, please tell me. I'm already scared to say or do the wrong thing."

"All I expect from you is to be yourself." Jan moaned as she sipped her coffee, moving until she was standing between Morgan's legs. "Be you, that's all I want."

"Don't take this the wrong way, but you seem remarkably calm for a woman who left her husband a week ago. Why am *I* the one panicking?"

"I don't know why you're panicking." Jan sipped her coffee again, then set it down on the counter beside Morgan. She palmed her thighs as she looked up at her, giving Morgan the perfect view of those deep blue eyes. "As for me, I don't see the point in worrying. Yes, I left my husband a week ago, but I'm finding it hard to hold onto any sort of feeling for him given how we ended."

Morgan reached out and held Jan's chin. "That guy is out of his fucking mind. Trust me."

"I don't want to talk about him. I want to spend my morning with you if you'll have me here."

"You *know* I'll have you here any time, any day." Morgan slid from the counter and wrapped Jan up in her arms. She nuzzled into her neck and said, "By the way, you can steal my clothes any time you like, too."

"It's a good job you said that. I'm going to need to borrow some after my shower if I'm staying here a while longer. Hopefully, you have a spare *unused* toothbrush lying around."

Morgan kissed Jan's forehead and sighed. "Anything you want."

Humming lightly as Morgan palmed her shin, Jan rested her head back on the couch cushions, feeling surprisingly relaxed given what had happened last night. They'd spent the last hour in this position, Jan's legs resting in Morgan's lap, the initial tension in the air no longer threatening upheaval. Jan didn't need that. She didn't want it. She was fully aware of what she was doing last night, and as she lay here, her only regret was that she wasn't still naked in bed with Morgan.

Back in the day, she'd had a healthy sex life with Phil. Healthy, just not quite as exciting as she would have liked it to be. But with work commitments and business plans often getting in the way over the last ten years or so, the sex had dwindled. So much so that Jan didn't even bother bringing it up in conversation anymore. There had been a period of time when she would have fought for their intimacy, a time when she would have surprised Phil with something that would get his heart racing, but Jan had known it had felt more like a chore to him. He never seemed happy at the end of it. That had really become an issue over the last year or so, and now Jan knew why. It wasn't because he had work on his mind or that he'd been at the office until a ridiculous hour. No, it was because he'd been getting what he needed from Anais.

"I miss my house," Jan said quietly as she stared up at the ceiling. "And my garden."

When Gillian had bought her new place, Jan was excited about its potential. It helped that Gillian had Finn—a joiner and an electrician by trade—and after seeing what Finn was capable of, she'd wanted that same expertise when she renovated her own home. Finn had truly taken her breath away with the new bespoke kitchen she'd designed and installed, but Jan hadn't had much of a chance to enjoy it. And soon, she wouldn't even be able to call it her kitchen.

"You know, you *can* tell him you want the house." Morgan eyed Jan as she squeezed her knee. "I'm pretty sure that sort of thing would go in your favour."

"He won't let me stay in that house unless I agree to work on the marriage with him. He loves it just as much as I do. There's no way I'm coming away with it." Jan wished she could stay in the house she'd dedicated twenty-odd years to. She wished Phil would just hand over the keys and walk away.

"You don't know that. If you get a good lawyer, they'll fight for you. For the house." Morgan turned on the couch a little. "You're the one he's fucked over, babe." Jan's heart fluttered at Morgan's term of endearment. She smiled, listening to Morgan's thoughts on this. "If you want something in particular, you tell him that.

Just because he loves the house too doesn't mean he should be entitled to a say on what happens with it. He's the one who had the affair. Not you."

Jan appreciated Morgan's support on this, but she didn't know if she had the fight or the interest when it came to splitting assets and whatnot. Emotionally, she was drained, and physically, well...she would prefer to keep her strength for whatever came after the divorce. She was really going to have to make decisions on what came next. "I know. It just seems easier to walk away with whatever he offers, I suppose."

"Why? Why should he dictate how this is going to go? Why should *he* be the one to pick and choose what he wants, only to leave *you* with the scraps of whatever's left?" Morgan frowned as she took Jan's hand. "You don't strike me as the kind of woman who will lie down and take this. Not at all."

"I don't know what comes next." God, had it *really* only been a week since she'd walked out on Phil? It felt that way when she was alone, but when she was with Morgan, it felt like a lifetime ago. Jan knew this was the shock talking, but in time, she would fight. She would have to if she planned to come away with anything remarkably decent. "I just feel like I need a few weeks to let it all sink in, and then I'll start making plans and decisions."

"Call him and tell him you're staying in the house until everything is sorted out. Tell him he's not welcome there and that you're not moving out."

"At the moment, I don't want to be there. While he thinks there could be a chance at reconciliation, he won't let it lie. He'll show up every day, and I wouldn't be able to stop him from doing that. I just...need the time alone first. To clear my head, you know?"

Morgan shifted until she was between Jan's legs, her arms braced on either side of Jan as she dipped her head and kissed her. "You'll know what the right decision is when the time comes. I just hate knowing you're at the hotel and not at home. Or staying with friends, whatever."

"I'm not really at the hotel, though, am I?" Jan quirked a brow as she fisted her hand in Morgan's T-shirt and pulled her down on top of her. The weight was calming. Morgan felt incredibly good against her. "I *definitely* wasn't there last night."

Morgan lifted her head and smirked. "No, you weren't."

"It's just a base for me. I'm rarely there. Maybe I'll start to look for places to live once I've had the house valued and I know what I'm working with." Jan brushed Morgan's hair from her face and searched her eyes. "Having you in my life right now is keeping me sane. I don't know what I'd have done with myself this past week."

Morgan's phone started to ring on the coffee table. She groaned as she lifted off Jan and reached for it. "It's just one of my staff," Morgan said, answering the call and putting it on speakerphone. "Everything okay, Ben?"

"Yeah, of course. Finn is here asking for you." He spoke low, probably aware that Morgan wasn't alone. He'd been the one to let Jan up here last night, so the fact neither of them had been down to the bar at any point today spoke volumes. "Should I pass on a message?"

"Yeah, um..." Morgan sat back and chewed her lip. "Tell her I'm stuck on a call with the brewery and that I have to head straight out after it."

"No problem," Ben said. "I'll tell her you'll be in touch later or something, yeah?"

"Thanks, Ben." Morgan ended the call and threw her phone onto the coffee table again. She crawled back between Jan's legs, the press of her body only firing Jan up all over again. "Finn is the last person on my mind right now. I have *you* all to myself, and I'm going to make every second of it count."

Jan took her bottom lip between her teeth as she gazed up at Morgan, only feeling slightly terrible for the lie Morgan had told Finn. "Sounds interesting."

Morgan crawled back slowly and dipped her head. She trailed the tip of her tongue down Jan's stomach, smiling against her skin when Jan gasped. "Mmm. The reaction I was hoping for."

"Morgan," Jan whispered, moaning as she buried her head in the cushion. "Oh, fuck." When Morgan lowered the waistband of the sweats Jan wore, Jan gripped the back of the couch. "I don't know how or why we've ended up here, but...don't *ever* stop."

CHAPTER 10

Dreading this conversation, Jan walked into the coffee shop where she was meeting Gillian and kept her head down. She needed another moment or two before she revealed her terrible secret, and right now, she was glad Gillian hadn't been available the day Jan had called. It meant Jan had given herself more time to process everything. By allowing herself that time, Jan no longer felt as though she would burst into tears the moment she laid eyes on Gillian.

As Jan looked up and scanned the room, she saw Gillian sitting with her back to the entrance. She quickly slipped off into the bathroom and stared back at herself in the mirror. Jan didn't know how honest she planned to be today, but she didn't believe she could come clean about Morgan just yet. Gillian would have a thousand questions, and Jan wasn't prepared for them. Of course it would be confusing for Gillian and likely everyone else, but Jan wasn't confused by the fact she had slept with Morgan. She also couldn't regret it. Because in that moment, as well as before and after, Jan had felt wanted.

You're almost fifty. Grow up!

Had Jan been so concerned about what she felt within

herself that she'd thrown caution to the wind that night? Perhaps. Had she wanted to feel some kind of emotion that *hadn't* been caused by Phil? One hundred percent. Regardless of the reasons why Jan didn't stop Morgan that night, it had been exactly what she needed at the time. Something that would help her to detach from everything swimming around in her head. Something...that made her feel and think and appreciate what she did have left. And right now, that was a heart. Jan didn't know how it was still functioning, but it was, and that was what she would cling to whenever life felt rough in the coming weeks and months.

She checked her makeup in the mirror, took her handbag from beside the sink, and made her way back out into the coffee shop. As she put on her best smile, Gillian turned around when the doorbell jingled, and someone else stepped inside. Jan lifted a hand and waved, then weaved through the small number of tables dotted about.

"Hi, love." Gillian stood up and embraced Jan. "I was wondering if you were going to cancel. You're never late."

Jan smiled as she took a seat. "Sorry, it's been a bit manic lately."

"Why? You're always on the ball. It's not like you to be stressed out. That's usually reserved for me." Gillian grinned, but it quickly faded when Jan just stared back at her. "Jan, what's going on?"

"I don't know where to begin..."

"You look tired." Gillian reached a hand across the table and settled it over Jan's. "Let me order you coffee, and then we'll have a good talk."

Jan spied the glasses of water on their table. "I'm okay with water for now. I've already drank five coffees, and it's barely one in the afternoon." The worry in Gillian was evident on her face. Jan would put her out of her misery soon enough; she just had to find the right words. "I..." Jan shook her head and managed a feeble laugh. "I'm divorcing Phil."

The cup of coffee Gillian had just lifted from the table froze in mid-air, her brows drawn. "I'm sorry?"

"Phil. My husband. I'm divorcing him."

"Yes, love, I know who Phil is." Gillian sat back in her chair. "I don't understand why."

"Because he's been seeing someone else, Gill."

Gillian lowered her coffee cup to the saucer with a clatter, prompting the people at the table next to them to look over their shoulders. But Gillian's stare didn't waver. She was almost burning a hole through Jan.

"Yes, I had the same reaction. Give it a minute, and the shock will wear off."

"And then what will I be left with?" Gillian asked, her lips barely moving.

"Anger. Disappointment. I don't know. He wasn't your husband."

"You're right, he wasn't. But having been through this, I have to wonder if I'll feel as sick to my stomach as I did with Dave or if something new will happen this time around." Gillian sighed and lowered her gaze. "No, I still feel sick to my stomach."

"I'll...be okay," Jan said, catching herself before her voice broke. "I just have to find my feet, and everything will be okay."

"How can you be so calm about this?" Gillian perched her elbows on the edge of the table and leaned in. "Seriously?"

"Because I've spent the last ten days or so crying. Because it's not going to change anything. Because I'm tired of feeling empty and lonely and unsure about where I go from here. If I lie to myself and say that everything will be okay, then surely it has to come true at some point." Though Jan hadn't expected it, that initial feeling of not knowing what to do was wearing off. She had Morgan to thank for that.

"Ten days? You've known about this for *ten days?*"

"Mm." Jan lifted her glass of water and sipped it. Maybe it would force the emotion back down her throat.

"Why are you only just telling me about this now? When Dave fucked me over, you were there from the moment I found out."

"I called. Finn answered. You were...busy." Jan didn't want to make Gillian feel bad, but she knew it was coming. Gillian had always been very good at punishing herself about the slightest of things.

And then Gillian lowered her head and sighed. Just as Jan had expected. "I'm so sorry."

"Gill, it's fine. You and Finn have a life together. I don't expect you to be there for me the way I was there for you. Phil was out of the country at the time, and you were on my doorstep beside yourself. Life is just different for us now, and that's okay."

"No, it's not okay. I'm your best friend, Jan. I should have been there for you from the second you knew the truth." Gillian reached out and squeezed Jan's hand. "I'm sorry, and it'll never happen again. *Anything* you need, I'm here for you."

"Please, don't worry about me. He's been fucking someone else, I know now, and all I can do is put one foot in front of the other until life moves on. I have no job and no home, but...I have my sanity. That's something, right?"

"No job and no home? Please tell me you didn't leave the house."

"I couldn't be there. He's there, and I can't even look at him, Gill. He's been fucking one of our colleagues. I just...I had to get my things together and get out. As for the job, well, like I said...it was one of our colleagues."

"*He* needs to leave. He's the one who caused all of this."

Jan shook her head. "I'm staying at a hotel, and I'm quite happy there until I decide what's next. I need space, space away from the home we've shared for so long, and then I'll figure something out."

"No, you're *not* staying at a hotel." Gillian held up a hand and scoffed. "You'll stay with me and Finn. It's simple."

"Don't take this the wrong way, but I don't want to stay with you, Gill. I love you and Finn so much, but I can't be around you both at the minute. Not at home, anyway." Jan sounded jealous and bitchy for saying that, she knew she did, but she couldn't spend her evenings watching Gillian and Finn snuggled on the couch. It just wasn't the right time for her at the minute. "You understand, right?"

Gillian nodded slowly. "I guess so."

"Good."

"I feel terrible." Gillian sniffled as she lifted a napkin and dabbed it beneath her eyes. "You've been dealing with all of this on your own, and now you have nowhere to live."

"Hey. I'll be okay. I know I will."

"But you should have the support of your best friend. My wife, too. I don't want you to live out of a suitcase and sit alone at night wondering what to do next. You should be surrounded by people who love and care about you."

"And I will be, eventually." Jan appreciated that Gillian wanted to offer the same support she'd received from Jan when she left her own husband, but Jan wasn't entirely alone. She had Morgan. *Oh, Morgan*. She somehow managed to suppress a smirk, choosing to look down at her hand in her lap while she pushed Morgan from her mind. "Please, Gill. Understand from my point of view, and just let me process this the way I know I need to."

"Okay." Gillian clenched her hands into fists as she lowered them to the table slowly. "But if I see him, don't expect me to be quiet about this. I'll tell him exactly what I think of him. The disgusting prick!"

Jan turned her watch towards herself and sighed. "I don't really have long. I need to go to the house and collect some more things. Phil will be home in the next couple of hours, and I'd like to do it before then."

"I'll come with you." Gillian pushed her seat back, but Jan held up her hands. "What?"

"I'm going alone. I'll be okay."

"Why won't you let me help you through this, Jan? Is it because you called, and I wasn't available?"

"God, no. Not at all." Jan rose to her feet and held out her arms. Once they were hugging one another, the weight of the morning falling from Jan's shoulders, she sighed. "But you won't always be around for me, and I need to stand on my own two feet. Just...do something for me?"

"Anything." Gillian drew back and searched Jan's eyes.

"Go home and tell Finn how much you love her. Be with one another and just love, okay? What you two have is rare." Jan had thought her love with Phil had been rare at one time, but seeing Gillian and Finn together... *That* was true love. Would Jan ever find that again? Probably not. She'd always been a firm believer in finding the one meant for you. Unfortunately, she had a feeling Phil had been her one. *What a depressing thought.*

"When Finn finds out about this, she's going to hit the roof. She always thought so highly of Phil, especially when he helped us out with the cameras." Gillian's face suddenly fell. "Then there was the wedding and the first-class tickets."

"Well, he was always generous. He just chose to be generous with his dick, too." Jan brushed a thumb under Gillian's eye. "Please don't cry for me. It's not worth the tears. Even my own seem to have dried up suddenly."

Gillian cupped Jan's face and regarded her with a look of ultimate sadness. "I'm so sorry for what he's done to you."

"Me, too."

Rummaging around in her handbag for her keys, Jan took a deep breath when she felt the cool metal reach her fingertips. She was glad she'd spoken to Gillian about the affair, and now she wanted to get a few more belongings and go. Quite frankly, she didn't feel anything when she looked up at the light blue front door that had once held so much love behind it. In this moment, as she pressed her hand to the wood and pushed it open, she felt that emptiness all over again.

You don't feel that way when you're with Morgan.

It was true. Jan knew she couldn't use Morgan as some kind of crutch, but when she was with Morgan, she barely thought about Phil and what he had done to her. Perhaps that was just Morgan's personality, Jan didn't quite know yet, but whenever she could have her mind taken off the dreadful days about to commence, she would.

She lowered her handbag to the floor in the hallway and threw her keys onto the side table. As with the last time, everything sat in place immaculately. It smelled like home. It looked like home. It just...didn't feel like home anymore. Jan had the chance here to see if that feeling ever came back, but she wasn't sure she wanted to take it. The one thing she had always promised herself before she married Phil was that she would walk if he ever hurt her in any way. Physically, emotionally, it didn't matter. This, what he'd done, was the ultimate betrayal. Friends could tell her to work it out, but Jan didn't want to. She would never trust Phil again, no matter how much grovelling took place.

Pulling her shoulders back, Jan walked down the hallway and pushed the back living room door open. She heard voices, and as she peered into the kitchen, Phil and Anais sat at the dining table. Phil's eyes immediately landed on Jan; the shock evident as he stared back at her.

"J-Jan. Hi."

"It's not enough that you fuck her everywhere else...now you have to bring her here, to the home I still own with you?"

Anais shot to her feet and turned to Jan. "Jan, I'm sorry."

"It's not me you need to apologise to. I couldn't care less about your conscience. It's your poor, distraught husband who couldn't even look me in the eye as he told me about the affair. That's who you should be speaking to and apologising to."

Anais sunk back down into the seat she'd been occupying when Jan arrived.

"But by all means, you have a seat at *my* dining table in *my* home."

Phil cleared his throat and crossed the kitchen. When he landed in front of Jan, the scent of his aftershave making her feel queasy, she took a step back. "Jan, we need to talk. I know you don't want to, but we should. It's important."

"No, no. It's not important." Jan backed further away. She placed a hand on the doorframe to steady herself and looked Phil square in the eye. "It's over, Phil. It doesn't matter *what* you say to me, we're over. Completely. Do you understand that?"

Phil shook his head. "I'll reject the divorce."

"You do that. Make it harder than it already is for me. You know, like the good husband that you are."

"For fuck's sake, Jan. I made a mistake. We both did. Anais is going back to her husband, and *I'm* coming back to you."

"I couldn't care if Anais took a long walk off a short pier—that's her decision and hers alone. But you? Oh, no. You're not coming back to me. I don't *want* you."

"But we have the house and the business. We've been together for so long, love. Give me a chance. Please?" Phil dipped his head and found Jan's eyes, but all she saw staring back at her was deceit. That...and a man she couldn't trust. "Jan, I know you still love me deep down."

"You know, if you'd come to me all those months ago and told me you were unhappy, I would have tried to work it out with you. That's what I thought we were already doing by going to counselling. But you didn't. You found what you needed with someone else, and now I'm done with you entirely."

Jan calmly walked away from Phil and took the stairs. When she landed in the bedroom and eyed the wardrobe where her large suitcase was hidden away, she took a deep breath. At forty-eight, she never imagined she would be leaving the house she had turned into the most beautiful home. When she'd woken up on what felt like a very distant Monday morning just last week, she hadn't anticipated packing up her clothes so she could retreat to a lonely hotel room. But here she was, still sure and *still* ending the only thing she'd known for as long as she could recall.

"Jan," Phil spoke quietly from the bedroom door. "Can we just sit down and talk?"

"The only time I'll be sitting down to talk to you is with a lawyer present." Jan glanced over her shoulder at Phil. The colour had drained completely from his face. "I don't want to fight with you, Phil. I just want to get what belongs to me and go. Is that so hard for you to understand?"

"But I love you."

Jan spun around. "I slept with someone else."

"W-what? When?" Phil lowered himself to the edge of the bed and rubbed at his stubble. "In the past?"

"On Monday," Jan said matter-of-factly. "So, there we have it."

"You did it to get back at me, and I understand that. Let's call it quits and figure our marriage out together."

Jan barked a laugh at that. "I did it because they wanted me. I did it because I spent the most amazing evening with them. I did it because while *they* were inside me, I wasn't fucking thinking about *you* and how much you hurt me."

Oh, you would have enjoyed it regardless of why it happened.

Phil's face fell, but Jan wasn't surprised. She didn't make it a habit to be so crass, but perhaps he would understand what she was saying if she approached it in this way.

"You can think what you want of me; I don't care, Phil. The moment you climbed into bed with that woman downstairs was the moment you were no longer my husband. So, please, let me get what I need so I can be gone. You're probably waiting to bring her up here anyway. Or have you already had her all over the kitchen?"

"Do you have to speak like that?" Phil scoffed and got to his feet. "This isn't you, Jan. I never once thought this would be your reaction."

"No, I know you didn't. What you *thought* would happen and what has *actually* happened is quite shocking to you, isn't it? You thought your good little wife would roll over and take it lying down. You thought I'd forgive you because you're my husband. Well, you're wrong," Jan paused when she heard the front door slam shut. "And now...you're on your own." She cocked her head and smiled, but Phil stared through her. "There's a microwave meal in the fridge. Enjoy it and get used to it because I sure as hell will never cook you another meal again."

With his shoulders sagged, Phil blew out a breath and turned for the door. "You're making a mistake, but if you want to go, I won't stop you."

Jan cleared her throat. "Hey, Phil?"

He turned, and if Jan was judging this right, Phil seemed... hopeful as he smiled back at her. "Yes?"

"Do me a favour and fuck off."

CHAPTER 11

Feeling the music pumping through her veins, Morgan bopped her head as she poured Finn a pint of her usual beer. They'd kept the conversation light since Finn had entered the bar some ten minutes ago with Gillian, and Morgan had a feeling they now both knew about Jan. Not that Morgan had slept with her—at least she hoped they didn't know—but that Phil had *foolishly* been having an affair.

As Morgan stood behind the bar, she still found it hard to get her head around. Jan was the kind of woman you wrapped up in cotton wool. Not someone your eye wandered from. Then again, Morgan knew many men out there who didn't know a good thing when they had it. Most of them ended up residing at the end of her bar until closing. But Phil? She'd seen them with one another on several occasions in here, and Morgan hadn't once gotten that impression from him. Still, it had happened, and now all Morgan could do was be there for his wife.

She toyed with her lip ring, smiling to herself when Jan wandered into her mind. Just a few nights ago, she had stood in this very position while Jan moaned and writhed against her. Morgan hadn't expected it, not in the slightest, but would she go there again if the chance presented itself? Fuck yes. She would have to be physically held back in order to keep her hands off Jan. *It was one night. You'll be lucky to see her again!*

"What are you smirking at?" Finn asked, her eyes narrowed as Morgan looked up at her. "Well?"

"Just...happy." Morgan lifted a shoulder as she set Finn's pint down. "White wine for the missus?"

"Yep."

Morgan turned her back, but she still felt Finn's eyes on her. No matter what, she couldn't do *anything* to give away what had transpired here recently. Yes, Finn was a good friend, but Jan meant more to Morgan right now. She wouldn't dare out her. Jan was going through enough already. Morgan filled a glass and turned, placing it down on the counter between them. "There you go. Card or cash?"

"Cash." Finn handed a twenty over and puffed out her cheeks. "Hey, you know Jan? Well, her husband has been having an affair. You fancy hiding the body with me when I get my hands on him?"

Morgan closed the cash register and handed Finn her change, trying to keep her facial expression neutral. "You're joking?"

"Honestly. I can't believe it." The anger in Finn's eyes was quite a surprise to Morgan. She knew Finn and her wife thought a great deal about Jan, but Morgan hadn't seen this side of her before. "He better hope I never see him again." Finn ran a hand down her face. "I mean, who does that to someone?"

Morgan decided to steer the conversation in a different direction. If she opened up about how she felt when it came to Phil, the cat would be out of the bag within the next few minutes. "Amanda. She *also* does that to someone."

"No way!" Finn's mouth hung open.

"Turns out she has a husband. Found out last week." Morgan wasn't sad that their fun had come to an end. How could she be when Jan had so unexpectedly turned up in her life? "I guess everyone is at it lately. Affairs."

"Fucking hell." Finn clenched her jaw. "I'm sorry she turned out to be another disappointment."

Morgan waved off Finn's apology. "It is what it is."

"But look, you *will* find someone, you know. You'll be standing there one night, and the love of your life will be sitting on a barstool. You just don't know it yet."

Morgan swallowed when she imagined Jan sitting on the very barstool Finn was standing beside. She knew it wouldn't come to anything, Jan had just left a significantly long marriage, but the thought was nice in her head. "Yeah, sure. We don't all have happy endings like you." As Morgan peered over Finn's shoulder, she caught Gillian staring her out. "As always, the wife is glaring at me. You'd better get back with your drinks."

Finn lifted her brows and exhaled a breath. "You're so dramatic. Gillian is looking at *me*, not you." With a wink, Finn left Morgan standing next to a beer pump, grinning as she glanced back over her shoulder.

Morgan rolled her eyes playfully and inconspicuously took her phone from the shelf under the counter. Maybe she would see if Jan would be joining her friends tonight. Morgan could certainly spend the night watching a beautiful woman. And yes, Jan *was* that beautiful woman.

Gillian and Finn are at the bar. Are you joining them?

She looked up briefly. Gillian and Finn were chatting amongst themselves. Morgan couldn't recall a single time before Gillian when she'd seen Finn so happy, and right now, it was lovely to see. While it usually made Morgan grimace, she was in a slightly different headspace this week. And it meant there was hope for everyone else out there. Finn had always claimed she didn't have the time for attachment, but the moment Gillian turned up in this bar, Morgan knew Finn was madly in love with her. She just carried herself differently. If Finn could find someone, Morgan knew she could too...someday.

Maybe if you give yourself the chance to meet someone, it may just happen!

Morgan's phone vibrated in her hand. She looked down, her heart racing when Jan's name sat waiting for her.

Not tonight. I don't think I can stomach seeing them so in love right now.

Morgan understood that, but it didn't make her any less disappointed. Did she want to see Jan? Of course she did. But Morgan suspected Jan was avoiding her. They hadn't spoken to one another since she'd left Morgan's place on Tuesday morning, more than satisfied.

I know Monday night was a bit of a shock to us both, but I can forget about it if that's what you want me to do. I don't want you to feel uncomfortable coming here. I'm sorry if that's what this is.

Lowering her phone to the shelf again, Morgan straightened herself out and moved along the bar. She hadn't considered that Jan would feel awkward before now, but it did make sense. That woman had just come out of a marriage that spanned far more than half of Morgan's life. Of course she would be feeling weird about it all. Wanting to reassure Jan that everything could remain the same between them, she rushed back to the other end of the bar and lifted her phone.

If it makes any difference, I wish you were coming here tonight. Even just so I know that we're okay.

Her message showed a read receipt no sooner than it had landed in Jan's inbox, but she wasn't replying. *Just leave it alone.* If Jan wanted to see Morgan, she would patiently wait for that moment. Until then, she would do what she did best and make sure her customers had everything they needed for their Friday night ahead.

Aware that she felt incredibly nervous tonight, Jan stopped outside Morgan's bar, clutch bag under her arm as she shook her hands at her sides. She didn't want to come across as uncomfortable—that was absolutely not the case here—but she also didn't want to feel as though Finn and Gillian could potentially know something about Jan and Morgan just from the way they behaved around one another. The last thing she needed was the looks and the questions. They'd slept with one another, and Jan didn't know if it would ever happen again. If it did, she would cross that bridge when she came to it. If not, she would hold the memory of that night close to her heart.

Before she had left her hotel room around the corner, Jan had texted Gillian so it didn't seem odd when she arrived. Thankfully, her best friend had insisted Jan join them when she'd questioned whether the couple were headed out tonight. It wasn't uncommon for Jan to meet up with them, especially when Phil was working away, but she knew tonight would be different inside The Corner bar. Even if she hadn't slept with Morgan, Jan had told Gillian about the affair, so it was naturally going to be a strange atmosphere.

Jan quickly checked her hair in the window of a parked car, ran her fingers through it, and braced herself as she walked into the bar. Morgan stared back at her, but before Jan could say hi to Morgan, Finn was on her feet and rushing towards Jan. "What can I get you? Whiskey? Something strong like that?"

Jan frowned. "Whiskey? When have you *ever* known me to drink that, Finn?" *Oh, you were quick enough drinking whiskey with Morgan.*

"Just thought you would have wanted a stronger drink with everything that's going on. Usual glass of red instead?"

Jan smiled and guided Finn back to the table. "You have a seat and calm down. *I'll* go to the bar. Can I get either of you anything?" Finn looked as though she wanted to argue, but Jan held up a hand. She quickly eyed their glasses. "White wine and a beer, yes?"

Gillian nodded and regarded Jan with an understanding smile. "Yes. Thanks, love."

Jan turned and made a beeline for the bar. Morgan was wiping down an area as she stopped at the counter, her eyes straying towards Jan the second she realised she was waiting. "Hi." Jan beamed a smile at Morgan, very happy to see her this evening. "A red, a white, and Finn's beer, please."

"Coming right up." Morgan offered a single nod, then got to work on Jan's order. Once she'd set the two glasses of wine down, Morgan lifted a glass and poured Finn's beer. "How are you?"

"Not uncomfortable if that's what you're still thinking." Jan leaned in a little but not enough for it to look suspicious. "Do you want me to tell them about Monday night?"

"I'm sorry?" Morgan kept her head down but chanced a look in Gillian and Finn's direction. "You mean...us?"

"Mm. I'd prefer to keep it to myself while I figure everything else out, but I also don't want you to think I'm hiding you, Morgan."

"Oh, um...that's not what I was thinking. And no, I don't want you to tell them. Not unless it's something you plan on telling them anyway."

Jan appreciated that greatly. While Gillian would have a lot to say about something so huge, Jan didn't care. If she wanted to sleep with a woman, then she would do that. And she had. *Oh, what a night it had been*. Jan was glad she hadn't been drunk on Monday night. At least by being *mostly* sober, it couldn't be used against her as a reason or an excuse. "I will, when I'm ready to." What if Morgan didn't want anyone to know? "Unless you'd rather I didn't." Jan frowned, not knowing what the right thing to do was. All she knew in this moment was that she would prefer it if Gillian and Finn weren't here. At least then, she could sit around chatting with Morgan all night. "Sorry. Maybe that's something we should have a conversation about.

Morgan set Finn's pint down next to the wine glasses. "A conversation is a good idea. Just give me a call when you're free, and we'll get together, yeah?"

Jan took the corner of her bottom lip between her teeth. Morgan was giving her that look. The one that made her legs feel like jelly. "I will. I'll call you."

Morgan rested her forearm over the top of the beer pump and smiled. "Have a lovely evening, Jan. I'll be waiting for that call."

Feeling a little hot under the collar, Jan took the tray of drinks to the table and joined Gillian and Finn. They both looked back at her as though someone had just been laid to rest, and this had been precisely why she'd considered *not* coming here tonight. She didn't want the sympathy. She didn't want people to try to work out what was going on in her mind. She just wanted to enjoy a glass of red wine and forget the rest existed.

Except for Morgan. Oh, she wanted her to exist.

"Can we not do that?" Jan sat in the booth beside Gillian, giving her the perfect view of Morgan. "I'm fine. Nobody died. Let's move on."

Finn sat forward, frowning. "I'm sorry, but you can't expect us to not be worried, Jan."

"I'd prefer it if you weren't. Or if you insist on it, at least keep it to yourself. Tonight, I want to forget about everything going on around me."

Finn nodded slowly as she sat back. "Fair enough."

"So, how is everyone?" Jan knew it was weird to sit here and dismiss her issues with Phil, but he was the last thing on her mind right now. Maybe one day she would need Gillian's advice when it came to Morgan, but for now, she wanted to keep it a secret. While it was exactly that, nobody could ruin it or tell Jan she was out of her mind. "Finn? How's the degree going?"

"Fine, yeah. Another assignment down. Another...God knows how many to go."

"Good. That's good."

Silence fell over the three of them, and then Jan felt her phone vibrate in her clutch bag to the side of her. She took it out quickly.

You look gorgeous tonight, by the way.

Oh, Morgan. Jan held back a smile, but inside, she was beaming.

Thank you. I wasn't sure if you'd want to see me in your bar again.

With the knowledge that Morgan had only recently stopped seeing Amanda, her biggest fear was that they were just using one another to numb the pain. That wasn't true for Jan, but they hadn't really had much of a conversation about what came next. Did they spend time together? Did they put it down as a one-night stand? Jan didn't know, so Morgan would have to tell her what was happening here.

I'll always want to see you in my bar. I quite enjoyed seeing you in my bed, too.

Jan's heart thumped a little harder at that. She looked up when Gillian cleared her throat, praying she hadn't said something she shouldn't out loud.

"Everything okay?" Gillian asked as she nudged Jan's shoulder.

"Yes, why?"

"It's not like you to sit on your phone during a night out."

Jan lowered it, screen down on the table. "Sorry. It's just one of the girls I used to work with. She's keeping me updated on what's happening around the business."

"You've really quit your job?" Finn cut in.

"I have, yes. At least, I think I have. Going back isn't something I can think about right now, but never say never and all that." Jan scanned the bar, her eyes locking on Morgan's a second or two later. She continued to watch Morgan as she said to Gillian and Finn, "Do you mind if I just reply to this text message? Then I'm all yours for the rest of the night."

"Knock yourself out, love. Do what you need to do." Gillian turned her attention back to Finn, giving Jan the opportunity to finish whatever was starting on the last message.

I enjoyed being in your bed.

Deciding to leave it at that for the time being, Jan locked her phone and placed it next to her thigh. She would surely have the chance to see Morgan again soon, so she would spend a few hours with Gillian and Finn, and if she got lucky, she might just find another few minutes to watch Morgan behind the bar. If either of them questioned it, Jan would simply tell them she was in a world of her own.

Mm. A world that includes Morgan Tate.

CHAPTER 12

Noticing that Jan was sitting alone, Morgan came out from behind the bar and approached the table. She had no idea where Finn and Gillian had gone, but they certainly hadn't said goodbye. If they'd left, Morgan would be pulling Finn up about that. No matter what, they *always* said goodnight to one another. Just because Finn was married, that wouldn't change.

Morgan reached down and collected the empty glasses on the table. "They gone home?"

"No. Not yet. Gillian has gone to the loo, and Finn is outside trying to get a cab."

"And you?" Morgan asked, quickly scanning the room. "Are you going back to your hotel?"

"I don't know, Morgan." Jan gazed up at Morgan with those gorgeous blue eyes, stealing every last thought she possessed. "Am I?"

"I mean, you know you're welcome to stay a while. Or the night. Whatever you feel like." Even though Jan was going through a lot, Morgan didn't feel as though any of this was superficial. This flirting or whatever it was...was one hundred percent genuine. "If you just wanted to talk, that's also more than okay."

"I saw Phil today," Jan said, lifting her wine glass and finishing its contents. "And the woman he's been sleeping with."

Morgan nodded slowly. "Yeah, I think you should definitely hang back when they've gone. If you can think of a reason to, anyway."

"Do I need a reason other than I'm not ready to leave yet?" Jan quirked a brow, sending Morgan's heart rate through the roof. Fuck, this woman was sexy. Morgan had pushed any of those thoughts from her mind a long time ago, but seeing Jan in this light, yeah, Morgan was more than interested. "They're not my parents. What I do with my life is my decision."

"Yeah, it is." Morgan heard the drop in her voice as she said that, but it was hard to have a coherent thought around Jan lately. "I'll speak to you in a few minutes then, okay?"

"Mmhmm." Jan turned back towards the table, twisting her empty glass as she did so. She would order another drink once Gillian was back from the bathroom and hope her best friend wouldn't insist they drop Jan off on the way home.

"Cab will be here in five," Finn said as she came strolling back through the door. She reached for Gillian's bag, downed what was left of her beer, and cocked her head towards the door. "You're coming, yeah?"

"Actually, no. I think I'll have another drink before I leave."

Finn lowered herself into a seat and propped her elbows on her knees. "Jan, I know things are really tough for you at the minute, but you know you're welcome to stay with us. We'd *expect* you to stay with us."

"I'm doing just fine at the hotel." Jan reached out and cupped Finn's cheek. "But thank you for thinking of me. I appreciate it."

"What's going on here? Are we *finally* having a heart-to-heart?" Gillian's voice cut through the air. "Did you get a cab, baby?"

"Yeah. It'll be here in a minute." Finn sat back and dragged a hand through her short, cropped hair. "I thought Jan was leaving with us, but it seems not."

"We'll drop you off at your hotel on the way home." Gillian took her bag from Finn and grabbed her coat from the corner of the booth. "It's only around the corner. Come on."

"No, I'm not leaving yet. I'm having another drink, Gill."

Gillian nodded. "Okay. Finn, cancel the cab until Jan is ready."

"What? Don't be ridiculous." Jan scoffed and got to her feet. "I don't need you to babysit me. I'm having another glass of wine, and then I'll head back. You two keep the cab and head home."

"I'm not letting you walk back to your hotel on your own. No way." Gillian held up her hands, looking to Finn for support. "Right?"

"I mean, if Jan wants to stay a while, we can't stop her, babe." Finn looked around the bar, stopping when she landed on Morgan. "Hey, Morgan?" Finn waved her over.

"What's up?"

"Would you do me a huge favour? Would you walk Jan back to her hotel when you close?"

Morgan smiled but didn't make eye contact with Jan. "Of course. Anything to look after my customers."

"Promise me, Morgan. I don't want to fall out with you when I find out you let her go without walking her back."

"Hey, I promise you." Morgan placed a hand on her chest. "I'll make sure Jan is safe. Don't worry."

Finn's phone pinged twice in her hand. She looked down at it and sighed. "Babe, the cab is here. What do you want to do?"

Gillian took a step towards Morgan and studied her. Eventually, she nodded and agreed. "I also don't want to fall out with you, Morgan. You get my best friend home safe, okay?"

"I will. She'll be okay here with me. You two get home safe." Morgan turned and walked away, whistling along to the low music playing as she did so. Jan wanted to admire her, but she would wait until she was alone. One hint of her looking and the game would be up. A game, it seemed, neither Jan nor Morgan had intended to play with one another.

"Come here. Give me a hug." Gillian opened her arms to Jan and held her tight. "Call me tomorrow. *Please.* I know you think you can manage all of this on your own, but you can't, Jan. You need friends around you, and I'm going to do everything I can to be there for you. We both will."

Jan drew back. "I'll call you tomorrow at some point." She eyed Finn. "You may think I need looking after, but you make sure *my* best friend gets home safe."

Finn saluted Jan. "Got it."

Once Gillian and Finn left the bar, Jan breathed a sigh of relief. She caught Morgan watching her, and Jan could only smile back. She would be spending some time with her bartender tonight, and as she sat here, she couldn't wait.

"Thought they'd never leave you alone," Morgan said as she approached the table again. She watched Gillian and Finn pull away in their cab, and then Morgan took a seat next to Jan, her hand out of view of the few customers finishing their drinks. "Hey, you okay?"

"Me? Yes." Jan dipped her head, blushing. "Thank you for getting them off my back."

"It's what I'm here for." Morgan slung the towel she was holding over her shoulder and settled a hand on Jan's thigh. The thrill that rushed through Jan's body was the very same thrill that had led to her guiding Morgan's hand down the front of her pants just a few nights ago. "You want another drink? It's on me, obviously."

"I'll have another red and a bottle of water, please."

Morgan squeezed Jan's thigh, not moving from her position. "You wanna stay over here with me tonight?"

Did she? Was it a wise decision? Right now, Jan didn't care. She enjoyed being with Morgan rather than alone in a hotel room. "Yes."

Morgan grinned. "O-oh. Great. I'll, uh...I'll be locking up in a few minutes. You okay to hang around here until then or did you want to go up to my flat now?"

"I can't sit here admiring you if I'm upstairs, can I?"

It was Morgan's turn to blush this time. She shook her head lightly. "No, I guess you can't."

Morgan double-bolted the door to the bar and put the shutters down. It hadn't been easy to get rid of Eric, one of her regulars, but eventually, his long-term friend Ged had convinced him it *was* midnight and that the bar was now closed. Eric had been coming here since Morgan bought the bar four years ago, and he was a permanent fixture every Friday night. He'd lost his wife the year before Morgan moved in here, and most of the time, she enjoyed listening to his stories from the past. But tonight, she had somewhere much more important to be.

She turned around, smiling when Jan stood in the middle of the bar, her clutch bag gripped in her hand. "All done?"

"Yep. Locked up and free." Morgan closed the distance and took Jan's free hand. "I meant it before when I said you look gorgeous tonight. I haven't been able to take my eyes off you."

Jan tugged on Morgan's hand and pulled her closer. "I don't care if they know about us."

"Neither do I, but I'm not sure you're in the right place for them to know at the minute. Once they talk you down from whatever ledge you're on, I probably won't see you again. Once will never be enough for me, not when it's with you." Morgan lifted a hand and stroked her knuckles against Jan's cheek. "Please, can I have you for just a bit longer before we go our separate ways?"

Jan walked backwards towards the door she knew would take them upstairs. Her back connected with it, and Morgan pressed herself against Jan. "Who says I'm going anywhere?"

"If Gillian and Finn have anything to do with it, neither of us will have any choice. They're protective of you, and I get that, but I don't know. I have a feeling they won't like this when they find out. *If* they find out."

"Because they'll insist that I'm straight."

Morgan switched her gaze from Jan's eyes to her lips. Could she just kiss her from now until they were forced apart? "Yes. Exactly that."

Jan drew her hand up Morgan's stomach beneath her shirt. Morgan shuddered, wetness gathered between her thighs, and right now, she knew she should just stop talking. If this was what Jan wanted, then Jan could have it. "If I want you, that's my decision."

"Do you want me?" Morgan pressed her hand to the door beside Jan's head and leaned in. Their lips brushed, she felt Jan practically melt into the door, and then their eyes locked. "Well?"

"Oh, I want you," Jan whispered against Morgan's lips. "I don't know what the hell I'm doing, but I want you. Make no mistake about that."

Morgan wrapped an arm around Jan's waist and opened the door. She held Jan against her, brought her lips to Jan's ear, and whispered, "I'm all yours until you say otherwise."

"Are you done down here now?"

Morgan smiled. "I am."

"Good. Upstairs is much more exciting." Jan turned and took the stairs, her arse teasing Morgan as she watched it in her figure-hugging, navy blue dress.

Morgan bit the inside of her cheek, wondering what the fuck she was doing lately. This woman had come out of nowhere but had somehow ended up in Morgan's flat on several occasions now. "You're incredible, you know that, right?"

"Just...hurry up." Jan stood at the top of the stairs with her hip jutted. "I've been dying to get you alone all night."

Morgan didn't need asking twice.

She quickly took her flat key from her pocket, shot up the

stairs, and opened the door. The moment they were locked away inside, Jan pressed Morgan to the back of the door and clawed at her belt buckle. If this was how Jan felt when she was with Morgan, then Morgan wasn't going to complain. No way.

"You have to admit that this turns you on..." Jan slowly lowered Morgan's zip and forced her jeans down her thighs. "Hiding away up here."

"All of you turns me on." Morgan held Jan's chin in her fingers and smiled. "Don't ever forget that."

"I wish you wouldn't say things like that to me."

"Why? It's the truth. All of you is exceptionally beautiful, Jan." Morgan took her bottom lip between her teeth when Jan slowly lowered herself to her knees. Fuck, this woman was going to be the death of her. Without a doubt. "Oh, shit."

Jan looked up at Morgan with hooded eyes.

"Do you have any idea how fucking sexy you look in this position?"

Jan traced her tongue across her bottom lip and tugged on Morgan's boxer shorts. They pooled at her feet with her jeans, and she couldn't step out of them quick enough. Jan palmed her thighs, and as she moved higher, spread Morgan's lips and dove right in. Morgan pressed her head to the back of the door, desperately trying to grasp onto anything she could hold, but the moment Jan sucked her clit into her mouth, Morgan's knees shook.

"O-oh, fuck!" Morgan grazed her nails through Jan's luscious blonde hair and rocked against her mouth. Considering Jan hadn't been with a woman in thirty years, she sure as hell knew what Morgan needed. "Yes. Fuck, that feels good." Morgan allowed the smile she was wearing to spread wider. In this moment, everyone they knew had been pushed firmly to the back of her mind. The only woman that existed was Jan. The only woman she cared about was Jan. People could have their opinions, but, ultimately, Morgan was going to enjoy this woman and whatever came with it.

As Jan lavished Morgan's clit with her tongue, she eased two fingers inside her. Morgan's pulse whooshed in her ears, and her knees continued to tremble, but Jan's mouth felt incredibly good on her. It had a few nights ago, and tonight was sure to be even more explosive. Any hesitancy Morgan may have felt when they'd first slept together didn't exist in this moment. Jan knew what she was doing, and she most definitely knew what she wanted. Jan drew back and looked up at Morgan as she picked up her pace and fucked her a little faster. "Correct me if I'm wrong, but you quite enjoy seeing me on my knees."

Morgan grinned as she pushed her head harder to the door. If Jan kept talking, Morgan wasn't going to last much longer. "Oh, I think you enjoy being down there just as much as I do."

"Mmhmm." Jan took a long, slow, teasing lick between Morgan's lips and moaned. "Oh, I do."

"J-Jan." Morgan panted, her lips bucking with every push of Jan's fingers.

"You need to come."

Yep. That would do it. "Y-yes."

"And you're so wet." Jan sunk deeper as she filled Morgan with a third finger. It didn't take a lot for Morgan to be wet around this woman, but tonight, it was far more than she expected. For most of the evening, Morgan hadn't thought for one moment that Jan would walk through her door. For the night to be ending like this, yeah, Morgan was very happy and very wet.

"I... It's what you do to me, and I don't give a fuck who knows it." Morgan's stomach tightened when Jan enveloped her clit with those delicious full lips once again. She flicked her tongue, bringing Morgan to the edge of what was surely only the first of many orgasms tonight. "J-Jan, I—"

When Jan sucked harder, Morgan's world turned black. Jan lifted a hand to Morgan's stomach, holding her in place, and hummed as Morgan came in her mouth.

"Fuck." Morgan pressed a hand to her forehead, her chest

heaving as she caught her breath. But it was clear that Jan wasn't finished. She eased out of Morgan, climbed to her feet, and unzipped the side of her dress. Once it was on the floor and Jan stood before Morgan in nothing but heels and lingerie, Morgan knew that she had to do whatever she could to make this work. Losing Jan just wasn't an option for her. "Do you have any idea how gorgeous you are?"

Jan stepped forward and pressed herself to Morgan as she said, "I'm sure you'll remind me once we're in the bedroom."

Morgan took Jan's hand and guided her across the room. She would spend the rest of her life reminding Jan how beautiful she was given half the chance, and tonight, it would be an honour.

CHAPTER 13

Jan woke up to the most beautiful sensation. Morgan pressed against her and sleeping soundly. Naked and as one. She hadn't thought about staying last night—she'd just about managed to make it to the bar at all—but she was glad she'd decided to hang back. By doing so, she'd just spent *another* night in Morgan's arms. A night she would add to the previous one and hold onto forever.

She watched Morgan as she slept. Jan hadn't had the opportunity to do so the last time she'd woken up in Morgan's bed. No, she'd lay here alone for a few moments before she'd gone searching for Morgan, only to find her mildly panicking out in the kitchen. Not this morning, though.

God, she's beautiful.

Had Jan thought about Antonia over the years? Several times. But it wasn't necessarily Antonia she was thinking about. When Jan's sex life with Phil had started to rapidly decline, Jan's mind often wandered off to the days when she'd found her attention fixed firmly on women. It was hard to remember at times, it had been so long ago, but the memories made Jan smile. She knew that much.

"I know you're watching me. I can hear you blinking."

Jan snickered as she took her bottom lip between her teeth. Morgan was sexy *and* hilarious. Jan hadn't laughed so much before she met Morgan. Well, became more acquainted with her, at least. "I don't think eyelids make a sound."

Morgan cracked one eye open and smiled. "But you admit that you *were* watching me?"

"What happens if I do admit it?" Jan teased as she stroked a thumb against Morgan's hip.

"You get a lot of kisses. Maybe a lot of something else, too." Morgan snuggled closer again and rested her chin on the top of Jan's head. "Five more minutes before I have to deal with life."

"I told Phil."

Morgan drew back and frowned. "Told him what?"

"That I'd spent the night with someone else." Jan wanted to always be on the same page as Morgan. Even though Morgan was unavailable because of her work commitments, it was important to maintain that level of full transparency.

"O-oh. Right. Um..."

"Don't worry. I *know* this isn't anything serious. You don't have to say anything. I just wanted you to know that he knows. I didn't say who it was, but he knows I've spent the night with someone else."

"Jan, I'm going at your pace here." Morgan rolled onto her back and looked up at the ceiling. "You say it's not serious, and I understand that you're not in a position to even think about a love life, but this isn't just fucking for me. Please don't ever think I'm using you to get off."

"God, I know. I hope you don't think the same about me." Jan hadn't meant to sound so blasé about her situation with Morgan. She just couldn't get her hopes up here. "I'm sorry if I said that wrong."

"If I knew you were in the position to do so, I'd be asking you out for dinner. Or a drink, whatever. A...date. But you're new to this all over again. You need time to decide what you even want in your future. While I *know* that's not me, it doesn't make me want you any less. It also doesn't stop me from thinking about the potential of us still doing this six months down the line."

Jan sat up on her elbow and traced a fingertip over Morgan's collarbone. "I wish it was you."

Morgan's brows drew together as she turned her face to Jan. "You do?"

"I love every moment we spend together, Morgan. But you've said it yourself. You don't have the time for a relationship."

"Oh, I'd make the time for you." Jan was surprised Morgan would do that. What was different about Jan compared to the other women Morgan had been with? "I'd hire more staff if I had to."

Jan smiled. "I appreciate that."

Morgan rolled over this time and stared deep into Jan's eyes as she encouraged her down onto her back. "I'm serious. You tell me the *moment* you're sure of what you want, and if that's me...I'm all yours."

Jan's heart started to beat a little harder. Could she really walk out of a marriage and directly into a woman's arms? People would likely tell her that she shouldn't...or *couldn't*, but this was Jan's life. It was her choice. "You really mean that? You'd be interested in a relationship?"

"Babe, I've always been interested in a relationship. I've just never really found anyone I want to work less for. It's been a string of bad mistakes to date, but you? Fuck, you're something else. I hope you know that."

Well, then. What could Jan possibly say to that? She wouldn't agree or disagree just yet—she needed to sort out all kinds within her life—but this conversation would remain at the back of her mind until a later date. "You're very good for my self-confidence."

"A woman like you should be filled with self-confidence. Don't let what he did to you take it away. What do you think drew me to you all those months ago when you started coming to the bar? I mean, other than your incredibly beautiful face and this body?"

Jan felt herself blushing. She had no idea how the hell she'd landed so perfectly on her feet here with Morgan, but she wouldn't take a single second of it for granted. "There were a few occasions when I had to concentrate on something else. You have the most intense eyes of anyone I've ever met, and it was hard not to gaze into them when you were speaking to me."

Morgan smiled. "Yeah?"

"It wasn't something I thought much of until I came here the other week. It's not as though I was in a position to do anything about it."

"No, I know. And thank God you didn't. This could have been a whole different story."

"Can I ask something of you?" Jan swallowed when Morgan shifted and pressed her body against her. "You're entitled to say no, of course."

"You can ask me anything at all. If I'm able to do whatever it is you want," Morgan said as she smirked. "Then you know I will."

Jan knew where Morgan's mind had just gone. If nothing else, the intimacy they shared was intense. "Can you stick around until I know I'm ready for a relationship? Can we...be together without actually being together until I know I can give my all?"

Morgan dipped her head and drew Jan into a slow, lingering kiss. Jan moaned when she wrapped a hand around the back of Morgan's neck, fairly certain she had her answer already. When Morgan pulled back and touched her forehead to Jan's, those dark eyes boring into her soul, Morgan grinned. "You can take as long as you need. I'm not going anywhere."

Carrying two cups of coffee towards the couch, Morgan handed one to Jan and took a seat beside her. While she didn't know much at the moment, she knew Jan brightened this place like nobody else ever had. Morgan loved her flat, she wouldn't want to be anywhere else, but she could certainly enjoy this space alone with Jan.

"Tell me how it went yesterday when you saw Phil and…whatever the fuck her name is."

Jan smiled. "Her name is Anais. Before all of this, I'd go as far as to say I considered her a friend. Okay, she was an employee before anything else, but we had a great working relationship with one another. We've also had many business nights out together."

Morgan puffed out her cheeks. Surely that only made all of this even worse. "Hard-faced bitch."

"Mm. My thoughts exactly." Jan sipped her coffee and rested it in her lap. But not before she draped her legs over Morgan's lap. "He was at the house with her. At first, I felt sick knowing she was in my home, but now I'm just ready to say goodbye to it all. I refuse to feel sad about something I can't control. I also refuse to give the two of them those emotions in me. They don't deserve them."

"God, I wish I had your mentality."

Jan looked down at her cup and shrugged. "I have a few more years on you, Morgan. When you reach my age, you learn to focus on what's important."

Morgan palmed Jan's knee. "And what's that, babe?"

"Giving my time to people who mean a lot to me. Being happy with what I do have rather than what I'm losing. Reminding myself that I'm still here and that I have a life to build all over again. *You*…you're important to me."

"You're important to me, too." Morgan leaned over and kissed Jan's cheek. "And I love having you over here with me the morning after. It's not something I afford myself most of the time."

"You have to have a life. The bar will survive. You've built it into something that simply cannot fail. And your staff seem great. Ben and Tyler are lovely guys. I'm yet to really speak to Megan."

"Megan doesn't have much conversation in her. She's a great bartender, but she's quieter than the others I've had in the past."

"Sometimes the quieter people are the people you should surround yourself with. They tend to have less issues and drama."

Morgan had to agree with that. The bartender Megan had replaced had done nothing but cause hassle for Morgan. First, she'd decided to invite her friends in whenever she was working so they could have free drinks. Then, she'd tried her hand at dipping into the takings on shift. Morgan couldn't have someone like that working for her. No matter what her reasons for stealing had been. "I have a good thing going here. Add you into it, and my life has been almost perfect lately."

"What would make it entirely perfect?" Jan asked, those blue eyes bright and so easy to get lost in.

"Knowing that you'll be here for a long time to come."

"When you say things like that to me, it makes me wonder why I even gave my marriage a chance." Jan swallowed as she shook her head. "If I'd been honest with myself in the past, you and I may be in a different position right now."

"How do you mean?"

"I know I've spoken about the counselling and how things felt off, but I'd been feeling it for far longer than I led myself to believe." Morgan appreciated it every time Jan opened up to her. It meant this was heading in the right direction. "Every day, I remind myself of something he used to do that I hated. Or the times when he just wasn't there...even though we were in the same room."

"I think we're all guilty of that. Nobody is perfect, neither are marriages, but we always want it to work out in the best way possible, so we settle or we look past things we know we shouldn't look past."

"You've done that before?"

"Oh, absolutely." Morgan was terrible for letting people off lightly. It was probably why she was single right now. Because she let people walk all over her until it either suited them or until she saw what was happening. "And not necessarily with love interests. Even with friends over the years."

"It never ends well, does it?"

Morgan wrinkled her nose. "Not really, no."

"I'm just glad Gareth came to me and told me. It must have taken a lot for him to sit down and tell me his wife was seeing another man. Then for that other man to be my husband...well, I'm not sure I would have had the balls to do it if the shoe was on the other foot."

"Oh, I don't know. I think you'd have done the right thing eventually. You seem like the kind of woman who only deals with the truth."

"The right thing would have been for Phil to come to me and tell me himself. I'd have felt less humiliated if he'd done it in the comfort of our own home. But instead, he left it up to Gareth to take care of."

"How did Gareth know about it?" Morgan hoped the poor guy hadn't walked in on it happening, but that was generally how it went.

"Anais told him she was away for the weekend. Gareth has been dealing with his mother's cancer diagnosis and helping her out where he can. He'd gone to stay with her that weekend but went back home for something he'd forgotten. Anais was in bed with Phil." Jan scoffed. "Does it make me a terrible person to be happy he caught them there and that it wasn't me catching them in my home?"

"Not at all, babe." Morgan took Jan's hand and held onto it. "Nobody wants to see that. I hate the thought of you walking in on your husband having an affair, so I'm also happy it wasn't you."

"Maybe men just want younger women these days," Jan said as she stroked her thumb against the back of Morgan's hand. "Maybe they've always been like that. I don't know."

"I think women can be equally as disgusting. I know that from experience. But I can understand why you feel that way. You've had one hell of a shock with all of this."

"I have. But you put me back together pretty quickly."

Morgan wasn't convinced that Jan was entirely put back together just yet, but it was nice to know that Jan appreciated Morgan being there for her. "If you want me to heal you, you say the word, and I'll do whatever I can to show you a different life. One that doesn't include affairs."

"That sounds like a nice idea to me. No affairs."

Morgan smiled and lay her head back against the couch. Another day with Jan by her side was another day when Morgan was truly winning at life. She lifted her head and laughed. "I can't believe you told him you'd slept with someone else. How did he react?"

"He thinks I did it to get back at him. I think he was ready to tell me he forgives me. Like I give a shit."

"So you actually had a conversation about it?" Morgan's mind was blown. Surely that meant she saw it going somewhere; otherwise, why bother saying anything at all?

"Brief, but yes. I may have made a comment about you being inside me. That was purely me twisting the knife, though. I wouldn't usually be so honest." Jan stroked her fingers up Morgan's forearm, sending a shiver down Morgan's spine in the process. "I don't know how or why, but it seems you bring a different side of me out."

"And is that a good thing...or?"

"Mmhmm. It's exciting." Jan lowered her coffee cup to the table and rose to her feet. Just when Morgan thought she was about to leave the living room, Jan straddled her on the couch and took Morgan's own cup from her. "Don't you think?"

"Something is exciting me." Morgan stared up at Jan, far more than excited, truth be told. "Can't possibly say what, though."

Jan reached down and took the hem of her T-shirt in her

hands. As she lifted it over her head, that long blonde hair cascading over her shoulders, it took everything within Morgan not to lean in and take a nipple between her lips. "Does this help?"

Aching to give this woman everything she deserved, Morgan palmed Jan's thighs and grinned. "Mm. It helps a lot."

Oh, today is going to be another perfect day!

CHAPTER 14

Rushing across the busy main street, Jan took refuge under a bus shelter. The rain had come out of nowhere this afternoon, and now Jan looked like a drowned rat. It hadn't been forecast, it was meant to be glorious today, but no such luck. Jan didn't often find the time to head into the city for retail therapy, her shopping sprees usually extended no further than online stores, so this was a nice change. With or without the rain.

She had already taken several bags back to the car, and in the next few minutes, she was meeting Gillian as she passed through on her way to a meeting in the city's central library. It would be brief, but at least Gillian would know Jan was still alive and surviving. She didn't know what images her best friend had been conjuring up in her mind, but Gillian texted Jan at least once a day to ask what she was doing and how she was feeling.

As Jan peered around the bus shelter, she could see the walkway to the main shopping area. It would only take her a minute or two to reach the next shelter, but did she want to risk it? The rain just wasn't letting up today. Still, if she wanted to spend a few minutes with Gillian, she would have to make a run for it.

Thank God you wore your Converse today.

She rushed from under the bus shelter and kept as close to the side of the buildings along the main road as she could. It didn't really help to keep her dry since the wind had the rain heading in all directions, but she could see Gillian in the distance. She'd always been the sensible one who carried an umbrella in her bag at all times.

Gillian laughed as Jan neared, quickly reaching out and pulling her under the umbrella. "I don't know when you're going to learn, I swear."

"Just...share the bloody umbrella with me and mind your own business." Jan grinned as she leaned in and kissed Gillian on the cheek. "Hi. Nice to see you."

"Come on. Let's stroll." Gillian linked an arm through Jan's. They wandered off in the general direction of the library, blue sky barely visible in the distance. Maybe it would stop in time for Jan to dry out before she got back to the hotel. "How are you?"

"I was feeling great as I got into the city and the sun was shining, but now...not so much." Jan wiped a raindrop from her nose and laughed. "At least it's not cold."

"Always a plus." Gillian squeezed Jan's arm against her. "Finn was asking about you. She said to say hi, and she wants to know when you're coming over for dinner."

Jan should probably make an effort and take up the invitation, but she was too busy dedicating her evenings to Morgan whenever she had a night off. "I'll come over next week, maybe."

Gillian side-eyed Jan as she lowered her umbrella once they were undercover again. "You seem awfully busy and unavailable for someone living in a hotel and who has no job. What exactly are you doing with your days while you're not working?"

Jan shrugged. "Just...finding a new routine. Enjoying some shopping. Taking time out for *me*." The day would soon come when Jan would have to tell Gillian about Morgan. She was just trying to put it off as long as she possibly could. "I may look empty-handed right now, but I have several bags in the boot of my car.

"Oo, did you buy anything you don't actually like that I can take off your hands?" Gillian wiggled her eyebrows and laughed. "You always used to pass things on to me."

"Probably. Give me a few hours to decide I hate one or two of the things I bought, and they're all yours."

Gillian sighed as they slowed their pace and perused shop windows. "Now that the jokes are out of the way, how are you really doing?"

"I'm...good. Great, really."

Gillian turned to Jan and gave her a knowing look. "You're the worst liar."

"I'm not lying, Gill. I *am* good. I'm feeling positive, and I guess in some way, I'm looking forward to a new future."

"Have you got yourself a lawyer yet?"

"Mmhmm. They came highly recommended from a friend at the office." Jan didn't know what the divorce would entail, but she would be fine. She had to be. "Any idea how long it takes for it all to be finalised?"

Gillian's brows rose as her eyes widened. "It depends entirely on how brutal either of you play this. If you don't agree on the terms set out, it's back to the drawing board. There will be a lot of compromising and whatnot. Probably a lot of grovelling from Phil, too. Just don't let him beat you down with some bullshit offer."

"I don't think he'd do that to me." Jan was brave saying that. Phil had just fucked another woman for a year behind her back, but when it came to their finances...he would likely be very fair. Jan had put in just as much as him over the years. "To be honest, I just want enough to move on. Find a place, keep myself afloat until I know what's next."

Gillian snorted. "If I was you, I'd be taking the bastard for everything he's got."

Jan could see why Gillian would say that, but it wasn't the woman Jan was. She couldn't do that to Phil. He'd met someone else, and that was the end of it. Jan wouldn't penalise him for falling out of love with her. "He claims he still loves me and wants us to work it out."

"At least you have that. Dave didn't want anything to do with me when I found out about the affair."

Dave had always been a completely different person to Phil. Even Phil kept him at arm's length. They'd known one another for a long time, but Phil always used to tell Jan that there was something about Dave that he didn't quite get a good feeling about. Seems he'd been right all along. Only now, they could add Phil to the same shit list that Dave was on. A usually decent guy or not, he had a black mark through his name as far as Jan and Gillian were concerned. "Phil is giving me space. The only time he tries his luck with apologies is whenever I see him."

"At least he isn't hounding you. That's something, I guess."

As they reached the end of the outdoor shopping area, Gillian turned to Jan. "Can we meet next week for a coffee at the hotel? Or something stronger if that's what we need on the day..."

"Yes. That would be lovely. I'll text you when I know what days I'm available, okay?" Jan's phone pinged in the pocket of her jeans. She would take care of it once Gillian had left. "I'm going to pick up a few more things and then head back."

"Okay, love. It's been lovely seeing you. And you look well, so that's naturally put my mind at ease."

Jan embraced Gillian and sighed. "Have you ever known me to fall apart?"

"No. But that doesn't mean you won't when you think nobody is paying attention." Gillian drew back and smiled. "Don't think you're alone. I can be there for you at the drop of a hat, and you know it."

"You're going to be late for your meeting. There is *no way* I'm letting you put the blame on me for that, so I suggest you get a move on, and I'll speak to you soon." As Jan watched Gillian take a couple of steps back, she reached into her pocket for her phone. "I *promise* I'll speak to you soon, okay?"

Gillian nodded. "Okay. Bye, love. Take care of yourself."

"I always do." Jan winked and offered a small wave in Gillian's direction. Her best friend walked away, that confidence Jan once possessed exuding from Gillian Masters.

She lifted her phone, grinning from ear to ear when she saw Morgan's name.

Hey. I know it's short notice but I'm in the city picking up a few supplies. Did you by any chance want to get some lunch with me before I start my shift in a few hours?

Jan pressed her back to the wall and sighed. Was this going to be a common occurrence between them now? God, Jan deeply hoped so.

I'm already in the city and I'd love to have lunch with you. Where should I meet you?

Morgan started to respond immediately.

Perfect. I'm outside La Casa right now. Fancy something to eat in there?

Jan would happily eat at a McDonald's if it meant she was sharing space with Morgan Tate.

I'm on my way!

Satisfied after a beautiful and unexpected lunch with Jan, Morgan took her hand as they reached the second floor of the multi-storey carpark. It wasn't something they could do in public—Morgan understood that—so while they were alone in here, she wanted to make the most of it. On so many occasions over lunch, she had *almost* taken Jan's hand, but Morgan would get used to less public displays of affection. She would have to if this was going to survive. Whatever *this* was, anyway.

"Thank you for lunch," Jan said as she leaned in and kissed Morgan's cheek. "I need to lie down now. I ate too much."

"Me, too." Morgan worked out in her head how long she could relax for once she got back. She was due to be in the bar at six, and it was only two now. "Maybe I'll get the chance. Depends if anyone manages to stop me between walking through the door to the bar and reaching the door to the flat."

"Is that an issue for you? Someone always needing something because you live above the place?"

"I think so, yeah. I'm kind of always just there, you know? I think people forget that I have a life that extends beyond the bar." As they reached Jan's car, she turned and rested against the bonnet. Morgan stood between her legs, drawing her into a kiss, smiling against Jan's lips as she tried to pull back. "Babe, it's fine. Nobody is around."

Jan laughed. "You think I care if someone sees us? No. I'm more concerned by the fact I stink of garlic."

Morgan lifted a shoulder. "I happen to *love* garlic."

Jan hooked her fingers through Morgan's belt loops and smiled up at her. "I don't want to leave you now that I've spent some time with you."

"Believe me, going to work is the last thing on my mind right now." All Morgan wanted to do in this moment was lie down and snuggle up with Jan. The fact it had rained all morning and afternoon only encouraged that mood. Warm, cosy, content. Those were the things Morgan was striving for these days. "But I always love to see you turning up at the bar, so you know, keep that in mind."

"I intend to show up at some point this evening—don't you worry about that." Jan wrapped a hand around the back of Morgan's neck and offered her a slow, lingering kiss. "A nice cocktail, a great atmosphere, and the perfect view. What more could I ask for?"

"A lottery win?" Morgan said with a quirked brow.

"Where would we run off to if I did win big?"

"Anywhere we wanted to." Morgan could happily daydream about that scenario for the rest of her life. "Somewhere hot. Somewhere with good food. Somewhere that makes *you* happy."

"I don't need a lot to make me happy, Morgan. This, right here, right now, makes me incredibly happy."

Morgan's brows drew together. "Standing in a cold carpark makes you happy?"

"If I'm standing in a cold carpark with you, yes."

Oh, Morgan was never going to keep hold of this woman. It just didn't seem possible if she allowed her mind to wander towards the future. Jan was worlds apart from anything Morgan could offer her. But for the time being, she would enjoy this. She would treat Jan the way she always should have been treated. "When you say things like that, it just reminds me that you're going to break my heart one day." Morgan drew a thumb across Jan's bottom lip. "But when you do, promise you'll go easy on me."

"I don't make it a habit to go around breaking people's hearts. Other people have that covered already." Jan dipped her head and toyed with one of the buttons on Morgan's shirt. "I don't know what the future holds, but I hope you'll feature in it."

"Yeah?" Morgan lifted Jan's chin with two fingers, her pulse quickening when Jan looked up at her with those blue eyes. "You mean that?"

"I do. And if that doesn't happen for some reason, please know that I'd never do anything to intentionally hurt you."

"I know you wouldn't." Even though Morgan was still getting to know Jan—they'd kinda skipped that stage and gone straight in for the kill—she could safely say that Jan didn't have the ability to intentionally hurt anyone. "I'm one of those people who prepares for the worst. It's easier than getting carried away with something that makes me unbelievably happy."

"I understand what you're saying." Jan regarded Morgan with

a small smile. "I hope I can prove you wrong and this grows to be something beautiful."

"Hey, I do, too. But I *am* mindful of what you're going through right now. I think it's important to remember that we're not just two single women who found a connection. Even though I want it to feel that way, that's not how it happened. We met one another when we were both having a rough time. You more so, but the point remains." Morgan stroked a fingertip up Jan's neck and smiled. "*You* are more than I ever expected. Don't forget that."

"Come back to my hotel room with me and rest for a while."

Morgan's smile spread wider. "I'd love to if I wouldn't be imposing."

"You could never impose." Jan pushed off the bonnet of her car and crushed her lips to Morgan's. It deepened, but Morgan would prefer to spend the next couple of hours kissing Jan somewhere far warmer than this carpark.

She drew back and wrinkled her nose. "Ew. You stink of garlic."

That earned Morgan a swat to the stomach from Jan, but they both laughed as Jan wrapped her arms around Morgan's waist. "Good thing you love garlic, isn't it?"

God, Morgan just wanted to spend forever kissing this woman. The day she lost it, she wouldn't know what to do with herself. She lay a hand on the side of Jan's jaw, their lips just millimetres apart. "Come on. Let's get out of here."

CHAPTER 15

O*ne week later...*

Yawning as she stood behind the bar, Morgan's shoulders slumped when she allowed the tiredness she felt to hit her. The bar had been packed last night—a hen party had practically owned the place until Morgan had to insist they leave because it was closing time—but by having them here, she had hit her weekly target in terms of takings in one night.

Jan had texted to see if Morgan was around, but she'd sadly had to let her down. It wasn't something she planned to make a habit of, but there would be times when Morgan just didn't have a second to stop and chat. Last night had been one of those times. Still, it hadn't all been bad. Jan was heading over now before the bar opened in an hour, so Morgan would apologise, and then they could move on.

As she took her espresso from below the spout of the coffee machine, Morgan's phone started to ring on the counter. She looked down at it and groaned. Amanda was calling, but Morgan couldn't give her any time. While Amanda wasn't in her head, life seemed straightforward. It *had* to remain that way.

A gentle knock on the window had her looking up from her phone, a huge smile plastered on Morgan's face when Jan waved back at her. Morgan lowered her cup, rounded the counter, and rushed towards the door. She quickly let Jan in, pressing her to the door as she locked up again and smiled into a kiss. Jan's hands found Morgan's hips, her handbag falling from her shoulder as they deepened the kiss. They moaned in unison, and then Morgan drew back. "Hi. It's nice to see you."

Jan ran her tongue across her bottom lip. "Mm. It would seem so."

"Coffee? I've just made myself one."

"God, yes. The coffee at the hotel is terrible." Morgan couldn't fathom why Jan was still staying there. Then again, she didn't suppose she had anywhere else to go unless Jan took Gillian up on her offer. For some reason, Jan was dead set against that idea. "Your coffee is so much better."

"Then have a seat, and I'll get that sorted for you."

As Morgan pushed off the door, she found herself unable to take her eyes off Jan. She wore light makeup today, but those eyes... Fuck, those eyes could undo Morgan right here, right now.

"What?" Jan asked, frowning.

"You're gorgeous." Morgan dipped her head and kissed Jan again, aware that they didn't have time to get too hot and bothered. Morgan had to work the bar alone until five this evening, and then she had to pack. "God, I wish we had more time."

"I'm not going anywhere. We have all the time in the world." Jan reached out and caressed Morgan's cheek, her perfume reminding Morgan of the nights they'd spent together so far. "Relax."

"I...won't be here next week," Morgan said as she took Jan's hand and guided her further inside the bar. "I've been so preoccupied with this place, and then you came out of nowhere, and well...

we both know what happened there. I completely forgot to tell you."

"Going anywhere nice?"

"The Canary Islands. Gran Canaria, to be specific." Morgan sighed and got to work on Jan's coffee. "I go for a week every year before the summer season starts. It's too hot for me once summer arrives over there."

"Oh." Jan sounded disappointed, but Morgan understood. She was even more disappointed. "Well, I'm sure you need the break."

"Now that you're here, I'd be happy to take a weeklong break locked away upstairs." Morgan glanced over her shoulder at Jan, smiling when she caught her checking out her arse. "Maybe I should just take the loss on what I've paid and stay here. I already know it would be worth it."

"No. You should go and enjoy your holiday. At least one of us should relax in the sun." Jan groaned. "Perhaps you can call me while you're there. I'll live vicariously through you."

Morgan turned to Jan and placed her coffee down where she sat on the opposite side of the bar. She waited a moment or two, wondering if the idea swimming around in her head was a possibility. She watched Jan, the disappointment still on her face, and decided to chance her luck. "Why don't you come with me?"

Jan's cup froze mid-air. "I'm sorry?"

"I have a double room booked. Four star. Adult-only pool." Morgan shrugged, trying to make light of the offer so Jan didn't feel pressured. "You're more than welcome to join me."

"I shouldn't. I have things to take care of here."

Morgan nodded. "You do. I understand that. But...it'll still be here when you come back, won't it?"

Jan smiled and lowered her eyes. "It will. I just...I can't *just* leave the country with you. People would wonder where the hell I am."

"I mean, you can tell them whatever you like. You can go on holiday. It's nobody else's business but your own."

"You'd be tired of me within a day."

Morgan gave Jan a knowing look. "You're not serious?"

"I am. I'm serious." Jan looked away as she shook her head. "Phil couldn't find the time for us to go on holiday. There must be a reason for that."

"Whoa. No." Morgan stopped in front of Jan and took her hands. "Whatever is going through your mind right now, forget about it. If Phil couldn't be bothered to stop working for a week so he could take his *incredibly* beautiful wife on holiday, that's his problem." Morgan leaned in and captured Jan's lips. "But I'd be *honoured* to have you there with me."

"Morgan," Jan mumbled against her lips, one hand gently pressed to her shoulder. When Morgan inched back a little, she knew she'd overstepped.

"I'm sorry. I shouldn't have even asked." Morgan ran a hand through her hair and sighed. "I thought it could have been nice for you to get away. To get out from under all the shit you're dealing with."

"Could we really do that?" Jan asked, hope—perhaps excitement—resting in those blue eyes. "Go on holiday together?"

"Of course we could."

"It wouldn't seem weird?"

Morgan pondered that for a moment. She didn't believe anything between her and Jan was weird. It was hard to feel that way when she adored spending time with this woman. "Weird how?"

"Well, I'm, what, three weeks out of a marriage." Jan scoffed. "People are going to think I've lost my mind when they find out about us."

Us. Morgan wanted to smile at that, but she didn't know what 'us' meant to Jan. Was it just that they were sleeping together, or did Jan really feel that connection Morgan was clinging onto? "What exactly is it that you're worried about them finding out?"

"That I'm sleeping with and spending *a lot* of time with another woman," Jan said as she tugged on Morgan's belt loop and pulled her between her legs. "And I wouldn't say it's worry that I feel. It's more...apprehension for people's reaction."

"That's completely understandable. Everything you're feeling is valid, Jan." Morgan had wondered on several occasions now if people would think she'd taken advantage of the situation Jan was in, but Jan had made the first move. Jan had insisted Morgan take her right back up the stairs again the moment she came undone in this bar two weeks ago. None of this could be considered as taking advantage. Not in Morgan's eyes, anyway. "Forget about the holiday. It's not important. But I will be thinking about you until I see you again." Morgan brushed her knuckles along Jan's jawline and smiled. "Every hour of the day."

"God, I hate feeling like this." Jan threw up her hands. "I hate not knowing what I'm doing with my life. Well, what little life I have left at the moment anyway."

"Everything will become clear when it's supposed to." Morgan stepped back and gave Jan some space. The last thing she wanted was for Jan to feel suffocated. "You've got this, okay?"

Jan simply nodded and lifted her coffee again. Silence descended over them, just the sound of Morgan prepping for another day at the bar keeping them company in this moment. Morgan wanted to convince Jan that a trip away would be good for her, but what right did she have to do so? Morgan didn't believe they were at that place with one another yet. They likely never would be.

You really have to stop looking so far ahead.

This woman was still married. For all Morgan knew, Jan could change her mind and decide to try again with Phil. It was easy to claim the answer was simple in the moment it was all happening, but Jan had every right to try to save her marriage. Just because she had told Morgan otherwise, it didn't guarantee a thing.

"Life," Jan said quietly.

Morgan's head shot up from the sink she stood at. "I'm sorry?"

"Life. I should be *living* my life. I should be taking what I can get whenever I can get it. Isn't that what he's been doing? Enjoying his life...with someone else."

Morgan didn't know where Jan was going with this, but she would listen and be ready with a response either way.

"I'll come with you. To Gran Canaria. If people don't like it, I cannot change that. It's out of my control."

Morgan clenched her hands at her sides and out of view of Jan. If she hadn't just done that, she would have squealed with joy. That wasn't a good look in front of the woman she was trying to impress. "You're serious? You'll come with me?"

"Why not." Jan shrugged and slid from her stool. She stepped behind the bar, approached Morgan, and pressed her to the sink. "Do you promise to look after me?"

"You know I will."

Jan draped her arms over Morgan's shoulders and sighed. "Then I guess I should go back to the house and pick up everything I need."

"I can't believe this is happening." Morgan laughed nervously. "I can't believe you even exist in my world, but I definitely can't believe I'm going to spend a week with you abroad."

Jan winked and lowered her arms from Morgan's shoulders, instead wrapping them around her waist. "I'll look forward to seeing you in a bikini."

Morgan's world aligned at the mere thought of Jan laid out in a bikini, her bronzed skin sparkling against the sun. She cleared her throat, imagining a refreshing cocktail instead. "Only if I get to see you in one, too."

With her arms tightening around Morgan's waist, Jan leaned in and said, "Try and stop me!"

How the hell did your life end up like this?

Jan didn't have the answer to that, but right now, she didn't care. In two days, she would be flying out of the country with Morgan, and the truth was that she couldn't wait. Not only would she have the chance to *truly* relax for probably the first time in twenty years, but she would have Morgan beside her on a sun lounger while she did so.

You're a little bit crazy!

Maybe Jan was, but it beat staying with a man who had no issue dropping his pants for another woman. In time, Jan knew this would all come crashing down around her. She knew that she would probably have a meltdown at the idea of her marriage being officially over. But for the time being, she was going to enjoy having no work to deal with, and she was going to enjoy something for herself. Not anyone else. Just herself. That enjoyment came in the form of Morgan Tate.

Only it's not simple enjoyment, and you know it!

As she stepped out of the lift and walked through to the bistro within the hotel she was staying at, Gillian was waiting with a smile at a table further back in the room. Jan had called her this morning, knowing she didn't work Wednesdays, and here she was... about to reveal her plans for the next week or so.

"I haven't ordered yet," Gillian said as she stood and kissed Jan on the cheek. "I wasn't sure what kind of afternoon this was going to be, so I thought it was best to wait."

"I think I'll stick to coffee for now. I have a few things to sort out, and I need to call to the house for my passport."

Gillian nodded. "Identification. Always handy to have it on you."

"For the holiday I've just booked, actually." Jan sighed as she lowered herself into one of the comfortable leather bucket seats dotted around the expansive room. She hadn't technically booked a holiday, but she had booked her seats on the flights. The fact they were available next to Morgan on both legs of the journey told Jan it was meant to be. "Fly out in two days."

"I'm sorry, what? A holiday? Jan Bartlett...is leaving the country?" Gillian's eyes widened, but Jan saw the humour. It wasn't often she gave herself the chance to unwind in the sun. "Where are you going?"

"Gran Canaria." It wasn't the first place Jan thought of when she imagined a holiday, but she trusted Morgan to take her somewhere she would enjoy.

"You don't strike me as the Gran Canaria type, love."

"It's something different." Jan shrugged, ordering a cappuccino when the server came to their table. Gillian ordered the same. "And the weather is gorgeous there at the moment. I'm not staying in the area with all the clubs. I'll need to take a cab there if I decide to venture to that part of the town."

"If you'd waited a few more weeks, we could have come with you. I don't like the idea of you travelling alone, and I certainly *hate* the idea of you in one of those clubs."

Jan rolled her eyes. "Plenty of people go on holiday alone, Gill. I'll be fine. I'm going to lie by the pool for the entire week and not think about anything else. It sounds perfect to me and *exactly* what I need right now."

"I know." Gillian regarded Jan with an understanding smile. "You'll call me and let me know how it's going?"

"If I even bother to pick up my phone while I'm away, yes." The very few holidays Jan *had* been on usually entailed some kind of business call while she was away with Phil. It seemed easier to be at the office than dare to take time off to relax in another country. "I've already logged out of my work email account on my phone. I'll log back in *if* I decide to return to the office, but until then, I'm a free woman."

"You're really going a mile a minute here, aren't you?"

Jan shook her head. "No. Going a mile a minute would mean

I'd already started divorce proceedings. This is just me taking time out to do something for myself. To stop worrying about the shit I'll be facing once I'm home."

"I like this side of you. Maybe if you stick to the idea of working less, we can finally have a holiday together at some point in the future."

Jan would like that. Preferably with Morgan in tow, too. She may not know exactly what her future held, but she did want Morgan in it in some capacity. Ideally as her partner down the line, but Jan knew she couldn't think that far ahead. It would be a mistake for the both of them. As it stood, Jan was taking each day as it came. If she dared to dream about her future right now, the impatient side of her would kick in. Being impatient would only bring issues with it. Jan wasn't stupid, she knew this was going to take time. Potentially *a lot* of time. "Sounds like a nice idea."

"You and I have *never* been able to day drink through the week because of our jobs. At least if we were abroad, we'd have an excuse, and nobody could judge us." Gillian winked and sat back. "Finn sends her love, by the way."

"Once I'm home, I'll come over, and we'll drink wine. Finn will drink beer, obviously."

Gillian suddenly gasped and leaned in. "What if you *don't* come home? You could meet some Spanish hunk and fall in love with him."

At least Gillian seemed open to the idea of Jan falling for someone else. That was a positive to take away from this conversation. Only if Jan had her way, it wouldn't be a Spanish hunk. It would be a gorgeous English bartender...*and* a woman. "Who knows who I'll meet now that I'm single."

Gillian's smile faded quickly. "Hearing you say that feels strange. It's always been Jan and Phil. Christmas cards, invitations, in conversation."

"Well, now it's just Jan." Jan smiled at the server as she set their cappuccinos down. She instantly brought hers closer and added one sugar cube. "And you know what, I quite like that."

"One thing I *never* expected was you to be happy if your marriage ended." Gillian eyed Jan as she stirred her own cappuccino. She knew her best friend was trying to read her. "Is this just a front, love?"

"Actually, it's not. I do feel good about the future. Once I've found a place I can call my own, the world is mine for the taking."

"That's a good attitude to have."

"I think watching you go through your divorce just reminded me of what I never want to happen. The thought of just existing in a house all day, only leaving it to go to work, cutting myself off from everyone around me. You know?"

"I'll admit that I didn't deal with my divorce very well, but look at me now." Gillian opened her arms out and grinned. "I'm happier than I've ever been."

"And that's what I'm holding onto. Knowing you recovered… then I know I can, too." Jan couldn't be any prouder of Gillian for the way she'd handled the last couple of years. Yes, there had been many times when she thought she was losing Gillian, but as they sat here now, Gillian looked incredibly happy. "I know it was tough for you, and you know I was there for you any time you needed me, but I *will* come to you if I think I'm drowning in all of it. I promise."

"I know you will. You always could handle things better than me."

"I don't think it's a case of handling it better or worse than one another. Everyone deals with life and their issues differently. It doesn't make any one person stronger or weaker. We just choose to deal how we deal."

"You always were better with words than me, too." Gillian smiled as she rested her head in the palm of her hand. "I do have to say, though, that you're looking very happy. Healthy and unbothered by all of this."

Mm. It's hard to care when a beautiful woman shows up in your life unexpectedly.

"I can't change what he did. Why bother letting it fester and make me feel miserable? I have a life to live, Gill. I have a whole entire world out there to explore. Who knows where it leads."

Gillian raised her cappuccino cup between them. "You know what, I'll cheers to that."

"Me, too." Jan clinked her cup to Gillian's and exhaled a contented sigh. "Phil is doing what he wants, and I'm going to do the very same thing!"

CHAPTER 16

"So," Morgan spoke quietly as she grazed her nails through Jan's hair. They'd been spread out on the couch for the last two hours, but Morgan was beside herself, knowing she would be alone with this woman for an entire week. "Did you happen to come across those bikinis we talked about?"

Jan grinned as she tilted her head back and eyed Morgan. "I wondered why you were so quiet. Have you been fantasising?"

"Would you hate me if I said yes?"

"Never." Jan splayed a hand across Morgan's chest and gazed back at her. Almost lovingly. "I've already been thinking about you in a bikini."

Morgan's chest expanded. Being with Jan was incredibly fulfilling. And every little thing she learned about Jan was only willing Morgan towards a future with her. "I think we're going to have a great time out there with one another."

"It's all I've had on my mind lately." Jan dipped her hand beneath Morgan's shirt. "Do you have plans for out there already?"

"Not really. I usually take it day by day, depending on the weather. If it's too hot, we can travel north where it's a little cooler for the day. If it's windy, then the pool is your best option in terms of sunbathing. Trust me, you don't want to be on the beach when it's windy."

"I'm glad you know your way around the place. I won't have to worry about a single thing. I'll just take your lead."

Morgan's stomach rippled when Jan dragged her nails across her skin. "Mm. That feels nice."

"All of you feels nice." Jan dipped her head and pressed her lips to Morgan's stomach. "And I'm dying to be alone with you in another country."

"Why?" Morgan asked, brow furrowed.

"I don't know. I just feel as though we can be ourselves out there."

Morgan understood what Jan was saying. The number of times Morgan had wanted to stride across her bar and kiss Jan in front of everyone were too many to count. When they met up for lunch, she wanted to take her hand and pull Jan that little bit closer as they walked around town. One day, it would be possible, but right now wasn't the time. "You'll feel less on edge."

"Exactly."

"I wish you didn't have to leave the country to feel safer." Morgan kissed Jan's forehead when their eyes met. "Being out isn't something I've ever worried about."

"One day, I won't have to worry either." Jan sat up and shifted into Morgan's lap. "And it's not that I'm worried—we've already established that. I just don't want to bump into friends at the moment. None of them would understand. And I certainly don't want to come across anyone who could go to Gillian and tell her before I've had the chance to do it myself."

Yeah, that wouldn't end well. Gillian would hit the roof if she didn't hear this directly from Jan. "I don't really want to be on the receiving end of Gillian's wrath if *that* ever happened."

"Me neither." Jan laughed. "But you and I are the only thing I care about right now. I just want to be with you like this." Jan wrapped an arm around Morgan's shoulder and touched their foreheads. "This is where I enjoy being the most."

"I hate it when you have to go back to that hotel room." Morgan wanted to offer her space to Jan again, but she didn't want to come across as pressuring her. "Maybe we need to discuss that while we're away."

"Discuss the hotel?" Jan drew back.

"Yeah. Figure out what's next. You can't stay there forever, babe."

"I know. And I won't. I'm just enjoying my own space at the minute. Even if I was at home, it wouldn't be the same. It wouldn't *feel* the same. I think that's why I got what I needed and left, to be honest. Until I feel ready to think about what's going to happen with the house, I don't want to be there." Jan's voice trembled ever so slightly. "If I'd refused to leave, it would only be harder down the line when it came to selling up."

"I hope it doesn't come to that. When you speak about your home, your eyes light up." Morgan couldn't imagine packing up her life and leaving her flat. She'd only been here four years, so she couldn't begin to think about how Jan must feel knowing she'd have to deal with boxes and moving companies. "And if it means so much to you, I'd love to see it. I bet it's gorgeous."

"It's where I feel at my most comfortable."

"I know." Morgan leaned in and kissed Jan. "But if you do get sick of looking at your hotel room, you know I'll make space for you here. It's not something I even need to think about."

"Thank you."

"You know how you don't wanna come down from something?" Morgan sighed, feeling immensely proud to have Jan in her arms. "Well, I don't wanna come down from you. From *this*."

"Then let's not worry about ever coming down. Let's just... appreciate one another and have some fun." Jan rested her head against Morgan's shoulder, but Morgan felt her smiling. Knowing someone like Jan *wanted* to be here, wanted to be alone with

Morgan, had her feeling several types of way, but Jan was right. Appreciation was enough for Morgan for now.

"I may have done something when you agreed to fly out to Gran Canaria with me." Morgan brought her hand to the back of Jan's neck and grazed her nails against her skin.

"What did you do?" Jan barely managed to say those words out loud. It was almost a whisper.

"Upgraded our room."

Jan beamed a smile as she tilted her head. "You did?"

"Only the best *for* the best."

"Please let me contribute towards all of this. You can't take on the cost alone. It's not fair to you."

Morgan would have paid triple if it meant she had the chance to go on holiday with Jan. It was no problem that she'd upgraded at all. If anything, it only made her far more excited. "This is my gift to you to help you relax before the shit hits the fan here."

"Then I'm expecting you to find the nicest restaurant you can so I can take you for a fancy dinner while we're there."

Morgan shifted down the couch a little, her eyes half-lidded as she allowed the peacefulness to lull her into the tiniest nap. "It's a date."

Sitting comfortably on Morgan's couch, Jan glanced around the room and smiled. Morgan seemed like one of those women who didn't need much in her life. Of course she had the big TV, the sound system, and everything else most people owned these days, but her flat was clean and tidy. It didn't have random stuff strewn across it. A lot like Jan's home. Only this place felt much more homely. It felt lived in. While Jan felt that way at her place, it felt lonely a lot of the time.

She reached for her phone on the coffee table as it pinged.

Morgan was currently down in the bar picking up their takeout from the delivery driver.

It was Gillian.

Fancy a few glasses of wine tonight?

Jan would usually take her best friend up on an offer like that; wine night had been a regular thing in the past when Phil was out of the country. But Jan was giving her body a rest. She knew what Gran Canaria would likely entail, so she was off alcohol until they flew out in a couple of days.

I'm a little busy at the moment running through some figures. Can we do it some other time?

Jan hated lying to Gillian. She couldn't recall a time before meeting Morgan when she had done so. Still, Jan was only doing this to protect herself. And to put less pressure on herself. It was bad enough that Phil had fucked everything up for her; she didn't need to continue it by fucking it up for herself, too.

Can you not do that another time? Finn and I miss drinking with you.

Jan smiled. She appreciated that her friends missed her, but it wouldn't change her answer. How could she even think about drinking wine on the couch when she had Morgan's undivided attention?

My liver needs a rest before Spain. You know, with all the sangria I'll be consuming!

Jan sunk further into the couch and sighed. Sunshine, heat, the ocean. Fun, laughter, not a care in the world. Good food, great wine, and...Morgan. God, she couldn't wait to get on that flight. She couldn't wait to wheel her suitcase out of her hotel and pick Morgan up for their early morning travel to the airport.

Why does everything feel so good with her?

Jan didn't know how to begin making heads or tails of this. Morgan shouldn't have been the woman she was besotted with. No woman should. Fuck, this was really going to throw everyone in her life into disarray. As Jan thought about that, she found that she didn't particularly care.

Her phone buzzed.

Fine. I'll just have to drink without you! Call me tomorrow!

The door to Morgan's flat opened suddenly, slamming shut as Morgan pressed her back to it, pizza boxes in one hand. "Fuck. That was close."

Jan frowned. "What was?"

"They're in the bar. Gillian and Finn." Morgan splayed a hand against her chest and sighed. "Fucking hell. My heart is racing."

Jan got to her feet and crossed the room, taking the pizza boxes from Morgan before her shaking hand dropped them. "Give those to me and breathe for a moment."

"Finn was *obviously* suspicious. I swear she has the scent and intuition of a fucking bloodhound!"

Yeah, Jan had to agree with Morgan. Finn always seemed to know what was going on when nobody else did. Jan was just glad that Finn couldn't possibly know that *she* was up here. She may be good at sniffing things out, but she wasn't that good. "Hey, relax. Finn doesn't know I'm here."

Morgan snorted. "I'm glad you're confident of that because I'm not."

"How could she know, Morgan?"

Morgan pushed off the door and followed Jan into the kitchen. "She's just that kind of person. I don't know how she does it."

Jan left the pizza boxes on the kitchen counter and turned to Morgan. She reached out a hand and pulled her closer, kissing her the moment she possibly could. "I need you to relax. Your eyes are about to bulge out of your head."

"I just don't want people to find out like this. It seems secretive, and that's not who I am." Morgan shook her hands at her sides, and then she looked up at Jan. "I don't want *you* to ever feel like a secret."

"I don't feel like a secret. And correct me if I'm wrong, but *I'm* the one who asked if we could keep it to ourselves for a while longer." Jan cupped Morgan's cheek and smiled. "If you're not able to do that, I understand. I don't want you to ever feel as though you're deceiving people."

"I'm not risking this. No way." Morgan leaned into Jan's touch and smiled. "Feels too good to care about deceiving people."

"Gillian texted me while you were getting our food. Asked me if I wanted to drink wine with her. I assumed she meant at home, but she must have meant here."

"Did you want to? I can always get you out the back exit without them knowing."

"No. That's not why I told you. I don't want to leave here until I absolutely have to. Spending the evening with you is becoming one of my favourite things to do."

"You've really spent a lot of time alone, haven't you?"

Jan shrugged. "It's...whatever. I chose to put up with it. And I can't really complain. Phil was out there drumming up business for us and taking care of meetings, so *I* didn't have to be the one travelling around the country. It's only recently that he's strayed." At least, Jan hoped that was the case. If she found out Phil had been having affairs whenever he could, she would go down fighting when it came to the divorce. "Come on. Let's eat this in front of the TV."

"That's why you're here, isn't it?" Morgan narrowed her eyes, but Jan noted the smirk immediately. "Because I don't make you eat at the dining table like you probably do at home."

Jan threw up her hands. "You caught me. Guilty."

Morgan held Jan's jaw gently and drew her into a kiss. "Fuck, I *hate* it when you have to go. I don't *want* you to go."

Jan grinned as she took the pizza boxes and headed for the couch. "Maybe I won't. Who knows."

Morgan rushed behind her with the box of wedges and various dips. "Wait, you're serious? You might stay over tonight?"

Jan had no reason to go back to the hotel. She had left a few items of clothing here for future 'the morning after' situations, and she had brought over a spare washbag. "Would you like me to stay over?"

"Can't believe you even think you have to ask that," Morgan snorted as she flopped down onto the couch. "But yes, I *would* like you to stay over."

"Then I will." Jan leaned over the couch and kissed Morgan. And then she smiled against her lips. "God, I'm going to get myself into a lot of trouble here."

"Trouble is the fun part, babe."

"Mm. Trouble is sexy."

CHAPTER 17

Jan stood out on the terrace of the ground-floor apartment Morgan had surprised her with, the sun setting in the distance. They'd landed some five hours ago—Meloneras was a beautiful area from what Jan had seen so far—and now Morgan was taking them out to dinner. They'd decided on a quiet, slower evening, reserving the fun and excitement for the rest of the week. Morgan had sat yawning repeatedly as they'd lounged around at the pool bar a couple of hours ago, so something simple and relaxed was the focus for the rest of the night.

As she continued to watch the fading daylight over the ocean, Jan felt saddened by the thought of Morgan usually being out here alone. She spent enough time stuck at the bar or up in her flat. Gran Canaria—or Meloneras, to be specific—seemed like a place couples would holiday, and if Jan had things her way, this wouldn't be the last time they visited the island together. For Jan, this was, without a doubt, the start of something truly special for her. Forget what was going on back at home. Forget the fact that she hadn't told Gillian and Finn about Morgan yet. The only thing she cared about for the next seven days was being here, sitting in the peacefulness of a Spanish island, with Morgan by her side.

Jan had spent the mid-haul flight out here taking stock of everything that had happened since she'd walked into her office the day Gareth came by. Her marriage was over—there were no two ways about that—but her life wasn't. She had meant it when she told Gillian she had the world at her feet, and Jan was going to make every last second of it count. If that meant cutting everyone off until they came to terms with her decisions moving forward, then so be it. If it meant hearing the opinions of not only those she cared about but those she didn't, so be it.

In this moment, Jan was happy and fulfilled. She was content with whatever direction her life took, so long as Morgan was firmly planted in it. Yes, it may have only been five weeks since she'd left Phil, and yes, being with Morgan so quickly after the end of her marriage was quite startling, but Jan struggled to care. How could she step back from what was happening here? How could she even consider a world without the happiness Morgan had given her so far?

The answer was simple: she couldn't.

From a very young age, Jan had always known what she wanted. Love, a stable home, and to feel accomplished every night when she climbed into bed. While she didn't have the stable home right now, that would return in one form or another. As for love... Well, she felt that in some capacity from Morgan, regardless of the fact they weren't exclusive. And lately, she *did* feel accomplished. Whether that was as she climbed into a *still* unfamiliar hotel bed or Morgan's was beside the point. She felt it, and that was what mattered.

She heard Morgan approaching from behind. Before Jan had time to turn around, Morgan wrapped her arms around Jan's waist, kissed her neck, and then rested her chin on her shoulder. "You look stunning."

"Thank you." Jan had only gone for a pair of white linen pants and a white tank top this evening. The humidity was still in the air, and if they were walking for a while, she wanted to be comfortable. "How was your shower?"

"Amazing. It's woken me up a bit." Morgan sighed as she looked out at the ocean with Jan. "Gorgeous here, isn't it?"

"It is. It makes me wonder why Gillian said that Gran Canaria wasn't really my kind of place." Jan frowned at the reminder of that comment. If *this* wasn't Jan's kind of place, then she had no idea what was. "Remind me to ask her about that."

"I know why she said it." Morgan lifted her phone in front of them, brought her lips to Jan's cheek again, and snapped a selfie of them. "It can be a bit of a party island depending on where you stay, and just down the road from us is a huge outdoor space that's considered to mostly cater towards the LGBTQ+ community."

"O-oh." Jan's brows lifted.

"But once you tell her the area you're actually staying in, I'm sure she'll realise that this is the perfect place for you to unwind."

It suddenly dawned on Jan that people could put two and two together. "Out of interest, where did you tell your friends and family you were going for the week?"

Morgan tensed at that. "Friends away from the bar know I'm here. Ben and Tyler also know, but they're not stupid and realise that we're keeping this under wraps. If Finn asks, I'm elsewhere in the country."

"And your family?" Jan asked, sensing there was something to be discussed when it came to Morgan's blood relatives.

"They don't get to know anything about me or my life. They lost that right when they cut me off at nineteen."

Another realisation dawned on Jan. She had no idea how old Morgan was. "And that was...how many years ago now?"

"I'm thirty-two, if that's what you're asking." Morgan unravelled herself from Jan and stood beside her instead. "If that's an issue for you, please tell me that when we get home. Not while we're out here watching the sunset with one another."

Jan took Morgan's hand and entwined their fingers. "It's not an issue for me. Not in the slightest."

Morgan regarded Jan with a small smile as she glanced in her direction. "That's what they all say."

"Well, I'm not *all*. I'm *me*. And I have no issue with any of this." Jan tugged Morgan to her and turned, wrapping an arm around her waist. "I would like to know more about you, though. Your family and how that came about."

"I'm an open book." Morgan lifted a hand and cupped Jan's cheek. "Anything you want to know, that's fine by me."

"I know that this is a little bit up in the air at the moment, and you've practically whisked me away on a whim, but...I *am* serious about this with you, Morgan. I don't pretend to know the answers to everything that's going to come, but standing out here tonight has reminded me that even though I'm going to lose a lot, I'm also going to gain something incredibly special to me. *You*. What we have. *This*. It's so beautiful, and making new memories with someone else is what I'm aiming for when the mess back at home has been cleaned up. That someone *is* you, okay?"

Morgan dipped her head and sniffled. "I'm sorry if I ever feel as though I'm pulling away. That's not intentional. Not...most of the time. I just," Morgan said, sighing as she paused for a moment. "I'm used to *not* getting the happy ending."

"Hey," Jan whispered as she lifted Morgan's head and held her chin in her hand. "I get it. I really do. Do you think I expected any of this to happen? To end up here with you, feeling immensely happy when *technically*, I should be miserable?"

"No. This has to be just as crazy for you to come to terms with."

"Then let's just enjoy ourselves and live life."

Morgan drew Jan into a slow, soft kiss. When they broke apart, a smile spread on Morgan's lips. "Believe me, all I've been doing since you walked into my bar that night is live my life."

That was all Jan could ask for. To know that Morgan was also finding a new normal, it was all she needed to be happy in life. "Good. Now, I'm starving, so should we head off and have dinner before we come back here and relax for the rest of the night?"

Morgan nodded as she leaned in and pressed a kiss on the tip of Jan's nose. "Sounds like the perfect date with the perfect woman."

Morgan sat across from Jan, the table they'd reserved offering them the most beautiful view of the lit walkway along the beachfront of Meloneras. Jan hadn't stopped smiling since they'd landed earlier today, and every time Morgan glanced in her direction, the hairs on her arms stood on end. It was a feeling Morgan was new to, more so because it was so intense. Jan, quite simply, was all she'd ever dreamed of. Every last bad mistake and dead end would have been worth it if it had led to this. Tonight, Morgan couldn't take her eyes off Jan.

She sat back in her seat and sipped from her glass of red wine. "How's the food?"

"Delicious." Jan eyed Morgan over the rim of her own glass, wearing a shy smile. "Yours?"

"I brought you here because I know how amazing the menu is."

Jan slid a hand across the table and settled it over Morgan's. She was no stranger to holding another woman's hand—Morgan had been a lesbian since forever—but when Jan did it, it ignited a multitude of feelings from deep within her. "Thank you for the perfect first day. It's been lovely."

"You're okay with heading back and just relaxing? If you wanted to see some of the island, I'm happy to show you."

Jan stifled a yawn as she shook her head. "Relaxing for the rest of the night sounds perfect. I don't have much left in my tank, to be honest with you."

Thank God for that. Considering Morgan was significantly

younger than Jan, she was really flagging now. All she wanted was to sit out on the terrace and talk about anything that sprung to mind. Walking, partying, and drinking just were not on her agenda tonight.

"Did *you* want to head out somewhere? I'm the one who has gate crashed this holiday. I'd hate to think you were changing how you usually do things because I'm here."

"Believe me, I *want* to relax at the apartment tonight." Morgan turned her hand over and smiled. "This is nice. Sitting here, hand in hand."

Jan sighed. "This just reminds me of what I can look forward to once we're home. Because if I'm learning anything being out here with you on day one, it's that I don't want to go back to hiding once we get home."

"You're not hiding, babe. You're just...finding yourself. Nobody, friends included, can begrudge you that."

Jan snorted. "Oh, I beg to differ. You really think Gill won't have a meltdown once she finds out about this?"

"I mean, I know she's your best friend, and I'm really close to Finn, but what right do they have to an opinion on how you choose to handle things? You're a grown woman, Jan. If you're not ready to face the world with me, that's your decision and your decision alone."

Jan softened as she squeezed Morgan's hand. "I appreciate your support more than you know."

"So long as you're okay, I don't care about the rest. If I have to spend the next several months sneaking you into my flat, then I'll do that. Don't *ever* feel pressured to do what you think is the right thing. We're good, babe. Really good." Morgan lifted a hand and smiled at the waiter when she signalled for the bill. "You still don't want a dessert?"

Jan placed a hand on her stomach and puffed out her cheeks. "No way. You'll have to carry me back if I dare to put another thing in my mouth."

"Okay." Morgan grinned, then lifted her glass and finished her wine. "Hey, out of interest. How *do* you think Gillian and Finn will react?" Morgan wasn't bothered about what they thought of her; she had what she needed sitting right across from her, but the idea of them being less than impressed with Jan *did* weigh on her mind at times. "You think they'll be happy for you?"

"I think Gillian will be confused, and I think she'll sit there shocked for several minutes. But then it'll wear off, and she'll be happy knowing that I'm happy. That's all we've ever wanted for one another."

"And Finn?"

"I know Finn a lot less than I know Gillian, but Finn is a sweetheart, and I know she'll be equally as happy as Gillian. Don't forget that you're a close friend of hers. Why would she possibly be anything other than happy?"

"Finn can be...surprising when she wants to be. I don't see any issues arising, though. Finn is too busy hanging on Gillian's every word to care what I'm doing with my life." Morgan lifted a shoulder. "But seeing her so happy really does make *me* happy. She used to sit alone in my bar, nursing pint after pint, dreading going home to the same old routine."

"I'm glad she's out of that routine. I know she would do anything for her mum, but she deserves to have a life, too."

Morgan nodded and thanked the waiter as he set their bill down in the middle of the table. She took a wad of euro notes from her back pocket and left the cost of the bill, plus a tip, on the small silver tray. "I think everything is going to be fine. I mean, it's Gillian and Finn. We *know* them. We're friends with them."

Morgan had nobody to answer to these days, and if either of them thought she would answer to them, they had another thing coming. Morgan focused on herself and the woman in her life. Everything else was simply background noise as far as she was concerned.

"How did you and Gillian meet?"

"University. I was studying business, and she was studying architecture. We were eighteen, with no idea what the world had to offer." Jan smiled. "Within a few weeks of our first year beginning, we just gravitated towards one another. We were inseparable, and we have been ever since."

Morgan lifted a questioning brow. "So…she knows you had a *filthy* lesbian fling during university?"

Jan cast her gaze on her lap. "No. That's not something I've ever divulged."

"Because?"

"At the time, I was worried about everyone's reaction. Antonia also didn't seem overly comfortable being out either. I'd arrange to see her whenever I knew Gillian had plans elsewhere."

Morgan guessed that made sense. Jan and Gillian had been at university a long time ago now. Life and society were entirely different some thirty years on. Though, at times, Morgan had to wonder if much had changed at all.

"That's not why I'm holding back this time, though." Ah. Jan had taken Morgan's silence to mean something else. "I'm so ready, Morgan. I just…feel so much more when I'm with you."

"Yeah?" Morgan stroked her fingers against the back of Jan's hand. "You think I'm worth coming out for?"

"One hundred percent. Without a doubt."

"Then that's all I need to know." Morgan rose to her feet and guided Jan up with her. "Should we stroll back?"

"Yes." Jan touched a hand to Morgan's chest and leaned in to kiss her. "Thank you for dinner. It was exceptional."

"Thank you for being my date. It's been a pleasure."

CHAPTER 18

Relaxing back on her lounger, Jan shoved her bottle of sun lotion underneath it and angled her face towards the sun. She was surprised her body hadn't gone into shock at the slightest hint of sun and relaxation, but so far, so good. Now that she'd recharged last night, Jan planned to go full steam ahead into the rest of the holiday.

She glanced to her left and smiled as Morgan hummed along to whatever was playing in her earbuds. Jan had opted for a romance novel rather than music today, and if she had the chance to nap once she turned onto her stomach, she was going to enjoy that snooze and not feel guilty about it. Didn't she deserve a decent holiday after being rushed off her feet for so long? Damn right she did.

Jan continued watching Morgan, noting just how relaxed she seemed out here. It was hard not to be when you woke up to the sound of the ocean, but Jan hadn't anticipated the difference in Morgan compared to back at home. Then again, did anyone *truly* feel happy and at peace when they knew they had to get up for work each morning? Some did, most didn't. She reached out a hand and took Morgan's where it sat on the very edge of her own lounger. Morgan lifted a brow behind her sunglasses as she turned her face towards Jan, that delicious smile lighting up her face as they looked back at one another.

"Enjoying yourself, babe?"

Jan's stomach somersaulted every time Morgan called her that. She would get used to it, but for the time being, she would enjoy the way it made her feel. Like a teenager all over again. "Absolutely."

"Good. I've just ordered us a couple of white coffees and some nibbles."

Jan frowned. When had Morgan got up from her lounger? "Um...you did? Did I drop off to sleep without realising it?"

"They have an app linked to our room. We can order whatever we like, whenever we like...from the comfort of our loungers."

Wow. Holidays abroad had really come a long way since Jan had last flown out of England. They barely had cars on the road the last time she'd gone away, never mind apps connected to room and pool service. "I'm impressed."

Morgan winked in Jan's direction. "You're hanging with the cool kids now."

"Mm. It would seem I am." Jan made a mental note to let Gillian know the name of the hotel where they were staying. This kind of place would be right up her street. And Finn, well, she was happy to follow Gillian around like a lost puppy, so she would jump at the opportunity.

Morgan turned on her side and removed her earbuds. "I don't think I ever want to come here alone again. Who knew being away with someone you care about could make it so much better?"

"I hope you're still saying that by the end of the week." Jan knew how to have fun, and she knew how to laugh, but the lack of holidays over the years did play on her mind. Phil was quite happy wandering off abroad to 'network' or whatever other excuse he could think up, but Jan was never invited. Why? Did her soon-to-be ex-husband not want Jan on his arm? *Does it really matter anymore?* Jan pushed her marriage out of her mind as she said, "And if not, keep it to yourself, and I'll be none the wiser."

"I have a feeling by the end of this holiday, I won't want to go home." Morgan gazed back at Jan, those soft brown eyes staring deep into her soul as she lifted her sunglasses. "And I'll want *you* to stay with me."

"Don't even threaten it. I'm the one who has nothing to get back for. Not really." Jan's gaze swept up Morgan's bikini-clad body. The curve of her hip as the sun bronzed her skin. God, Jan couldn't believe she was even lying here right now. "What plans do we have for this evening?"

"I thought maybe we could head further along the coast. In a cab, of course. I know what your relationship is like with your heels." Morgan toyed with her lip ring as she smiled. "I'm close to having an intimate relationship with them myself."

"Come again..."

"You in those fucking heels," Morgan said as she closed her eyes and took her bottom lip between her teeth. "Any chance I'm going to find you dancing against me wearing a pair of them later?"

Fucking hell. Did this woman make it her life's mission to make Jan feel good about herself? It was certainly working. "I'm sure I can manage that."

"Yeah? You promise?" While Jan loved Morgan's enthusiasm, she hadn't expected her eyes to light up the way they just had. "Babe? Seriously?"

"Yep." Jan smirked and focused on the sea and sand ahead of her. "Now, you should get back to your music before I drag you inside the apartment and have my way with you."

"You do realise that's not a threat, right?"

Jan's skin prickled when Morgan drew her fingertips up the inside of her wrist. "Morgan..."

"Talk to me, gorgeous."

"I can't. Every time you do something as simple as that, it leaves me breathless." Jan wasn't worried about being honest with

Morgan. If anything, she encouraged Jan to be exactly that. "I'm not used to this kind of attention."

"That only hurts my heart...and makes me want to give you even more attention."

"That won't be necessary. You give me plenty of everything already." Jan smiled. "I'll keep an eye out for the coffees arriving. You enjoy your music."

"I enjoy watching you more than I enjoy any music. Just...so you know." Morgan lowered her sunglasses over her eyes, her face still turned towards Jan. She knew Morgan was doing exactly what she'd said—she was watching Jan. So, Jan decided to give her something to look at by removing her bikini top and lying on her back once again. Morgan moaned quietly as she said, "Fuck. Me."

"Maybe later."

Even though Morgan had sworn herself off any work while she was away, she had found herself stepping away from the table a few minutes ago to take a call from Ben back in England. Jan had insisted that she didn't mind being left alone, but it wasn't something Morgan would make a habit of. This was their holiday, and it was their chance to unwind. Ben knew that, he had repeatedly apologised during the call, but Morgan had taken care of what she needed to take care of, and now she could dedicate every last second to Jan again.

She returned to the table and sat down. "I'm sorry about that. Ben doesn't usually call me when I'm away."

"It's fine. No harm done." Jan slid her hand into Morgan's. Tonight, Jan had chosen the seat next to Morgan rather than the seat facing. They could enjoy the sunset together from this position. "Is everything okay back at home?"

"Yeah. The brewery hasn't turned up with the kegs I ordered

before we left England. Ben just wanted to know if he should chase it up on my behalf."

"He's a nice guy. I like him."

Morgan liked him, too. So much so that she was planning to promote him. "You think he'd make a good manager if I asked him?"

"Oh, absolutely." Jan nodded as she stroked her fingertips against the back of Morgan's hand. Whenever she did it, butterflies wreaked havoc in Morgan's stomach. "Is it something you're thinking about?"

"If I want this to work, then it's something I have to do."

Jan frowned. "I'm sorry?"

"You and I. If it's going to work, I have to change the way I live my life right now."

Morgan knew that Jan wouldn't hold it against her when it came to how much she worked, but the inability to make plans and take trips away just wasn't something she wanted to bypass any longer. Morgan was serious about a relationship here, and that meant she wanted to be around for Jan more often.

"I appreciate what you're saying, but I'm sure we can work around schedules and stuff. I'm only available as much as I am right now because I walked away from the business."

Morgan smiled. "I know. But I'd still like to see you more often. Evenings and weekends whenever you're available and you can make some time for me. You're not going to be unemployed forever, I don't imagine."

"I...think I'm going to go back to my job." As Morgan side-eyed Jan, Jan was chewing her lip. "Phil and I have worked hard to make it what it is. It seems a shame to let it all go and find something else that I likely won't be happy with."

"I think that if you can come to some kind of agreement with him, then there's no reason why it can't work as well as it has so far. It's important that you do something you love, and if that's staying on at the business, then you do that, babe." Morgan leaned in and kissed Jan's cheek. "But I'm still going to ask Ben how he feels about the promotion."

"It would be nice to spend more time together," Jan said, resting her head on Morgan's shoulder. They'd finished dinner some thirty minutes ago now, so sitting back and watching the world go by on the beachfront with a cocktail was the perfect end to this day. "When I'm with you, I feel as though I'm where I'm meant to be."

Morgan's pulse quickened at that. While she knew Jan enjoyed spending time with her, she hadn't expected her to feel *that* particular way. "You really mean that?"

"I do mean it."

If the shoe had been on the other foot and Morgan had said that to someone other than Jan, they likely would have run a mile in the opposite direction. But Morgan wasn't afraid of love or commitment. She wasn't afraid to be herself with this woman. Right now, Morgan was just incredibly happy to have Jan sitting beside her. "That means a lot to me."

"It's important that I'm honest about how I feel. With myself more than anything." Jan lifted her head and faced Morgan. "I don't know what I'll be dealing with when we go home, so I have to remind myself of these moments when the shit inevitably hits the fan."

Morgan reached out a hand and stroked the back of it against Jan's cheek. "I know things aren't going to be easy for you if you're planning to reveal our relationship, but you *do* have my support, okay?"

"I appreciate that."

Morgan wasn't sure this was a good idea, but she would say it anyway. "And if we get back to England and you decide that having me in your life is going to cause too much confusion for people or make you lose friends and family, then I understand if you won't want to see me anymore." Morgan hoped they could remain friends should that happen, but she couldn't offer that right now.

Having Jan and then losing her... It wasn't something Morgan was sure she was strong enough for when it came to a friendship down the line. "I'd miss you, of course I would, but you know." Morgan lifted a shoulder. "I just want you to be happy with whatever works for you."

"I think you and I will be just fine."

Jan was far more optimistic than Morgan was, but she'd been here before, and she'd seen how people could turn on those they loved when they didn't conform to what society saw as 'right'. She didn't want to burst Jan's bubble, and she wouldn't, but Morgan *could* have her own worries about it all...while keeping them to herself. "I know."

"So, what are the plans for the rest of the night?"

Morgan inhaled a deep breath. "Honestly? I don't care what we do or don't do. I'm just happy and loving every moment of this holiday."

"I spied a cute little ice cream shop on the way down here. The mint choc chip looked delicious, and I think it would be the perfect dessert."

"You *want* mint choc chip ice cream, you *get* mint choc chip ice cream." Morgan drew Jan in and planted a kiss on her lips. As she pulled back, holding Jan's chin, Morgan grinned. "I still can't believe you're here with me."

"I can't believe it either." Jan dipped her head. "But I wouldn't want to be anywhere else."

Morgan sighed contentedly as she relaxed back in her seat. Five more minutes, and she would call for the bill. Right now, she just wanted to memorise this moment so she could add it to all the others. Then, if things did turn sour back at home, she would have something beautiful to look back on when she sat alone in her flat.

CHAPTER 19

Taking in the quietness of the morning, Jan sat out on the terrace, angling her face towards the sun. She sat in nothing but a towel—she'd showered some forty minutes ago—and now she was waiting for Morgan to decide on a destination for their day out. They'd both agreed that sightseeing was on the itinerary today, perhaps some lunch elsewhere on the island, and then tonight was a club night. Jan hadn't been clubbing in well...she didn't dare reveal just how long it had been. But if she guessed, she would say Gillian wasn't even married to Dave at the time, and Jan had a questionable fashion sense. She vaguely recalled being at a club back home, wearing blue eyeliner and a boob tube dress. Jan shuddered at the mere thought of it.

She lifted her phone from the table and brought up Gillian's messages.

Do you remember the 90s at Club Secret?

God, that felt like a lifetime ago. It *was* a lifetime ago. But they were memories, and Jan loved nothing more than creating memories. Yes, she may cringe and wince when she looked back on them, but she wouldn't change any of it.

My God! How could I ever forget?

Jan laughed.

I was minding my own business sitting out in the sun reminiscing.

She wouldn't divulge the fact she was heading to various clubs that evening, Gillian *would* have an aneurysm, but Jan was excited to do something she hadn't done for so long.

I still have every photograph taken. They're safely away in preparation for your 50th! Social media won't know what's hit it!

Jan groaned as she sunk down into her seat and lifted her legs onto a small stool. If Gillian dared to make those pictures public, Jan would die of embarrassment.

I WILL fall out with you, Gill! Mark my words!

While Jan enjoyed this back-and-forth with her best friend, her mind constantly drifted to Gillian and Finn's reaction when she told them she'd been seeing Morgan. Jan didn't know why she felt anxious about that day—neither of them had ever done anything to suggest they wouldn't like the idea of Jan with another woman—but something was causing her to feel that way.

Her phone buzzed.

How's the holiday going? Met anyone you like the look of yet?

Oh, Jan had absolutely met someone. It just hadn't happened on the island.

I'm here to relax and unwind. I have enough to deal with when I return. I don't need a holiday romance on my mind. I'll try to call you tomorrow. Say hi to Finn for me.

She locked her phone and placed it face down on the table. Jan could hear Morgan getting ready through the open patio doors, but she wanted a few more minutes of this view before she dared to tackle her own side of the wardrobe they were sharing. The sun was holding her hostage, so what?

"Babe?"

Jan glanced over her shoulder. Morgan stood further inside the patio area, half-dressed. She wore a pair of short denim shorts and her bra. There was something incredibly satisfying about having this woman all to herself for an entire week. If Jan had realised anything recently, it was that she quite enjoyed being with someone who cared about her. Someone who cared about her happiness. Morgan had only been around for a little over a month, but God, she *did* make Jan happy. Far happier in this setting than Phil ever had. "Yes?"

"I've booked a transfer to take us to Firgas for the day. It's north of the island, very traditional, and authentic Canarian."

"Sounds perfect." Jan eyed Morgan from behind the privacy of her sunglasses. Her skin was bronzing nicely, and several small tattoos were visible on her hip, thigh, and forearm. The other arm was entirely covered with a sleeve tattoo. "Should I get ready?"

"We're not being picked up for nearly two hours. It was the earliest time slot I could get, so no, take your time. No rush."

Jan hummed as she angled her face towards the sun again, lifting her towel a little higher where it sat against her thighs. Maybe they could have coffee here at the apartment before she got ready to head out with the most beautiful woman in the world. "Perfect."

The heat of the sun suddenly disappeared as a shadow cast over her face. She opened her eyes to see a smiling Morgan looking down at her. "Can we stay here all day while I just sit around looking at you in your towel?"

Jan smirked, allowing the feeling that started low in her belly.

"I mean..." Morgan lowered Jan's legs from the stool and spread them as she got to her knees. "I can't really think of anything else I'd rather do." She palmed Jan's thighs beneath her towel, that look in Morgan's eyes sending Jan's mind into a spin. This woman *really* wanted her. *Fuck!* "I somehow managed to restrain myself once I knew you were showering before."

Jan sat forward and drew Morgan into a kiss. It was heated, almost frenzied, and as Morgan wrapped a hand around the back of Jan's neck and grazed her nails against her skin, wetness pooled between Jan's thighs. "You just know all the right things to say, don't you?"

Morgan inched back with her bottom lip between her teeth. She ghosted her hand higher beneath Jan's towel and lifted a brow. "I know what makes you wet. Why *wouldn't* I say the right things?"

Jan gasped lightly when Morgan brushed the back of her hand against her soaked pussy. "Oh, fuck." They had neighbours next door—Jan had heard them returning from what sounded like a very drunken outing last night—but they had a wall separating them, as well as a wall obscuring the view of anyone sat out at the pool. "Morgan, I—"

"Unless that sentence ends with 'want you', I don't care." Morgan looked up at Jan with hooded eyes, toying with her lip ring as she grinned. "I prefer to begin my day with the taste of you on my mind...and my lips."

Well, then. Who the hell was Jan to turn that down? She sunk back in her seat and spread her legs, enamoured by everything Morgan was as she licked her lips and dipped her head. This woman was changing Jan's life, her existence, without likely realising it. She had so many things she wanted to say... "Wait, I—"

Morgan quirked a brow as she wrapped her hands around Jan's thighs and shifted her closer to the edge of the seat. This... wasn't Jan's life. It had *never* been Jan's life. But sitting here with Morgan between her legs, that look of undeniable desire in her gorgeous dark eyes...Jan never wanted to go back to anything she'd ever known before. She didn't want to return home and go back to the daily grind the way she had over the last twenty-seven years. No, she wanted this to be a permanent fixture in her life...while making memories with Morgan just like this one. Jan shook her head lightly. "N-nothing."

Morgan took a long, slow, teasing lick between Jan's lips. Jan slapped a hand to her mouth when she almost let out a guttural moan, mindful of those around them. "So fucking good." Morgan sat up on her knees and leaned in, slipping her tongue into Jan's mouth. She moaned, grinning when Jan also found it hard to remain silent, and held Jan's chin in her hand as she pulled back. "You're a dream come true," Morgan whispered as she searched Jan's eyes. And then she slowly eased two fingers inside Jan, her stare unwavering. "*Everything* about you is a fucking dream come true."

Jan tightened around Morgan's fingers, rocking against them when that intense heat started to build from deep within her. "Oh, Morgan..."

Morgan touched her forehead to Jan's. "I...want you to be mine, Jan. I *need* you to be mine."

Jan wrapped an arm around Morgan's shoulders, her mouth hanging open when Morgan fucked her a little harder...a little faster. "F-fuck, I-I want to be yours." Jan lowered a hand and touched her fingertips to her sensitive clit. Their breath mingled, Morgan picked up her pace again, and all Jan could think of in this moment was the future with Morgan Tate. The mornings they would wake up with one another, the nights they would sit down and discuss their day, the milestones still left to achieve. Jan lashed her fingers against her clit, nodding slowly. "Y-yes. Just like that."

Morgan sat back on her knees and dipped her head, enveloping Jan's clit with her lips. She sucked and teased with the tip of her tongue, but those fingers inside Jan were bringing her closer and closer to the edge. Jan gripped the arms of her chair, meeting every last thrust of Morgan's fingers, and came hard against her tongue. "Mm." The vibration of Morgan's hum reverberated through Jan, her back arching as she offered everything she had. "Fuck, you taste like nothing else in this world."

Exhaling a shaky breath, Jan slumped into her seat and placed a hand on her forehead. "That's certainly got my day going."

Morgan laughed as she slowly eased out of Jan and brought her fingers to her lips. "I aim to please, babe. And tonight...you're all mine. Every last inch of you."

Morgan strolled hand in hand with Jan through the charming town of Firgas, astonished that she wasn't making this familiar trip north of the island alone. In all the years she had been coming here, Morgan had never brought another woman to her favourite quiet getaway. Meloneras was lively and electric all year round, but Firgas was...peaceful. Its calm streets, cobbled and winding, meandered between pastel-coloured houses that were adorned with wrought iron balconies and spilled with bright flowers. The air was fresh; it always had been here, carrying that familiar scent of salt from the nearby coast.

The crown jewel of Firgas—a cascading thirty-metre waterfall—streamed elegantly down the heart of the town, bordered by vibrant tiles. Each tile represented the crests and emblems of different towns in Gran Canaria, blending history with the beauty of the place in a way Morgan adored. The waterfall was artificial, yet its delicate trickling sounds made it feel entirely natural. Then there was that hum of life around them—locals chatting on shaded terraces and the occasional chip of birds—that only added to the charm of Firgas.

"This is..." Jan shook her head in awe as they stopped at the foot of the waterfall. Morgan understood, though. The air here had always seemed lighter, and the people...well, they were the reason Morgan came back time and time again. Red, purple, and yellow blossoms spilled from nearby planters, their colours bursting so vividly that it was hard not to love the place. "Wow."

"You like it here?" Morgan asked.

"Oh, I love it, Morgan." Jan sighed as she let go of Morgan's hand and slowly spun around. She held a palm to her chest, her smile widening with every last detail she took in. "It's so different to where we're staying."

"I know. I come here every year. Just for a few hours to unwind. To sit and think."

Jan nodded slowly as she turned back to Morgan. "I can understand why. It's so...pretty."

Morgan appreciated that Jan could see the beauty of the place, but the truth was, she'd brought Jan here *because* she knew she would love it equally as much as Morgan. Jan wasn't a party island kind of woman. She wasn't someone who dragged herself home in the middle of the night, stumbling her way through towns and cities. No, Jan was elegant and poised. To a point, anyway. Morgan knew she was fun and great for a laugh, but this was absolutely Jan's style.

"This isn't the kind of place I imagined you'd be fond of," Jan said as she took Morgan's hand again and angled her head towards an empty table outside a restaurant. "But I'm glad you are. It means you appreciate the nature around us."

Morgan pulled out a seat for Jan and smiled. "I always appreciate nature and beauty." She sat facing Jan, settling her hand over Jan's on top of the table. "This town has a lot of memories for me. I try to stay connected to it whenever I can."

"Memories?"

Morgan smiled when a waiter came by. They ordered coffees and a seafood platter to share, and then Morgan remembered that Jan was waiting for an answer. "Yes. I used to come here with my parents when I was a child."

"I see."

"I don't have the luxury of doing it with them anymore, so I come here alone. Except for this time when I have you with me." Morgan dipped her head and smiled. "Which I'm really grateful for, by the way."

"Thank you for bringing me to a place that's special to you."

"I thought about not coming here this time around, but I

figured you'd enjoy being here and I wanted you to see another side to the island. Other places can be kind of intense and packed full of holiday makers who have been drinking since they got out of bed, but here..." Morgan glanced around and smiled. "Here is where I feel at my most comfortable."

"Can I ask what happened? Why you don't have a relationship with your parents anymore?" Jan turned her hand over and stroked the inside of Morgan's palm, effectively calming her into this conversation. "Please don't feel as though you have to divulge anything if you'd rather not, though."

"Just the usual. Found out their daughter was a lesbian, didn't approve, and turned the rest of the family against me." Morgan lifted a shoulder. She'd had this conversation on several occasions now. It was second nature to feel not very much about it all at this point. "We only have a small family anyway. I've always been the only daughter, grandchild, and niece. Mum only has one sister, and Dad is estranged from most of his family too, so I don't know a great deal about his side in terms of relatives."

"R-right."

"I tried to reason with them, but it just became a pointless task in the end. I miss them, of course I do, but I can't change who I am. I can't be someone I'm not for the sake of them."

Jan regarded Morgan with a sympathetic smile. "And I hope you never would."

"I did try for a period of time. I knew I was gay when I was, like, fourteen. I didn't come out until just after my nineteenth birthday. Before that, I wore the dresses Mum wanted to put me in and wore the makeup as I got older, but...I just didn't feel like me. I couldn't deal with who I was trying to turn myself into. We'd never had the conversation about my sexuality at any point before I came out, but Mum claims she always knew and tried to 'teach it out of me'." Morgan scoffed and shook her head. "I couldn't live a lie, no matter how much I loved them."

"Was there a reason she was so set against it?"

Morgan lifted a shoulder. "She just doesn't believe in it. That's what she's repeatedly told me over the years. I guess I could understand a little better if she had an *actual* genuine reason for feeling that way, but not believing in it just isn't good enough for me."

Jan's brows rose with surprise. "And that's it? No contact with you anymore?"

"Yep. I used to send cards on birthdays or at Christmas, and they would be returned to me. Calls are ignored, and messages are never replied to. When I came out, she gave me a week to get my things together and leave. I used to go over there, hoping one day they'd see I was still just me, but they rarely answered the door. When they did, they told me exactly what they thought of me." Morgan relaxed back in her seat and sighed. "That was a tough period of my life. I had nowhere to go and no money."

"W-what did you do?"

"Couch surfed with a few friends for a while. Stayed in a couple of hostels when they had a bed available for me. Did a stint under bridges and in doorways around the city for several months."

Jan cast her gaze on the table as her shoulders slumped. "God, I'm so sorry, Morgan."

"It is what it is. I came out of it, and now, I'm making a life for myself."

"How...did you come out of it?" Jan looked back up at Morgan, those blue eyes reminding her that she was safe here.

"My grandfather passed away when I was twenty-six. My parents didn't know that I still saw him and had a great relationship with him. I wasn't going to risk losing him by telling them, either. He...was my only supporter." Morgan wished she could have been around more for her grandfather during his final years, but he'd lived in a care home, and she couldn't exactly move into his room with him to take care of him. Still, whenever she could, she would drop in and spend hours upon hours talking about the past with him. "I've never seen Mum looking so pale as she was the day I was summoned to the reading of his will."

Jan's eyes brightened. "I have a feeling this story has a happy ending, even though it's terribly sad at the same time."

"He left everything he had to me. His care home fees were paid via his two private pensions, so his home was left to me, along with any savings he had." Morgan smiled, looking back fondly on her relationship with him. "He also told my parents what he thought of them via a letter he'd written a few months before he died."

"He saved you..."

Morgan cleared her throat when the waiter brought their coffees. "Gracias." She sweetened hers a little and nodded. "He did. He had no idea I was moving from place to place almost daily; I didn't have the heart to put it on him. I also didn't have it in me to move my stuff into his place and live there. I couldn't pay the electricity bills anyway, even if I'd done that, and again, he didn't know I was on the bones of my arse. He would have done anything he could for me, but I didn't want to put it on him. He'd already been the most amazing grandfather when I was growing up. I wanted him to just keep that image in his head and not worry about me. Because he would have."

"Oh, Morgan."

Morgan didn't want to ruin this afternoon. She would give Jan more information when it was appropriate. "Everything worked out in the end. That's what counts."

"Would you tell me about the bar and how you acquired it when you're ready to?"

"Absolutely. Just...not now. I don't want to waste this moment talking about the past when I could be enjoying the present with you, here like this." Morgan's mouth watered when their platter arrived. "And you won't get a single word out of me once I tuck into this, anyway."

Jan beamed a smile as she laughed. "That's fair enough. But... thank you for sharing a part of your past with me."

"I'm an open book, babe. Nothing is a secret in my life."

Except you, unfortunately.

CHAPTER 20

Was this what it felt like after a night of clubbing when you were nearing fifty? Jan slowly lowered herself to a seat in the shade and dropped her sunglasses over her eyes. She'd woken with a headache—dehydrated, too—while wondering if she could have made better life choices last night. Still, in that moment, Jan had *thoroughly* enjoyed herself. She'd danced like she hadn't done in at least twenty years. Morgan...was a revelation.

Jan didn't particularly blame her marriage for the lack of fun over the years, but she was learning that working herself into the ground to please Phil wasn't something she ever planned to do again. Whether she remained at the business or not, Jan was making changes to her life. Without a doubt. Morgan, too, given the conversation they'd had about her promoting Ben to manager. Could this really be the beginning of a new life? Could Jan honestly walk right into a full-blown committed relationship with Morgan?

Oh, you're already there. Don't fool yourself into believing otherwise.

She cleared her throat and lifted her phone. Jan had a call to make, and she wanted to do it before Morgan returned from the local grocery store. She didn't need anyone to talk her out of this decision. It was done. It was final. Jan was officially moving on. She called Gillian, not surprised when it barely had the chance to ring before she answered.

"What's it like? Is it hot? How's the hotel?"

Jan lifted her legs onto a stool and sighed. "Paradise. All of it is just...perfect."

"It's pissing down here. It has been since yesterday morning." Gillian sighed. "Thanks for calling me. I know you're away, but I like to know you're okay. Especially because you're there on your own."

"The hotel is gorgeous. It looks out onto the beach." Even though Jan was feeling a little fragile this morning, she didn't exactly have a hangover. It was tiredness more than anything. "I think I'll lie by the pool today. It's quite quiet at the moment."

"No sun bed wars?"

Jan smiled. "No. None. I also have the option of lying out on my private terrace if I want to."

"You have a private terrace?! Okay, I'm officially jealous." Gillian groaned, but Jan understood. Nobody wanted to be stuck at home while their best friend was sunning themselves abroad. "Maybe I could pull a sicky at work tomorrow and fly out."

Even though Jan knew Gillian was joking, she still felt a wave of anxiety at the prospect. "We should definitely arrange a holiday at some point. With Finn, too, of course."

"That would be great, love. You can count us both in." Gillian cleared her throat. "How have you been out there on your own? Has it given you time to decide what's next?"

"Yes. That's why I've called you." Jan lifted her glass of water from the table and sipped it slowly. "Could you do something for me?"

"Of course. What is it?"

"You're working from home today, yes?" Jan desperately hoped Gillian was. She *needed* her help.

"Mmhmm. Though, working is a bit of a stretch. Finn had a lecture this morning, and since she left, I've done nothing other than lay on the couch."

"Could you go to the house for me and meet the estate agent at two?" That anxiety flared up again, but it was time. She couldn't hold onto the place forever, hoping everything would magically sort itself out. "They emailed me this morning to say an agent was available to value it."

"O-oh."

"Gill, please. I want to know what I'm working with before I tell Phil I've had it valued. It's nothing concrete, but it *is* a step."

"You have my support. Of course you do. I just wasn't expecting you to call me saying you were having the house valued."

"If you don't want to get involved, I understand."

"I'm more than happy to get involved. Phil is dead to me as far as I'm concerned. I hope his dick falls off!"

Jan barked a laugh, quickly slapping a hand over her mouth when she realised just how loud she'd been. "As I say, it's just something to get the ball rolling. I have no idea how long anything will take, and I can't exactly look for a new place to live without knowing what kind of funds I have to do so."

"You're being sensible. There's nothing wrong with that. But if he turns up while I'm there with the agent, what am I supposed to say?"

"He won't. I've checked the online diary, and he's in Kent until tomorrow." Jan had been lucky to get an appointment so quickly. Perhaps it was fate. "You won't have to worry about that. He's probably taken *her* on some spa retreat. Fucking pig!"

"Jan, love."

"I'm fine. I don't care where he is or what he's doing. I just want him out of my life now, Gill. I want to put all of this behind me and live."

"Okay. I'll be there." Gillian groaned down the line. "God, whatever you do...don't fall for someone significantly younger than you. My body is *dying* this morning. I don't know where I find the strength."

Jan took the corner of her lip between her teeth to keep her from giggling like a teenager. She understood exactly what Gillian was saying, but Jan wasn't at the stage of wondering where she'd find her strength. She had plenty left for Morgan and that delectable mouth.

"Are you still there?"

"Yes. I'm here." Jan spied Morgan walking along the sidewalk between the pool area and their terrace. She quickly brought a finger to her lips when Morgan eyed her. "But I'm going to go now. I'd like to find a lounger before they're all gone."

"Okay. Well, lots of love, and I'll drop you a text when I'm home from yours later."

Jan smiled when Morgan lifted her legs from the stool and sat down, bringing Jan's legs into her lap instead. "Okay. Bye, Gill. Talk to you soon."

As she ended the call and slid her phone onto the table, Jan looked up at Morgan...seeing her in a whole new light this morning. Last night after the club had been intense, but it had been exactly what Jan had needed without her knowing it. Morgan, those hips, and that fucking mouth... "Hi." Jan planted her feet on the floor and leaned in to kiss Morgan. "I thought you'd got lost."

"Well, you were hardly moving when I was leaving before. I decided to stroll back and take my time." Morgan held Jan's chin as she tried to pull back. "My heart is still pounding when I think about last night."

Oh, God. They couldn't discuss it. Not yet. Jan was still wet thinking about it. "Please, not yet. I need to gather my thoughts before you say another word."

Morgan smirked as she trailed her tongue across Jan's bottom lip. "I have it playing on repeat in my mind. Give me a shout when you want a reminder."

Jan shuddered but allowed the smile working its way onto her lips to spread impossibly wide. "*You* are so bad."

Morgan rose to her feet and guided Jan up with her. She wrapped an arm around Jan's waist and pulled their bodies together as Morgan whispered, "And *you* are so fucking good."

With the patio doors open and the sound of the ocean floating on the breeze, Jan lowered the volume on the TV and gazed in Morgan's direction. Tonight, they'd decided to have dinner early, then head back to their apartment to relax. The whole clubbing scene had taken it out of Jan last night, and this morning, and Morgan didn't look to be in much better condition. Jan had spent the day rehydrating and trying to get her mind off the sheer filth Morgan had possessed last night when they'd returned from their night out. God, Jan hadn't known she'd had such stamina in her.

For the last hour, she'd spent every minute in her own head trying to figure out how to tell Gillian about what was happening here. After Morgan's heart-to-heart with her in Firgas yesterday, Jan was wary about coming out. That didn't mean she was considering staying in the closet, but she was hoping to deliver the news with minimal impact. Jan didn't have to worry about telling her own parents; her dad had never been in her life, and her mum had sadly passed away the year before Gillian divorced Dave. But Gillian *was* the closest thing Jan had in terms of family, and it was important that Jan had the support of her best friend.

"How did you and Finn meet?"

Morgan gazed back at Jan with tired eyes. "My grandad lived on the same street as Finn."

"Oh! Really?"

"Mmhmm. Finn was leaving her mum's place when I was clearing out Grandad's house after he died. Finn, as you know, is younger than me so we didn't hang out growing up or anything, but we got talking and she seemed kinda nice. Before I knew it, she was helping me to send his things to charity or wherever else they were being shipped off to."

That sounded just like Finn. From the moment Jan had met her, it was clear she had a kind heart. Even during those days when Gillian didn't know what to do for the best, Finn was only ever concerned about Gillian. It hadn't mattered what she, herself, wanted. Gillian was the priority. That had been the very moment when Jan knew they were made for one another. "Finn is...an old soul."

"She is. She's a great friend to have in your life, too." Morgan grazed her fingertips over Jan's knee and smiled. "She was the one who encouraged me to take on the bar."

"Oh?"

"Yeah, we were out having a pint together one night in the bar across from The Corner. It had a for sale sign up, and I made a throwaway comment about how it would be cool to open a bar. There are plenty of pubs in town, but we didn't have something that people could unwind in without it getting rowdy, you know?"

"I do *love* The Corner. It feels far more welcoming than some places in the area."

"And that was exactly what I wanted it to be when I was thinking up all those plans for the place. I didn't imagine they'd come to anything; I wasn't business-minded, and I didn't know a thing about bars and breweries." Morgan dragged a hand through her hair. The natural blonde highlights throughout it had started to lighten with the sun. "I was living at my grandad's place, but I'd always planned to sell it. It was far too big for me, and I was nowhere close to being ready for a relationship, so it would have just been me rattling around in there."

Jan regarded Morgan with an understanding smile. Right now, she *wished* she could rattle around in her own huge house. "That's how you came to live in the flat above it?"

"God, the place was a mess. The beams had rotted, the floor

was ready to cave in, and I just didn't feel good about anything I had to undertake." Morgan shook her head lightly. "Finn came in and ripped the place out. She was on an apprenticeship with a local joinery firm at the time and some of the guys she worked with offered a hand. Without her help, I probably would have given up and left the flat to rot further. I didn't *need* to live above the bar, but it was a no-brainer when I saw what Finn had done with the place. She's talented, I'll give her that."

"She designed and fitted my kitchen. I'll miss it when we've sold the place." Jan lay her head on a cushion and sighed. "It kind of became the centre of the house, you know? It was just so beautiful, and everyone was talking about it when they came to visit."

"It *could* still be your kitchen if you speak to Phil and mention the idea of staying in the house."

Jan sat upright and propped her head in her hand. "When you went out this morning for a newspaper, I called Gillian and asked her to do something for me."

"Okay..."

"She met an estate agent at the house this afternoon. She has a spare set of keys. They're going to value it, so I know what to expect once we put it up for sale." Jan's voice almost betrayed her as the severity of what was happening sunk in. "The time has come to get the ball rolling, and that means selling up."

"Babe, I didn't know you were doing that. I could have been here to support you if you'd told me you were making that call." Morgan took Jan's hand and brought it into her lap. "How do you feel about it all knowing you're getting it valued?"

Jan took a moment to find the right words. Her bottom lip trembled as she met Morgan's gaze. "Heartbroken."

"Come here." Morgan opened her arms and pulled Jan in against her. "I wish there was something I could do for you, but nobody knows I'm even in your life." Morgan lowered a kiss to Jan's hair as tears worked their way down her cheeks. "I hate that I can't be there for you. Not standing proudly beside you, anyway."

"That's my fault. I'm sorry." Jan sniffled and wrapped an arm around Morgan's waist. "If I wasn't such a coward, Gill would know I was here with you."

"It's not about being a coward. It's about doing things on your own terms. I've never not understood that. I just wish I could be there for you...out in public, you know?"

"I know. But this, right here, is just as good...if not better." Jan buried her face in the crook of Morgan's neck and sobbed as she realised just what her life was about to become. People would talk, friends would tell her she was stupid for not trying to repair her marriage, and Phil would walk away mostly unscathed. They always did.

"Hey, come on. Don't worry about it. Everything is going to be okay, babe." Morgan soothed a palm up and down Jan's upper arm. "You're strong, and you're doing what's best for you. Don't ever forget that."

Jan drew back and smiled when Morgan brushed a thumb under her eye. "It feels as though you're the only person who is going to understand. That's what scares me the most—nobody understanding that I don't want to stay with a man who has hurt me the way Phil has."

"Nobody else has a right to tell you what you should or shouldn't do. I get it completely, and I think walking away is incredibly brave."

If Jan could stay on this island with Morgan forever, she would. But neither of them could do that because they had lives back at home. They had friends and people who cared about them. Jan could only hope they would still care when the truth came to light. "Thank you for being by my side. It means the world to me."

"Hey," Morgan whispered as she smiled into a kiss. "Unless you tell me to, I'm not going anywhere, okay?"

Jan touched her forehead to Morgan's, allowing the sound from the ocean to calm her. "Okay."

CHAPTER 21

You should have booked a two-week holiday!

Morgan sighed as she brushed the sand from her feet and lifted her legs onto her sun lounger. Jan was reading beside her, the sun was blazing down on them, but Morgan's heart was heavy. Tomorrow, they would fly back to England. Tomorrow, everything Morgan could have ever dreamed of would end. She hadn't known just how important this holiday could be for them, but the mere thought of pretending Jan was nothing more than a customer at her bar ached deep in her chest.

What had she expected from this trip? Well, she'd expected fun and laughter, dancing and sangria, but what she was coming away with was so much more than that. For the first time in several years, Morgan had opened up and been her true self with another woman. Jan just brought it out of her without warning. She knew about Morgan's past, about her non-existent relationship with her parents, and it felt as though they were in an entirely different place with one another as this week drew to a close.

Morgan eyed Jan and her perfect, slender body. Was this really happening? Did Morgan *actually* have a future she could look forward to? It certainly felt that way. Jan was so at ease around her that it was hard to come to any other conclusion. Life was good, Jan was a breath of fresh air, and Morgan couldn't wait until they could be together back at home. She couldn't wait for the day when Jan would walk into the bar, step up, and kiss Morgan without any concern at all. The nights when they would stroll around town, hand in hand. Morgan wanted it all. She wanted *everything* Jan could offer. She wanted...to love this woman.

Jan closed her book and swung her legs over the side of her lounger. Morgan quickly focused on the ocean ahead of them, but she suspected she'd already been caught watching Jan. "Everything okay?"

"I...yes." Morgan cleared her throat and the unexpected emotion that had lodged itself there. "Do you need more lotion on?"

"No. I think I'm going to move into the shade for a while. It's hotter than I thought it would be today."

Yeah, it was hot. Ridiculously hot with this woman around. "I thought maybe we could give it another hour and then head for one of the restaurants behind us. Maybe have some lunch?"

"You heard my stomach growling, didn't you?"

Morgan hadn't, the crash of the waves drowned out every last noise around them, but she'd wished she'd heard it. It would only be another thing to add to the list of Jan's cuteness. "Yeah. Thought a tidal wave was heading for us until I realised it was you."

Jan swatted Morgan's hip as she laughed and got to her feet. "Stop it."

"I'm joking. If you're hungry now, though, we could head for lunch earlier. I don't mind."

Jan dragged her lounger under the parasol and fixed her towel. "I'm okay for a while longer."

Morgan narrowed her eyes behind her sunglasses, quickly climbing from her own lounger and situating herself on Jan's. She lowered her legs on either side and straddled it, then patted the space in between. "Sit. I'll share the shade with you."

Jan cocked her head and grinned, sending Morgan's pulse through the roof. She knew Jan wasn't used to little moments like this, but Morgan was going to continue doing the things that encouraged a smile from her. She got herself comfortable between Morgan's legs and rested back against her. "This is nice." Jan lay her head back against Morgan's shoulder and sighed. "I can't believe we'll be on a flight home this time tomorrow."

"I'm trying not to think about it." Morgan wrapped her arms around Jan's waist and rested her chin on her shoulder. "If I knew I could, I'd extend the holiday."

"I'm good for *at least* another month here, but I know you have to get back for the bar." Jan angled her head and smiled when Morgan laid a gentle kiss on her lips. "Right now, I'm grateful for the memories out here with you."

"There will be more. Whether it's at home or elsewhere, we will definitely make more memories." Morgan smiled against Jan's lips and tightened her arms around her waist. "You're so beautiful, and being out here with you has just...I don't know." Morgan paused briefly. "Made me appreciate you even more, I guess."

Jan regarded Morgan with a gorgeous smile. "I don't know what I would have done without you recently. You've made life so much easier for me, and all I want is to know you more."

Morgan felt the same way. One hundred percent. "Do you have any family back home that are going to take this badly?" Jan hadn't spoken about her family, but Morgan kind of understood. Given the shitshow of her own family, it didn't seem out of the ordinary to her. "Siblings? Parents?"

"Dad left when we were younger. Mum passed away a couple of years ago. I do have a sister, but she lives in New Zealand. She's been over there now for...God, it must be coming up to twenty-three years. She met her husband there while she was travelling, and now, they have three kids. Two girls and a boy."

"Oh, that's nice. Do you get the chance to see her much?"

"We video call when we can. The girls, Betsy and Katie, are in college. Noah, I believe, is about to start travelling himself. He knows if he finds himself in England, he has a place to stay with me."

"Correct me if I'm wrong, but the kids probably see you as the cool auntie."

Jan lifted a shoulder. "I'd like to think so, but I haven't seen them in the flesh since they were much younger. I miss them all, but it's a long way to travel for a catch-up, you know?"

"You and Phil never thought about taking a break and heading out there?"

Jan snorted. "He couldn't even manage Europe, never mind New Zealand."

"No, I know." Morgan sighed. "Maybe you could plan a visit now that you're no longer tied to him and the business. If nothing else, it may be a nice break for you. It'll give you the chance to recharge and make some decisions on where you see your future going."

"Maybe, I don't know. Catherine has her own business over there, so she's generally as busy as me. Well, when I was working, anyway." Jan looked out at the ocean and cleared her throat. "And going to New Zealand would mean not seeing you for several weeks. I'm not sure I like that idea right now. Not while I'm here, in your arms, *thoroughly* enjoying myself."

Morgan shouldn't allow it, but those words settled in her heart, ultimately sending a shiver up her spine. Jan didn't want to leave the country because she would miss her? Well, Morgan was surely doing something right. She lowered her head and kissed Jan's neck. "As much as I love *and* hate the idea of you missing me, it's something you should still consider."

"I'm quite content right now." Jan palmed Morgan's thighs and sighed. "This is where I want to be. Wherever you are."

Relaxing after a long but beautiful day in the sun, Jan rested back on the super king-sized bed she'd shared with Morgan for the last week and clasped her hands behind her head. Morgan was packing away whatever she wouldn't need for the last night here on the island, but Jan preferred to run around at the last minute. She wouldn't usually do that, but the moment she opened her suitcase, she knew she would be sad all over again. She'd already spent the morning feeling that way; there wasn't a chance she was allowing her mood to affect this evening, too.

Morgan appeared in the doorway with her phone in her hand. "Finn has texted me."

"Oh?" Jan sat up on her elbows and eyed Morgan across the room. "Is she okay?"

"She...wants to know why I decided to visit friends in England instead of going on my usual holiday abroad."

"It's a fair question, I suppose. If I had to choose between England or Meloneras, I know where I'd rather be."

Morgan stepped into the room and took a seat on the edge of the bed. "I don't know why I feel paranoid about her message, but I do. As though she's trying to catch me out, and she already knows about us, you know?"

"Trust me, if she knew about us, she wouldn't be texting you. She'd be calling me...or Gill would be, demanding answers." Jan took Morgan's phone from her hand and set it down on the bed. "Come and rest with me for a minute. Get out of your head and just enjoy our last night here together."

Morgan crawled towards Jan and smiled into a kiss. "You have a gorgeous tan. Everyone is going to be jealous when you get back."

"Mm. What we *didn't* think about was how you're going to explain your tan." Jan drew back and frowned. "No, really. How *are* you going to explain it? Gillian said it's been raining continuously."

Morgan lifted a shoulder. "Honestly, I don't really care."

Jan understood that, but it just made everything feel deceptive all over again. She hadn't had time to think anything through before she left England; she'd been too high on the idea of having Morgan to herself. "I'm sure you'll think of something if you happen to bump into Finn. You and I both know it's the first thing she'll pick up on."

"I know. Once again...she's like a bloodhound."

Jan fell back onto the mattress, gripping Morgan's tank top as she did so. Morgan landed on top of her with an 'oomph', and then those gentle fingertips found the side of Jan's neck, soothing her skin. "Maybe I should just send Gill a message and reveal all of this. If nothing else, I won't be there for her to give me a grilling."

"She means more to you than that." Morgan brushed Jan's hair from her face and smiled. "If you want to do it together, just say the word, and I'll be right there with you."

That wasn't the worst idea in the world, but Jan would prefer to sit down with Gillian alone and ease it into the conversation. Mostly because she had no idea how Gillian would respond but also because there would probably be a lot of questions and confusion. "I appreciate you for offering, but I'll be just fine doing it alone." Jan craned her neck and kissed the tip of Morgan's nose. "And once it's all out in the open, we'll all get together and have a great night out. Dinner will be on me."

Morgan sighed as she propped her head in her hand. "You think it'll be that easy?"

"Of course. Gillian isn't really in a position to question my sexuality when she's now married to a woman herself."

"Fair point."

As Jan considered how long they had to get ready—perhaps a roll in the sheets beforehand—her phone started to ring on the side table next to the bed. She reached for it, lifting her brows when Gillian's name was displayed on the screen. "Speak of the devil."

She pressed a finger to Morgan's lips and answered the call. "Hi, Gill. Everything okay?"

"Of course. I was just wondering if you'd heard anything from the estate agent yet?"

Jan smiled when Morgan shifted off her but rested her head against Jan's chest. Her hand found Morgan's luscious hair, everything within Jan settling as she stroked her fingers through her locks. "I called them this morning. They believe we're looking at offers over eight hundred thousand."

"Nice. You should be able to find yourself something really lovely when you start looking. Just...make sure it still has a decent-sized garden. You know I love your garden parties, and there's *no way* I'm giving them up because Phil is a disgusting prick!"

"Noted. I'll be sure to invite you along to any viewings. You'd have the final say, of course." Jan laughed. "I'm flying home tomorrow, so once I'm settled in again, I'll call you and come over for coffee."

"Lovely. I can't wait to hear all about your trip. Have a safe flight home."

"Love to Finn. Bye, Gill." Jan ended the call and lowered her phone to the bed. The silence of the apartment enveloped her, Morgan too, and in this moment, Jan just wanted to shout from the rooftops that she was happy and thrilled with the direction her life would soon be taking. "Remind me what time our dinner reservation is again?"

"Seven," Morgan said quietly as she draped an arm across Jan's stomach. "The last supper."

"The last of this holiday, yes. But just one of many everywhere else." Jan shifted further down the bed and wrapped Morgan up in her arms. The sun and the heat had really taken it out of them today, so a nap was required before she took Morgan for dinner at a place that had exceptional reviews...along with incredible views of the island. "In case I forget to tell you, you've made me the happiest woman in the world these last couple of months."

Morgan didn't say anything. Instead, she held onto Jan far tighter than she ever had before, nuzzled into her, and sighed.

It's time to live for yourself, not everyone else.

CHAPTER 22

With her hand sitting securely in Morgan's, Jan stared out of the plane window, the smile she wore unimaginably wide. She hadn't known what would come out of this week away with Morgan, and she hadn't strived for anything in particular, but Jan desperately hoped that this would continue back on English soil. She was done with worrying, and she was done with going back and forth in her mind. Being with Morgan had shown Jan a world she'd never thought possible. And as she sat here, surrounded by people who had no idea what she was going through, the idea of not waking up in Morgan's arms tomorrow physically hurt her heart.

She turned to Morgan and smiled when Morgan gazed back at her. "I wish this wasn't coming to an end."

Morgan squeezed Jan's hand. "The holiday is, but us... Well, I'm hoping you still see this going somewhere."

Jan dipped her eyes briefly, mesmerised by her hand in Morgan's. It felt freeing, and it felt right. "Do *you* still see it going somewhere?"

"I do." Morgan lifted Jan's hand and kissed the back of it. "I've had an amazing week with you, and it's not even because I was actually abroad with someone. I'm used to travelling alone and most of the time I enjoy it. This week with you has only reminded me of the things I've been missing over the last several years. It's reminded me that I want this again. Someone in my life. Someone I can sit down and watch TV with, someone I can wine and dine, someone I can feel complete with." Morgan smiled. "It's taken me quite some time to realise what I was missing."

"You've had that before then?" Jan didn't want to come across as shocked, but Morgan often spoke about the no-strings flings and the short-term relationships she'd had. But this time, something in Morgan's eyes suggested she'd once had something far more serious. "A long-term relationship?"

"Just once." Morgan laid her head back against her seat and sighed. "A long time ago."

"Who was she?"

"Lisa," Morgan said. "We were together for five years. She's one of the reasons I decided to move into the flat above the bar."

"Can I ask what happened?" Jan swallowed, noting the pain in Morgan's voice. "Or maybe we should wait until we're back in England."

Morgan turned on her side as best as she could, the side of her face pressed to her seat as she gazed back at Jan. "We still have a three-hour flight ahead of us. It'll keep us entertained if nothing else."

Jan lifted a hand and brushed Morgan's hair from her face. Her sun-kissed skin was even more beautiful than usual. "If you want to talk about it, okay. But if you'd rather we didn't, don't feel as though you have to."

"We met when I was in my early twenties. We'd known each other for a lot longer than that, we're from the same area, but she asked me out for a drink one night. I'd already kind of had my eye on her, so I said yes." Morgan's features changed ever so slightly. She seemed...distant. "We had a great relationship. Most of the time, we were inseparable. We lived together and had our finances together for a period of time...and then she dropped the bombshell that she wanted kids. She'd told me a few years before that she didn't, and then she changed her mind." Morgan sighed. "I never wanted kids, and I just didn't have it in me to give her what she wanted to make her happy if it was going to make me miserable."

"That's fair enough."

"She let it go for a while and then came the incessant conversations about it. The guilt-tripping. Threatening to leave me and then telling me she was staying. I didn't know if I was coming or going most days."

Jan could understand where Morgan was coming from. Having children didn't define a relationship. It didn't complete you. Unless that was what someone wanted, of course. Jan had never been fortunate enough to have children, and she'd made peace with that many years ago, but they had tried for a long time. When they found out that Jan couldn't conceive, Phil had been wonderful about it. As time went on and life passed them by, it hadn't seemed like such a big deal in the end. They were still happy as a unit of two. "Is that why you ended it?"

"She ended it. She came home one night and told me she'd been on a few dates with a coworker. That she wanted to make sure it would work out before she broke up with me. I believe they have three kids now. Twin boys and a girl."

"I think it's always important to do the right thing. If you didn't want children, then why should you force yourself into that situation?"

"Lisa didn't see it that way. She was under the impression that *all* women wanted children, and it shouldn't even be a conversation that needed to be had." Morgan laughed at that. "I don't know why people think everyone wants kids. It's just not something I've ever imagined for myself, and when I did allow myself to think about it, all I felt was dread."

"Do you ever wish things could have been different?"

Morgan shrugged. "No. Life is...it's forever changing. Nobody knows what's going to happen from one day to the next. Not really. We can try to plan and prepare for the future, but any one of us could be gone tomorrow. Lisa is happy, and since I met you... I'm also very happy."

"I don't know where I go from here," Jan said, her voice low as she stroked a thumb across Morgan's bottom lip. "I have so much to do and so many things to figure out, but I don't want to deal with any of it. I just want to live in this bubble and hope it all works itself out."

"Do you think you can find space for me in your life somewhere?" Morgan visibly swallowed. "Not immediately, I know you have a lot going on at home, but I don't know...maybe down the line? When it feels right for you?" They'd already had the conversation about being together, but Jan appreciated the time and the patience Morgan had given her so far. "After being abroad with you, taking you out on dinner dates and that...I'd really love to keep doing that back at home."

God, Jan would love nothing more than to go on a date with Morgan once they were back in England. But before she did, she *had* to tell Gillian about them. It didn't feel right to hide any longer. Jan was a grown woman, and she would make whatever decision was best for her. "I'd like that."

"Yeah?" A lazy smile spread across Morgan's mouth, those dark brown eyes piercing Jan's soul.

"I've just spent the most incredible week away with you. I'd be out of my mind if I decided that I didn't want to see you again."

"And you're prepared for whatever comes in terms of friends and family? Phil, too?"

Jan knew that Morgan was worried about Gillian and Finn's reaction, but Jan wasn't. Not anymore. Gillian had been through so much with her, and Jan knew that when the moment came, Gillian would be happy for her. So long as she was safe and healthy, that would be the only thing that mattered. As for everyone else...well, that was simply background noise that Jan wouldn't pay any attention to. At least, that was the hope.

"Will you still be there at the end of the day?"

Morgan nodded, her gaze fixed on Jan.

"Then they can ask all the questions they like. Whether I answer them or not depends on me."

Morgan reached out and cupped Jan's cheek. "Never thought I'd find a woman like you who actually *wants* a relationship."

"When I left my marriage, I thought that was it for me. The idea of dating was terrifying, and to be completely honest, I didn't have any plans to do anything of the kind. The only plan I had was to sit in that hotel room and stare at the wall crying." Jan hadn't known what the hell was coming as she'd closed the front door to her home and turned her back on everything she'd known for the majority of her adult life. "I certainly didn't think you'd show any kind of interest in me."

Morgan regarded Jan with an understanding smile. "I hate knowing you're alone at the hotel."

"That won't be the case for much longer. Now that I have the valuation for the house, I'm going to speak to Phil and tell him I want half sooner rather than later so I can set up a new home and a new life for myself. It's the least he can do after what he's put me through." Jan really hoped Phil was on board with the idea. She didn't want to wait until the divorce was finalised. She just wanted the cash to move on. "And providing he agrees to my terms, I'll be back at work soon."

"Good idea regarding the valuation. You do need somewhere to live, and you shouldn't have to stay at a hotel until the divorce has gone through." Morgan squeezed Jan's hand. "And I think going back to work will give you that routine again."

Jan grinned. "You're just saying that so I'm not propping your bar up every afternoon."

"Hey, I'd love nothing more than to spend my shifts with you at the bar. Don't *ever* think anything else. But you need the routine. You're far too good to sit in a bar day in, day out. Far too good."

"No chance of a job with you then?"

Morgan leaned in and kissed Jan softly. "I wouldn't even insult you by asking."

When Morgan drew back and sat in her upright position again, Jan sighed and looked out of the window. It was time for people to know about the woman in her life, and if there was a backlash, then so be it. Jan couldn't help who she was attracted to, and if everyone could understand that, all of this would be perfectly fine.

"Thank you for the most beautiful week." Jan lay her head on Morgan's shoulder and closed her eyes. "I hope it's something we'll do again in the future."

Morgan palmed Jan's thigh as she said, "I'm already planning the next one in my head right now."

Feeling torn for the first time in as long as she could remember, Morgan shoved their suitcases into the boot of Jan's car and lingered for a moment. More than anything, she wanted to take Jan back to her flat with her, but Morgan knew it would be wise to give Jan space. Because now that they'd landed, everything became very real all over again. *Hasn't a week of uninterrupted time with her been enough for you?* As Morgan stood behind Jan's car, she knew it would never be enough.

While Morgan knew she could be open and honest with Jan, she wasn't sure bringing it up again was a good idea. Jan knew where Morgan stood, and Morgan believed she knew where Jan stood, but in this moment, Morgan wanted more, and she wanted it right now. Not down the line, just...now. She would be miserable the moment they parted ways, and that misery wouldn't lift until Jan was back in her arms again. That was an unusual feeling for

Morgan, if she was being entirely honest. She was so used to being dropped or only having contact with women in the past when they wanted something from her that she rarely allowed herself to get emotionally involved. Amanda had been the most recent proof of exactly that.

Get out of your head and just enjoy what you can have.

Morgan cleared her throat and closed the boot. At least they had the hour-long journey home from the airport to spend together. That was better than nothing. As she climbed into the passenger seat and eyed Jan, Morgan could only smile and allow whatever she was feeling. Jan hummed along to the radio and tapped her fingers against the steering wheel, her tanned skin so soft and silky smooth.

"All done. Let's hit the road." Morgan clicked her seatbelt into place and sighed. "I hate coming home from a holiday. Don't you?"

"It's not something I've ever really had to worry about. As you know, holidays were few and far between for me." Jan reversed out of her parking space and began the ten-floor descent. "But I'm not enjoying coming home from this holiday, no."

Every time Jan spoke about her marriage and the lack of everything she deserved, Morgan found it hard to comprehend. Fuck, she would have given Jan anything she desired while they'd been on holiday together. As far as she was concerned, Phil deserved to lose this woman. He deserved to figure out a life without her. He sure as hell wouldn't find better down the line. "Wanker." Morgan muttered under her breath, but she felt Jan's gaze drift towards her. "Sorry."

Jan simply lifted a shoulder and concentrated on the road. "Maybe if he'd found the time or put in more of an effort, we wouldn't be in the situation we're in now."

Did that mean Jan wished she wasn't here in this car with Morgan? Was that a hint of hesitancy for what was coming? "I know you've seemed pretty adamant about what happens next, but are you one hundred percent going through with the divorce?" Morgan hoped it wasn't a knee-jerk reaction. She couldn't imagine seeing Jan and Phil together in the future. "No more counselling?"

"No. I'm done with him." Jan said that so calmly that Morgan was impressed by her cool, calm demeanour. If that had been Morgan, she wouldn't have known what to do for the best. Twenty-seven years was a long time to spend with someone. The idea of just stepping away from a relationship spanning almost three decades filled her with dread. "I feel like I don't know him anymore. I can't look at him unless I absolutely have to. And then when he texts me begging me to work things out with him, it only makes me loathe him more."

"Some time apart wouldn't work for you?" Morgan didn't know why she was trying to push Jan towards her husband—it would mean the end of whatever was happening here—but she was of the opinion that if something was meant for her...it would be.

"I've spent enough time apart from him over the years because of work. This doesn't feel much different, to be honest." Jan eyed Morgan briefly. "Looking back, I gave him a lot of leeway because of the business, but now that you and I have been spending time with one another, I'm beginning to realise I want so much more."

"More what?"

"Fun. Excitement. Unexpected trips away. Days when I lounge around. The opportunity to sit and enjoy reading a book. Just... more."

Morgan reached a hand across the console and settled it on Jan's knee. "I get that."

"More of *this*, Morgan." Jan lay her hand over Morgan's and smiled. "There have been so many times when I've been over at Gillian's, just watching the love they have for one another. At one time, I found myself craving the very same thing. But then I put it to the back of my mind because Phil has never changed. He's the very same man I fell in love with and married. He's always been less touchy and less romantic than my friend's partners. So, how could I miss something I'd never had with him?"

Oh, that was painful to hear. Morgan cleared her throat. "I think everyone deserves those things."

"Maybe. I don't know."

Morgan watched Jan as she drove through the dark streets and towards the motorway. There was just something about this woman that mesmerised Morgan on more than one occasion daily. She had an air about her that Morgan hadn't come across before. While Amanda had been very particular about everything in her life, often found in front of a mirror while she checked herself out, Jan was the total opposite. She still maintained that Jan was elegant and one hell of a woman, but she knew how to find the laughter in life, too. That was a huge plus in Morgan's eyes. If she could laugh and enjoy herself with another woman, she was winning. Without a doubt. "I've really had the perfect week with you, Jan."

"Perfect doesn't come close." Jan entwined their fingers as they took the ramp onto the motorway. It was quiet, almost secretive, to be driving along this stretch of road while they held hands, but Morgan wouldn't change anything. Being with Jan was all she could have dreamed of. "And now I have to go back to a hotel room with my life strewn across the place."

Morgan decided she would offer, even if she knew Jan likely wouldn't take her up on it. "You're welcome to come back to my place with me."

"I know, but I should spend the rest of the evening figuring some things out. I have to deal with my divorce sooner or later. No need to draw something out that cannot be salvaged."

"I know. I still had to offer."

"Believe me, if I didn't have things to take care of, I wouldn't *dream* of going back to the hotel. But I need to find a place to live, and I'd like to do that soon. I can't hold Gillian and Finn off much longer. They'll force me into their spare room eventually."

Morgan grinned when she noted that twinkle in Jan's eye. "They're good people. They care about you. We all do."

"And I appreciate that more than any of you know."

Morgan sat up in her seat and peered at the speedometer. "Hey, slow down a bit."

"I'm well within the speed limit."

"I know that, but the faster you drive, the less time I have with you before I have to let you go." Morgan relaxed into the leather seat when Jan decelerated. "Perfect. All of you is absolutely perfect."

CHAPTER 23

Jan exited her car, the gravel beneath her heels crunching as she pulled her shoulders back and walked towards the offices. She was mildly anxious to be here today—she hadn't stepped foot on business soil since Gareth had exposed the truth to her—but she had nothing to be ashamed of. Phil had done the dirty, not Jan. If the staff thought any differently, then she would set the record straight.

With a slight sense of love and belonging sitting in her chest at the brief thought of Morgan, Jan took the steps to the main offices and forced the heavy steel door open. Anais would be sitting at her desk, and Phil would be holed away behind his private office door. Clients and other employees would likely be milling about, some frantic...others not so much, but it was all just noise to Jan today. She was still high on life and the Spanish sun.

She stopped and scanned the room. Her eyes immediately landed on Anais, her appearance different today. Jan couldn't put her finger on what it was, but yes, Anais seemed different. As they glared at one another, Jan's stare didn't waver. She wouldn't be intimidated by the very woman who had stolen her husband. Only as Jan stood here, she found a smile curling on her lips. Anais may have stolen her husband, but after the last several weeks she'd spent getting to know Morgan, Jan was in some ways thankful for that. Morgan had tilted everything Jan had ever known. She had shown her what life could be like post-divorce...even before the divorce had been finalised. And instead of spending days, sometimes weeks, alone while Phil was out of the country on business, her evenings with Morgan were a refreshing change.

She turned and eyed Phil's office door. The small square window in it gave Jan a glimpse inside, and she could just about see the top of Phil's head. He would be on a call, he usually was, but Jan could wait. She didn't exactly have anywhere pressing to be right now.

She stepped towards the door and knocked lightly. Phil's head shot up, he peered at her through the window, and then he waved her inside. She entered quietly, took a seat, and waited for him to end his call. When he did, Phil looked up at her with tired eyes. Was he unable to sleep lately? Huh, Jan didn't have that problem. Perhaps it was the guilty conscience he possessed. "Jan, hi."

"I won't keep you long, I know how busy you are, but I just wondered if you had a few minutes to discuss the divorce?"

Phil nodded and lowered his eyes. "I was hoping you'd eventually change your mind, but as the weeks passed, I knew you wouldn't be coming here to tell me you forgive me."

"Is that what you need me to do in order for you to move on? Forgive you?" Jan didn't have it inside her to forgive Phil right now, she wasn't sure it would ever be possible, but she would lie if he desperately needed it from her.

"Your face has always given you away, so it's no use lying to me."

Jan nodded and watched Phil across his desk. He had something on his mind. Jan had spent long enough with him to know when he was stressed, and now was one of those times. Potentially the worst she'd seen him in many years. "Okay."

"I...have something I need to say to you." Phil clicked his pen, then set it down on top of the files in front of him. "Before we go any further. It's pretty important."

"What is it?" Jan straightened herself in her seat and watched her ex-husband expectantly. "Phil?"

"Anais is pregnant."

Jan's world slowed as she processed that information. It would take far longer than a few seconds in Phil's office. This was going to require a lot of contemplation. The only thing Jan knew in this moment was that she wouldn't give Phil the satisfaction of watching her thoughts unfold via her face. "I see. Congratulations."

"I'm sorry, Jan. None of this was ever meant to happen."

"I assume you'll be doing the decent thing and staying with her."

Phil chewed his lip. "It wasn't planned. I swear to you it wasn't."

"You're no longer my husband or my responsibility, Phil. What you do with your life is none of my business. But if you're doing this, if you're ready to become a father, then I wish you the very best."

"It's going to change things with the divorce, obviously. I'll have a child to take into consideration now."

Jan could scream and shout, she could seethe and be bitter, but what was the point of that? She would be the only one hurting. Not Phil or Anais. And no matter what she thought about either of them, it wasn't an unborn child's fault. "Can I give you my terms first and hope we can end this amicably?"

Phil rocked back in his seat, steepled his fingers, and nodded.

"I'd like you to give me whatever half of the house is worth. I don't know if you plan to sell it or keep it for your new… family, but I had it valued while I was in Spain, and the estate agent believes we'd be looking at offers over eight hundred thousand."

"You had it valued? And you've been to Spain?" Phil sat

forward and perched his elbows on the desk. "Why didn't I know about this?"

"Why would you have known about it? I'm not your wife anymore, Phil. The sooner you realise and understand that, the sooner we can all move on with our lives." Jan crossed her legs and settled her hands on her knees. "I'd also like to keep my position here at the office and remain a partner in the business."

"T-that's it? That's all you want?" Phil rubbed at his stubble, his brows drawn. "Half of the house and to keep your job?"

"My *position*, Phil. I built this business with you, and hell will freeze over before your new squeeze gets her hands on *any* of it. So, half of the value of the house and half of the business in the form of me remaining in my position as partner until I decide I no longer want to be here. If that day comes, you can buy me out."

Phil nodded. "Okay."

"When can I expect the money? I currently have nowhere to live...through no fault of my own."

"I'll have it sorted out by the end of the week. I'll call the bank and have everything you need ready to go when you find a place you'd like to put an offer on."

Well, that was that. Jan rose to her feet and smiled. "Thanks. I'd like us to remain as calm as possible through this. I have no desire to fight with you. I suggest you make sure Anais is on the same page as you regarding my position here, or you'll both have one hell of a fight on your hands. Understood?"

Phil pushed his seat back and stood up. "I don't want to fight with you either, Jan. I just want you to have what belongs to you."

Jan took a step towards the door and looked back at Phil. "Did you have the affair with her because you wanted a family?"

Phil lowered his eyes as he shoved his hands in the pockets of his pants. "Jan, I—"

"You knew for over twenty years that I couldn't have children. You told me we were okay as a couple and that we didn't need a child to complete us. If you'd explained that you needed more, none of this would have happened. I would have let you go to find someone who could give you what I couldn't. But to do it this way, to hurt me and humiliate me… I can't forgive you, Phil. I want to, I've spent the best part of my life so far loving you with *everything* I had inside of me, but I can't."

"I fucked up, Jan."

"You did." Jan nodded. "And *now*, you have to step up."

Jan pulled her shoulders back and walked out of Phil's office. She didn't look in the direction of Anais or any other employees, she simply strode out of the building and headed for her car. Once she was back in her hotel room, Jan could fall apart.

"Hey, Eric! Do you want another Guinness before I sit down for five minutes?"

Eric lifted his empty glass and nodded. "Go on then, love."

Morgan smiled and went about the usual routine. She poured half and left it to settle, wiping down the bar counter where a customer had recently vacated. Could she drop Jan a message to say she was thinking of her? She knew Jan was heading into the office today to discuss the divorce with Phil, but Morgan didn't want to come across as though she was fishing for information.

Jan's divorce wasn't her business. Not at all.

She finished pouring Eric's pint of Guinness and set it down in front of him. He handed her a five-pound note, sending Morgan on her way with a wink. She rung it up on the register, took her glass of lemonade from the shelf behind the bar, and perched herself on a stool. She chose not to sit with the customers today. She gave them enough of her attention when she was working her shifts. Morgan just wanted a moment to herself. Yesterday, she had woken up in Spain, and right now…she would rather be there. It hadn't stopped raining all morning, but thank God the sun was beginning to break through the clouds.

As she reached for her phone, her brows rose. Jan had sent her a text about thirty minutes ago.

Are you free to talk? I'm on my way over x

Morgan would always make herself available. That wasn't a question Jan ever needed to ask.

Of course. I'll see you when you get here x

As Morgan locked her phone, Jan walked into the bar and headed directly for her. Honestly, she looked like she'd seen a ghost. "Hey, are you okay?"

Jan's hand shook as she held on tightly to her handbag, frown lines between her brows concerning Morgan. "I, um…I've parked my car up outside. Will it be okay there until tomorrow?"

It was Morgan's turn to frown this time. Jan *knew* it would be okay there. She'd parked it up on a few occasions now. "What's going on?" Morgan slid from her stool and took Jan's hand. "Babe?"

Jan eventually looked up at Morgan. "Could I make coffee upstairs? W-would you mind?"

Morgan guided Jan towards the door to her flat and turned her back on her customers. "You know you're welcome to come here and *be* here whenever you need or want to."

"I need a moment to myself, and then I'll explain. I just… couldn't face going back to that hotel room on my own."

Morgan felt Jan trembling. She hated seeing her like this. Still, Jan would talk to her when she was ready to. "Go up. Do what you need to do. Put the TV on and get comfortable. The moment I'm able to, I'll come up and see you, okay?"

"Don't worry about me. You're working, and I understand that. I just feel…better here. Less alone." Jan smiled weakly. "That's pathetic, isn't it? To feel alone. While he's happy and looking forward to a new future."

Morgan wrapped Jan up in her arms, not caring who could potentially walk in. "You're *never* alone. Not while I'm here. I promise you that. And it's not pathetic. It's completely understandable."

"Thank you for always being here." Jan turned her face into the crook of Morgan's neck. She inhaled, and then Morgan felt her smile against her skin. "You mean a lot to me, Morgan. I hope you know that."

"Hey," Morgan whispered as she drew back. "I've got you. Whatever you need. Okay?"

Jan smiled. "I know. I'll just...head up."

Morgan reached out and opened the door for Jan, sighing as she watched her take the stairs slowly. She had no idea what Jan was about to face, but it had certainly shaken her up. Morgan closed the door again and eyed the clock on the wall. Ben was due in for a shift in the next ten minutes, so Morgan would wait impatiently, and then she would be with Jan for as long as she possibly could. She didn't make it a habit to leave her staff alone on a shift, but Ben had been here since Morgan opened the bar, and he knew what he was doing. Unless they had a huge influx of customers, Morgan wouldn't likely be needed at all.

As if someone had been listening to her wishes, Ben came through the door with a huge smile on his face. "Hi, Eric. Nice to see you here again."

"Is he being funny, Morgan?" Eric piped up from the other end of the bar. "Thinks he's a bloody comedian, this one."

Morgan laughed and smiled back at Ben as he approached her. "God, am I happy to see you."

"Everything okay?" Ben took his rucksack from his shoulder and shoved his phone in the pocket of it. "I'm not late, am I?"

"You've never been late. I just have a few things I need to take care of. Can you hold down the fort here?"

"Oh, yeah. No problem at all." Ben cleared his throat. "Tyler called me when I was on my way in. He's looking for an extra shift or two a week, and I told him I'd run it by you. No harm asking and all that."

Morgan nodded. Someone *had* to be looking over her today. "Any chance he can make it in today? I'll pay you both extra if I can have the rest of the day *and* night off."

"I don't need extra. But I'll call Tyler now and see when he can get here. You go and take care of whatever it is you have going on." Ben sat a hand on Morgan's shoulder. "I'll just text you and let you know what he says."

"Thanks, Ben. I owe you one." Morgan took her phone from the shelf and rushed up the stairs to her flat. When she opened the door, Jan was sitting on the edge of the couch with her head in her hands as she whimpered. "Hey." Morgan was with Jan in seconds, crouched on the floor in front of her. "Babe, come here. Whatever it is, it'll all be okay."

Jan sobbed uncontrollably into Morgan's shoulder. The longer it went on, the more concerned Morgan became, but she would never show Jan that. She needed someone who could listen without judgement. Not someone panicking and worrying alongside her.

As Jan pulled back, trying to catch her breath, she wiped a hand across her cheek. God, the look on her face was devastating. Morgan wasn't sure she even knew how to console Jan in this moment. "Take a minute. Relax. No matter what's going on, you're safe here, and you don't have to talk about it until you're ready to."

"She's pregnant," Jan said, quite clearly deflated beyond belief. "The woman he's been seeing...she's pregnant."

Morgan sat back on her knees and sighed. No wonder Jan was beside herself this afternoon. Anyone with a heart would be. "Fuck. I'm so sorry."

"And it's not even that I'm bothered." Jan reached out a hand and stroked Morgan's cheek. "I'm in a different headspace now that you're in my life. It's just...I have to wonder if he did it because he wants kids."

"It's not something you ever talked about when you were

married?" Morgan frowned. Surely, Phil would have had that conversation with Jan in the early days. "I mean, you can't just decide randomly that you want kids. Or can you? I don't know." This wasn't really Morgan's area of expertise. But she would still do anything she could to ease Jan's pain. If that meant talking this through, then so be it.

"I can't have children. We found that out very early on in our marriage." Jan plucked a tissue from the box on the coffee table and dabbed at her eyes. Her mascara was already down her face, but Morgan would never point that out. It wasn't necessary. "I already feel humiliated and inadequate because he was having an affair with a woman much younger than me. This just adds another blow to how I feel about myself."

Morgan placed a hand on Jan's cheek and sat up on her knees. "I can't imagine how hard this must be for you, but I am here for you. Your friends will be here for you too when you tell them this latest development. But you *have* to let them in, Jan."

"I don't want to let anyone into my bubble with you. Because whether I tell them about Phil knocking up our employee or whether I tell them about us, you're in my bubble. In my life. You're the only thing that makes any sense lately. And in all honesty, that's a pretty fucked up place to be in my head." Jan scoffed. "I mean, you're a woman. I'm only just out of a marriage to a man. Yes, my university days happened, but I still didn't think I'd ever find myself in bed with a woman."

Morgan swallowed. She had to prepare herself for the possibility that Jan wouldn't want to do this anymore. Eventually, she would come to her senses. Morgan knew it. "If you need space and to not be here with me, I get it. I just want you to do the best for you, babe. Nobody else. Just you."

"And what about you?" Jan held Morgan's hand against her face.

"I'm used to women deciding they don't want to be with me. I've lost count of how many have walked away. It's nothing new in my life." Morgan hadn't expected her voice to break, but it did. "Just promise to be honest and upfront with me. If you don't want to do this, if I'm not potentially in your future, please tell me that. Don't ghost me. I'd hate to never see you again."

"I would *never* do that to you."

Morgan's phone pinged on the table. She reached for it quickly, wanting Jan to know she had her full attention.

Tyler is on his way in. He can be here within the hour. He said he'll lock up tonight with Megan.

Morgan shifted to the couch and sat beside Jan, relaxing into the soft leather. She turned her face to Jan when Jan also sat back and sighed, searching her eyes. "You wanna get out of here for a while?"

"Wouldn't that be lovely?" Jan inched her hand towards Morgan's and took it. "And for the record, I'm not walking away from you. You're the only person I look forward to seeing lately."

Morgan's heart thrummed. God, she'd got lucky here. She just hoped it could last. "I look forward to seeing you, too."

"You should probably get back down to the bar." A sadness settled in Jan's eyes. "I'll get myself together and head back to the hotel."

"I have the rest of the afternoon and night off." Morgan shifted closer to Jan and wrapped an arm around her shoulders. "I asked Tyler to work so I could be here for you."

Jan sat up and turned to Morgan, a look of disbelief flashing across her face. "You...took the rest of the day off for me?"

"Yeah. Wanted to be here because you walked into the bar in a terrible state."

"Morgan, I—"

"We don't need to talk about it. I *want* to be here with you." Morgan leaned in and kissed Jan gently. "After the week we've just spent together, I hated not being with you last night." Morgan was always mindful of what she said to Jan, aware that this could turn in a split second. "I know I have no right to feel that way, to miss you, but I can't help how I feel."

"Does it make me needy if I say that knowing you miss me makes me feel better about all of this?"

Morgan smiled. "No, not at all."

"I...missed you too last night."

Okay, Morgan hadn't expected Jan to feel the same way. How could she when she had so much to deal with? "O-oh."

"Don't sound so surprised. Is it not quite clear that I enjoy being with you?"

"Well, yeah. I just...I don't know. I couldn't tell you the last time anyone missed me."

Jan smiled into another kiss, her hand palming Morgan's thigh. "Knowing what you're capable of, I bet Amanda misses you."

"Amanda has been the furthest thing from my mind since you came up here with me the night you were in the bar. Trust me, what I had with Amanda is *not* what I have with you."

"Maybe we *should* get out of here for a while. If we don't, we're going to be very naked very soon."

"You make that sound like a hardship for me," Morgan whispered against Jan's lips. Her palms grew clammy, her pulse thundered in her ears, but Jan was right. Maybe getting out for a couple of hours was a good idea. Some fresh air would do them both the world of good. A little rain wouldn't stop them. "But yeah, let's get outside for a bit. Then hopefully, I can have you all to myself here later."

Seated at a table in the window of a local coffee shop, Jan stared down at her hands in her lap, trying to get her head together. She didn't know how she felt about Phil and the pregnancy, but she did know that she couldn't let it eat away at her. No matter what, they were getting divorced. Did Jan really need to let Phil becoming a father get to her so much? She didn't want to—she planned to discuss it with Morgan and then forget any of it existed—but Jan also had to consider how it would affect her down the line. She hadn't *really* dealt with anything that had happened recently, and at some point, it would surely come crashing down around her.

Or maybe it won't. She smiled as Morgan came sauntering towards her.

"Cappuccino," Morgan said as she lowered a cup to the table in front of Jan. "And a slice of lemon drizzle cake."

Jan looked up at Morgan and regarded her with an appreciative smile. "Thank you."

"I'm hoping it'll put the colour back in your face." Morgan slid a hand across the table as she sat down, only to hesitate and pull it away again. "Sorry. I forget sometimes."

Jan took the lead and held onto Morgan's hand before it fell away from the table. "I'm tired of hiding. If I want to sit here holding your hand, then I'll do that."

Morgan entwined their fingers. "I just... I think you have enough going on right now. The last thing you need is someone coming in here and seeing us together. You can do without it."

Jan couldn't care less who walked in here. And yes, that included Gillian or Finn. Or both. Christ, Phil and his newly formed family could walk in here, and Jan wouldn't bat an eyelid in this moment. Morgan was her safe space, and Morgan was her future. "I appreciate what you're saying, but I'm going to see Gillian tomorrow, anyway. She'll know about us then."

Morgan's face paled suddenly.

Jan pushed the lemon drizzle towards her and smiled. "Maybe you need this more than me."

"No, I..." Morgan fell silent and shook her head.

"You don't want me to tell her." It wasn't a question; it was an observation. "Will that be a long-term thing, or..."

Morgan's gaze shot up at Jan. "No, that's not what I'm trying to say. Not at all. The moment I can be with you like this everywhere is a moment I *cannot* wait for, babe. Believe me when I say that."

"Then what's the problem?"

"I'm worried about you. I think you're dealing with too much, and us being together isn't something that needs to be discussed with anyone else right now. I'm not going anywhere; I'm perfectly happy to wait until the rest of your life has sorted itself out. So please...don't do this because you think it's the right thing to do or that you'll lose me if you don't. That's so far from the truth." Morgan leaned over and kissed the back of Jan's hand as she lifted it. "Figure out the divorce and this new development first. *Then* we can focus on us."

Jan understood what Morgan was saying, but the decision was final. She didn't want to wait any longer to tell Gillian about Morgan. "Is it strange that I don't really feel anything about the pregnancy? Does that make me heartless...or cold, at least?"

"No, gorgeous. It doesn't make you either of those things." Morgan regarded Jan with the most beautiful smile. "I *do* have to admire how you're handling everything, though. Even though I'm worried about you, you're the strongest woman I know."

Jan appreciated Morgan's worry, but she was doing just fine. If, down the line, everything came crumbling down around her, she would deal with it then. But until that moment came, Jan was taking each day one step at a time...while holding onto Morgan's hand whenever it was possible.

"I promised myself I wouldn't wallow and cry myself to sleep at night. I promised that I would pick myself up and live my life. Sitting back while everything falls apart around me just isn't an option. It was *never* an option. And I know people will find that hard to understand; as women, we're used to being the emotional ones or made to feel as though the world has ended. But I'm not doing that. I don't *want* to do that." Jan placed the lemon drizzle cake between them to share. "If I had done any of that, I wouldn't be here with you right now. I wouldn't have shared the most wonderful memories abroad with you. You...wouldn't exist in my world. Not in this capacity anyway."

"That's something positive to take out of it all, I guess."

"It's the most important thing to take away from it all." God, Jan wanted to be alone with this woman. She wanted to be held on the couch, talking about everything and anything that came to mind. "You've been there for me from the very day everything happened. But you've become such a huge part of my life that I barely remember that day. It's not something that eats away at me. Maybe that won't always be the case, maybe I will have some almighty meltdown when I least expect it, but I have you in my life, and I couldn't ask for anything more."

"Right back at you." Morgan's smile lit up the entire coffee shop as she looked down at their hands. "And this is nice. This is... yeah, it feels right."

"It's never felt wrong with you. I don't know why that is, but I'm grateful for you. Every single day when I wake up, I'm far more than grateful for you." Jan wanted to finish up here and get Morgan alone. "When I'm with you, I feel things I've never felt before."

Morgan gazed into Jan's eyes. "Yeah?"

"So much, Morgan. Far too much for me to process."

"Good feelings, though, right?"

Jan beamed a smile as she squeezed Morgan's hand. "The very best feelings. Trust me."

"We should eat this cake and head off. I know a few things I'd like you to be feeling in the not-too-distant future."

Jan giggled at that, taking her bottom lip between her teeth when Morgan offered her that sexy smirk. "I can also think of one or two things that would certainly take my mind off anything I don't want to be thinking about."

"It's that one particular thing, isn't it? You know, the one with my tongue when I—"

Jan pressed a finger to Morgan's lips suddenly. "*Don't* finish that sentence." She leaned over the table and kissed Morgan, then drew back and whispered, "I can't concentrate when I think about you inside me."

"Fuck," Morgan spoke through gritted teeth, her eyes closing as Jan's breath washed over her lips. "If nothing else, you know how to make me wet in an instant."

"Mmhmm. Welcome to the club, baby."

CHAPTER 24

Jan had no idea how today would pan out, but she was thinking of all the potential positives. Gillian would know about Morgan, Finn too, and nobody would have to sneak around or feel as though they were keeping a secret any longer. She had already called Gillian on the way over here, wanting to ensure she could come right out and say it rather than wait for another day or time if her best friend was unavailable. Gillian was home, Finn was at university, so here Jan was...unsure as to how she should even say the words out loud.

She knocked on Gillian's front door and took several deep breaths. Not only did she need to tell Gillian about Morgan, but she had the bombshell to drop regarding the fact that Phil was going to be a father. Jan didn't know which would be more shocking to Gillian. Hopefully, it was the pregnancy. Jan didn't need *anyone* to be shocked or have an opinion when it came to Morgan.

The door opened suddenly, and Gillian threw her arms around Jan's neck. "Oh, it's so good to see you!"

Unable to breathe, Jan pulled back and frowned. "It's only

been ten days since I saw you. We've gone far longer than that in the past."

"Are you still at that fucking hotel?" Gillian urged Jan inside the house and closed the front door. "I seriously don't know why you don't take one of our spare rooms. It seems silly to spend all that money on a room until God only knows when."

Jan lifted a shoulder. "It's on the business credit card, so Phil is paying, too."

"Oh, that's brilliant!" They retreated to the back living room, and as Gillian turned to face Jan, she started to laugh. "Maybe you should upgrade to the best suite they have."

"Believe me, I *have* thought about it."

Gillian rested back against the dining table and regarded Jan with a sympathetic smile. "How are you doing, love?

Jan lowered her handbag beside one of the chairs and took a seat. "You know what, I'm great. I'm feeling refreshed and ready for whatever comes next."

"When I left Dave, I didn't want to face the world. I couldn't even imagine looking anyone in the eye."

"I know. You avoided *me* whenever you could." Jan gave Gillian a knowing look. "But look, it happened. I can't change it even if I wanted to."

"And...do you want to?" Gillian pulled a seat closer to Jan and sat down. She took Jan's hands and stared deep into her eyes. "I can't believe I'm asking you this, but do you *want* to forgive him and try again?"

"No. Things have changed significantly for me over the last several weeks. And even if they hadn't, I still wouldn't have given him another chance."

"W-what does that mean? What's changed?"

"Gill, I...slept with Morgan. From the bar. The Corner bar." Jan didn't know why she was giving specifics; Gillian knew *exactly* who Morgan was.

Still, Gillian's face fell as Jan spoke that out loud. She couldn't begin to imagine what was going through Gillian's head, but as she drew her hands away from Jan's, Jan knew she wasn't going to have the support she expected. Not so easily, anyway.

"Please say something, Gill."

"I...I don't know what to say." Gillian sunk back in her seat and sighed. "When did it happen?"

Jan lowered her eyes. "The week after I found out about the affair."

"Wow. That was...swift."

Jan frowned. What the hell was Gillian implying? "I'm sorry?"

"I just...did you give yourself a moment to realise the severity of your marriage ending before you fell into bed with another woman?"

Jan scoffed. While she understood that all of this *was* huge, she hadn't expected Gillian to lead with that. Jan wasn't sure what reaction she'd wanted, but something a little more supportive would have been nice. Perhaps even to be asked if she was happy. "Of course I did. I know ending my marriage is big, and it's messy, but..." Jan shook her head. She wasn't going to come clean about the amount of time she'd spent with Morgan. If she did, she had a feeling Gillian would just continue to judge her. "I think I'm just going to leave." She reached down for her bag and rose to her feet. "You know, of all the people I have left, I expected more from you, Gill."

"You've just dropped something *huge* on me, and you expect me to jump for joy?" Gillian stared back at Jan with a frown. "Seriously?"

"What I *didn't* expect was immediate judgement from you. Anything else I could have handled, but you went right for my throat, didn't you?"

"Forgive me, but I'm confused." Gillian carded a hand through her dark hair and exhaled a deep breath. "You and...*Morgan*. Really?"

"Yes, really."

"Well, this is going to be an interesting conversation with Finn."

Jan didn't really care how the conversation with Finn went. Whatever Finn had to say, that was her business alone. "I don't know why it matters to either of you."

"Look, Jan. You *know* I love you, but you spent twenty-seven years with Phil, and what? You're just going to shack up with some bartender just *weeks* after you left Phil?"

"*He's* the one who has been fucking another woman for a year. *He's* the one who destroyed those years we were together. Why am *I* the one being judged here for my decisions?" Jan couldn't do this. She refused to stand here and be chastised for wanting a life again. "And for the record, Morgan is so much more than just a bartender. I'd appreciate it if you gave her a chance. You don't know the first thing about her."

"Because until today, she *was* just a bartender to me, Jan. She was the woman who used to bring us drinks on a night out. But now...now she's what? Your girlfriend?" Gillian's brows drew together. "I mean, is it serious?"

"It's...going somewhere, yes." That was all Jan was prepared to offer right now. Just because Gillian was her best friend, it didn't make her automatically entitled to Jan's feelings.

Gillian nodded slowly. "Right. Does Phil know yet?"

"He knows I'm completely done with him. As for him knowing about Morgan, it's none of his business." Jan turned and walked towards the door that led to the hallway. She shoved her handbag up on her shoulder and turned back to Gillian. "I'm sure you and Finn will have a lot to talk about when it comes to this development, but please respect what I have going on with Morgan and leave her out of this. Whatever you think of her or me, she doesn't need to hear it. She's done nothing wrong. And neither have I."

"There was never any hope for me and Dave, but until the day you found out about the affair, you were madly in love with Phil."

Gillian ran her hands down her thighs and sighed. "Has something been going on that I don't know about? Was everything okay at home before you found out he'd been sleeping with someone else?"

Jan chewed her lip. She didn't want to do this right now, but she would give Gillian more information when she was ready to. "He had an affair, and that's that."

"Then all I can ask is that you give yourself some time." Gillian regarded Jan with a faint smile. "Figure out what comes next, maybe without Morgan being around."

Jan's bottom lip quivered as she blinked back tears. "Phil is about to become a father, Gill. I'm *not* putting my life on hold for him or anyone else. You included."

The shock on Gillian's face was precisely what Jan had expected. "He...what?" She shot up from her seat and crossed the room. As she took Jan's hand and held it tight, Gillian shook her head. "No. This can't be happening." Gillian pinched the bridge of her nose and exhaled a long, slow breath. "That piece of shit has got his new woman pregnant?"

"Yes." Jan jerked her hand from Gillian's. "I'm going to head off. You're up to date on my life, and whatever you think of me, I can't change it." Jan searched Gillian's eyes, unable to read what her best friend was thinking. "I know this is a lot, and I know I landed it on you suddenly, but I came here hoping for your support, Gill. Not your judgement."

"Jan—"

"I'll see you when I see you. Say hi to Finn for me."

Jan turned and left Gillian's home as quickly as she could. Just last year, Jan had been consoling Gillian night after night when Finn left her. For so many weeks, she had tried to navigate their issues with her best friend. Perhaps it was foolish for Jan to expect the same from Gillian, but she wouldn't make that mistake again. Right now, Jan felt as though she was in this alone, but she would fight every damn day for a happiness that suited her. If that could possibly involve Morgan, then Jan was going to grab it with both hands and never let it go.

What a beautiful day...

Morgan sat on a stool at the end of the bar, not too concerned that none of her customers were in yet. The weather was glorious, and unfortunately, Morgan didn't have the space outside the bar to add outdoor furniture. But it was set to rain in a few hours, and she knew they would come rushing back indoors then.

Right now, the peace and quiet was exactly what she needed. Just a few days ago, Morgan had returned from the most amazing week with Jan, and while her...lover had a lot to contend with in the near future, Morgan wasn't worried. It was hard to find anything to worry about after their conversation on the flight home. Jan was *not* going back on her divorce. She *did* want to keep seeing Morgan. They'd hit it off, and Morgan guessed the rest would be history. They'd made a connection—one so deep that Morgan was in a different headspace post-Spain—and to know that Jan felt the same way was blowing her mind. All of this...it was so much more than just fucking.

The bar door swung open, and Finn came bursting through it suddenly. "You and I need to talk, so you'd better make yourself available right now."

Morgan frowned as she turned her watch towards herself. "It's a bit early for you, isn't it? Don't you have a lecture you should be at?"

"Are you serious?" Finn scoffed. "You're *actually* seeing Jan?"

Ah. They knew.

Morgan had a feeling it was only a matter of time before they had to explain themselves, but that was the beauty of Jan. She made Morgan forget everything that was going on around her. To Morgan, Jan didn't feel like some terrible secret. No, she just felt like a woman Morgan wanted to keep to herself for as long as possible. "First of all, lose the fucking attitude, Finn."

"I'm sorry, but I'm really fucking confused." Finn threw up her hands and laughed. "We *are* talking about the same Jan, right? Jan Bartlett...Gillian's best friend? Y-you...and Jan Bartlett?"

Morgan wasn't sure how Finn had meant that to come across, but it hurt. *Deeply*. Neither Finn nor Gillian had any idea what Morgan and Jan had shared to date. Perhaps if they had, Finn wouldn't find this so funny. "And there I was, thinking you were my friend." Morgan slid from her stool and made her way back behind the bar. "If you have nothing nice to say about all of this, you can fuck off and find somewhere else to drink with your wife."

"No, I need you to lay this all out for me. Like...honestly, how did that even happen?"

Morgan shrugged. "I don't know what you want me to say, Finn. How do you think it happened? You've been a lesbian a long time...you know where I'm going with this."

Finn strode across the room and braced her hands against the bar counter. "I'm going to say this to you as your friend. You need to end this now."

Morgan nodded slowly, her chest aching for the position she found herself in. Of all the people in Morgan's life, she thought Finn would be the one to understand. She thought Finn would back her when it came to this. Even when she'd worried about them finding out, she didn't think the reaction would be this severe. "You want me to stop seeing her. Of course you do." Morgan sighed. "I told Jan this would happen."

"Jan has just left her husband of near on thirty years. She doesn't know what she's doing from one day to the next." Finn may well believe that, but nothing about Jan suggested that she was confused or unsure about where she was at right now. "Please tell me you didn't take advantage of her."

"I'm sorry?"

"Was it a one-night stand or something?" Finn asked, her

brows drawn. "I mean, it doesn't really matter what it was...you have to end it, Morgan."

"Why? Because *you* say so?" Morgan lifted a brow. She didn't appreciate Finn coming here and telling her what to do about her personal life, but it would be the last time that she did. "Have you even asked Jan how she feels about any of this? You sure as shit haven't asked me!"

"I... What?"

"You've just come in here claiming I should do what you want me to do with no idea what's happening or how long it's been going on." Morgan rested her forearm on a beer pump and glared at Finn. "I know you both think that Jan is some fragile flower, but I can assure you that she's not."

"It doesn't change the fact that she's having a really fucking hard time right now."

Morgan sort of understood where Finn was coming from, but when Jan was with her, she didn't see that hard time. No, she saw fun and laughter. She saw flirting and the batting of Jan's eyelashes. What she saw when she looked at Jan Bartlett...was a woman who wanted to live her life and the excitement that came with it. "I know what's going on with her ex-husband, I've *always* known, but that doesn't mean Jan doesn't know what's best for her."

Finn pulled herself up onto a stool. "How did this happen, Morgan?"

No. Morgan wasn't doing this. She wouldn't sit here and discuss her relationship with Jan unless Jan was also present. But she *would* remind Finn of the support she'd given her back when she fell in love with Gillian. "You know when you met Gillian and eventually told me how it came about?" Finn nodded. "Did I *once* judge you for fucking your lecturer? Did I *once* tell you that it was a mistake and that you should cut her off?"

"No."

"Imagine if I had. How would you have reacted to that?"

Morgan watched on as that sunk into Finn's mind. Was she finally realising that she couldn't control what two people did? God, Morgan hoped so. "Imagine if I'd told you that it would only end in disaster or that it was wrong...or that Gillian had no idea what she wanted."

Finn sighed. "Morgan."

Morgan turned her back on Finn. She needed a moment to gather her thoughts and her emotions. She hadn't expected this at all, and as she stood here right now, she had to wonder what Gillian would fill Jan's head with. It wouldn't be anything good; Morgan knew Gillian didn't like her. She just...didn't know why. "I'm honestly not interested, Finn. Whatever you think of us, please keep it to yourself. I don't have time to give a shit what people think of me, and yes, that includes *you*."

"You're both going to get hurt."

"Are we? Can you see into the future?" Morgan rounded the counter again and took a seat on a stool next to Finn. "I know it's a shock, and I know Gillian is probably thinking about all the ways she can keep me away from Jan, but I'm not going anywhere. For however long Jan wants me in her life, I'm going to be there for her. You and Gillian *cannot* and *will not* stop that."

"When did it happen?" Finn asked. "When did you sleep with one another?"

Morgan lifted a shoulder. "Can't remember, and I've lost count since."

"Y-you've been seeing one another?" Finn's face paled. "For how long?"

"When did she leave that wanker of an ex-husband?" Morgan's brows drew together. "Six weeks ago? Seven?"

"It's coming up to eight, actually."

Morgan smiled. "Seven weeks then."

Finn sighed and lowered her head on her shoulders. "I can't believe you've kept this from me. I mean, Jan is *straight*, Morgan.

And once the divorce proceedings start, her head will be up her arse."

"And when that happens, I'll be there for her. The way I have been so far."

"But you're not hearing what I'm saying. Jan is straight!"

Morgan smirked. Jan was far from straight. At least, when she was beneath Morgan, she wasn't straight. Or when she'd spent an hour watching Morgan down at the water's edge on the beach. Or when she'd tugged on the string holding Morgan's bikini bottoms in place and gone down on her just hours after they'd landed in Gran Canaria. No, Jan *wasn't* straight. "I can assure you, she's not."

"I can't deal with this." Finn exhaled a breath. "And I can't even begin to understand how it happened in the first place."

"Why do *you* have to deal with it? And why do *you* have to understand it? I'm happy with Jan, and she's happy with me. Can't you and Gillian just be happy *for* us?"

Finn slid from her stool and made her way towards the exit. As she turned back and eyed Morgan, Finn shook her head. "Someone is going to get hurt here. I fear it's going to be you."

Maybe Morgan would get hurt, but for the first time in so many years, she felt as though she was in a place where she could be happy. And sure, maybe it would fall apart, and Jan would realise that Morgan wasn't good enough for her, but Morgan had to try. She needed to enjoy what she currently had because if it did end, she knew she'd never find anyone quite like Jan ever again.

"Hey, Finn?"

Finn turned as she pulled the bar door open.

"You and your wife should probably find somewhere else to drink from now on." Morgan hated to do this to someone she considered a friend, but she wouldn't entertain *anyone* in her bar who thought it was okay to throw their opinions on her life around. "And if Gillian has a problem with that, she knows where to find me."

CHAPTER 25

With a huge smile on her face, Morgan's heart beat a little harder when Jan walked through the bar door. After Finn's arrival here yesterday, she didn't think she would see Jan any time soon. But it was the text Jan had sent Morgan last night explaining that she wouldn't be heading over to the bar that really had Morgan worried. She one hundred percent expected Jan to cut all ties with her.

Morgan's smile suddenly faded when she realised that could still happen. Jan looked worn out. She didn't look like the same woman she'd spent several weeks with now. She seemed bothered by something. Morgan just hoped they could remain amicable if Jan was here to let her down gently. It tracked in terms of who Jan was as a person. Morgan didn't believe she had it in her to text and say she wouldn't be around anymore.

"Hi." Morgan swallowed when Jan pulled herself up onto a stool. Thankfully, the bar was quiet right now. "Can I get you anything to drink?"

"No, thank you." Jan tried to stifle a yawn but failed. "I didn't sleep at all last night, so I've already had three coffees back at the hotel."

"I thought their coffee was terrible?"

"It is. But it was better than nothing at all." Jan set her bag down on the bar counter and finally looked up at Morgan. "I'm sorry I couldn't make it over last night. Once I'd been to Gillian's, I just needed some time alone."

Morgan nodded and waited with bated breath.

"It didn't quite go as planned." Jan's voice trembled as she put that out into the world. "Her reaction was...unexpected. It knocked me off kilter."

"What was her reaction?"

Jan sighed and propped her head in her hand. "I don't really know how to describe it. She sort of implied that I'd wasted no time in moving on. It's just...the way she said it that I didn't like. As though maybe she was judging me and slut shaming me."

"I'm sorry," Morgan said as she rounded the bar and placed a supportive hand on Jan's shoulder. She wanted to do so much more than that, but she wasn't sure she was entitled to do so. "I, uh...I know what happens now."

"Pardon?"

"I know what happens now," Morgan repeated. "And you really don't have to do this, Jan. I got involved with you knowing you were dealing with a lot. I probably shouldn't have encouraged you." Morgan ran a hand down her face, saddened that this was ending. Because for her, it hadn't been some meaningless fuck. It hadn't been passing the time with Jan to keep her company. It had been so much more. "But I need you to know that I don't regret any of it. What we've had over the last couple of months, I can't explain it. You've reminded me that I can be happy again. That means a lot to me. *You*...mean a lot to me."

"I don't understand what you're trying to say."

"You've come here to tell me you can't do this anymore, right?"

Jan lifted a hand and cupped Morgan's cheek. Her blue eyes

were brighter than they had been when she arrived. "I haven't come here to do that to you."

Morgan frowned. "You haven't?"

"No. Never."

"It's just that Finn—"

Jan suddenly lowered her hand. "Finn, what?"

"She came here yesterday afternoon. I'm guessing it was after you'd been to speak to Gillian." Morgan reached behind her for the nearby stool and dragged it closer. Once she was sitting comfortably, her hand in Jan's, she continued, "She said I should end things with you. There was a brief mention of taking advantage of you, too."

Jan cast her gaze on their hands and shook her head. "God, I'm sorry she said those things to you."

"I don't care what she thinks of me, I don't care what anyone thinks of me, but are you sure that I'm the one you want to *possibly* do this with? I mean, I know we've spoken about it on a couple of occasions now, but I don't really know what's happening here. I'm scared to ask because of what you're going through and how sudden this is."

"What is it that you want to ask specifically?"

Morgan searched Jan's eyes. Could she really ask the question she wanted to ask? She had nothing to lose, she guessed. "Just like...are we dating? Or could we be instead of whatever this currently is?"

The smile that spread on Jan's mouth didn't quite settle Morgan's heart rate. She would need a little more to go on before that happened. "I don't see why we couldn't say we're dating."

"But is that what you want, Jan?" Morgan squeezed Jan's hand and dipped her head to find her gaze. "Seriously, is it what *you* want?"

"Yes. It is."

"Even with everything you're dealing with? Even though you're barely out of a marriage? I'm happy to wait until the time is right for you or until you decide that this isn't the right thing for you. I just...I need you to tell me how this is going to work."

"We're dating. If people can't deal with that, then it's their own tough shit."

"And by people, you mean your best friend and her wife?" Morgan wasn't sure this was going to go to plan if Jan didn't have Gillian and Finn's support. Jan was so close to her best friend that this was surely going to create a huge rift between them.

"Them and anyone else who has something to say about it." Jan slid from her stool and stood between Morgan's legs. She drew Morgan into a soft kiss, smiling against her lips before she pulled back a little. "I understand that people are confused and concerned, but why should I put my life on hold just to appease them? Why should I do exactly what Gill did and lock myself away...refusing to deal with the world? That just doesn't make sense to me."

"Nor me." Morgan smiled. "I just don't want you to lose the people who mean the most to you."

"I won't. They'll realise that I have the chance to be happy again, and everything will be okay."

Morgan lifted her brows and exhaled a deep breath. "I hope you're right."

"In time, you'll realise that I'm always right." Jan winked and rounded the bar. "Now, I quite fancy an espresso. May I help myself?"

Morgan laughed. "You may."

Settled into a booth at Morgan's bar, Jan brought up several estate agent websites, prepared to trawl through the copious amounts of homes available to buy. Now that she was refreshed from her holiday, it was time to look at what was available. Jan wanted a place to live in, and today, that process began. She refused to put it off any longer.

She brought her cappuccino closer, smiling as she eyed Morgan behind the bar. She wouldn't stay here all day—Morgan was going to be sick of the sight of her soon—but she had wanted to be here while she looked for a place to live. If she was torn between several, she could at least ask Morgan's opinion. That would have usually been Gillian's job, but their friendship was strained at the moment.

I could strangle Finn!

Now wasn't the time to recollect the information Morgan had given her about Finn coming here yesterday. She could deal with that another time. And she would, without a doubt. While she understood that her friends wanted to protect her, their concern should be directed towards Phil for ever putting her in this situation, *not* Morgan.

As she scrolled through the first website on her list, the dread started to settle in all over again. Jan was almost forty-nine. She didn't want to have to pack up her life and go through the hassle of redecorating and picking out new floors. She shouldn't *have* to do it. What she should have been doing right now was planning a dinner party or a garden party. Exactly as she did every year. But she didn't have a dining table or a garden she could use right now. She didn't even have a bed she could call her own.

"Hey," Morgan said as she appeared at the booth. "I brought you a bottle of water, and Ben has just been out to pick up lunch, so I asked him to get you something, too." Morgan set down a plate with a chicken club sandwich sitting on it. "You should eat something while you're sitting here doing that. I know you'll only forget otherwise."

"Thank you." Jan reached out and took Morgan's hand. Did she already know Jan well enough to assume that she would forget to eat lunch? Huh, women *were* far more attentive. "I might need your help if I come across something I'm interested in. Only if the bar is quiet, though."

"Mid-week is always quieter. Just give me a shout if you need some advice. Though, you probably shouldn't take it from me. I live in a one-bed flat above a bar."

Jan frowned. "Hey, I *love* your flat. It's cosy, and it's where we've spent many nights together. Your flat means a lot to me."

Morgan dipped her head as her cheeks reddened. "I know. It's still not really what I had in mind for myself."

"Well, it suits you just fine at the moment." As Jan was about to offer Morgan a seat, her phone started to ring on the table. It... was Phil. "Hello?"

"Hi. Um, are you around for a quick chat? About the divorce?"

Jan cleared her throat. "Yes, what's up?"

"Can we do this face-to-face instead? I know you don't want to see me, and I understand that, but I don't want it to be this way, Jan. I don't want to lay out terms and shit over the phone to you or via a lawyer neither of us know the first thing about. I'm close to the hotel you're staying at, so I can be there in a few minutes. I'll wait in the reception for you."

"I'm not at the hotel. I'm at a bar around the corner." Jan eyed Morgan and mouthed 'Phil'.

"What's the name of it? I'll come right there now. I don't want to keep you waiting any longer than you already have."

"Give me a minute." Jan brought her phone away from her ear and covered the mouthpiece. "Phil wants to meet with me about the divorce. Should I tell him I'll meet him elsewhere?"

Morgan shook her head. "No need. Tell him to come here. Saves you packing everything up and traipsing across town." Morgan pushed the plate towards Jan. "And you still need to eat."

Jan appreciated that Morgan was willing to accommodate Phil, but she didn't want to make her uncomfortable. Not at all. "Are you sure? I don't mind meeting him somewhere else."

Morgan stepped closer and laid a hand on Jan's shoulder. "I promise you, it's fine."

Jan cleared her throat and brought her phone back to her ear. "I'm at The Corner bar. It's—"

"Yep. I know where it is. I'll be there in five minutes."

The call ended, and Jan looked up to where Morgan had situated herself back behind the bar. This really wasn't ideal, but Morgan was right. Jan would have to pack up her laptop and leave the lunch Ben had so kindly picked up for her if she wanted to do this elsewhere.

She sighed when she saw Phil's distinctive royal blue Range Rover pull up outside. Jan had no idea what he wanted to talk about; they'd already decided on who was having what. But she would give him the time to discuss this if that's what he needed. At some point in the near future, they'd have no reason to talk to one another unless it was something to do with the business.

Phil strode through the door and smiled at Morgan. She returned the slightest one of her own, and then she moved to the other end of the bar and started talking with a customer. He eyed Jan, his face still holding that tiredness she wasn't used to seeing. "Hi, love. Thanks for meeting me."

Jan waved a hand towards the seat facing her. "Have a seat."

He peered over the top of her laptop as he sat down, regarding her with a small smile. "Found anything you like yet?"

"No. None of them are my home." Jan shut her laptop lid and clasped her hands on the table. "So, what can I do for you?"

"I've already spoken to my lawyer this morning. Set new terms. He wants me to fight for X, Y, and Z, but I'm not interested in all that. I just want you to have what you *rightfully* deserve."

Jan sat back in her seat and exhaled a deep breath. They'd already agreed on terms—why had Phil changed them now? "What's going on, Phil?"

"The house. I don't want you to have half of it. I want you to have all of it. I've already found a smaller place, and the offer has been accepted on it. The deeds will be changed into solely your name." Phil lifted a hand towards Morgan. When she arrived at the table, he looked to Jan. "Glass of wine?" Jan didn't see why not, so she nodded. "Red wine and a beer, please, Morgan."

"No problem." Morgan turned away, not making eye contact with Jan.

"As we've agreed, you'll stay on within the business. Your usual role and remain as partner. I've already had my lawyer go through the finances, and your half of what's in the joint account should be with you within a few days. To your own personal account."

"R-right." Jan's head was whirring with this information. She hadn't asked for half of the finances, even though she was entitled to them. She just wanted money to buy a place, but now...she wouldn't have to? This was a pleasant surprise. It certainly made life easier for her.

"I've upgraded your car. They'll be at the house next week to collect the old one and drop off the new one. Business fleet, as usual." Phil reached for his beer the moment Morgan set it down on the table and slid Jan's glass of wine towards her. "Thanks."

"Why the sudden change of the terms?" Jan wasn't ungrateful, she just hadn't expected any of this.

"I fucked this all up, Jan. Our marriage. I thought I knew what I wanted, and I didn't think about you in the process. I'd like to believe I'm still a half-decent man, and I want you to have what belongs to you. I don't want you to go without or spend your time looking for somewhere to live. That house wouldn't have been *anything* without the love you put into it. For us. And I fucked that."

Jan nodded slowly. "You did. I just hope you and Anais will be happy with whatever you decide between you."

"It's...strained at the moment. But what will be will be." Phil swigged his beer and sat back against the booth. "How are you?"

"I'm doing okay." Jan appreciated him asking, but even if she wasn't okay—and she was—she wouldn't tell him that. "I'm not sure what day it is at the moment, but it'll be nice to get back home and move on."

"I *am* sorry, Jan." Phil chanced a hand across the table and settled it over Jan's. She stiffened ever so slightly but allowed it. "I do have to ask... If Anais wasn't pregnant, would there have been *any* chance of us getting back together?"

"No. None." Jan glanced in Morgan's direction to find her staring at their hands. She slowly pulled it away. "You know how I feel about affairs, Phil. You know exactly what I told you when Dave cheated on Gill."

"I know. I still had to ask." He smiled weakly and sighed. "I can't believe how stupid I've been."

"Was it me? Did I not give you enough or make you happy enough?"

Phil's brows rose at that. He seemed shocked by Jan's question, but she couldn't fathom why. Wasn't that the first assumption when it came to cheating? "No, love. Never."

"Then why?" Jan didn't particularly care for his reasons. Phil had done it regardless, but she would like to move on with her life, knowing the truth.

"Honestly?" Phil puffed out his cheeks. "Because I could? Because I wasn't thinking about the life I already had? Because I'm a fucking idiot who has just lost the best thing to ever happen to him..."

Well, it was nice to know he thought that of Jan at least.

"We had a good run, didn't we?" Jan's voice broke as she said that, but it wasn't a sadness for where she was at right now. It was a sadness for the years she'd put into something...only for it to end the way it had. "We had fun."

"We did, Jan. We had a lot of fun." Phil finished his beer and took some cash from his wallet. He left it on the table and got to his feet. "You'll look after yourself, yes?"

"I will." Jan did regard him with a genuine smile this time. Phil was a good man. He'd just proven that by handing the house over to Jan, but it wasn't meant to be any longer, and that was okay. "And before you hear it from anyone else, I'm dating."

Just...dating? Or are you off the market before you even had the chance to be on it?

Jan probably should have spoken to Morgan before she'd informed Phil, but she didn't get the impression that Morgan would mind. Gillian and Finn knew now, so it was only a matter of time before they were seen out in the city with one another. Jan had no reason to hide with Morgan. Looking back, she never should have approached this in that way.

"O-oh." Phil's shoulders slumped even though Jan knew he hadn't wanted anyone to be aware of that. "Who is he?"

"That's all you need to know for the time being. When I'm ready, people will know more. Can you give me that? The chance to figure this all out before I reveal anymore?"

Phil held up his hands and nodded. "Of course."

Jan looked back at Phil. She couldn't believe what had just happened here today, but she was grateful that he was doing the right thing. "Oh, Phil?"

"Mm?" He stared back at her as he checked his pockets.

"Did you and her ever...you know, in the house?"

"No. Never. That day you walked in and she was there, that was the first time she'd ever stepped foot inside the house." Phil shook his head. "I know I made a huge mistake, but I would never bring another woman into our home. Never, Jan."

"Okay. Well, just let me know when you want to collect your things from the house. I'll give you space to do what you need to do and make myself scarce that day."

"Thanks." Phil hitched a thumb over his shoulder. "I'll go, but if you need anything, just call me."

"Goodbye, Phil." Jan watched her soon-to-be ex-husband leave Morgan's bar, her shoulders relaxing the moment the coast was clear. She hadn't realised she'd been so tense while he was here, but she hadn't expected the call from him today.

"Everything go okay then?" Morgan's voice brought Jan out of her thoughts.

She turned to her left and looked up at the beautiful bartender. "Yes. What time are you finishing today?"

"Around five, providing nothing goes wrong."

Jan beamed a smile as she said, "Would you like to come over to my place for dinner tonight?"

"I'm sorry, your place?" Morgan lowered herself into the booth beside Jan. "I don't follow."

"I'll explain later. I have a sandwich to enjoy right now."

CHAPTER 26

Still utterly confused by Jan's request earlier today, Morgan stopped outside a house in an area she wasn't familiar with and gathered her thoughts. Jan had sent her the address not long after she'd left the bar this afternoon, but she hadn't revealed any other information in the meantime. Morgan *hoped* Jan was back here to stay, but if she was...what were the terms? Would Phil still be around? Fuck, Morgan hoped not.

She slowly pushed the garden gate open and relaxed her shoulders. Jan would never invite her over if Phil could potentially walk through the door. Even if he meant nothing to Jan anymore, she still wouldn't do it. Nobody other than Gillian and Finn knew about Jan and Morgan, and look how that had ended. To think that anyone else would be outwardly supportive of them would be ridiculous.

Morgan cleared her throat and knocked on the door. She'd picked up a bottle of Jan's favourite wine on the way over here, and now she was praying that they would crack it open to celebrate rather than to commiserate. Finn's opinion continued to plague Morgan's mind, but she was trying not to let it get to her. Jan didn't need someone who sat around while they were in their own head. No, she needed someone confident and sure around her. Someone who could guide Jan through this new stage of her life. *If* she genuinely saw something with Morgan.

When the door opened, Jan's gorgeous smile shone back at Morgan. "Glad you found the place. Come in."

Morgan stepped over the threshold, inhaling deeply as the subtle scent of Jan's home enveloped her. She immediately noted a warm mix of old wood and lavender. The house was unmistakably Edwardian, with its high ceilings and intricate crown moulding. The stained glass panels that framed the doorway were something to be admired, almost matching the worn runner that stretched down the hallway, the floral pattern faded but still elegant. *Just like Jan.* Morgan thought with a smile.

Framed photographs lined the walls, giving Morgan a glimpse of Jan at various stages of her life. Laughing at parties, holding a glass of wine, standing beside what Morgan assumed were family members. Then she spotted photos with Gillian and Finn on their wedding day in Vegas. Phil was still present in the image, but Morgan suspected Jan would de-Phil the place when she was ready to.

Morgan smiled as she cast her gaze to the heavy wooden staircase, the banister carved as it wound up to the next level. All in all, this place matched *exactly* who Morgan imagined Jan to be outside of the bar and her own flat. Strikingly elegant, a little chaotic, and unapologetically herself. "I found it just fine," Morgan said as she turned in the hallway. "But I still don't know what I'm doing here."

"I told you earlier. Dinner." Jan closed the door and pulled the bolt across the back of it. "But I know. You're waiting for an explanation." Jan stepped closer to Morgan and laid a hand on her chest as she leaned in and kissed her. "It's so good to see you here."

Morgan smiled against Jan's lips, holding her by the waist. "It's good to be here. You seem...different."

"When your home is handed back to you, it's hard to be

anything other than thrilled." Jan winked, took Morgan by the hand, and guided her through into the living room. "What can I get you to drink?"

"Oh, um...do you have a beer?" Morgan lifted the bottle of red wine in her hand and offered it to Jan. She would ask about the whole 'home being handed back' once they were sitting down and Morgan had taken it all in. "I picked this up for you on the way. I know it's the one you prefer."

"Thank you." That earned Morgan another kiss. One she didn't want to stop. As Jan deepened it, it seemed she was reluctant to end it, too. "You taste good. Real good."

As Jan stepped away, Morgan took her hand and held her back. "Hey, what's going on, babe?"

"Make yourself at home, and I'll be right back with drinks. Then I'll explain everything." Jan dropped a kiss on the tip of Morgan's nose and walked away.

Gorgeous place. Morgan eyed the sleek glass coffee table, its steel legs gleaming where the light from the chandelier above it caught. The Edwardian charm coupled with the modern design enveloped Morgan like a warm hug. The dark wood panelling, polished to perfection, stretched halfway up the walls until it met muted soft grey paint. She turned her attention to the impressive marble fireplace, imagining just how warm and cosy this place must feel in the winter. And then she eyed the plush grey couch adorned with geometric scatter cushions and matching throws. The blend of historic and contemporary worked *very* well.

Glancing towards the floor-to-ceiling windows, dressed in sheer white curtains with velvet drapes beneath, Morgan appreciated the natural light they let in. She exhaled, wondering what the hell a woman like Jan could ever see in her if this was the kind of life she had. Morgan couldn't say she'd *ever* come across someone who could pull off a Persian rug so well in such a modern living room.

"Okay, I know you're confused, but you could have at least

taken your shoes off and sat down." Jan handed Morgan a beer and grinned. "I'm home now. This is *my* place. A place you've earned more than the right to make yourself comfortable in."

Morgan's heart swelled as Jan gazed back at her. "He's agreed to walk and leave it to you?"

"Basically, yes." Jan sat down on what looked like a luxurious couch that would hold you hostage the moment your arse cheeks met it. "He's already found a place to move his little family into."

Morgan sensed a sarcasm in Jan's tone, but she couldn't blame her. It was one thing to find out your husband had been playing away, but to know he had a child on the way, too? No. Morgan couldn't fathom how that must feel.

"You know," Jan said as she reached out a hand and pulled Morgan down beside her. "I've been wondering what he would have done if I hadn't found out about the affair. Would either of them ever come clean? Would Anais have pretended it was Gareth's?"

"Yeah, that's a fucked up situation to potentially be in." Morgan blew out a breath. "Doesn't bear thinking about really."

"Thankfully, I'm not in that situation, and it's not something I have to think about." Jan curled her legs to the side of her and rested against Morgan when Morgan lifted an arm and hung it loosely around Jan's shoulders. "Because I have you." Jan tilted her head and kissed Morgan, sighing contentedly when she drew back. "And I really love having you over here."

"Thank you for inviting me over. This place must have a lot of mixed feelings attached to it for you." Morgan rested her beer bottle between her thighs and brought her hand to Jan's cheek. "God, you're so gorgeous that it hurts my heart."

"Do you have to be at the bar in the morning?" Jan asked as she rested her head on Morgan's shoulder. "Early…or at all?"

"I'm working the evening shift. Ben is opening up tomorrow."

Jan slid a hand beneath Morgan's hoodie and grazed her nails against her stomach. "May I introduce you to my bed tonight since I've spent *so long* acquainting myself with yours?"

A thrill rushed up Morgan's spine at the mere thought of it. She'd hated that Jan was ever at the hotel, even though she spent most of her time at Morgan's flat or the bar. Knowing that wouldn't be something she had to worry about anymore only relaxed Morgan beyond belief. "I'd *love* to acquaint myself with your bed."

Considering they'd had Gillian and Finn to contend with over the last couple of days, Morgan felt remarkably good about this with Jan. And Jan... Well, she seemed to be on cloud nine. Could this last, or would Morgan come to find the same old thing she usually did? A broken heart and a tear-stained face. *That's not important right now*. Morgan pushed those worries from her mind and kicked off her shoes. She would move them out of the way the next time Jan unwrapped herself from around Morgan.

"I don't want you to run, but since I came back here this afternoon, this is all I've wanted. Being held on my couch by *you*. It's something I've thought about on several occasions now, but this evening is just...going to be perfect."

Morgan sunk further down into the couch and sighed. "I'm so grateful to be here with you."

Why did you ever leave this place?!

Jan hummed along to the radio playing on the windowsill in the kitchen, preparing coffee before she woke Morgan and began her day. She didn't have anywhere to be, Morgan didn't either, but she did want to discuss the idea of Jan visiting Finn and setting the record straight. Morgan wouldn't go for it—she and Finn went back many years now—but Jan just didn't have it in her to leave it alone. How could she? If she didn't address this, then Gillian and Finn may just sit back and wait for Jan and Morgan to break things off. Jan didn't see that happening, so now her main worry was that she would lose touch with Gillian. That wasn't something she was willing to risk.

She lifted her phone from beside the radio and considered whether she should send Gillian a text. Jan didn't really want to warn them that she would be visiting. Not if either of them still had issues they needed to deal with regarding Jan and Morgan. So, she lowered it again and focused on the coffee cup under the spout filling with delicious, smooth caffeine.

As she lifted her cup and turned, resting against the counter, Jan looked up to find Morgan standing between the kitchen and the living room. She wore a T-shirt and boxer shorts, those long legs on display for Jan's eyes only. She cleared the instant arousal from her throat. "Good morning."

"It *is* a good morning. It always is when I have the pleasure of seeing your face before anyone else's." Morgan's tone of voice, coupled with the look in her eyes, told Jan that things were about to get real heated, real fast. "Is it always so quiet around here?"

"Mm. It's one of the reasons I was dreading finding somewhere else to live." Jan knew that now was the perfect opportunity to mention paying a visit to Gillian and Finn. Then they could continue giving one another their undivided attention until Morgan had to leave later. "What time do you have to head off?"

Morgan lifted a shoulder. "Probably around three. My shift begins at five."

"Okay. I'm...going to visit Gillian and Finn once you leave. I'd like to clear the air with Finn and explain to her that the things she said to you are *not* acceptable."

"Babe, you don't need to do that. It's honestly not worth it." Morgan crossed the kitchen. "Don't fall out with them over me."

"It is worth it. *You* are worth it." Jan didn't care what people thought of her. That was something she would have to get used to once everyone knew she was not only divorcing Phil but now dating a woman. "It's something I have to do, okay?"

"Okay."

Jan smiled behind her cup. Her hands always itched to reach out and touch Morgan, and this morning appeared to be no different. "Coffee?"

Morgan rounded the kitchen island and took Jan's cup from her. Her lips explored Jan's neck before she had time to realise what was happening, and then the belt on her silk robe was slowly being tugged on. "I've got all the energy I need right here, *only* for you."

"Mm." Jan tilted her head back and enjoyed Morgan's delicious lips on her skin. Fewer things in life could ever compare. Phil, included. When Morgan teasingly opened Jan's robe, goosebumps prickled her skin. "Oh, God. What the hell are you doing to me?"

Morgan tweaked a nipple and smirked against Jan's ear. "Everything you could *ever* dream of." She grazed the back of her hand between Jan's thighs, gasping quietly when she found her wetness. "And when you wake up wet and ready for me, it only makes me want to give you the fucking world."

Jan clenched her jaw when Morgan dragged two fingers between her lips. Any further conversation regarding Gillian and Finn could take a backseat. Forever, if needs be. Right now, Morgan was all she felt and all she wanted for the rest of this day. "Morgan, please..."

Morgan halted her movements and drew back, staring directly into Jan's eyes. She touched her forehead to Jan's, that gaze unwavering as she eased inside her with two fingers. "You're so fucking perfect, babe." Morgan took Jan's bottom lip between her teeth, then released it slowly. "Feel good?"

"S-so good." Jan pressed her back harder to the counter, aching to sink down on Morgan's fingers. She was close. Her walls had tightened around Morgan's fingers the moment they were inside her, but she wanted to feel *everything* Morgan was for a moment longer. Jan's knees shook when Morgan slowly massaged her walls.

Fuck, she was sure she'd died and gone to heaven the moment she first kissed this woman. "Y-yes."

Morgan traced the tip of her tongue along Jan's bottom lip, smiling when Jan's knees started to tremble. "You gonna come for me, gorgeous?"

"Oh, shit." Jan gritted her teeth when Morgan pressed the heel of her hand against her clit. The pressure built deep within her, rising faster with every move Morgan made. "C-close."

Morgan drew back and locked her eyes on Jan. "I want to watch you come."

Jan gripped the counter as she came hard and fast, barely managing to keep her eyes open. When Morgan smiled back at her, Jan felt nothing more than love holding firm in her chest. Which was potentially an issue given the sheer state of her life. But then Morgan guided her away from the kitchen counter and through to the hallway, that sexy smile not fading. No matter what, Morgan was here, and she was present. It was all Jan needed right now.

"Were you busy before I came down here?"

Jan blinked, unable to form a thought, never mind a sentence. "N-no."

"Back up the stairs then. I need to clean you up."

CHAPTER 27

With a mixture of apprehension and disappointment settling deep within her, Jan knocked loudly on Gillian and Finn's front door for the third time. Her best friend was home, the white Audi out on the street proved that, and Jan didn't have time to stand around on the doorstep. She knocked again, pressing the doorbell, too.

"Alright! I'm coming!"

The door swung open, and Gillian stared back at her. She wore her reading glasses, a pen in her hand, quite clearly working from home today. Jan would say what she needed to say, and then Gillian could carry on with that work. "J-Jan, hi."

"Hi. Do you have a minute?"

"Oh, um...yes. Come in." Gillian frowned as she stepped aside, oblivious to the reasons Jan was here. "Look, I know we left things the way we did the other day, but—"

Jan held up a hand and cut Gillian off. She wasn't doing 'buts' today. She'd had a gorgeous night with Morgan and an even better morning. "You've already made it clear what you think of me, Gill. What I *won't* have is Finn showing up at the bar, demanding that

Morgan stops seeing me." She shook her head. "I'm a grown woman. I *can* take care of myself."

Gillian's eyes widened suddenly. Had Finn not told Gillian about visiting Morgan? Huh. "Just...relax. Go through to the living room, and we can talk about it."

"Would that be an *actual* conversation, or are you going to talk *at* me?" Jan didn't enjoy falling out with anyone, but the last person she wanted to lose was Gillian Masters. They'd been through practically an entire lifetime together already.

"Fucking hell. What's got into you, Jan?"

"I don't appreciate people offering their opinion on something that has nothing to do with them." Gillian may have thought Jan was overreacting, but she was actually holding back right now. The look in Morgan's eyes when she'd gone to the bar yesterday only to find out Finn had been over to stick the boot in had been heart-breaking. As though Morgan had done something wrong, and she felt terribly guilty. Jan never wanted her to feel that way, and she wouldn't allow anyone else to do so, either. "Is Finn home? It's her I've come to see."

"Yes, she's in the living room." Gillian wrapped her arms around herself and sighed. "This is all really unnecessary."

Jan chose not to respond to Gillian. She was here to deal with Finn and Finn alone. She dropped her handbag at the bottom of the stairs and strode into the living room. Finn was lounging, watching TV, refusing to meet Jan's eyes. "Can you turn off what-ever you're watching for a moment?"

"When you learn to speak to my wife with respect, yes." Finn sat up and muted the volume, her hands clasped under her chin as she stared down at the floor. "I don't appreciate you coming here speaking to Gillian like that."

"Hurts, doesn't it?" Jan lifted a brow. "When someone comes at you or the woman you care about."

"I'm sorry?"

"You. Going to the bar and telling Morgan that she should end things with me." Calmly, Jan took a seat on the couch and waited for Finn to make eye contact with her. When she did, Jan continued. "I don't appreciate it, Finn. Not at all."

"Jan, you know we love and support you. I'm just finding it hard to understand how you and Morgan ended up in a relationship with one another."

"Morgan has been there for me since I found out about the affair. She's sat, and she's listened. She offered me her bedroom for the night when I'd spent the evening sitting in her bar with nothing I owned. I'd been so disgusted by Phil that I left the house within minutes of getting home from the office. I had my phone and my purse." She smiled when she reminded herself of Morgan and everything she had done for Jan so far.

Finn snorted. "And what? You thought you'd sleep with her to say thanks?"

"Finn!" Gillian admonished from the other side of the room.

"I'm sorry." Finn ran a hand through her hair. "But from what Morgan told me, you've been sleeping with one another since you found out about Phil.

"When I started sleeping with Morgan has nothing to do with you." Jan's brows drew together. "And I'm failing to understand why you *think* it does."

"You're my friend. I care about you. I'm worried that this is going to fall apart, and then you get hurt. You don't need that right now. Not when you're already dealing with a divorce *none* of us saw coming."

"And you think I *did* see it coming?" Jan scoffed as she glared back at Finn. In this moment, she wasn't sure this was the Finn she had become so fond of. "I was as shocked as you two, believe me."

"Jan—"

Jan softened a little, but not enough to be less angry with Finn. "Morgan means a lot to me."

"Morgan is...she's complicated. I'm sure she would agree with me when I say that. She doesn't really do relationships, and that bar is her life." Finn shook her head. "Look, she was sleeping with someone else just before you left Phil. Amanda. Morgan kind of just takes life as it comes, you know? No commitment kind of thing."

Jan understood that Finn knew a different Morgan from the one she knew herself, but that wasn't the impression she got from Morgan at all. She'd been honest about her situation with Amanda, and that was all Jan needed. Honesty. "And the moment she found out that Amanda had a husband, she cut her off. At least she's capable of doing that. Unlike my fucking husband, who can't keep his dick in his pants!"

Finn shifted from the couch to her knees in front of Jan. She took Jan's hands and gazed back at her with a pleading look. "Whatever you want, we'll support, but please think about this. Decide if Morgan is *really* who you want to be with."

"We're officially dating now."

Finn sat back on her knees and lowered her head. "I don't know what to say."

"Then please, say nothing." Jan drew her hands away from Finn's. "If you and Gill can't give me the time I need to work out who I am or where I'm headed, then all I can ask is that you keep your opinions to yourself and stay out of my personal life."

"Of course we can give you time." Gillian joined Jan on the couch and placed a hand on her shoulder. "We're just worried about you, that's all."

"But you're not. Not really. You're worried about who I'm sleeping with, and I *cannot* for the life of me understand why, Gill." Jan knew this was a pointless conversation. It wasn't going anywhere, and it certainly wasn't getting any better. "While you two see the woman I'm sleeping with, I see so much more. She just...she's the only person I feel I can go to when I need to talk. She listens and doesn't judge me." Jan sighed. "I know leaving Phil is a shock, and I know it hasn't been long since all of this happened, but why should I sit around feeling sorry for myself when I can be happy? Can't that be enough for you?"

"Jan," Finn said as she placed a hand on her knee. "Are you seriously expecting to just fall *out* of love with Phil and *in* love with Morgan?"

"I fell out of love with Phil the moment he told me the affair was true." Jan swallowed, reminded of that day and all the pain it had brought with it. Only that pain had been short-lived, and that was because of Morgan. "He's having a child with another woman. He has a place of his own now." Jan turned to Gillian. "I know you want me to fall apart like you did, and I know you want me to need you, but I'm okay. I'm alive, I'm healthy, and I'm okay, Gill."

"I *never* want you to go through what I did, Jan. That's *not* what this is."

"Then I don't know where we go from here. I don't know what you want from me." Jan ran her palms down her thighs and rose to her feet. "It would have been nice to have my friends by my side while I try to move forward with my life, but I guess we don't always get what we want." Drained and disappointed that this hadn't progressed in the right direction, Jan swallowed down the emotion lodged in her throat and stepped around Finn, where she still knelt on the floor. "All I want is to be happy. To find a new normal and not sit at home existing for the sake of it. My own husband was finding the happiness I couldn't give him with another woman, yet *I'm* the one being told to hang back and decide what I want. I've told you what I want...and that's Morgan. I don't know how much clearer I can be about that."

"Jan, please don't go." Gillian followed her out into the hallway. "Stay, and we'll talk."

"I don't want to talk. I'm sick and tired of talking. I shouldn't have to defend myself." Jan's bottom lip quivered as she stared back at Gillian. "I'm just going to head off and sort out my life."

"Jan, I don't want you to be alone."

Jan lifted her handbag from the floor and opened the front

door. She turned back when she stopped in the doorway, saddened that her best friend couldn't just accept this. "I won't be around for a while. Please don't call me. I just want to be alone while I deal with the divorce." Maybe Jan *did* need time away from everyone. Morgan included. Only as she pondered that, she felt entirely miserable. "Tell Finn to fix her friendship with Morgan. I'll...lay low. If she finds someone else, then I'll make sure you and Finn are the first to say you told me so."

Jan took the steps down to the garden path, aware that Gillian was still watching her. She didn't know what came next, and she didn't know where to turn, but Jan was certain that Morgan didn't need any of this. It was unfair to expect her to put up with Gillian and Finn interfering with their relationship.

She climbed into her car and locked the doors, then rested her head back against the seat. Being with Morgan over the last couple of months had fulfilled Jan in ways she never knew possible, but she did need to step back and decide if all of this was worth putting a potential love interest through. *Potential?* Jan scoffed inwardly. There was nothing *potential* about this at all. Jan knew what she wanted, she knew she would always crave to know more and do more with Morgan, but maybe she wasn't entitled to that. Maybe only Gillian and Finn were supposed to have the happy ending.

I don't know what I'll do without her. Jan brushed a tear from her cheek and sighed. That applied to both Morgan *and* Gillian. They'd always come as a pair—Jan and Gillian—but Jan expected far more from her best friend. As for Morgan, well, Jan wasn't sure she would ever find anyone quite like her again. She turned the key in the ignition and pulled away from the pavement, the ache in her chest prominent. As the sun began to set in her rearview mirror, she felt the happiness of this morning fading along with it. "Go home. Lock the door. *Exist.*"

CHAPTER 28

Excited to surprise Jan at home this evening, Morgan had spent the last hour clock watching, her foot repeatedly tapping against the floor. She hadn't heard from Jan since she'd left her place earlier today, but Morgan was taking it as a good sign. Hopefully, Jan was sitting drinking coffee with Gillian, and all of their issues were a thing of the past. Even though Morgan didn't know Gillian as well as she would have liked to know her by now, Gillian wasn't the kind of person to let Jan go through everything alone. It just didn't seem possible. Jan was her best friend. They were joined at the hip. Gillian *was* going to come through for her. Without a doubt.

Just as Morgan was dreaming about her evening with Jan, Finn came through the door. She didn't know why she was here—Morgan had told Finn to find somewhere else to drink—but the bar was busy tonight, so she wouldn't make a scene. *Maybe she's here because Jan and Gillian are having a heart-to-heart.* As she watched Finn cross the room, Megan and Tyler came in behind her. She smiled and offered a small wave, knowing she would have to give her staff a decent summer bonus for having her back today. They'd agreed to work what was left of the evening shift and lock up once midnight came. Morgan didn't plan to be back here before the morning, and she'd told them as much when she'd called them.

Her phone lit up on the shelf. It was Jan.

With excitement building in the pit of her stomach, Morgan grinned as she lifted her phone. If Finn had something to say, she could wait until Morgan had replied to Jan. Jan...who had no idea Morgan was cutting her shift short and heading over there.

As Morgan opened the message, her heart sank.

I'm sorry. I need space.

Morgan glared at the screen when another message came through.

None of this is about you. You've been amazing, Morgan. But my friendships are falling apart and I'm already picking up the fragments that I have left of my life.

Morgan did give Finn her full attention this time. She stared through her, determined not to get upset while she was standing behind her own bar. But it would be a struggle. Morgan felt the waves of emotion beginning to build within her. "What the fuck have you done?"

Finn frowned. "Excuse me?"

"You and Gillian. What the fuck have you done?"

"I, uh...what?" Finn asked as she rested her elbows on the bar. "I've just come in for a pint. I'm not here to fall out with you, Morgan, and I'm not here to get involved in your relationship with Jan."

"I told you to drink elsewhere."

"Well, yeah, but I wanted to apologise to you." Finn held out a hand. "Truce? I don't like fighting with people. Especially not you."

"Nah. You can fuck off. Both of you." Morgan took a step back and frowned. "And thanks for fucking it all up with Jan. You'll be thrilled to know that she wants nothing to do with me anymore."

Finn slowly lowered her hand and visibly swallowed. “What are you talking about?”

“Jan. She’s just texted me. Said she needs space and apologised.”

Finn pulled herself up onto a stool and nodded. “I mean, I can understand why she’s asked for space. She’s been through a lot, as you know. Maybe she’s realised it’s time to stop and reflect on the last couple of months.”

“She said it was because of her friendships. I’m guessing Gillian got into her head. And *you*, more than likely.” Morgan had truly believed this was going somewhere with Jan. Until Jan had gone over to see Gillian this afternoon, everything was going really well. And now, Morgan had no idea what to do. Did she still go over there? No, she couldn’t. Jan had asked for space, and Morgan had no choice but to give it. “I honestly thought you were one of my friends, Finn.”

“What? You *are* my friend.” Finn softened, but Morgan didn’t. No, she was ready to blow. “Morgan, relax. It’ll blow over. If it’s meant to be, it’ll be.”

Tyler and Megan came from the room that led to the cellar and slipped past Morgan. They got chatting to customers, but they may as well not be here. Morgan was now paying them for no reason. She didn’t have anywhere she needed to be anymore. She focused back on Finn. “Enjoy your night. I’m going to bed.”

“Morgan, wait.” Finn rushed to the side of the bar and stopped Morgan from opening the door that led to her flat. “I don’t want us to be like this. I can’t change what’s happened, but I *don’t* want this.”

“Newsflash: my life isn’t on your fucking terms, Finn.” Morgan shoved past her and rushed up the stairs. For the first time in so many years, Morgan was going to break down. She felt the tears stinging her eyes and she felt the swell of emotion rise up in her throat. She forced her key into the door at the top of the stairs as tears slid down her cheeks. Only as she tried to close the door once she was inside, Finn's foot was stopping it. "Seriously, Finn. You need to back off."

"Let me in. I want to talk to you."

Morgan didn't want to talk to anyone right now. Unless Jan turned up here, she was all out of conversation. "I just want to be on my own."

Finn shook her head and stepped inside Morgan's flat. "I know I shouldn't have got involved or even said what I was thinking, but the shock of finding out you've been sleeping with Jan *still* hasn't worn off." Finn dropped down onto Morgan's couch and dragged a hand through her hair. "We can't believe she's getting divorced, let alone sleeping with you."

"God, I wish you'd stop saying that." Morgan clenched her hands into fists at her side. Why did people keep making their blossoming relationship seem less than it actually was? "We're not just fucking one another, Finn. She's just spent a week in Spain with me. We're together most nights. Whatever ideas you have in your head about us, I can promise you that they're all wrong. Every last one of them."

"She went to Spain with you? I thought you were visiting friends down south?"

"I told you that because I wanted Jan to feel comfortable. I didn't want her to feel pressured to come out to you and Gillian. When I asked her, I thought she'd say no. Only she didn't. She came with me, and we had the most amazing week together." Morgan scoffed. "Taking her away was something her ex-husband should have been doing all these years." She reached for a bottle of whiskey on the kitchen counter, took two glasses from the cupboard, and joined Finn on the couch. "I know you think I'm not good enough for her, and I know Gillian hates the fact that I live and breathe now, but she made me happy, Finn."

"She is lovely." Finn smiled. "I think she's the reason me and Gillian got back together."

"I *know* that this won't last. I *know* she's going to break my heart when she realises I'm just me and she could do a million times better. But you know what? I would have been happy with the pain and the hurt down the line if it meant I'd had the chance to be with her. Even briefly." Morgan had spent years pushing potential love interests away. Women who deserved her undivided attention, not an hour here and there when Morgan could take a break or had a random day off. "I was finally in a place where I enjoyed being with someone again. She made me feel as though something more was possible."

"You've only just left Amanda, and she's only just left Phil." Finn offered a single nod in thanks when Morgan handed her a glass of whiskey. "How can either of you be in a position to date? I mean, you *hate* dating."

"I don't know how many times I have to tell you that it *wasn't* serious with Amanda. We were *never* together. She used to show up here when she wanted a fuck, and that was the extent of it. Even *I* felt dirty in the end because I realised it was why she was coming here." Morgan wouldn't make that mistake ever again with another woman. "But Jan was different. She was...everything I'd dreamed of." Morgan smiled when Jan's face flitted into her mind. "I've been into her since the first time you guys brought her here. But I knew she was married and I'd never—"

"Is that why you kissed her? Because you knew she'd left him?"

"She kissed me. Everything that happened was on Jan's say-so. Not that I didn't agree, but *she* kissed *me*. She instigated it all. I was too much of a coward to make the first move. Mostly because it's Jan but also because I knew what she was going through."

"You're really into her, aren't you?"

Morgan nodded as she stared down at her glass. Her eyes burned, and as she sniffled, Finn pressed a hand to her shoulder. "Like I've never been into anyone before, yeah."

"Shit." Finn sunk back into the couch. "She came over before. She didn't stay long, but I told her you weren't really the commitment type. Because...for as long as I've known you, you haven't been." Finn sighed. "I'm sorry, Morgan. I'll make it right. I promise you."

"Just...leave it alone. It's probably for the best, anyway." Morgan knew that was a lie, all she wanted was to be with Jan tonight, but if they'd filled her head with bullshit, Morgan would let Jan figure it all out in a way that suited her best. "I just wish you could have given me the benefit of the doubt."

"I wasn't thinking. I was so worried about Jan that no matter what she said to me, I dismissed it. Instead of just supporting what she wanted, what she was saying, I told her to think about what she was doing."

"She was so happy Phil had decided to give her the house. That look on her face as I knocked on the door and she was in her own home... God, I wish I could have taken a picture." Morgan sipped her whiskey. "It was like she'd finally relaxed, knowing she didn't have to worry about finding somewhere to live. Even though I'd told her she never should have had to. He should have done the right thing from the start and left."

"Wait! She's back at the house?" Finn asked as she sat forward and scooted closer to Morgan. "Their house?"

"*Her* house. Phil has a new place."

"She didn't tell us she was back at home." As Morgan turned to Finn, she noted the guilt in her eyes immediately. "Though, I don't suppose she had the chance to."

"Do me a favour?" Morgan sniffled as she found the courage to say the words to Finn. "Look after her. Make sure she's okay. Just... be there for her." Morgan closed her eyes as tears rolled down her cheeks. "I don't blame her for cutting me loose—I'm not exactly reliable given the job I have. But I *was* trying, Finn. I'd brought staff in tonight so I could surprise her at home."

"You never get staff to cover your shift."

"Says a lot about what I thought of Jan then, doesn't it?" Morgan forced down the emotion in her throat, but the tears wouldn't stop. "She was so worth it for me. We connected, and I couldn't help how I felt about her. Then when we spent the night together, I expected her to be gone by the morning. I thought she would have freaked out and left before I woke up. But...she didn't. She stayed. She actually didn't leave this place until I started my shift that evening." Morgan smiled. "She's a great cuddler."

"You cuddled?" Finn's brows rose, but Morgan understood. All of this was so far from who Morgan portrayed herself to be that Finn was bound to be surprised. "Fucking hell. She's turned you into a new woman."

"Nah, she just reminded me of who I am deep down." Morgan knocked back her whiskey and poured another. She got to her feet and crossed the room to her bedroom door. "Close the door on your way out."

"Morgan?"

Morgan sighed as she met Finn's gaze. "Yeah?"

"I *am* sorry. I feel terrible."

Morgan simply shrugged. If Finn wanted to feel terrible, that was her own choice. But this would be the last time anyone *ever* meddled in Morgan's life. "Whatever you told her, you're probably right. She probably sensed it, and that's why I'm here, alone, once again."

"Let me fix this. Please."

"I understand that you're sorry, but I don't need you turning up at Jan's place with a guilty conscience. It won't help anything. She's asked for space. She's told me where she stands. I have to respect that. As Jan's friend, I'd hope you'd respect it, too."

"Gillian will—"

"Gillian won't do shit. She hates me. She'll be glad to see the back of me." Morgan leaned back against the wall next to her bedroom door. "Why *does* she hate me? And don't tell me she doesn't because I see right through it."

"She's never once said that to me. As far as I'm aware, she has no problem with you." Finn's eyes held a sincerity, but Morgan wasn't convinced. "I swear to you, she's never said anything bad about you."

Morgan nodded. She couldn't be bothered to discuss this any longer. The only person she cared about, the only person she wanted to defend herself to...was gone. Even if Jan hadn't specifically stated that she'd called it quits, Morgan knew she had. She felt it in her heart. "I really have nothing left to say."

"Then I'll say what I have to say." Finn rose to her feet and lowered her glass to the coffee table. "I've known you for a while now. In that time, all I've seen is a multitude of one-night stands come and go. Whenever I ask you about settling down, you dismiss the conversation, or at one time, you would have thrown it back at me. I'm now learning that I don't fully know the real you, but what I do know is that you're a good person, and I've hurt you. By trying to protect one friend, I've hurt another. You may not believe me, but it was *never* my intention for this to happen, Morgan. When Jan left our place earlier, she didn't once insinuate that she wouldn't be seeing you again. The way she spoke about you, how her eyes lit up when she brought up your name...even *I'm* surprised she's not here." Finn's shoulders slumped as she sighed. "It's...why I came here. To apologise to you together."

Morgan's bottom lip quivered as Finn spoke from the heart. "I'm very good at showing what I want people to see. With Jan, I was myself. She liked it...I think. You know, what she saw in me." Morgan stared down at the floor. "But I don't think I'll ever have the chance to settle down. Not after this. I can't deal with being dropped all the time." How could Morgan look forward to settling down when even her own friend had been against it? "I did think the potential was there with Jan, but I realise now that I was wrong, and I was hoping for something completely unobtainable."

"Morgan—"

"I know you feel bad. Part of me is happy that you feel that way. You put those thoughts and ideas about me in Jan's head. The rest of me just feels sad. For losing Jan and for losing you."

"You haven't lost me." Finn's brows drew together. "Why the hell would you think you'd lost me?"

"Because I choose to walk away from this friendship, Finn. I choose to put myself first and not keep people who don't want to see me succeed in my space. I want friends who back me. I want friends who fight for me. You...you basically stabbed me in the back, and I won't hang around long enough for you to twist the knife a little deeper."

Finn stood open-mouthed, blinking repeatedly. "Morgan, this is all going to work out. I know it will. Just give it some time with Jan. As for me... Well, I understand that I've hurt you, and I know I've fucked our friendship up."

"Jan is never going to risk losing Gillian, and I'd never expect her to. But I do wish people would back me once in a while. Trust that I'm a decent person, you know?"

Finn looked back at Morgan with tears in her eyes.

"She's going to need you both, Finn. Please take care of her." Morgan stepped towards the counter and took cash from her wallet. "Pick some flowers up for me and take them over. A second housewarming or a 'sorry I took advantage of you'. Whatever shit you decide to feed her on arrival."

Finn's shoulders slumped. "You should take flowers to her."

"She doesn't *want* to see me." Morgan felt her anger beginning to rear its head again. "What part of that don't you fucking understand?!"

Finn held up her hands. "Okay, okay. I get it. You want me to leave."

"I wanted you to leave the moment you walked into the bar." Morgan did step into her bedroom this time, a shiver working its way up her spine when she caught a subtle hint of Jan's perfume. "You know the most fucked up thing about all of this? I was falling for her, Finn. The only reason I forced myself not to was because Jan isn't in a place where she can even consider a good, strong relationship right now. But I was. I was falling hard."

Morgan slammed her bedroom door shut and turned, pressing her back to it as she slid to the floor. Whatever the future held, it wouldn't involve Jan.

She took her phone from her pocket, gave herself a moment to breathe, and typed out a message.

You know where I am if you ever need anything. Having you, even if only briefly, has been the greatest pleasure of my life. Take care of yourself, Jan x

With a deep sense of loss sitting in her chest, Morgan sniffled and jumped a little when she heard her front door close. Today had started out so perfectly, and now, Morgan didn't know where to turn. The one friend she usually talked things through with had actively destroyed what she was building. If Morgan had learned anything recently, it was that she had to look after herself and never rely on anyone else.

CHAPTER 29

Jan stared back at herself in the bathroom mirror, her eyes sunken from her lack of sleep. Realistically, her sleep troubles should have been because of Phil, but they weren't. She missed Morgan *deeply*. Her laugh, that smile, the ease Jan felt around her. She missed turning up at the bar, knowing she would be in the best of company. But most of all, she missed the way Morgan's arms felt wrapped around her.

When she'd left Gillian's place a week ago, she hadn't known what the next step would be. All she knew was that she needed to lock herself away at home and pray this nightmare would be over sooner rather than later. Nothing made any sense, and most of the time during this last week, Jan felt as though she was on the outside watching her miserable life unfold.

She felt detached. She felt so far removed from the life she'd once had that she was struggling to come to terms with it...or see a way forward. When she'd texted Morgan, she hadn't been thinking straight. All she saw down the line was more pain. More judgement. More turmoil. Jan never wanted to be the woman who brought that to anyone's life, so she'd fled. Not very far, but to her home. The one thing she could call her own.

Gillian had called her once or twice, but it seemed she'd taken the hint after the second day of trying, and if Jan knew Finn the way she believed she did, she was probably lying low. They were the reason she'd ever sent that message to Morgan in the first place. If Jan had things her way, this week wouldn't have felt so lonely. No, she would have been making more memories with Morgan, and she would have been unapologetic as she did so.

A sudden hammering on her front door made Jan jump, a hand splayed across her chest as she took a breath. Nobody knew she even had this place back. Chances were, Gillian and Finn knew she was back home—Morgan had probably told them—but neither of them would bang Jan's door down. It wasn't their style.

She shot down the stairs wearing a hoodie Morgan had left there and pulled the front door open.

Gillian stared back at her with tears in her eyes. "I know you don't want to see me, but if you'd sent me a text telling me to fuck off, at least I'd know you were okay."

"How did you know I was here?"

"Morgan told Finn the night she went to the bar." Gillian visibly swallowed. "That's how I knew I'd really fucked up. You would have told me otherwise."

"As you can see, I'm alive, and I'm fine." Jan attempted to close the door, but Gillian stopped her with a hand. "Gill, please. I don't want to speak to you or anyone else."

"Jan, can we talk? Please?"

"I have nothing to say. Until you showed up here, I hadn't spoken to another soul in seven days."

Gillian regarded Jan with a faint smile and stepped over the threshold. "Let me put the kettle on, and then I'll leave if that's what you really want." As Gillian placed a gentle hand on Jan's hip, the floodgates opened. "Oh, Jan. Come on. Sit down and take a minute."

"A minute for what?" Jan barely recognised her own voice.

"Right now, I don't know. I just need you to sit down, and then we can talk about what's going on."

Jan scoffed and wiped the backs of her hands against her cheeks. "You know *exactly* what's going on. Don't try to deny it."

Gillian lowered herself to the couch opposite Jan and hung her head. Did she feel terrible? Jan hoped so. For so long, she had held Gillian together. She had lain in bed with her nightly at one time, praying she wouldn't cry herself to sleep. Everything Jan had done...had basically been thrown back in her face.

"As you can see, I'm fine. So, you can go now."

Gillian looked up at Jan with tears in her eyes. "You're not fine. You're in a terrible state, Jan."

"I was doing good. I had this place back, and I was dating Morgan. My life was...exciting again. Something I hadn't had for a long time." Jan sniffled as she plucked a tissue from the box on the side table. "I know it was a shock to everyone, and I know I've kept things about my marriage from you, but I *was* happy, Gill. She made me *so* happy without even having to try."

"What things about your marriage?" Gillian clasped her hands in her lap as she sat back. "If you want me to understand all of this, you need to be honest with me, love."

Jan guessed it was time to come clean about her failing marriage. "We were in counselling. We had been since the end of last year. I felt like I was losing him and myself, and I didn't know how to tackle it. Something just didn't feel right. Gut instinct, I don't know."

"Why didn't you tell me sooner?"

"Because it was *my* marriage, Gill. I tried to make it work, to be better, but it still wasn't enough for him. He was changing, and I didn't know how to make him love me anymore." God, that was sad. Why should anyone put themselves in a position where they were fighting for a lost cause? Fighting to force a love that didn't exist anymore. "We barely spoke to one another some days. I put it down to work and how busy he was, but I think we both know why he was falling out of love with me now, don't we?"

"Oh, Jan. I had no idea."

"For the briefest time, Morgan made me forget about the humiliation he put me through. She made me feel wanted. She looked at me in a way I'm not sure Phil *ever* had." Jan closed her eyes and smiled. Even though they'd never have that again, Jan would never forget the care and support Morgan had shown to her. The exhilaration and the laughter they'd shared. "I just...hope she sees in herself what I saw. I hope she takes something positive away from our time together and uses it to find someone meant for her."

"She's...devastated."

Jan didn't need to hear that. She wanted people to tell her Morgan was glad to see the back of her. "Morgan will be just fine. She has so much ahead of her."

"And you?"

"I signed the divorce papers two days ago. They were picked up by courier this morning. I don't know what's next for me now. I'm going back to work; Phil has agreed to keep me on as partner, so that's something to keep me busy." Jan looked around her huge living room. "I've always loved this house. It was my dream from the moment we bought it. But it feels too big for me alone. I hate the thought of putting it on the market, but...it seems silly to stay." Jan scoffed. "Maybe Phil will want to buy it for his new family."

"I know I haven't been the greatest friend to you lately, but I can't walk out of here after seeing you like this. I just... I don't have it in me."

"Has Finn been looking after Morgan?" Jan found it hard to believe that Morgan was upset—or devastated, as Gillian had claimed—but if she was, she needed to know she had people there for her.

"We're not welcome at the bar anymore. She doesn't answer

Finn's calls. They haven't seen one another since the night you sent Morgan the text."

That hurt Jan's heart. It wasn't necessary to fall out with people, and certainly not because of Jan. "So, she's alone?"

"I... Yes. I think so." Gillian swapped seats and sat down beside Jan. "Finn has been trying to be there for her, but Morgan is angry with us." Gillian took Jan's hand and squeezed it. "I've been really worried about you."

"Why?"

"Because I made a mess of our friendship. I'm scared we'll never be the same again." Gillian's voice broke, but she cleared her throat and looked up at Jan. "I had no idea just how much you cared about her, Jan. You've kept everything so close to your chest that I had no idea what was going on."

Jan understood from Gillian's point of view; it was hard not to. Perhaps this was the moment when they tried to work on their friendship. "I do understand why you were both worried about me. Especially when I told you about Morgan. I guess I just tried to see the best in it and hoped you would, too." Jan wrung her hands in her lap. "Maybe if I'd spoken to you before I actually came out with the truth, this may not have happened."

"You had your reasons, and neither of us had any right to try to dissuade you." Gillian curled her fingers around Jan's shaking hand. "But we know now, so we can help you figure all of this out."

Jan sat confused. What was there to figure out? "I'm sorry?"

"Do you miss her?" Gillian asked, a wry smile settled on her mouth. "Truthfully, do you miss her?"

"So much, Gill." Jan swallowed down the emotion lodged in her throat and closed her eyes. "More than anything in this world." She had never really needed much company in life; she had friends and colleagues she spent enough time with. But she couldn't describe or understand the feeling she had when she thought about Morgan. She couldn't process any of this because it had all ended so suddenly. To know now that Morgan was equally as upset... That surely meant something. Was this Jan's chance to make it right with her? "I don't know what to do."

Gillian turned side-on and studied Jan's face. "About what, love?"

"About Morgan. About any of this." Jan didn't want people to meddle in her life *or* Morgan's life anymore. She just wanted to move on with whatever the hell was about to come for her. "I fear I've ruined it with her."

"I don't think you have. She knows you're going through a lot, and I know she understands that your life is up in the air."

"You don't even like her." Jan snorted. "I don't know why you care if I see her again or not."

"God, I wish people would stop saying that. I *don't* dislike her. I *don't* hate her. When I met Finn, I was wary of her, that's all. I guess she sensed that, and we've just never tried to get to know one another."

"She means a lot to me, Gill."

"I know." Gillian wrapped an arm around Jan and rested her head on Jan's shoulder. "Now you have to decide what your next move is."

"I don't follow."

"With Morgan. This surely isn't the end. If Finn and I could make it work, then you two can surely figure it out."

"People will talk. I don't want my life to be that way. I don't want to be the topic of conversation. I just...want to be happy." Of all the things Jan could have said, she hadn't expected that. She couldn't care less about other people, and deep down, she never had. If Jan was happy, that was what mattered.

"Fuck them." Gillian nudged Jan's shoulder and smiled. "If you want her, then you go and get her."

Could Jan do that? Walk into the bar and demand Morgan give Jan another chance? They hadn't gone their separate ways on bad terms, but Jan still should have gone to Morgan and spoken to her before now. Told her the reasons for Jan needing space. Instead, she had left Morgan to fend for herself while expecting Finn to be the one to pick up the pieces.

"Am I out of my mind?" Jan swallowed as she gazed back at Gillian. Before she'd asked Morgan for space, it didn't feel that way, but now...now, Jan was doubting herself.

"Not at all."

"That's why I texted her, you know. Because that's how it felt when I left your place that afternoon. As though you were accusing me of being crazy. That it was ridiculous to think I could date her."

Gillian shook her head and sighed. "I could have handled it all so much better than I did. But I'm sitting here right now telling you that you have my support. I just want you to be happy, Jan. If Morgan makes you happy, then you should see where it goes."

"It's been *so long* since I've been with a woman, but the moment I kissed her, I knew it was what I wanted."

"I'm sorry...what? You've been with a woman before?"

Jan waved a hand and got to her feet. "It was back in university. It...was a lifetime ago."

"University?" Gillian almost shrieked as she said that. "Who?"

"Antonia."

Gillian's brows rose. "God, I'm finding out a lot of things about my best friend lately. Shacking up with the local bartender, going to *Spain* with her, being with women in the past. I feel like I don't know you anymore."

Jan winced as she turned around and eyed Gillian from the other side of the room. "Sorry I didn't tell you about Spain. Everything was happening really fast, and I didn't want what ultimately happened to happen sooner than it did. I just wanted to enjoy being with her while nobody knew. Less pressure and all that."

"How was it over there with her?"

Jan smiled. "I can't describe it."

"That good?" Gillian lifted a brow.

"Far better than good." Jan turned to the mirror on the wall, disappointed by the state she was in. If she was going to see Morgan again, she really had to book an appointment at the salon. "When I'm with her, nothing else matters, Gill. Phil doesn't exist in my head, and I just feel calm. Almost...loved."

"Then you know what you have to do. You *have* to go and see her, Jan."

"I know, and I will. I just need to get my head straight, and then I'll go to the bar. I need a few days, a week at the most. Maybe if I go back to work and get into my routine again, everything will be clearer. Right now, I don't think I'd know what to say to her."

Gillian nodded and crossed her legs. "That sounds like a sensible idea."

Not wanting to dive too deep into her own mind, Jan pulled her shoulders back and searched Gillian's eyes. Whenever they had a dilemma between them, Gillian's face gave her away. But in this moment, she was a picture of calm...a calm that Jan was going to hold onto. "I guess I should start making myself look and feel a little more presentable then."

"Shush. You're gorgeous even when you're having a meltdown."

Jan flopped down beside Gillian and laid her head against Gillian's shoulder. She allowed herself a moment to breathe, to... stop panicking about everything, and then she laughed. "Who would have thought us two would be striking up mind-blowing relationships with women in our forties!"

Gillian snorted. "If Morgan is *anything* like Finn, I know exactly what you're in for." She pressed a kiss to Jan's hair and drew back. "I hope to God you're going to wash that mane before you even think about going to the bar!"

"I will. Don't worry." Jan closed her eyes and enjoyed the

silence. While she hadn't wanted to come face-to-face with Gillian today, she was glad she had. "Five minutes of peace and quiet before you have me run ragged again."

Gillian sighed. "Five minutes."

CHAPTER 30

Another day.

Another mindless shift spent behind the bar.

Morgan usually enjoyed a night off a week, but with no reason to spend any time at her place, she hadn't bothered to schedule any days off. She had worked every day and night since Jan had asked for space, and two weeks on, nothing had changed. Morgan had craved to reach out, to ask Jan how she was doing, but she wasn't sure what would come out of her mouth if they did speak. Morgan would probably say a few things Jan didn't need to hear—about how much Morgan missed her—and it would only make everything worse.

Right now, it was bad enough.

She lifted a hand and waved as Eric came limping through the door. He'd spent most of this week reeling off story after story to Morgan, but she'd appreciated it. It stopped her from thinking about Jan, and it stopped her from walking the streets night after night. She just felt...lost.

You're not lost. You're stupid.

Morgan laughed and shook her head. She rarely found herself speechless when it came to women, but Jan wasn't just any woman. For the time Morgan had spent with her, Jan was her world. Everything she did each day was done with Jan on her mind. When she woke up alone, Morgan didn't *feel* alone. Because she knew at some point, she would see Jan again. To have that so intensely and then lose it so suddenly, Morgan found it hard to wrap her head around.

"Morgan?"

Morgan sighed and turned towards the voice at the end of the bar. "Yes?"

"The bar is quiet. Come and chat with me."

Morgan didn't know why Amanda was there. Morgan sure as hell hadn't invited her. They hadn't spoken since Morgan had cut her loose over two months ago, so when Amanda had come strolling through the door over an hour ago, Morgan hadn't known what to do. She could have asked her to leave, but it was a customer, and it wasn't ideal to turn that down. Thankfully, Amanda had been respectful and mostly quiet since she'd arrived. "I'm good here. I have customers."

Amanda lifted a brow. "Are they invisible? Because I don't see anyone who needs serving."

Morgan groaned inwardly. She was beginning to wish she *had* taken the night off. At least then, she could have lied and told Amanda she wasn't home. "I have a job to do. I can't stand around talking to you all night."

"You used to."

"Yeah, well, things are different now. You know this." Morgan approached Amanda and lowered her voice. "If you've come here expecting something more, you can leave. I've told you where we stand with one another and that's that."

"I do miss you." Amanda stroked the tips of her fingers over Morgan's hand, where it rested on the counter. Morgan drew it away, not wanting to give this woman an inch. If she did, Amanda would think something was happening here. It absolutely *categori-*

cally was not. "My marriage is complicated. I didn't tell you about him because I didn't think it mattered."

Morgan scoffed and shook her head. "You're joking, right? Why *wouldn't* it matter?"

"Because we weren't serious, and you made sure I knew that every time I came here."

"That's beside the point, Amanda. Whether we were serious or not doesn't change the fact that you're married." Morgan ran a hand through her hair. "Do you have any idea how affairs affect people? What it does to them and their self-confidence?"

As Morgan said that, her thoughts instantly turned to Jan. The pain and turmoil on her beautiful face the night she sat in the very spot Amanda had taken on arrival. She couldn't *ever* put herself in that position with a married woman ever again. In future, if there *was* anyone else, Morgan would insist on knowing the truth before she dared to continue.

"Is that what this is about? You've been cheated on in the past, and now you're hurt that I didn't tell you about my husband?"

"No. It's nothing to do with that. I just don't like knowing you put me in that position. I mean, what if he'd found out and turned up here one night? If he'd had something to say to me in front of all my customers? I'd look like a right twat then, wouldn't I?"

"He never would have known. He barely knows I'm in the same house as him at times."

Was Amanda in the same situation that Jan had never realised she was in? Was she also living through a one-sided marriage? God, Morgan hoped not. She couldn't deal with two divorcing women. No way. "If you're not happy with him, you should tell him that."

"It's not that simple. It never is." Amanda curled her finger and beckoned Morgan closer. As Morgan dipped her head, expecting maybe an apology, Amanda brought a hand to her cheek. "*You* were who I wanted to be with. I wish you could have given me another chance."

Morgan peeled Amanda's fingers from her cheek and stepped back. "You have a husband. I could never give you another chance." A whoosh of cold air hit Morgan as the bar door opened. Thank God she had a customer to see to. The longer she stood here talking to Amanda, the more she felt inclined to ask her to drink elsewhere. "And now I have to get back to work."

She turned away from Amanda and puffed out her cheeks. Morgan just didn't need this right now. She was dealing with her own shit.

With a forced bright smile, she moved further along the bar and looked up. And then everything within her froze, her pulse thundering in her ears as she gazed across the room.

Jan...was standing there.

Jan gazed back at Morgan, almost smiling when Morgan's mouth hung open and she blinked repeatedly. Was that a good sign? Was Morgan happy to see Jan? God, she really hoped that's what this reaction was. If Jan had got this wrong and Morgan didn't want to see her ever again, then she would walk out of here feeling embarrassed. Only she knew Morgan, and Morgan would never make her feel that way. She would accommodate Jan, then let her down gently in private. Even after Jan had done the one thing she'd never wanted to do...leave Morgan without answers.

"H-hi." Morgan cleared her throat. "I, um... I didn't think I'd see you in here again."

Jan hesitated but eventually moved closer. She felt eyes on her from the other end of the bar, and as she looked in that direction, everything within her recoiled. Amanda was here. The very woman Morgan had told Jan there was no chance of reconnecting with. The only reason Jan even knew it was Amanda was because she had tried to re-add Morgan on social media once Morgan had removed her from her profile.

You spent too long figuring your life out...and now it's too late.

She held her composure as she focused her attention back on Morgan. Yes, she was disappointed, but she wouldn't show it. Morgan was free to do whatever she pleased. "You...have company."

Morgan held up her hands. "She's a customer. Nothing more."

Jan could only take Morgan at her word. She hadn't lied to her before; there was no reason to think otherwise this time around. "Could I have a glass of red, please?" Jan decided *not* to take a seat at the bar. She had no intention of sitting within striking distance of Amanda. No way. She took some cash from her purse and handed it to Morgan when her glass of wine arrived in front of her.

"It's on the house." Morgan pushed the note back towards Jan and smiled. "How are you?"

"I'm...doing much better." Jan threw a thumb over her shoulder as she scrunched the note in her hand, aware that tonight wasn't the night to talk things through. To apologise to Morgan. Part of Jan had hoped Morgan wouldn't be working when she'd arrived—she was almost certain it was usually her day off—but it didn't really matter. It was just nice to be out of the house and somewhere familiar again. "I'll just take a seat. It's good to see you."

Jan crossed the room and smiled at Amanda when their eyes met. She had no desire to fight with another woman for Morgan's attention. She had enough going on. Jan took her phone from her clutch bag and slid into the booth she usually shared with Gillian and Finn. Right now, she wished they were here with her.

How much does Morgan hate you at the moment? I could really do with some company at the bar.

She set her phone down on the leather beside her and sighed. Perhaps coming here had been a mistake. Even if Jan had felt good about it as she left the house some thirty minutes ago, she was starting to have second thoughts.

Her phone pinged.

Do you want us to meet you there? I'm not sure of the reception we'll receive, but I'll be there for you if you need support.

Jan wouldn't say it was support she needed. She just didn't want to sit here looking like a lost soul while Amanda was around. It was quite clear that she and Morgan had been having some kind of heart-to-heart when Jan had arrived.

I'll be okay. I'll finish my wine and leave. The woman she was seeing before I came onto the scene is here. It's a little awkward. I'll call you tomorrow.

As she locked her phone and shoved it into her bag, Jan sat back in the booth and stared down at the table. Was this what her life would be now? Lonely evenings in bars. Dinner for one in a fancy restaurant. Days on end without human interaction outside of work. It was a depressing thought but one Jan had to prepare herself for.

She reached out and brought her drink closer to her. The deep red liquid sloshed around in the glass, almost spilling over the side. Jan lifted it and sipped, only to lock eyes on Morgan, who was now standing at the end of her table. "Is everything okay?"

"You're here."

Jan's brows drew together. "Do you want me to leave?"

"I can't believe you're here. Just...sitting here."

Jan cast her gaze on the table again. "I'll go. I'm sorry. I probably should have called to ask if it was okay to come." She set her bag down on the table and slid towards the end of the booth. "I had hoped you had the night off so we could talk."

Morgan stepped back as Jan got to her feet, one hand shoved in her jeans pocket. "You wanted to talk?"

"Yes. But right now isn't ideal. I understand that." Jan's eyes drifted towards Amanda very briefly. She was watching their interaction intently. "I didn't realise she was around again."

"She's not. She turned up about an hour ago. I didn't know she was in town."

Jan searched Morgan's eyes. Genuine, as always. "Then I'll come back when it's a better time for you."

Morgan chewed her lip for a moment. "When you say you want to talk...is it *us* you wanted to talk about?"

"Mmhmm. If there's any chance of an us, anyway." Jan didn't want to imagine never being with Morgan again, but she didn't know how Morgan felt about her anymore. Jan had fallen off the face of the earth for two weeks. "I know I should have come to you and explained why I needed some space, but my head wasn't in the right place the night I texted you."

"Hey, you don't have to explain." Morgan took a step closer. "I know what you're going through, and I'd always prepared myself for a message like that. Granted, I wasn't expecting it, given how great things were going between us, but I get it. I just wanted you to be okay."

"I am. I'm okay." Jan inched a hand forward and took Morgan's, which hung at her side. "Thank you for understanding."

"I wanted to call you, but I didn't think you'd appreciate it. I've been worried about you." Morgan entwined their fingers and stepped closer again, the softness of her eyes melting Jan. It was nice to know that hadn't changed. "It's so good to see you, Jan."

"Are you sure?" Jan wrinkled her nose, even though Morgan looked happy to see her. "I don't expect you to be very happy with the way I left us, but it really wasn't anything you'd done. You've been amazing. You've been patient and understanding. You... care."

"Of course I care. You mean the world to me, babe."

Jan's heart fluttered. She'd missed these moments with Morgan. God, she'd missed everything about her. "I know I've shown up here tonight unannounced, but would you consider giving me another chance? I don't expect an answer from you in this moment, but I would be grateful if you'd think about it. About us."

Morgan beamed one of those delicious smiles. "I don't need to think about it."

Jan practically pressed herself to Morgan, a hand placed on her chest, and drew her in to enjoy the sweet taste of her lips. Even though she'd spent the last week sorting her life out, Jan had taken any opportunity she could to remind herself of this woman. Of everything Morgan brought to her life. Happiness, laughter, excitement. Reluctantly, Jan pulled back and took her bottom lip between her teeth. God, she'd wanted to kiss Morgan in public for so long. Spain hadn't counted—nobody knew either of them there—but here...where they had friends and acquaintances, she'd ached to do it.

They gazed back at one another, the heat between them quite clear and a stark reminder of what Jan had almost lost. She smiled as she said, "I guess we should arrange that date we've *continuously* spoken about."

The sound of a stool scraping along the floor had Morgan turning around suddenly. Amanda was aggressively shoving her phone and purse into her handbag. Jan wouldn't get involved in this, so she took a seat and watched whatever was about to happen unfold.

Amanda crossed the room and stopped in front of Morgan. She looked down at Jan, scoffed, then held a hand up in her face. "I don't know who *the fuck* you are or where you came from." She glared at Morgan. "Have you been fucking her behind my back?"

Morgan's brows rose. "Really? You actually think you have *any* right to ask me that?"

"Have you?" Amanda lowered her hand from in front of Jan's face and stepped closer to Morgan. "Is this why you were so quick to drop me?"

"I dropped you before I met Jan." Morgan squared her shoulders. "Let's not forget that *you're* the cheat, not me."

Jan rose to her feet and cleared her throat when she noticed several customers watching. "I think you should leave. This is Morgan's bar, and she has customers in."

Amanda turned to Jan. "And I think this conversation has nothing to do with you."

"Thankfully, it doesn't." Jan took Morgan's hand as she stood right beside her. This woman wouldn't make a scene in here, not on Jan's watch. "But it doesn't change the fact that people are watching, and you should know better than to cause a scene in here. It's very childish."

Amanda folded her arms across her chest. "Who exactly are you?"

"That's not relevant to this conversation." It didn't matter who Jan was. It was time for Amanda to leave. "Get your belongings and go."

"Are you going to let her speak to me like that?" Amanda side-eyed Morgan.

"Trust me, she's being far more respectful than I would be. Jan is right. It's time for you to leave." Morgan stepped away and took Amanda's handbag from the bar and her coat from her stool. She handed them over and smiled. "And please, don't come back."

With sheer disbelief etched on her face, Amanda stepped around Morgan and walked out the door. Jan's shoulders relaxed immediately, but people were still looking over at them. She turned to Morgan and kissed her slowly. "Am I staying until you close, or am I going home to warm the place up for your arrival?"

Morgan grinned as she wrapped both arms around Jan's waist. "I'm not letting you go. You'll have to stay so I have something beautiful to look at."

Jan brought a hand to Morgan's cheek, reminding herself of Morgan's soft skin. "I've spent two weeks thinking about you. You'll have to forcefully remove me from your premises."

"The only place I'll be forcefully removing you from is that booth so I can take you upstairs and have my way with you."

And just like that, Jan's world lit up once again. All she felt was Morgan. All she saw was Morgan. And if she had her way, it would be for a very long time to come.

CHAPTER 31

The disbelief Morgan felt as she sat here with Jan was quite startling. She hadn't expected her to walk through the bar door tonight, and when she had, she hadn't thought for one second that anything positive could come out of it. But...here she was, with her hand in Jan's. Here she was...with the biggest grin spread on her mouth, knowing this woman was back in her life. How had this happened? Two weeks ago, when Jan asked for space, Morgan hadn't seen a way forward. She'd wanted to reach out and tell Jan that she understood—that she accepted the position she was in—but Morgan had been unable to find the right words in those moments when she'd stared at her phone.

As Morgan scanned the bar, completely empty for the first time this week, she was glad no customers were sitting around. If they were, Morgan wouldn't be able to spend this time with Jan. If they were, she certainly wouldn't be aching to press herself to Jan and remind them both of everything they'd shared so far.

"You okay, babe?" Morgan turned her body inwards and lay a hand on Jan's thigh. "I really want to take this upstairs so we can talk, but I usually have an influx around nine-thirty."

Jan drew Morgan into a kiss. One that had her head spinning

and her palms clammy. When she pulled back a little, Jan smiled. "I'm fine. I'm perfectly okay sitting here."

"Can I get you another drink or something?" Morgan felt slightly nervous, but she couldn't fathom why. Perhaps it was the unexpectedness of this night. Maybe she was subconsciously worried that this would fall apart again. It had been so sudden the last time around that it was possible.

"Hey," Jan whispered against Morgan's lips. "Relax. Take a minute."

Morgan cast her gaze between them as she leaned against the booth. "I'm sorry. I...didn't think I'd see you again. I don't know what to do with myself."

"That's understandable." Jan's acknowledgment of the situation meant a lot to Morgan. She hadn't walked in here and expected all to be forgotten. "I should have come here sooner. Or called, at least."

"Have you been okay?" Morgan searched Jan's eyes, enamoured by the blueness of them tonight. Had they always been so intense, or had Morgan just missed Jan so much that everything seemed heightened? "While you took some time away, were you okay?"

Jan regarded Morgan with a wry smile. "The first week, no. Then Gillian came to see me, so the second week was better." Morgan was glad Gillian had been around for Jan. She hated the thought of her just existing at home. "She...said you've cut ties with Finn."

Morgan hadn't come face to face with Finn in a fortnight now. Part of her hoped that would continue, but the rest of her was just sad to have lost a friend. Though, was Finn really a friend if she could interfere the way she had when it came to Jan and Morgan? If that was considered acceptable, then Morgan didn't want friends like that. Regardless of the fact Finn was trying to look out for them both in her own way, it had still resulted in Morgan losing Jan. "Yeah. The night you texted me."

"Could it be repaired?"

Morgan pondered the idea for a moment. She didn't know the answer to that because it wasn't something she'd thought about until now. Did she miss seeing Finn around the place? Yes, of course she did. But Morgan *would not* risk this again by having someone in her life who thought they could meddle without consequences. She didn't care who it was; it just wasn't an option moving forward. "Honestly, I don't know."

"If it makes any difference, I'd like to see it repaired." Jan squeezed Morgan's hand and smiled. "Life is too short to fall out with people."

"She's the reason you and I haven't seen one another for two weeks." Morgan frowned, a little perplexed that Jan would want her to forgive Finn for fucking this all up. "I don't forgive very easily. Not when someone has taken something so special away from me."

"But...I'm sitting here right now telling you I want to be with you, Morgan. Everything else is irrelevant at this point."

"And Gillian? Is she going to come in here and tell me what she thinks of me, of *us*, and I'm expected to let it go?"

"No. Gillian won't do that. She's supportive of my decision." Jan cleared her throat. "I haven't spoken to Finn yet. I think she may be avoiding me."

"She's lucky I didn't smack her in the face when she came here the other week. You'd just texted me and she walked through the door. I was so fucking angry with her." Morgan ran a hand down her face and sighed. "I don't care who she is to you or anyone else —I'm not putting up with shit like that. I'm not losing you again so they can either get on board, or they can just deal with me being around."

Jan shifted closer, though Morgan didn't know how it was possible. She already felt as though she was wrapped around her. Jan brought a hand to Morgan's cheek and gave her a knowing look. "And I'd never expect you to put up with it. What you and I do is nobody else's business." She stroked a thumb against Morgan's skin, reminding her of what every last touch had once felt like. "I think you did the right thing in cutting Finn off. She has to understand that she can't behave like that and get away with it."

"Y-you agree with me?"

Jan smiled. "If nothing else, I think it may have reminded her of what she could potentially lose."

"As it stands, she *has* lost me. I'm not going to bend over backwards to make her feel more comfortable in my life, and if the time comes, I'll tell her that." Morgan was sick and tired of her love life forever going wrong. She wasn't doing it anymore. If she had the chance to be happy—and she did here with Jan—then everyone else could fuck off. It was that simple. "I care about you, and I care about a relationship with you. If that means Finn and I are no longer friends, and I avoid situations that involve her and Gillian, then so be it."

"They do understand that they're in the wrong. They realise they should have kept their opinions to themselves, even if their worries for us both came from a good place," Jan said as she drew her hand away. "I texted Gillian tonight when Amanda was here, and she didn't seem overly enthused about coming. Because they're not welcome here."

"Maybe if they both changed their attitude towards me, I wouldn't have to tell them they weren't welcome here." Morgan lifted a shoulder and got to her feet. She wasn't sitting here talking about either of them any longer. "Glass of red?"

Jan smiled and offered a single nod as she said, "You're a good person, Morgan. I'm grateful to have you in my life."

Morgan rounded the bar and grabbed a beer for herself, then poured Jan a glass of red wine. "Then that's all that matters." As she gazed back at Jan across the room, the door opened, and a frantic Gillian stared back at Morgan.

"H-hi, um...I know you don't want to see me, but I was

wondering if you knew where Jan was? I can't get a hold of her, and I'm worried."

Morgan cocked her head towards the booth they'd been occupying for the last twenty minutes or so. "She's sitting right there."

Gillian frowned as she stepped further into the bar. "O-oh."

Morgan watched their interaction, choosing to remain behind the bar until Gillian had said what she needed to say. Only as she started to wipe down the counter, the door opened again, and Finn walked in. Morgan turned her back and took her stock folder from the shelf beneath the bar, aware of the tension in the room as Finn's eyes burned through her. "Your wife is at your usual table."

"Morgan."

Pinching the bridge of her nose, Morgan exhaled a deep breath and focused on the various bottles of whiskey along the back wall. "Yeah?"

"C-could we talk?"

Morgan turned around, anxiety written all over Finn's face as she wrapped a hand around the back of her neck and cleared her throat. Morgan remained silent while she mulled over the idea of sitting down to talk with Finn. Since Gillian was also here, she would likely chime in when it was necessary. At least, that's what Morgan hoped for, judging by what Jan had said a few minutes ago. While Morgan didn't particularly care for or need either of their support in this, it would absolutely make life easier. She didn't want Jan to have to split her time or be mindful of bringing her best friend up in conversation around Morgan.

"I can just leave if you want me to. Jan is fine, thankfully, so if you'd rather not do this...I get it."

Morgan nodded towards the stool on the other side of the bar. "Have a seat."

Finn's eyes lit up as she smiled, but the atmosphere was... strained. Morgan had no idea what would come of this conversation, but she would allow Finn the space to say what she needed to say. "Thanks. I appreciate it."

"If a customer comes in, I'll have to deal with that." Morgan remained behind the bar, stepping towards the beer pump holding Finn's usual beer of choice. "You want a drink?"

"Please. I haven't had a good pint since...well, you know when."

Morgan nodded as she lifted a glass towards the pump. "Plenty of places serve your beer, Finn."

"And none of those places are my local or a bar I'd prefer to be at." Finn sighed as she looked over her shoulder at Gillian and Jan. "Could Gillian—"

"Have a glass of white wine?" Morgan quirked a brow.

"Y-yeah. If that would be okay?"

Morgan groaned inwardly. Finn had never been lost for words before; she didn't need to start that habit now. "Look, if you have something to say, just say it, Finn." Morgan stared at her. "Jan is here, I haven't seen her for two weeks, and I know where I'd rather be. It's *not* standing behind this bar waiting for you to figure out your feelings."

"I'm sorry. For everything." Finn shook her head and cast her gaze on the pint Morgan had just set down in front of her. "I feel like an absolute prick, and I'm so sorry."

Morgan nodded slowly. "Okay."

Finn's brows drew together when her head shot up. "What? That's it? You're not going to make me suffer?"

"We're not okay, not by a long shot, but Jan is back in my life, and that's all I care about right now." Morgan leaned over the bar and lowered her voice. "But I'm warning you, what's happened over the last few weeks...it'll be the last time you *ever* get involved in my personal life again. Got it?"

Finn held up her hands. "I know. I was out of line."

"Now, go and join your wife while I get her a glass of wine." Morgan turned and walked away, rolling the tension out of her shoulders as she closed her eyes and took a moment to settle again. If she just focused on Jan, everything would be okay.

"Morgan?" Jan's voice had a smile spreading on Morgan's face faster than anything else in this world ever would. "Is everything okay?"

Morgan turned with Gillian's drink and nodded. She handed Jan her own glass, grabbed her beer, and eyed their table. "Yeah, of course. I'll sit with you while this place is still empty."

Jan met Morgan at the end of the bar and wrapped an arm around her waist. She searched Morgan's eyes, narrowed her own ever so slightly, and then simply nodded. "Okay. If you're sure."

"I am. Let's sit down together while we can." Morgan followed Jan and approached the booth. Finn and Gillian looked as though they were ready to run out the door the moment anything confrontational happened, but that wasn't who Morgan was. She'd never found happiness out of bickering with people. "Your drink," Morgan said as she set it down in front of Gillian.

"O-oh. Thank you."

Gillian clearly hadn't expected Morgan to be so welcoming, but she could kill people with kindness when it suited her. In this moment, Morgan had everything she needed sitting right beside her. Jan...and only ever Jan. "No problem."

"I..." Gillian shook her head and sat up straight against the booth. "I wanted to speak to you."

Morgan lifted a brow. "Me?"

"Yes." Gillian quickly took a sip of wine and eyed Jan briefly. Morgan had no idea what was about to happen, but the tension she'd felt as Gillian and Finn arrived had quickly faded. "I believe you're under the impression that I don't like you. Not only after everything that's happened recently, but before then, too."

Morgan rested her ankle on her knee as she relaxed back. "I don't expect to be friends with everyone, Gillian. So long as we can all be amicable, that's enough for me."

"It's not true. That I don't like you." Gillian's eyes softened for the first time ever in Morgan's company. "I'll admit that I was a little standoffish when I met you through Finn. I was dealing with a lot, and my job was potentially on the line if anyone knew about us. But I don't dislike you. I don't know you to dislike you."

"That's fair."

"Did I wonder if you and Finn had ever been together? For all of five seconds, yes, but that's where it ends. I guess we've just never really given one another the opportunity to get to know each other." Gillian lay a hand over Jan's on the table. "But you're dating my best friend, and I'd like to finally get to know you."

"I'd...like that, too." Morgan hadn't expected Gillian to be so lovely this evening, but she was thankful for this conversation. "I just want everyone to be okay with this." Morgan turned her attention to Finn, holding up a hand when Finn opened her mouth to respond. "I admire how protective you both are of Jan, but she's safe with me. She's happy with me. And I'm fucking insanely happy with her."

Finn nodded as she smiled. "I know."

"So, like...can we all just stop being weird and get back to normal? Every time someone pipes up with their opinion, I lose precious time with Jan. I'm not risking that anymore."

Jan palmed Morgan's thigh beneath the table. "I've lost enough time with you over the last two weeks."

Morgan turned her face to Jan and grinned. "We have all the time in the world to make up for it. You know that."

Jan leaned in and placed a hand to Morgan's chest as she kissed her. When Morgan had expected her own body to tense—it was the usual reaction when Jan did something like that in front of people—the opposite happened. Everything within Morgan relaxed. Any doubts slid from her mind, and all she could think about was the moment she woke up with Jan in her arms again.

"Okay, *that's* going to take me a minute to get used to." Gillian's voice broke Morgan and Jan apart. "I'm so used to seeing you kiss Phil and his stubbly face..."

Jan laughed. "Yes, I don't miss that at all."

"Why would you?" Gillian shrugged. "Nothing in this world could compare to the softness of another woman."

Jan melted against Morgan at that. "Oh, you're not wrong."

As Morgan brought her beer to her lips, the bar door opened, and a customer walked in. She groaned and rose to her feet. "Right. Have fun. Some of us have work to do."

CHAPTER 32

Roused from a deep sleep by the sound of the coffee machine, Jan cracked one eye open and groaned. She hadn't moved from this very position all night, and now she had a dead arm and pins and needles in her shoulder. The moment they'd locked up the bar and headed up here last night, Jan and Morgan had crashed. It had been an emotional evening, so it was to be expected, but now Jan felt refreshed and ready for whatever this day threw at her.

She stretched herself out in Morgan's bed, smiling when she heard Morgan humming along to the radio in the kitchen. God, she'd missed this. She'd missed *her*. Everything that Morgan was... Jan had craved. There had been moments when she'd lay in bed just staring at the ceiling all night, and there had been moments when she'd woken up on the couch the next morning because the bed had felt too lonely to even climb into. But she was here, and she had been all night. Safely in Morgan's arms.

Jan brought the material of Morgan's T-shirt up to her nose and inhaled as she smiled. There was something incredibly pleasing about waking up in Morgan's washed-out Ramones T-shirt. It reminded Jan of not only the moments they'd already had together but everything that was to come. Happiness, excitement, something different. But for now, Jan simply wanted to snuggle into Morgan's bed and leave the world outside.

"Morning, babe."

Jan brought the material away from her face and grinned when she saw Morgan standing in the bedroom doorway holding two coffee cups. "Hi."

"Coffee?"

"Yes, thank you." Jan sat up and took a cup from Morgan, then slouched back against the headboard. She brought it to her lips, moaning as she inhaled the scent of fresh coffee. "Smells amazing."

"I thought it might wake you up a bit. I barely got two words out of you last night once we'd got into bed."

Jan pulled the cover back and cocked her head towards the empty space. "Come and keep me warm for a bit longer."

Morgan rounded the foot of the bed and climbed in on her side. Jan had to smile at that. She had a side of the bed here. As Morgan faced her, she frowned. "What are you grinning at?"

Jan cast her gaze on the cup in her hands and shook her head. "Oh, nothing."

"No, tell me."

Clearing her throat as she set her coffee down on the bedside table, Jan shifted closer to Morgan and sighed. Usually, she would try to find the right words without putting pressure on this, but she didn't care this morning. She took Morgan's hand and brought it to her lips. "I...have a side of the bed here."

"Of course you do. You'll *always* have a side of the bed here, babe." Morgan's gorgeous brown eyes gazed back at Jan, making her heart jump and her pulse race. She felt so many things when it came to Morgan, but wasn't it too soon to say them out loud? Jan...didn't know. "And anything else you want to have here."

Jan hummed when Morgan pressed a kiss to the tip of her nose. "And the same goes for you when it comes to my place."

"I'm just really happy you got to keep your place. The rest doesn't matter."

Jan sensed a hint of apprehension in Morgan's voice. She understood. Jan had walked away just two weeks ago, but she was here, and she was staying in Morgan's life. Nothing in this world could change her mind on that, especially now that Jan had support from Gillian and Finn. "I know this has been a lot, and I'm so deeply sorry for losing my head, but I'm in this with you, Morgan. All of it...I want, okay?"

"W-what are you saying?" Morgan's brows drew together as she searched Jan's eyes.

"I'm saying that I don't just want to date you. I want to be with you. Exclusively. I want to wake up with you every morning if I can, and I want to share all of *me* with all of *you*."

Morgan blinked back tears. "You mean that?"

"Every last word of it." Jan wrapped herself around Morgan and nuzzled into her chest. Nowhere had ever felt safer. Nowhere would ever feel better. "I've signed the divorce papers, I'm back at work, and I'm here. I have everything I want, Morgan. I feel... happier than I have in a long time, and that's because of you."

Morgan sniffled when she pressed a kiss to Jan's hair and held her close. "I've missed you so much."

"I'm sorry."

"Please, don't apologise." Morgan drew back and brought a hand to Jan's cheek. "I understand why you needed to step back, but it didn't make me miss you any less." Tears slid down Morgan's face, but her smile was something to be admired in this moment. "The longer I went without hearing from you, the more I wondered if I'd ever see you again." As Morgan's voice broke, the floodgates opened. *Oh, God.* Jan's heart broke when Morgan lowered her head and sobbed against her shoulder. "I can't believe you showed up for me."

"Hey," Jan whispered as she soothed a palm up and down Morgan's back. "I'll *always* show up for you." Jan squeezed her eyes shut when her own tears threatened to surface. "I made a mistake asking for space. I should have thought about what you needed in that moment, and not just myself."

Morgan shook her head against Jan's shoulder. "You know I only care about what's best for you. I've always been honest about that."

"And I now realise what's best for me."

Morgan lifted her head and brushed the back of her hand against her cheeks. Her bottom lip continued to tremble, but Jan appreciated Morgan's vulnerability in this moment.

"You, baby. *You* are what's best for me."

"I don't know how you ended up in my life, and I don't know what you see in me that could possibly make you happier than you've been in the past, but I'm so fucking in, Jan. Every last piece of me is entirely in where you're concerned."

"I know." Jan stroked her thumbs beneath Morgan's eyes and regarded her with a smile. "I don't like seeing you cry."

Morgan scoffed as she lifted a shoulder. "I rarely cry."

"I hope that I'll never be the reason you cry again." Jan drew her into a kiss, one hand wrapped around Morgan's neck when she pressed herself to Morgan's warm body. "From this moment on, we go back to what we had before I stupidly sent that message to you. Only this time...without hiding."

Morgan relaxed and touched her forehead to Jan's. "I'm so ready."

"And...I was hoping I could spend the weekend here with you while you're working."

"Ben took the promotion. I asked him last week, and he didn't even have to think about it."

Jan was thrilled to hear that. Ben was such an integral part of Morgan's team, and he was a lovely guy. "That's brilliant news."

"So, I have every other weekend off now. As well as a few nights a week."

Jan beamed a smile. "Please tell me this weekend is your weekend off..."

"It is." Morgan pulled Jan into her lap and wrapped her arms around her waist. "And I don't want to spend it here with you."

"Maybe my place?" Jan quirked a brow. "We haven't had the chance to spend much time there together."

"I'd love to spend the weekend with you at your place, but could I take you out for dinner tomorrow night?"

"It's a date," Jan said as she smiled into another kiss. "With the most beautiful woman in the world."

Morgan blushed and cleared her throat. "You uh...you said you're back at work."

"We can talk about that later. Once we're back at my place... maybe with a takeout."

"Perfect." Morgan practically lifted Jan out of her lap and sat her in the middle of the bed. She got to her feet and opened her wardrobe. "Guess I'd better sort a weekend bag out for myself."

"Mm. Maybe you should just pick out some clothes that you can leave at my place. After all, you'll be spending a lot of time there when you're not working."

Morgan spun around and grinned. "Seriously?"

"As serious as a heart attack, gorgeous."

Watching Jan from the archway that separated the kitchen from the dining room, Morgan smiled to herself. She'd spent the entire day with Jan—something that wasn't often possible—and now they were about to sit down in the living room with takeout. Moments like this were something Morgan rarely afforded herself, but with Jan, she wanted so many more of them. Taking life at their own pace, lounging around if they felt like it, just being with one another. Tonight, this was all Morgan could have dreamed of.

She stepped towards Jan and wrapped her arms around her

waist from behind. "Something smells good, and it's not the food."

Jan glanced back over her shoulder and smirked. "That was something I missed. The way you smell."

Morgan lifted a brow. "Oh, really?"

"Mmhmm. Your perfume always reminds me of the first night we slept together." Jan relaxed back and settled her hands over Morgan's. "Down in the bar...with you pressed against me. It's something I remember vividly."

Dropping a kiss below Jan's neck, Morgan inched a hand lower and slipped it just past the waistband of the sweatpants Jan wore. "I've had dreams about that night on several occasions now."

"It's good to know I'm not the only one." Jan turned in Morgan's arms and drew her into a kiss. She tasted of everything Morgan had craved over the years. Safety and promise. Contentment and love. "Ready to eat?"

"Yeah, come on. I'll get the food." Morgan stepped away from Jan and gathered everything they needed onto a tray. Once they were in the living room, the coffee table cleared so they had space to lay everything out, Morgan lowered herself to her knees and started to plate up. "I've had a great day with you, by the way. I didn't realise how much I wanted to do these things with you until it wasn't happening anymore."

"We've not really had the chance to spend entire days with one another, have we? I know we had Spain, and I know there was the odd time when you didn't have to work, but knowing that we'll be able to enjoy at least every other weekend together is something to look forward to."

"You said you're back at work. I won't know what to do with myself now that you won't be strolling into my bar whenever you like."

Jan grinned. "Actually, my work schedule has changed. My choice."

"Oh?"

"I only work from the office two days a week now. The rest of the time will be from home." Jan cleared her throat. "I don't want the awkwardness of being there every day. Once Anais is showing, people will just start to talk more than they already are."

Morgan hated that Jan felt as though she would be better off working from home. Even if it meant she got to see Jan more often because there wouldn't be a commute to contend with every day, it didn't make Morgan hate Phil and his new woman any less. "You own that business, babe. Don't let her make you feel awkward."

"Oh, she can't even bring herself to look at me." Jan scoffed and shook her head. "And working from home means you can come over and lounge around if I'm busy. It keeps you out of the bar when you're not working. A change of scenery, you know?"

"You don't know how much I'd love that." Morgan glanced up at Jan and smiled. "Sort of makes me never want to have to work again."

"I'm just grateful for any time I can spend with you." Jan helped herself to a spring roll. "It was nice to see Gillian and Finn last night."

"Yeah, it was." Morgan was glad they'd had a conversation last night. She didn't need the animosity between them. "Finn apologised, and now we can all move on."

"I think she was under the impression that she'd ruined your friendship entirely. Judging by what Gill said to me last week, anyway." Jan sighed as she stretched her legs under the coffee table and relaxed against the couch. "I'm glad that's not the case."

"Nah. It's not like that at all. I just...I don't like confrontation." Morgan lifted a shoulder. "The night she came to the bar, we had a pretty rough discussion. She realised she'd fucked up then, but I wasn't going to roll over for her. She deserved to feel the way she did. I'd just lost you, and it was mostly her fault."

"Everyone is where they're supposed to be now." Jan lifted her plate from the table and moaned when she stabbed a fork into a sui mai. "You're a bad influence. I *never* eat takeout."

Morgan stopped mid-chew and side-eyed Jan. "I... You don't?"

"No. It always seemed a waste to order something in for me alone."

Fucking hell. Phil had been so absent in their marriage that Jan couldn't even enjoy something simple like a takeout on a weekend. That was sad. Truly sad. "But you enjoy takeout, right?"

"I do. It's nice to not have to cook one night a week."

"In that case, let's make it a weekend thing. And if I'm working, we'll make it a midweek thing." Morgan nudged Jan's shoulder. "You can have anything you want with me, babe."

Jan regarded Morgan with a sexy smirk. "Yes. I'm beginning to realise that."

No matter what, Morgan was going to spoil this woman in any way she could. Jan deserved it. She deserved so fucking much. "We're a good team, don't you think?"

Jan gazed back lovingly at Morgan, those blue eyes soft and inviting. "We make a very good team."

"I'm enjoying having other things on my mind lately. It's always just been work, but now? Work is generally the furthest thing from my mind." It wasn't often Morgan fell asleep at night with a woman on her mind, but she was enjoying the change. And Jan, of all women? Well, Morgan would sleep soundly for many years to come. "I fall asleep thinking about you, and I wake up the very same way."

Jan reached for the TV controller on the coffee table and powered it on. "Mm, even when you're sleeping next to me, you're in my dreams too."

If Jan kept saying things like that, Morgan was going to say some things that she probably wasn't ready to hear. *Change the subject!* She quickly cleared her throat. "Hey, um...I don't want to put you off me, but could I put the football on? It's being televised tonight."

Jan laughed. "Of course you can. I don't watch much TV, so help yourself." Jan handed the controller to Morgan and turned her face towards Morgan's shoulder. She pressed a kiss to the skin not covered by her tank top, then returned to her food. "And for the record, it would take a lot for me to be put off by you."

Morgan whooped when she saw the score line. Her team was winning one nil.

"Which team is yours?"

Morgan smiled. "The team wearing blue."

"Are they good...or?"

Hmm. That was a debatable question. "At the moment, yes. But it's been a tough season for us. Things are looking up now, though. New manager and all."

"Excellent. You can explain the rules around football to me some other time."

"While I appreciate the enthusiasm, you don't have to take an interest in it if it's not your thing, babe." Morgan would talk to Jan about everything and anything, but she found it hard to believe that she would *ever* be remotely interested in football.

"It's an interest of yours, so it's an interest of mine."

And just like that, Morgan fell harder in love with this woman. She didn't know how that would go down when she eventually found the courage to tell Jan, but that was a problem for another day. Tonight, Morgan just wanted this. To be alone with Jan.

CHAPTER 33

One week later...

With her chores for the day done and dusted—literally—Jan relaxed back against the kitchen counter and sighed. She hated cleaning; there had been a time when she'd considered hiring someone only for Phil to insist that he would do it. But Morgan was headed over this evening once her shift was over...and Jan wanted to finish anything that needed doing beforehand. The thought of doing anything other than giving Morgan her full attention tonight filled her with dread. Morgan had worked the late shift last night, followed by the day shift this morning, so time together was all Jan wanted.

She turned for the coffee machine and powered it on. A quick caffeine fix would see her right, and then she could prepare for that beautiful evening with Morgan. Because, yes, evenings had become exciting since she'd met Morgan. Gone were the days of Jan sitting at home alone, waiting on a call from Phil from wherever he was in the country. Gone were the days of settling simply because that's what was expected of her. Morgan made her feel, made her think, but more than anything, she had made Jan fall back in love with life. That said a lot about who Morgan was if she could pick Jan up so suddenly, given what had happened over the last few months.

As she sat a cup under the spout of the coffee machine, the doorbell rang. Her pulse quickened at the thought of Morgan waiting on the doorstep, arriving earlier than planned, so she rushed down the hallway and yanked the door open.

"Oh, Finn. Hi."

"Hey." Finn dipped her head and scuffed her boots against the ground, her hands shoved in her pockets. "Do you have a few minutes?"

Jan frowned. "Sure. Come in."

"Thanks. I won't stay long. I'm sure you're busy." Finn brushed past Jan and moved down the hallway and into the dining room. When she turned, she smiled and shifted uncomfortably. "I just wanted to touch base with you."

"Touch base?"

"Yeah. I haven't stopped by to apologise properly for the way things went the other week," Finn said as she cleared her throat. "And I'd really like to do that."

"Okay." Jan had to smile at that. Finn wasn't a bad person—far from it, actually—but she appreciated that she'd come here to apologise fully. It meant a lot to Jan. "Maybe we could have coffee?"

"Yeah, that would be great, thanks." Finn slid her jacket off and hung it over the back of a dining chair. She sat down and clasped her hands in front of her on the table, chewing her lip. "Morgan not here today?"

"She's working. She's coming over this evening."

"Nice." Finn nodded slowly. "I think we're allowed back in the bar after us being there last week, but it feels a bit strained still. Understandable, though."

"She hasn't said anything to me about either of you, so I

couldn't possibly explain anything regarding your friendship with her." Jan carried two coffees through from the kitchen and sat down facing Finn. "I'm sure she'd be happy to have a conversation with you about it if you think that's what needs to happen."

"Yeah, maybe. I...don't think she's bothered either way."

Jan knew Morgan would warm to Finn again when she was ready to. Until then, she wasn't getting involved. Morgan was entitled to feel whatever way she felt surrounding the fallout. "Give it time."

Finn wrapped her hands around her coffee cup and looked up at Jan. "And us?"

"What about us, Finn?"

"Do I need to give that time, too?" She stared back at Jan with a sadness in her eyes. "I would have come here sooner, but I wanted to give you and Morgan space to talk and stuff. I know I really fucked up, but I just...I can't deal with the thought of you hating me."

"Hate is a *very* strong word."

"Maybe it is, but you'd be well within your rights to feel that way." Finn's voice trembled, surprising Jan. "If that *is* how you feel, please don't see less of Gillian. I can go out when you come over if you don't want me there, or I can drive Gillian over here for girls' night. Just please don't make my wife suffer because I went behind her back and spoke to Morgan at the bar. I just...I was worried about you both. I didn't want either of you to get hurt." Finn shook her head. "I had no idea what had been going on between you, so my natural reaction was to worry about you moving too fast, you know?"

"Oh, Finn. I don't hate you." Jan reached a hand forward and settled it over Finn's. "We're okay."

"Why didn't you tell us about everything that was going on?" Finn frowned as she looked back at Jan. "Gillian is more like your sister than your friend, but we had no idea what was happening."

"I wanted to explore what I was feeling for Morgan. I wasn't ready to tell anyone." Jan could understand why Finn had asked that question. The three of them knew everything about one another at one time. "Morgan just wanted to do the right thing for me, which I appreciated at the time."

"I don't mean with Morgan. I mean with Phil. Gillian says you were in counselling before you found out about the affair."

Jan smiled weakly and cast her gaze on her coffee cup. "Everything has always been 'Jan and Phil'. Neither of us could do any wrong in your eyes or Gillian's. I guess I just wanted to work through our marriage problems and come out the other side with minimal impact. For nobody to look at us differently."

"We would have been there for you, you know."

"I know, and looking back, maybe I should have spoken to you both. Perhaps I would have seen what was happening sooner if I had," Jan said, pausing as she exhaled a long, slow breath. "But you and Gillian were only just repairing your own relationship. Then I saw how madly in love you were with one another, and I just couldn't bring myself to be honest about what was happening in my own life." Jan scoffed. "Pathetic, really, isn't it?"

Finn's brows drew together. "What is?"

"Wanting to present as the couple you and Gillian have always known. Wanting to pretend that life was just perfectly fine."

"I don't think it's pathetic at all. I think we all want our marriage to work, and when things go wrong, it's hard to open up about it." Finn lifted a shoulder. "I'm sure you look back now and see things you didn't see before. Moments when you realised you weren't as happy as you thought you were."

"I'm having a lot of those moments lately."

Finn took Jan's hand this time. "Are you happy now, Jan?"

Jan beamed a smile as she nodded. "So happy."

"Yeah?" Finn's smile mirrored Jan's. "Good. That's good."

"When I walked into the office that day and Gareth came to see me, I didn't think I'd be happy ever again. I knew I didn't want to give Phil another chance, and I wanted the divorce the moment

I knew the truth, but happiness wasn't something I had any intention of trying to find. Morgan just...came out of nowhere." Jan allowed herself a moment to appreciate everything Morgan had done for her. She smiled and dipped her head. "Even though I knew her as the owner of The Corner, that was the extent of it."

"She is great. I know I said some things to you that likely resulted in you walking away, and I know I said one or two things that were...well, terrible things to say about a friend, but she *is* great."

"She didn't take advantage of me, and she didn't use my situation to get whatever she wanted out of all of this. She...I don't even know how to explain it. She was there for me on a level I never once expected."

"I've never seen her so chilled out and enjoying life." Finn grinned. "She's always been a workaholic, and I was forever teasing her about settling down, but seeing her with you at the bar last week was eye-opening for me." Finn relaxed back into her seat, the tension in the air no longer lingering. "You mean a lot to her, Jan."

"We make one another happy, and that's all I care about. I don't need huge declarations, and I don't need someone to try too hard. I just needed exactly what she gave me, and that was *time*. All I wanted was time before I came to you and Gillian." Jan would never expect anyone to hide who they were or sneak around for her, but Morgan had done so without even being asked in the beginning. "I don't know what the future looks like right now, but Morgan will be in it for as long as I can have her."

"We *are* happy for you both. Now that the shock has worn off, we're really happy for you."

"Thank you."

"Would you maybe call us when you think we could all get together and go for dinner or something?" Finn asked, that apprehension still in her eyes.

"Absolutely. I'll speak to Morgan tonight and find out when she's available."

"Okay, but if she doesn't want to, would you at least keep in touch with Gillian? As I said, I'll make myself scarce if that's for the best, but Gillian misses you a lot. I do too, but I made my bed and now I have to lie in it."

As Finn got to her feet, Jan did, too. No matter what, she wasn't losing anyone she cared about. Jan opened her arms to Finn and smiled. "Come here. Everything is going to be okay."

Finn stepped towards Jan and accepted the hug. She sniffled when she rested her chin on Jan's shoulder, sighing as she relaxed against her. "I'm so sorry, Jan."

"I know you are." With a final squeeze, Jan drew back and cupped Finn's face. "We carry on as normal, okay?"

"Okay." Finn reached for her jacket and threw a thumb over her shoulder. "I'll head off, but you know where we are if you need anything."

As Finn strode down the long hallway, Jan cleared her throat. "Hey, Finn?"

"Yeah?" Finn turned with one arm through her jacket.

"How do you know when the moment is right?"

Finn stared back at Jan, utterly confused. "The...moment?"

"W-when did you know you were in love with Gill?"

The confusion clouding Finn's eyes quickly lifted, and her brows rose. "O-oh. Um, I think I knew I loved Gillian long before we were actually together. It was hard not to fall in love with her." Finn shrugged. "But I don't think you can really base it on our relationship. We spent so long trying to know what the right thing was that I probably told her I loved her a lot later than I would have liked to, you know?"

"It's just...I want Morgan to know what she means to me, but I'm worried it's too soon." Jan wasn't a fool, she knew she'd only separated from her husband near on three months ago, but did that really matter? If she was in love with someone, then surely it was okay to speak it out loud. "I'm worried she won't feel the same way...or that she'll think I'm being ridiculous for feeling the way I do when I only signed my divorce papers the week before we worked things out."

"You want my advice?" Finn smiled when Jan nodded. "Life is too short to *not* say what you're feeling, Jan. Dave was plotting to set Gillian's house on fire while we were figuring out how to be together, so yeah...you should say what you're feeling when the moment is right for you." Finn stepped towards Jan and squeezed her hand. "Fuck what anyone else thinks. If you're in love with Morgan, then you do what feels right to *you*."

"It's that easy?"

"Not always, but we don't need to make things harder than they already are." Finn let go of Jan's hand and opened the front door. "Whatever happens, though, *do not* tell Gillian I knew you were in love with Morgan before she did. I'll never hear the end of it."

Jan barked a laugh. "You're right. I also won't hear the end of it."

Finn puffed out her cheeks, her eyes wide. "Good talk."

"Thank you for coming over. It means a lot to me."

Finn stepped out into the garden and smiled. "Thanks for being lovely and not kicking my arse right back out the door again."

"I'll be in touch with some dates for dinner. Get home safe, Finn."

Jan closed the door and pressed her back to it, a million and one thought whirring around her head as she closed her eyes. Could Morgan come here tonight and learn what Jan was feeling? She didn't know, but she wasn't dismissing the idea completely. If the moment came, then Jan would do exactly what Finn had suggested...and do what felt right.

CHAPTER 34

With a bunch of flowers in her hand, Morgan rang Jan's doorbell and bounced on the balls of her feet. It was Sunday evening, Morgan was more than ready for a break tonight, and she knew this was the *only* place she wanted to be. In Jan's gorgeous, comfortable home. She hadn't realised it when Jan first mentioned Morgan spending her time off here, but it made sense. Morgan didn't have to worry about any of her staff knocking on her flat door because they needed advice on something. Instead, they could drop her a text while she was lounging on Jan's heavenly couch.

When the door opened and those blue eyes gazed back at her, Morgan fought the urge to cling onto Jan and never let her go. It wasn't necessary, and it wasn't a requirement now that they were in a relationship with one another. Morgan could be here whenever she wished to be, and Jan could come and go from the bar as she pleased. Life, right now, was fucking perfect.

"Hi." Jan wore a shy smile as she switched her gaze between Morgan and the flowers in her hand. "Are those for me?"

Morgan grinned as she stepped inside, lay a hand on Jan's hip, and kissed her on the cheek. "Of course they are."

"Oh, Morgan. They're beautiful."

Jan kicked the door shut and took Morgan's hand. As always, the warmth of Jan's home spread through Morgan, but it felt different here tonight. She couldn't put her finger on what the atmosphere was, but it was...calm. So calm she never wanted to leave here again. All of this made sense without Morgan understanding how it could.

"How was work?" Jan turned back and took the flowers from Morgan, inhaling as she brought them to her nose. "I wasn't sure if you'd get out on time because of the football."

"I have Ben, Tyler, *and* Megan working tonight. As soon as I knew I was seeing you, I made sure I had enough staff in so I could make a run for it the moment I knew I was able to."

Jan set the flowers down on the dining table and pulled Morgan in against her. "It's a strange feeling for me knowing you'd rather be here than anywhere else."

Yeah, Morgan understood that. "Just because certain people in the past haven't been appreciative to have you in their life, that doesn't mean I'm not. If I can ever choose where I want to be...it's here, with you." Morgan pressed a kiss to the tip of Jan's nose and smiled. "Remember that, okay?"

"Oh, I'll never forget it." Jan swayed them in the back living room to the gentle rhythm playing on the radio in the kitchen. "Can you believe we've made it to this point?"

"Honestly, no. I can't." Morgan stroked her knuckles gently against Jan's cheek and smiled. "Feels good, though."

"And Finn came over today to apologise to me."

Huh. It had taken that long? Morgan drew back ever so slightly. "I thought she would have apologised long before now. If I'd known she hadn't, I wouldn't have been so nice to her in the bar last week."

Jan lay a soothing hand on Morgan's chest. "She wanted to give me a more in-depth apology than a simple 'I'm sorry'. I appreciated it."

"That's fair enough. I'll let her off." Morgan guided Jan away from the dining table and into the main living room. "Do we have any plans for tonight?"

"No. Not unless you had something in mind," Jan said as she cleared her throat. "But while we're on the subject of Finn, she wanted to know if we'd like to go out for dinner with them."

"That would be lovely." Morgan flopped down on the couch, dragging Jan down on top of her as she did so. "Let me know when they're thinking, and I'll check my schedule."

"Perfect." Jan gazed back at Morgan with an intense yet unusual look in her eyes. "Thank you for coming over tonight."

Morgan had to wonder why Jan was thanking her. *She* should be the one thanking Jan for ever taking an interest in her. "No need to thank me."

"I know, but—" Jan cut herself off and made herself comfortable where she lay against Morgan, sideways along the couch. "I've spent the day going over a lot of things in my head and I have all these different feelings going on inside of me as a result of it."

"R-right." Morgan's brows drew together as she watched Jan intently. "Did you want to talk about anything you're feeling? If everything has become too much now that people know about us...I understand."

Jan propped her head in her hand and smiled as she toyed with the string on Morgan's hoodie. "Nothing is too much for me. I'm perfectly happy."

"O-okay. Then...I don't really know what else to say to you."

"Do you have any idea just how perfect you are?" Jan stroked a finger along Morgan's jawline, searching her eyes as that same finger traced Morgan's lips. "How much you've held me together over the last few months..."

"I'm far from perfect, but I hope you know that I always would have been there for you whether or not we were together. I didn't do it because I'm into you, babe. I did it because you needed someone, and that's just who I am. It's the right thing to do."

"I had no idea what my life would look like when I sat in your bar on that miserable Monday night. I couldn't imagine finding love again. Everything I'd always had, or *thought* I had, was gone. In a split second, I didn't feel as though I knew who I was anymore, and that was terrifying for me." Jan smiled weakly. "I hide what I want to hide very well, but inside, I was fearing being alone for the rest of my life."

"Someone like you could never be alone for the rest of your life." Morgan lifted a hand and cupped Jan's cheek. "There's always a second chance when it comes to love."

"I know that now. I have it right here with you."

Morgan's pulse hammered in her ears, Jan's gentle touch the only thing keeping her grounded. Jan surely didn't mean what she was saying, did she? "Jan, I—"

"I'm falling in love with you," Jan said, her voice soft but confident. Her eyes slowly lifted to meet Morgan's, holding something raw. Hope, maybe...or fear. "I didn't think I had it in me to give my heart away again so soon, but with you...it was effortless. It happened without knowing it. But I am. I'm falling in love with you."

Morgan's heart stopped for a beat or two, and then it started to race. The room that had once been filled with casual conversation was now as still as anything Morgan had felt before. Jan's words continued to hang between them. *I'm falling in love with you.*

A rush of warmth surged through Morgan, sending a tightness directly to her throat *and* her chest. She blinked repeatedly, wondering if she'd heard those words right, but no...Jan's gaze held firm on her, and Morgan knew she'd heard it exactly right. She also knew what Jan needed in this moment. Honesty.

A part of Morgan wanted to throw her arms around Jan, to tell her she felt exactly the same way, but the rest of her was hesitant. Morgan had been here before. She'd had the love, and she'd had what *she thought* was everything she needed. Only for it to fall apart and for Morgan to be left understanding that sometimes love could be a complicated road.

She swallowed hard. Jan's stare hadn't once wavered, and Morgan knew this moment was as real as it got for her. The uncertainty, the warmth, and the crippling excitement all swelled deep inside of her. She wanted to say something, *anything*, but all the words seemed too small, too...insignificant. Instead, she leaned in and kissed Jan. The kiss deepened, but there was nothing frantic or hurried about it. It was soft, deliberate...it was Jan. Morgan drew back slowly and smiled. "I'm falling in love with you, too."

Any tension in Jan quickly slipped away as she lay her head on Morgan's chest and sighed. The moment had happened, and now calmness resided in Morgan's head and heart. "Thank you for being the one to show me what happiness really is."

Morgan lowered a kiss to Jan's hair and whispered, "Thank you for trusting me."

Situated behind her computer in her home office, Jan wore a smile that hurt her face. Morgan was still sleeping, but Jan had been up and about preparing for a day of work for the last two hours. Back when she was married to Phil, Jan hated Mondays. Sunday night, too, when she had to prepare everything for the office, but this particular Monday morning was probably the greatest of her life. A little dramatic, perhaps, but the truth. How could she feel anything other than euphoric after her moment with Morgan last night?

The sex had been off the charts once they'd both come down from their emotions—raw and uninhibited—and this morning, Jan was aching in places that hadn't seen a hint of exercise in a long time. She grinned to herself as she rocked back in her chair and stared through the screen. Maybe she shouldn't be working today.

She sure as hell couldn't concentrate on anything that was required of her.

Thankfully, it was a slow-ish day. Beth had sent a few blueprints over for her to take a look at, and she had some files to update on the system, but that was the extent of Jan's 'work' today. *And I have her to myself all day, too.* Jan hadn't specifically timed her conversation with Morgan last night to coincide with the night off...followed by the next day, but it certainly helped.

As she brought up the first blueprint on her screen, she heard footsteps on the stairs. Jan smiled and peered over her shoulder, her heart pumping that little bit harder when Morgan landed in the hallway and strode confidently into the back living room. Jan was situated in the corner, her desk a mess of papers. "Good morning."

Morgan yawned as she stretched. "You should have woken me up."

"Why?"

"I don't know," Morgan said as she leaned down behind Jan and kissed the side of her neck. "If I've never told you before, you look incredibly hot wearing your reading glasses."

Jan rolled her eyes playfully. "God, you're such a lesbian."

"Guilty!" Morgan spun Jan's chair around and got to her knees in front of her. That gaze penetrated Jan in all kinds of ways, but the softness always remained in Morgan's eyes. The gold flecks did little to quell the love she had for this woman. "Do I need to remind you of just how much of a lesbian I am?"

Jan took her bottom lip between her teeth and smirked. "Maybe you do."

Morgan hooked her fingers around the waistband of Jan's—okay, they belonged to Morgan—sweatpants and urged her to lift her hips. When she did and Morgan dragged them down her legs, Jan felt that all too familiar heat rise throughout her. It didn't take a lot for Morgan to get her going, but since their conversation... since they'd told one another they were falling, it was so intense that Jan felt as though she could burst from the slightest of touches. And she had…on several occasions last night.

Morgan palmed Jan's thighs before she leaned back in to remove her underwear. The cool air prickled Jan's legs with goosebumps, but it was Morgan's soothing, warm breath that she focused on as she sat up on her knees and drew Jan into a fiery kiss. "Working from home just got exciting." Morgan smiled against Jan's mouth as she lowered her hand and dipped it between her legs. She brushed Jan's lips with her knuckles, kissing her way along Jan's jaw and towards her ear. "Mm, you're wet."

"W-what do you expect?"

Morgan's eyes flickered a shade darker when she urged Jan towards the edge of her chair. In all her life, nobody had ever dropped to their knees and gave Jan what she needed. Not Phil, not…anybody. "Fuck, I could taste you every minute of the day." Morgan licked her lips and inched closer. "You're so fucking beautiful. Every last thing about you."

Jan's heart swelled. Morgan had no issues with being vocal in their relationship, and in this moment, Jan believed it was top of the list in terms of what she loved about her. Communication was hugely important to Jan, even if she'd struggled with it herself recently. "Morgan, please…"

She dipped her head and licked a slow path between Jan's lips. Jan gripped the arms of her chair, pressed her heels into her seat, and gave herself over to Morgan. Her hips moved rhythmically, every inch of her skin burning with the orgasm already building deep in the pit of Jan's stomach.

"F-fuck." Jan gasped when Morgan slowly eased her tongue inside of her and wrapped her fingers around her thighs. "Y-yes. More."

The shrill of Jan's phone pierced the air, chiming on her desk as a call came through, but Morgan didn't let up. She eased deeper and moaned. Jan rode her face, thankful when her phone stopped ringing, and tangled her hand through Morgan's hair.

And then the ringing started again.

Fucking hell!

Morgan drew back reluctantly. "Answer it."

"N-no." Jan shook her head, desperately needing the release Morgan had built up inside of her. "It can wait."

"Just...answer it."

Jan blindly reached for it and answered with a frustrated huff. "Yes?"

"Did you get the blueprints?" Phil asked, his voice pulling her far from whatever Morgan had been doing between her thighs just moments ago.

"Yes, Phil. I have the blueprints." Jan rolled her eyes as she looked down at Morgan, but Morgan simply smirked, dipped two fingers inside her, and rolled her tongue over her clit. "I...uh, d-do you need anything else?" Jan's fingers ached as she wrapped one hand around the arm of her chair again. "I... Y-yes." She cleared her throat. "I'm b-busy."

"Where the hell are you?"

Morgan eased a third finger inside her, and Jan's head fell back against her seat, her eyes closing as she slowly fucked Morgan's fingers. "At home. W-working."

"You're taking the piss, right?" Phil scoffed. "You don't sound like you're working. You don't even sound like you're at home. If you can't deal with this, and I can't trust you to work from home, then tell me that, Jan!"

Morgan sucked Jan's clit between her lips and brought her to the edge of what would surely be an explosive orgasm. She needed to end the call now before it was too late. "I said I'm busy—I have to go!" She ended the call and dropped her phone to the desk with a clatter. "That was cruel."

Morgan drew back and lifted a brow. "I don't give a fuck."

"Since you feel that way, you can fuck me harder to make it up to me." Jan hooked her legs over either side of the chair, opening herself fully to Morgan. "Go on. Make me come."

Morgan's eyes blazed with a fire Jan had never encountered before. These were the moments they were both living for recently. Fun and fucking...while falling deeply in love with one another. "Babe, I'm so fucking wet for you."

"Then touch yourself and come with me."

Morgan slid a hand down the front of her pyjama shorts, moaning when she brought herself towards the edge. "Shit." She watched as her soaked fingers slid in and out of Jan with ease, the sound of their wetness blanketing the silence of the room. "Fuck, you're so tight."

"I-I'm close."

"M-me, too." Morgan's mouth fell open, the most beautiful smile teasing on her lips as she fucked Jan faster, her own hand moving frantically inside her shorts. "C-coming. Oh, fuckkkk."

Jan came around Morgan's fingers, her body shaking and slumping in her seat. She placed a hand to her forehead, gasping when Morgan withdrew her fingers and lapped up her wetness. "Baby," Jan whispered as she pressed a palm to the top of Morgan's head. "Oh, shit. Fuck...t-that..." She shuddered and moaned, shockwave after shockwave flowing through her. "H-how the hell am I supposed to work after that?" As she lowered her legs, Jan felt the slickness coating her thighs, but she didn't care. Morgan wanted her, Morgan craved her...and Jan, well, she was feeling the very same thing but on another level entirely.

"I love you, and I *do* want to spend my life tasting you." Morgan leaned up on her knees and crashed her lips to Jan's. "You have the sweetest pussy in the world." She brushed her hand between Jan's legs and smirked against her mouth. "So fucking perfect."

CHAPTER 35

Closing down her computer and gathering her belongings from her desk, Jan rested back in her office chair and slipped her heels on. Even though she was glad to be back at work, she wasn't impressed by how tired she felt today. Though, the late night had been worth it. It always would be when Morgan took control and rocked her world.

She smiled, her eyes closing as she rested her head back against her chair. Morgan had dropped Jan at work this morning and had promised she would be here to pick her up when she was finished for the day. Morgan had to work this evening, but Jan didn't mind. She could do with a few hours out of the house after being cooped up in her office all day. So what if she would only be propping Morgan's bar up.

A gentle knock at the door startled Jan, but as she looked up and peered through the glass, she smiled. Gareth was waiting outside. She waved him in and rose to her feet. "Hi, Gareth. How are you?"

He smiled. "I'm okay. Getting used to a new normal, but okay."

"I'm glad you decided to keep us on your route." Jan rounded her desk and rested against it, crossing her legs at the ankles. "Have you been taking care of yourself?" Jan's first observation was that Gareth looked great. Perhaps he'd done what was best for himself, too. "You look well."

"It wasn't great for the first few weeks, but after a couple of blowouts with the lads at the pub, I realised that letting her go was the best thing I could do. She wasn't happy with me, and I'm not staying with a woman who can't communicate that when it matters most."

"How do you feel about the latest development?"

Gareth sighed. "It's something I try not to think about. Once we're divorced, I won't have to see her again."

Jan understood that. And it had been one of the reasons she'd got the divorce going the moment she could. Why hold onto something that couldn't be fixed? Why remain tied to someone via a piece of paper when that someone was about to have a child with another woman? "I think it's important to remember that neither you nor I have done anything wrong and however we choose to move forward is the best thing for us. Not them. If not seeing her again is better for you, then I'm glad you recognise that."

"Do you still see him?"

Jan folded her arms across her chest as she lifted her brows. "I don't have much choice. We co-own this place."

"That...must be difficult for you."

As Jan was about to respond, her phone buzzed on the desk. She briefly eyed it and smiled. It was Morgan. "Actually, it's not been a problem for me. I took some time off work and, in the process, met someone else."

"Really? Wow." Gareth seemed shocked by that development, but Jan didn't expect everyone to understand. She hadn't even told Phil about Morgan yet, but Jan didn't particularly care. Phil wasn't a part of her life any longer. He'd also lost the right to know about Jan and her life the moment he got into bed with Anais. "Well, congratulations."

Jan regarded him with a warm smile. "Thank you."

"Anyway, I just wanted to drop in and see how you were doing. I should head off so I can clock out a little earlier than usual." Gareth stepped towards the door and smiled over his shoulder. "Take care of yourself, Jan."

"You too. I'm sure I'll see you again soon."

The moment Jan was alone, she lifted her phone and read the message Morgan had sent her.

Hi, babe. I'll be with you in five minutes. Temp traffic lights on the way in. I love you x

Jan's pulse quickened when she reread the message. Even though they'd told one another they were falling in love, seeing it so freely on a text message had Jan feeling all kinds of emotions. Emotions that hadn't really surfaced for a long time before she'd met Morgan. She locked her phone and shoved it in her bag, then turned out the light and stepped out into the main area.

As she rummaged around for her makeup mirror in her bag—wanting to look presentable when Morgan arrived—Anais walked through the door. "O-oh." Anais cleared her throat, suddenly lowering the files in her hands to cover her stomach. "Hi, Jan. I-I was just dropping some files off to Beth."

Jan held out an arm towards the cluster of desks to her left. "Well, don't let me stop you."

She watched Anais as she strode towards Beth's desk, her bump visible as she turned to the side. Jan focused on it for a moment or two, and then she cleared her mind, pulled her shoulders back, and left the office building. She glanced to her right and towards Phil's offices, smiling when she saw him standing outside talking to a contractor. He offered her a small wave, Jan returned one of her own, and then she took her sunglasses from the side of her bag and slid them on. Even though it had been raining on the way in this morning, there wasn't a cloud in the sky now.

Morgan's car rolled to a stop further down the car park, but Jan could do with the stroll. It would stretch her legs after being sat at her desk all day. Not being at the office was something she was getting used to now, and usually when she was working from home, she would take a break and walk around the local park. Being at the office didn't offer the same thing. Someone *always* needed something from her.

"No car, love?" Phil's voice pierced through the air.

She turned to him and smiled. "No, I got a lift in this morning, and I'm being picked up. See you next week."

When Jan turned back towards Morgan's car, she had already exited it, and she was resting against the bonnet. Her dark blonde hair shone against the sun, her tongue poking out and playing with her lip ring as Jan approached her. Morgan was checking her out, Jan felt it as the intensity of Morgan's gaze spread all over her skin.

"Hi, babe." Morgan reached out a hand and pulled Jan between her legs. "Good day?"

"It was. Productive, mostly." Jan splayed a palm against Morgan's chest as she leant into a kiss. It deepened, and every swipe of Morgan's tongue reminded Jan of the life she had now. "Mm. You've been drinking coffee without me."

"Guilty," Morgan said against Jan's lips. "But you don't begrudge me a good cup of coffee before I have to work, do you?"

"Never." Jan braced one hand against the bonnet of Morgan's car and went back in for another kiss. And another. "Should we head off? I wouldn't want your boss to tell me off for making you late for work."

Morgan pushed off the car, still holding onto Jan's hand, and opened the passenger door for her. Once Jan was safely inside, another kiss from Morgan place to her lips, she looked through the windscreen to see a pale looking Phil staring back at her, open mouthed.

Doesn't feel good, does it? Jan relaxed and clicked her seatbelt into place. Morgan was by her side not a moment later, her hand heading directly to Jan's thigh. "Ready?"

"Mmhmm." Jan watched Phil from behind her sunglasses. "I think Phil is about to go into shock."

"Well, the stupid bastard should have thought about someone else kissing his ex-wife before he decided to have an affair." Morgan snorted, squeezing Jan's thigh lightly. "Still can't fathom what the fuck was going through his mind when he made that choice."

"I'm...glad he had the affair."

Morgan hit the brakes, almost skidding along the gravel of the car park. "I'm sorry, what?"

"I'm glad he had the affair."

"How could you possibly be happy about something like that, Jan?"

Jan kicked her heels off in the footwell of Morgan's car and turned ever so slightly in her seat. She lifted a hand to Morgan's face and searched her eyes. "Because I've found someone ten times better than he'll ever be."

Morgan swallowed as she leaned into Jan's touch. "Babe."

"I mean it. I had no idea how terrible my marriage had become until I left him."

"Then I'm happy I could give you something that makes you happy." Morgan turned her head and kissed Jan's palm. "You're all I've ever dreamed of."

"And you were a dream I didn't know I so desperately wanted." Jan leaned up over the console and kissed Morgan. "Now, let's go. I want *at least* an hour alone with you before I lose you to your customers."

Thankful that the evening rush hadn't started yet, Morgan rested against the bar directly opposite Finn. Jan and Gillian had snuck off into the bathroom a few minutes ago, and neither of them had reappeared yet. Morgan knew why; Gillian was probably wanting to know everything about their relationship, but Morgan wasn't worried. If that's how women like Jan and Gillian did things, she wasn't getting involved. No, she was quite happy standing here while Finn sunk a pint in record time.

"Fucking hell. Did you even take a breath then?"

Finn grinned. "Trust me, after the day I've had, I deserved that."

"The house you're working on still pissing you off?" Morgan quirked a brow as she poured Finn another pint. "Have they paid you yet?"

"Nope. Still waiting. I've downed tools until I see the cash I'm owed. If they don't pay up, the place will be left as it is, and I'll walk."

"Finn, they owe you *thousands* already! You can't just walk away." Morgan knew that was exactly what the homeowners were waiting for. Finn *had* to remain at that job. "They'd rather you walked than have to fork out grands. They haven't lost anything then. The place was a ripped-out shell anyway."

"I know, but I just can't be arsed with all the chasing." Finn groaned and lay her head down on the counter. "Fuck sake!"

"Hey, if you're going to walk away from the job, at least take out everything you've already done. The kitchen is finished...but they haven't paid you. Take the whole lot with you. I'll even come and help you get it out if you want."

Finn smiled as she lifted her head again. "I'm glad we're okay now. Thanks for texting and inviting us over."

"You know the score. I'll knock seven shades of shite out of you if you *ever* get involved in my relationship again!" Morgan winked and moved along the bar. Eric was situated in his usual place, his walking stick hanging precariously on the edge of the counter. "Another Guinness?"

"Oh, go on. Why not? No place else to be."

Morgan grinned and got to work on Eric's drink. As she watched the dark liquid fill half of the glass, the door opened.

Morgan briefly looked in the direction of it, and then her heart sank. Phil was glaring back at her. "Can I help you?"

He hiked a thumb over his shoulder, the vein at the side of his head visible from across the room and throbbing. "Outside. *Now.*"

The moment Finn heard Phil's voice, she spun around on her stool. Morgan didn't know what was going to happen in the next few minutes, but she wouldn't have anyone causing a scene in here. Finn shot down from her stool and approached Phil. "The fuck are you doing in here?"

"I'm here to see your *mate.*" He sneered at Finn and focused back on Morgan.

"I don't know when you decided you could speak to me like that, but you can turn around and fuck off, Phil." Finn stood toe-to-toe with him, her chin jutted. "You're not welcome in here."

"No, but my wife is, isn't she?"

"Ex-wife," Finn corrected with a sarcastic smile.

Morgan quickly set Eric's Guinness down in front of him and rushed from behind the bar. She knew what Jan meant to Gillian and Finn, and she didn't know what Finn was going to do the longer Phil stood in the middle of the bar. She cleared her throat and lay a hand on Finn's shoulder. "Sit down. I've got this."

"You sure?" Finn turned to Morgan with fury in her eyes.

"I'm sure." Breathing a sigh of relief when Finn nodded and walked away, Morgan focused her attention on Phil. "If you want to talk, we can talk. But we do it outside."

"Why? So your customers don't know you've been fucking a married woman?!"

Morgan took Phil by the elbow, turned him around, and shoved him out the door. He almost lost his footing as he landed outside on the pavement, but he quickly gathered himself and faced Morgan.

"The fuck are you doing, Morgan?"

"Well, I'm trying to run a business." She shoved her hands in the pockets of her jeans and stood tall. Phil wouldn't intimidate her, no matter how hard he tried. "As for my relationship with Jan, I don't believe that's got *anything* to do with you."

"How long has it been going on?"

"Why? She's not your wife anymore, and that's nobody's fault but your own." Morgan studied Phil's face. Was he...accusing Morgan of sleeping with Jan while they were still together? Fuck. "Hang on, you think this started before you knocked up your employee?"

"Jan wouldn't meet anyone so soon. That's not who she is. She doesn't spend her time in bars, fucking random bartenders!"

Morgan stepped forward, almost forehead to forehead with Phil. "Have some fucking respect for your ex-wife."

"She's worth ten of you!" Phil's eyes bulged as he roared that in Morgan's face. "You're fucking nobody!"

While that hurt, Morgan wouldn't show it. "That may be true, but at least I actually give her attention and show her affection. At least I care that she's in my life. But you? You've no idea what you've lost. Or maybe you do, and that's exactly why you're here trying to put me down." Morgan turned her back, hoping Phil got the message. "Go home, Phil. You're making a fool of yourself."

As Morgan stepped back inside the bar, the weight of what Phil had just said pressing down on her, she cleared her throat and swallowed down the emotion lodged in it. Finn, Gillian, and Jan stared back at her from across the room, but it didn't need to be discussed. What was the point?

"Another round?"

Jan sighed as Morgan bypassed her and chose not to take the hand she held out. It wasn't something anyone needed to dwell on. Morgan just wanted to get on with running this place.

Finn stepped up to the bar and lowered her voice. "You okay?"

"Yeah."

"Morgan—"

"I'm fine, Finn." She braced her hands against the counter and exhaled a deep breath. "I just wish people would stop telling me

I'm not good enough for Jan. I *know* I'm not, but I don't know how to change that."

"H-he said that to you?" Finn clenched her hands into fists. "That piece of shit had the fucking audacity to say that to you?"

Morgan pushed off the counter and held up a hand. "I don't want to talk about it anymore. I'm sick of not being able to go more than a few days without someone fucking it all up."

Finn dipped her head and found Morgan's eyes. "You *are* good enough for her. No matter what *anyone* says. She fucking loves you, and that's what matters."

As Morgan shook her head and got back to work, Jan and Gillian came from the other side of the room. Morgan briefly made eye contact with Jan, swallowing down the lump in her throat as she offered her the smallest smile.

Jan's brows drew together. "What's wrong?"

"Fucking Phil!" Finn clenched her jaw as she lifted herself onto her stool again. "He's got some balls coming here after what he's done."

Jan looked between Morgan and Finn, her face draining of all colour. "He's been here?"

"Yeah. He's not happy, which I guess is understandable." Morgan cleared her throat and wiped down the counter. "He made sure I knew what he thought of me, that's for sure."

"When did he leave?" Jan set her handbag down on the bar and moved towards the door. "Will I catch up with him?"

"Just leave it, babe. He's not worth the hassle."

Instead of taking her seat beside Gillian, Jan turned for the exit.

Great. More drama.

Rushing out the door, Jan looked down the street, spotting Phil before he rounded the corner. She didn't know what had just happened between him and Morgan, but she knew it wasn't anything good. When Morgan had stepped back inside the bar only moments ago, she looked as though she was going to burst into tears. If Phil had been responsible for that, Jan was about to lose her rag *very* quickly.

She strode down the road as fast as her heels would allow, catching up with Phil and his slumped shoulders outside a local bakery. "Hey, Phil!"

Phil glanced over his shoulder but continued walking.

Jan reached out and gripped onto his arm. "*Don't* walk away from me!"

He spun around, his face red as he glared at Jan. "Are you for real? Fucking a woman? You're pathetic."

Jan studied his face, searching his eyes for the person she'd once known. But all she saw staring back at her was a sad, pathetic man she didn't recognise anymore. Which was a shame really because Jan didn't want life to be this way. If Phil was happy with Anais, then good luck to him. But Jan would also find her own happiness, and Phil couldn't do anything about it.

"Did that make you feel better back there?" She threw a thumb over her shoulder. "Did it feel good coming into the bar trying to assert some kind of dominance over Morgan?"

"I don't give a fuck about Morgan! But *you*...you're ridiculous! Anything to get back at me, right?" He scoffed as he pointed his finger in Jan's face. "You need to be very careful, Jan. Don't fucking rile me up because you won't win!"

"Point your finger in my face *one more time*, and I'll rip it from its fucking socket!" Jan stepped closer to Phil, regarding him with a look of complete disgust. "I may no longer be your wife, but don't you *dare* scream and shout at me in the street."

"You're not even gay! What the hell are you doing?" He threw up his hands. "Is this some tactic to try to make me feel small and incapable?"

Jan laughed and shook her head. "Oh, no. You did that all by yourself."

"I can't change what happened with Anais. It's done and I can't take it back. But you don't need to humiliate me at work and give everyone a show while you've got your tongue down some fucking dyke's throat."

Taken aback by Phil's awful attitude, Jan stepped away and held up her hands. "I'm done with you. I don't even know who you are anymore. You're disgusting." Jan turned on her heel and slowly made her way back to the bar, taking stock of what had just happened.

"You didn't even give me a chance to make it right." Phil's voice bypassed the noise of the traffic and reached Jan. "You just... left."

Jan turned slowly and frowned. "Y-you wanted me to stay with you while you fathered a child with another woman?"

"W-we could have made it work, Jan. If you'd given *me* the chance to figure everything out, I would have given *you* anything you wanted." He shoved his hands in the pockets of his suit pants and sighed. "I never wanted to lose you."

"I don't know if this will ever register in your brain, but I *don't* love you anymore, Phil. I *won't* fall back in love with you. You've been seeing another woman, got her pregnant, and quite frankly...I don't ever want to look at you again." Aware that this would be the last time she saw Phil outside of a business relationship, she stepped closer and said, "If you never wanted to lose me, you shouldn't have fucked her for the best part of a year." She took a breath. "I'm in love with Morgan and I'm happy. If you care about me at all, you'll accept that and let me live my life however *I* want to live it."

Calmly making her way down the road, Jan pulled her shoulders back and swallowed. Gillian was standing outside the bar, but she wasn't looking at Jan. No, she was glaring at Phil and probably plotting his demise.

“Are you okay?” Gillian took Jan’s hand as she stopped in front of her. “Love?”

“I’m fine. I’ve said what I need to say. I’m done with him.”

Gillian smiled and guided Jan back inside the bar. “*Large* glass of red please, Morgan.”

Jan looked up and met Morgan’s eyes. She still seemed haunted by whatever Phil had said to her. Jan cleared her throat and strode behind the bar. “Hey.” She held onto Morgan’s hand and pulled their bodies together. “I don’t know what he said to you, but I love you and that’s the only thing you need to remember, okay?”

Morgan smiled as she drew Jan into a gentle kiss. “I love you, too.”

CHAPTER 36

T*hree weeks later...*

Fixing her earring into place, Jan took a final glance in the mirror and smiled back at herself. Morgan had insisted she wear this dress tonight, a little black dress that apparently 'left her breathless'. Jan laughed to herself. She couldn't believe this was her life now. In love with a woman who would do anything for her, a woman who had no issue complimenting Jan and showing everyone in town what Jan meant to her. It was a stark contrast from what she'd had with Phil, but she wouldn't change any of it. She wouldn't dream of wanting anything other than what she had now. Morgan Tate was her everything.

Now she understood exactly what Gillian and Finn had with one another. While Jan had loved seeing her best friend ridiculously happy, she hadn't always understood the obsession they had with one another. But now, she did.

She makes me feel like nobody else in this world exists.

And when they were together, that was true. Jan had never felt so...wanted. She'd never felt so blissfully happy. She'd never felt so in love with her life. She didn't know when or if that sense of ultimate accomplishment would end, but deep down, she desperately hoped it wouldn't. She *needed* these moments. She *ached* to always be the centre of Morgan's world. Morgan was certainly all Jan could think about. Morning, noon, and night, the obsession was only becoming stronger.

Her phone beeped on her dressing table.

I can't wait to see you tonight. I love you x

Jan placed a hand to her chest and smiled. Morgan had worked until five, and though she would usually head right over here the moment her shift ended, she had opted to get ready at the bar. It would have only meant less time for her to get ready otherwise.

Jan quickly snapped a picture of herself in the mirror and attached it to her reply.

I can't wait to see you either. Was this the dress you wanted me to wear? I love you, too x

Jan knew she was teasing Morgan, but Morgan would thank her for it. She had five nights ago when Jan had texted her filthy pictures, and this was tame in comparison. *Very* tame.

Fuck, babe. You look amazing. I can't wait to taste you later. You'll be all mine once the night is over x

A thrill rushed up Jan's spine as she took her bottom lip between her teeth. She hadn't imagined she would fall in love with a woman fifteen years younger than her, but it worked. It worked so well that neither of them had thought about the age gap for a single moment. If Jan could catch the attention of Morgan, then she was doing something right. Wasn't that the only thing that mattered? Age was...irrelevant.

She lowered herself to the edge of her bed and sent off a quick response to Morgan.

Maybe I'll make you wait until tomorrow x

She wouldn't dream of it, not in a million years. But Jan had realised that the more she teased Morgan, the hotter the sex was when they eventually found themselves alone together.

And maybe I'll fuck you behind the nearest closed door if I feel like it...

Morgan ended the message with a smirking emoji, but that only left Jan feeling incredibly aroused as she sat here waiting to call a cab. Usually, she would brush Morgan's suggestion off, but tonight she couldn't be sure that she wouldn't allow Morgan a moment like that. Her body generally told her what she wanted and when, and in this moment, it wanted Morgan and her delectable mouth. She wanted those lips to blaze a path of fire over every inch of her skin. And that tongue, oh that tongue was capable of so much. Far too much for Jan to handle at times.

You tell me when and where and I'll make sure I'm soaking wet for you x

Okay, that was enough. Jan would never make it to the bar if she continued this back and forth. Her legs simply wouldn't carry her down the stairs and into the cab if she didn't put a stop to the flirting she'd foolishly started. *She makes you feel good. So what?*

Jan's phone pinged in her hand again.

You should come over a little earlier than planned. I could take care of you before we even head out. It would be my absolute pleasure x

Could Jan do that? Of course she could. But she also knew that the moment Morgan got her naked, any plans to head out with Gillian and Finn would be long forgotten. Once Morgan's skin was pressed to hers, she wouldn't surface from Morgan's flat for at least an entire twenty-four hours.

Tame your thoughts, baby. We'll have one another all alone at the end of the night. Makes it all the more exciting. You and I both know that x

Jan locked her phone and rose to her feet. She needed to finish getting ready. Jan didn't do late arrivals. She was *always* on time. And if she was late, Gillian would make sure she knew all about it.

For the first time in so many years, Morgan was ready for a night out on the town with the woman she loved, and their friends, and she was going to make the most of it. She had spent at least twenty minutes in the shower trying to recall the last time she'd done something like this, and sadly, it had been too long. At least five years, she had guessed by the time her skin had wrinkled, and she realised she was standing staring at the tiles in her shower cubicle.

There had also been a moment when she'd brushed a tear from her cheek, feeling incredibly blessed to be in the position she was in now. Life with Jan was flourishing before Morgan's eyes and there wasn't a thing she could do about it. She didn't *want* to do anything about it.

She's so fucking beautiful.

Morgan smiled as she turned out the light in her bedroom—the very room that had a constant faint linger of Jan's perfume—and fixed her watch to her wrist. Jan would be downstairs waiting, and Morgan didn't want her to wait a second longer. That woman didn't deserve to sit alone on a stool at the bar. No, she deserved every last ounce of Morgan's attention. And tonight, it would be *solely* focused on her. Whether Gillian and Finn were in the room with them or not was irrelevant. Morgan only saw Jan. Morgan only cared about Jan. It was that simple. But she knew Finn understood better than anyone when it came to love and the idea of Morgan never wanting to leave Jan's side. Finn was disgustingly in love with Gillian, and Morgan was on her way to feeling the very same thing she'd spent so long teasing Finn about.

She checked herself over in the mirror on the chimney stack and nodded slowly. Morgan had managed to get into town this morning before the bar opened at midday so she could pick up a new outfit. That was just another thing she wasn't used to doing. She rarely bothered to splash out on herself...what had been the point in the past?

A key in her flat door had Morgan spinning around in front of the TV. It would be Jan, nobody else had access up here, but it only made Morgan's pulse quicken. Jan had her one and only spare key. God, she loved that more than she probably should. It was only a key, after all.

No, it's not only a key. It's a symbol of what you share with one another.

Morgan cleared the sudden emotion from her throat and beamed a smile at Jan. "Sorry, babe. I was about to head down. I didn't mean to keep you waiting."

Jan shoved her key into her clutch bag and crossed the room. "I've only just arrived." Her gaze swept up Morgan's body, leaving a trail of heat behind. "You look *very* good tonight."

Morgan wrapped a hand around the back of her neck and blushed. "Thanks."

"Gillian and Finn are running a few minutes late. They texted me when I was in the cab. Something about Gill's hair being trapped in a zip."

Morgan dragged her bottom lip between her teeth to keep her from laughing. If she knew Finn the way she believed she did, something had gone wrong during a quick fumble. "Right. I'm sure *that's* entirely innocent."

"Don't. It was immediately where my mind went as well."

Morgan held out a hand and pulled Jan in against her when she took it. "God, you look stunning tonight." She drew Jan in, arm around her waist, and lay a careful kiss on her lips. The last thing she wanted was to ruin her lipstick. That would come later. "So stunning. All of you."

Jan hummed lightly as she pressed her cheek to Morgan's and swayed them. "The bar is packed tonight. It's a good job we're heading away from here. Even the owner wouldn't get a seat."

Morgan lifted a shoulder. "Maybe not, but I'd have found you one. You know that."

"Thank you for being perfect." Jan pulled back and gazed at Morgan, her blue eyes soft.

"I love you. I'll always find a seat for you in a crowded bar."

Jan smiled. "I know."

"You were at the office today, right?" Morgan didn't want to get involved in that side of Jan's life, but if she found out Phil had said more of the disgusting things he'd already thrown at her, Morgan would be at his office *so fast* that he wouldn't have time to blink.

"I was. Phil is away, thankfully."

Morgan frowned. "You're not worried about seeing him again, are you?"

"No, I'm not. I just don't want it all to start at the office, too. I had no idea he could be so cruel with his words and now I have to wonder if he's going to try to push me out."

Morgan snorted. "You own fifty percent. He owns fifty percent. If he knows what's good for him, he'll get on with his job and leave you alone."

"I'm sure everything will be fine. He's not at the office as often as I usually am. He's always been the traveller out of the two of us." Jan stepped away and helped herself to a glass of water. "Anyway, we don't need to talk about him. I'd rather enjoy my night out with you, having fun, while he sits at home dealing with his new family. He's happy, and I'm happy." Jan sipped her water then smirked. "Though, I'm sure *I'm* the happier out of us both."

"Ooh, that was smooth." Morgan grinned as she stepped up behind Jan and pressed herself to her. "I can't wait to get to your place later. The whole weekend to ourselves." Morgan dipped her head towards Jan's ear as she said, "Whatever will we do?"

"I can think of a few things." Jan turned and eyed Morgan. "But for now, you need to behave yourself." Jan hooked her fingers over the waistband of Morgan's jeans and tugged her closer. "It'll be interesting to see if you can keep your hands to yourself until we get home later."

Morgan wanted to see that as a challenge. She wanted to hold back just to prove she could. But the truth was...there wasn't a chance she could control herself this evening. Until she could devour Jan later tonight, she was going to take what she could get whenever it was on offer. If that meant getting a little handsy in a booth—she'd booked a VIP area that none of them knew about—then so be it.

"You just worry about yourself, babe. I'm good."

Settled in a booth at a new club in town, Jan looked around and grinned. Gillian was sitting beside her, while Morgan and Finn stood at the bar discussing the football. It wasn't either of their thing, so Jan had insisted they retreat to their comfortable and surprisingly private area while they could. She didn't care for the offside rule or VAR discussion.

She turned to Gillian, smiling when she noticed her best friend staring at her. "What?"

"You look like a completely different woman lately."

"I am." Jan was glad people were noticing how happy she was. First one of the girls at the office, and now Gillian. "Don't know why I didn't climb back into bed with a woman sooner."

Gillian barked a laugh at that. "I'm still trying to get my head around how you kept it quiet back in university."

"You were too busy being all academic and applying yourself." Though Jan hadn't taken university lightly, she had been more of the loose cannon between them. "And Antonia was terrified of being caught. Her parents were high up in the church and she was convinced they'd condemn her to hell."

Gillian snorted at that. "I've been to hell, it's where all the cool kids hang out."

Jan's eyes strayed towards Morgan and Finn as they laughed together. Just a month ago, they hadn't been in the best place with one another, but Jan was glad Morgan didn't hold grudges for too long. This was a new start for Jan, and she wanted her closest friends with her on the journey. "It's nice to see them happy again."

"I know." Gillian smiled when she followed Jan's line of sight. "And us."

"I did think about holding out a little longer, but I couldn't do it." Jan lifted a shoulder and turned to Gillian fully. "I never expect you to react the way you did, but we're a long time dead and I want to make the most of everything I have now. You and I are too old to fall out with one another."

"I was a shitty friend."

"You can make it up to me by paying for the next spa weekend we go on."

Gillian frowned as she brought her wine glass to her lips. "We… don't go on spa weekends, love."

"We do now. I've already found the next hotel I want to try and you're coming too. If Finn is missing you, she can sit and be miserable with Morgan. It's about time you and I had a weekend away together."

"When?" Gillian groaned as she rolled her head on her shoulders. "I'll probably go into shock the moment I have a facial. It's been so long since I took time out for myself."

"That's precisely why I'm taking you." Jan twisted her wine glass on the table, still focused on Gillian. "As for the when…it'll be during the next half-term. So, a month away?"

"Oh, God. I can't wait." She eyed Finn across the club. "Though, I think you can be the one to break it to my wife."

"Fine by me." Jan shrugged and then turned, feeling Morgan's presence close by. Just as she'd suspected, Morgan was passing through the rope with the help of security. "Hi. Nice of you to join us."

"Finn thinks she can get tickets to the game in a few weeks. She was asking if I fancied it. You wouldn't mind if I go, would you, babe?"

Jan settled a hand on Morgan's thigh the moment she was seated beside her. "Of course not. You love the football, and this is an important game, if I remember right."

Morgan cocked her head. "You were actually listening to me that day when I was rambling on? I thought you were just smiling and nodding to make me feel better."

"I *always* listen when you're talking." Jan squeezed Morgan's thigh as she leaned in and kissed her just below the ear. "Anything you say is incredibly important to me."

As Jan drew back, Morgan took a hold of her chin gently and brought her back in for another kiss. She smiled against Jan's lips, the muscle beneath Jan's palm tensing as she inched a little higher. "You are *so* getting anything you want later."

"Mmhmm. I thought as much." Jan cleared the arousal from her voice and turned back to Gillian. Only now Finn was sitting beside her, and they were both staring at Jan and Morgan. "What?"

"Did you want us to just leave?" Finn grinned as she cocked her head towards the exit. "You both seem a bit busy, ladies."

Jan rolled her eyes playfully. "You have no right to say *anything* like that to me when you've had the audacity to answer one of my calls during sex!"

"What? I... We... Nah, we'd never do that." Finn shook her head, the look on her face saying she was certain about that.

"Oh, really? Explain the night I called when I'd just left Phil then?"

Finn lowered her eyes and nudged Gillian. "You can take that one, babe. I'm not getting involved."

Gillian sighed. "We're sorry about that. You never used to call me in the evening unless that dickhead was away, so when you did, I panicked. I told Finn to answer the phone in case something terrible had happened." Gillian swallowed. "And it had, but we didn't know it."

Jan softened. "Actually, it turns out it wasn't terrible at all. I think we can all agree on that, can't we?" Jan rested back against Morgan, holding onto the hand she'd just draped over her shoulder. "Does this look terrible to either of you?"

"Well, no, but at the time...when you eventually told me what he'd done, it felt terrible."

Morgan leaned forward a little. "For the record, I did suggest that telling you and Finn about Phil was something Jan should consider. So she had plenty of people around her." Morgan paused and held up a hand. "But then Jan flourished and came into her own right in front of my eyes, and I knew I didn't need to push her to do anything at all. When the time was right for her, she'd know."

"And I appreciated that so much," Jan said, turning her head and kissing Morgan. When she focused back on their friends, Jan smiled. "I knew what I needed...when I needed it."

"When you said that I wanted you to deal with your divorce the way I did..." Gillian shook her head. "That wasn't what I wanted at all. Never, Jan."

"I was angry with you. I couldn't understand why you seemed so upset that I wasn't broken and falling apart. But I also realise that Morgan and I were quite a shock. It was for me, to a point. Not enough for me to care about slowing down, but enough for me to briefly question if I even had a heart because I felt *nothing* for Phil the moment I knew he'd been seeing someone else." Jan sipped her wine and smiled. "But he knew what would happen if he ever strayed. I'd always been honest about that. When you left Dave, I reminded him of my stance on it all."

"I admire you for being able to turn around and walk away with such ease, I really do." Gillian dipped her head towards Finn. "I think it's time you went to the bar for a bottle of champagne, baby. I think we all have so much to celebrate, but Jan and Morgan more so."

Jan's heart thrummed at just how perfectly tonight was going. Gillian and Finn had been on board for several weeks now but tonight felt like the beginning of something truly beautiful. Something Jan had never known she'd needed so much. "You'd better make it two bottles, Finn. You know what we can all be like."

Finn rose to her feet and smiled. "Two bottles of the finest. Got it."

EPILOGUE

T*en months later...*

Morgan bounced on the balls of her feet as she checked her watch for the millionth time today. Gillian and Finn sat on stools across the bar from her, appearing equally as excited as Morgan, so now she was waiting for Jan to arrive before the truth was revealed. She'd never really been the type to spontaneously do something so big, and definitely not without Jan's say-so, but Morgan couldn't resist. For the last two months or so, Jan had been running the business alone while Phil took time off to be with Anais and their child.

For so many nights, Morgan had held Jan on the couch while she dropped off to sleep against her. For so many days, Jan had just about managed to smile fully, her eyes tired and worn. Morgan hated seeing her like that. Yes, she'd agreed to take on the bulk of the business for the period of time Phil would be away, but Jan hadn't known about the new contractors Phil had been in talks with for several weeks beforehand. When her girlfriend already had enough on her plate, Phil had intentionally added to it without being forthcoming in terms of the truth. Morgan didn't like that, but Phil had turned on Jan the moment he knew she was dating a woman...and he hadn't backed down since.

"Any idea what time she's arriving?" Gillian sighed and shifted in her seat. "I'm not very good at being patient."

"She texted me about ten minutes ago to say she's at home dropping off her laptop and files, and then she'd be here." Morgan lifted her bottle of beer and sipped it. As of an hour ago, she was on leave. Something she rarely afforded herself prior to meeting Jan. "You haven't said anything at all to her?"

"No, but mostly because Finn threatened to divorce me if I dared to let it slip."

Finn nodded as she set her pint down. "Correct. This is Jan's surprise and it's *Morgan's* job to reveal all. Not yours, babe."

"I know. I know." Gillian held up her hands and rolled her eyes. "God, I wish you wouldn't all gang up on me like that. You two forget that Jan and I have been best friends since university. Lying to her *isn't* something I enjoy."

"You're not *really* lying, though," Morgan said. "You're just not telling her about something in particular."

Gillian pursed her lips. "Mmhmm."

"Now, if Jan had specifically asked you about something and you didn't tell the truth, that's another matter. But I know she hasn't because she has no idea about any of this. I don't think she's going to hold it against you when she finds out you and Finn are in on it all."

Finn groaned and flopped back against her seat. "Now you're making me worried because what if Jan *does* hold it against us?"

"She won't. Trust me." God, Morgan couldn't deal with these two and their nerves for much longer. Anyone would think she'd asked them to help move and hide a body the way they were behaving. "Another drink to calm your nerves?"

Gillian emptied the last of her wine down her throat and lifted a shoulder. "I guess it wouldn't hurt."

As Morgan busied herself behind the bar, Jan strode through the door. As usual, she looked tired and in dire need of a nap. "Hi, babe. I didn't think you'd be here so soon."

"Large red please. Before I lose the will to live, I'd like to enjoy just one glass."

Morgan stepped out from behind the bar and wrapped Jan up in her arms. "Another tough day?"

"Not really. Just..." She sighed and drew back. "I'll sit down and explain."

Morgan's heart threatened to fall into her stomach. As of right now, Jan was *supposed* to be on a two week break from work. Something in her eyes told Morgan that was no longer the case. *Fuck!* "R-right, yeah. You sit down and I'll get that glass of red for you."

Morgan watched Jan for a moment or two, trying to decipher what was about to come next, and then she looked to Gillian who seemed equally as apprehensive. Was this about to turn to shit? Morgan really hoped not.

"What's going on at work, love?" Gillian took control of the conversation, laying a hand over Jan's on the bar counter.

"Phil came back to the office today, which I'm glad about." Jan lifted her glass the moment Morgan set it down in front of her. She quickly sorted out Gillian and Finn's drinks, but she listened intently. "What I didn't expect or want was for him to bring the baby into my office, introduce us to one another, and then have the fucking audacity to refer to me as Auntie Jan."

Morgan almost dropped the pint glass in her hand, horrified that he would do something like that to his ex-wife. "Nah, you're not serious, babe." Morgan glared, unable to comprehend how Phil could be so cruel. "Please tell me that never happened."

"It happened."

"And why *the fuck* would he think it was okay to do that?"

Morgan clenched the hand at her side into a fist, turning her attention to Finn. Why? Because Finn understood *exactly* what she was feeling right now. "You think we have time to go over there?"

Finn snorted. "I'm game. I'd be more than happy to pay him a visit and remind him that he's a piece of shit!"

"I just want to forget about everything for the next two weeks and relax. I've been so busy that I don't feel as though I've had time to do anything meaningful." Jan shook her head lightly as she looked up at Morgan. "You've been so patient with me this month and I want to spend whatever time I can with you while I have the chance. Just...enjoying life again."

Morgan toyed with her lip ring as she held back a smile. "Me too, babe. Fuck Phil and his shitty attitude."

Finn cleared her throat. "Yeah, Jan. He's not worth getting upset over."

Morgan eyed Gillian, but it seemed she didn't share the same opinion as her wife. If Morgan focused hard enough, she was sure she would see steam coming from her ears. "You good, Gill?"

"No. No, I'm not." She exhaled a deep breath as she pinched the bridge of her nose. "I just...what the fuck is wrong with these men who claimed they once loved us? I don't understand how they can just become so bitter towards us."

Jan nudged Gillian's shoulder and smiled. "They don't like that we're succeeding and happy. Fuck them. Morgan and Finn are right."

The door that led to the flat opened and Ben stepped out. "Sorry about that. Mum called me about coming over this week to see the flat."

Morgan grinned. "That's no problem. There have been plenty of times over the years when I've been late. It's no big deal." She took her set of keys for the bar from her pocket and tossed them in Ben's direction. "The place is all yours until I'm back." She rounded the bar and pulled up a stool next to Jan, beer in hand. "I have a fortnight with a very special woman and I'm going to make the most of it."

Jan leaned in and kissed Morgan. "How about we finish these drinks and head home. *You* still have a box or two lying around the place and I'd like to see the back of them."

"Sorry, babe. I'll be a little bit too busy for that." Morgan winked at Jan as Ben wheeled out Gillian and Finn's suitcases from behind the bar. "But we can head home for a little while. Just to make sure we've got everything we need."

Jan's brows drew together as she looked down at the suitcases then back up at Morgan. "I'm sorry?"

"I've got the passports and all the documents. Gillian even packed your case for you. I just want you to double check that I haven't forgotten anything."

Jan glanced in Gillian's direction. "What's going on?"

"We have it on good authority that Gran Canaria is *excellent* for unwinding when a particular ex-husband has been giving my best friend a hard time." Gillian nudged Jan's shoulder and smiled. "We have a flight to catch in around five hours so I suggest you get that glass of red down your neck and then we can all be on our way to some relaxation for the next ten days."

"T-ten days?" Jan's eyes widened as she turned to Morgan again. "Baby, is this true? We're all going on holiday together *today*?"

"Mmhmm."

Jan shot down from her stool and stood between Morgan's legs. She cupped her face, searched her eyes, and blinked away a tear or two. "God, I love you."

Morgan tucked a strand of Jan's blonde hair behind her ear. "I love you, too. It's important that you take a break and recharge. Why not do that in the sun...on a beach...with our friends?"

"The last of your boxes can wait. Right now, we have a plane to catch."

"You excited, gorgeous? To be back in the place where it all really began for us?" Morgan wrapped her arms around Jan's waist. "And I know we'd been together here for a little while beforehand, but Meloneras just...reminds me of you. Of us. The early days and how we didn't quite know what was coming."

"I'll *always* be excited to return to Meloneras."

"In that case, you should call a cab as soon as you're ready so we can head back to our place." Saying that, knowing Jan's place had recently become *their* place, it still sent Morgan's mind into a spin. But she was getting used to it. Everything just felt so beautiful when they closed the door at night and locked the world outside. "I've already booked a guy to take us to the airport at five, so we have until then to be ready."

"Yes, let's go! We can hail one on the street."

Morgan's brows rose at Jan's sudden enthusiasm. She'd known Jan wouldn't turn down a holiday, but the doubt had crept in once Jan had walked through the door before. Thank God her mood had lifted and now they were all happy again. But Morgan *would* keep an eye on Phil when they returned. If he needed taking down a notch, then so be it. "You're so fucking gorgeous when you smile."

Jan hung her arms loosely around Morgan's neck and drew her into a slow, lingering kiss. "All I seem to do when I'm with you is smile. But that's not surprising since you're the only thing I need in life to make me happy."

With a kiss placed to Jan's temple, Morgan sighed with contentment and stepped away, shoving Gillian and Finn's suitcases towards them. "Let's get this show on the road. I'd rather be sipping a cocktail on a beach than in here."

SIGN UP TO WIN!

Sign up to my mailing list to be the first to hear about new releases, and to be in with a chance of winning books!

www.melissaterezeauthor.com

DID YOU ENJOY IT?

Thank you for purchasing Heal You.

I hope you enjoyed it. Please consider leaving a review on your preferred site. As an independent author, reviews help to promote our work. One line or two really does make the difference.

Thank you, truly.

Love,
Melissa x

About the Author

Oh, hi! It's nice to see you!

I'm Melissa Tereze, author of The Arrangement, Mrs Middleton, and other bestsellers. Born, raised, and living in Liverpool, UK, I spend my time writing angsty romance about complex, real-life, women who love women. My heart lies within the age-gap trope, but you'll also find a wide range of different characters and stories to sink your teeth into.

SOCIAL MEDIA

You can contact me through my social media or my website. I'm mostly active on Twitter.

SCAN ME

Also by Melissa Tereze

Another Love Series

The Arrangement (Book One)

The Call (Book Two)

Before You Go (Book Three)

Mrs Middleton Novels

Mrs Middleton

Teach Me (Co-write with Jourdyn Kelly)

Vanessa

The Ashforth Series

Playing For Her Heart (Book One)

Holding Her Heart (Book Two)

The Stepmother Series

The Stepmother (Book One)

The Show Must Go On (Book Two)

The Hush Liverpool Series

Discovery (Book One)

The Hideout (Book Two)

A Little Light (Book Three)

Any Kind of Life (Book Four)

The Study You Series

Study You

Choose You

Other Novels

Life After

It's Always Been You

It's All About Bex

Privately Investigated

Behind Her Eyes

At First Glance

Always Allie

Breaking Routine

In Her Arms

Forever Yours

The Heat of Summer

Forget Me Not

More Than A Feeling

Where We Belong: Love Returns

Naked

Titles under L.M Croft (Erotica)

Pieces of Me

Printed in Dunstable, United Kingdom

67842428R00214